MAGNOLIA PARK

MAGNOLIA PARK

A Comic, Pornographic Novel of Erotic Obsession and Other Horrors in the Deep South

W. A. Moltinghorne

iUniverse, Inc.
New York   Bloomington

Magnolia Park
A Comic, Pornographic Tale of Erotic Obsession
and Other Horrors in the Deep South

The cover image, "Bible's Motive", is by Planem Penov; the cover design is by Luis Alicea; the back cover design is by Chris Gerrard.

iUniverse books may be ordered through booksellers or by contacting:

iUniverse
1663 Liberty Drive
Bloomington, IN 47403
www.iuniverse.com
1-800-Authors (1-800-288-4677)

ISBN: 978-1-4401-4258-1 (sc)
ISBN: 978-1-4401-4257-4 (ebk)

Printed in the United States of America

iUniverse rev. date: 6/22/2010

The scientific study of the psychopathology of sexual life necessarily deals with the miseries of man and the dark sides of his existence, the shadow of which contorts the sublime image of the deity into horrid caricatures, and leads astray aestheticism and morality.

Krafft-Ebing, *Psychopathia Sexualis*

'Tis therefore Nature that must be seized when one labors in the field of fiction, 'tis the heart of man, the most remarkable of her works, and in no wise virtue, because virtue, however becoming, however necessary it may be, is yet but one of the many facets of this amazing heart, whereof the profound study is so necessary to the novelist, and the novel, the faithful picture of this heart, must perforce explore its every fold.

Marquis de Sade, quoted in Walter Kendrick, *The Secret Museum: Pornography in Modern Culture*

The passion caused by the great and sublime ... is Astonishment; and astonishment is that state of the soul, in which all its motions are suspended, with some degree of horror. In this case the mind is so entirely filled with its object, that it cannot entertain any other, nor by consequence reason on that subject which employs it. Hence arises the great power of the sublime, that far from being produced by them, it anticipates our reasonings, and hurries us on by an irresistible force. Astonishment ... is the effect of the sublime in its highest degree; the inferior effects are admiration, reverence, and respect.

Edmund Burke, *A Philosophical Enquiry into the Sublime and Beautiful*

The daemonic-divine object may appear to the mind an object of horror and dread, but at the same time it is no less something that allures with a potent charm, and the creature, who trembles before it, utterly cowed and cast down, has always at the same time the impulse to turn to it, nay even to make it somehow his own.

Rudolf Otto, *The Idea of the Holy*

The pure prove their purity by wallowing in filth and emerging unspotted.

A. D. Nuttall, *The Alternative Trinity*

1

"Do you want to hear what that woman is up to or not, Clinton?" Billy's mother glared at Billy's father, daring him to say no.

Billy Mayden and his parents were having dinner. Billy bowed his head and poked at the food on his plate. He pushed his new glasses up on his nose and idly wondered if they would help his jump shot. Stupid things kept slipping down. He was in a hurry to get out of there but couldn't seem to get moving.

It was late Saturday morning, two days before Labor Day, in the year 1957, three days before classes started up again at Southern Bible College where Billy was enrolled. Sometime before next Tuesday morning he would have to tell his mother that he wouldn't be going back to college and that the tuition money he had earned writing tracts for the Evangelical Society had gone to buy the new-fangled gadget the three of them watched five nights a week until 8:00 pm when Channel 5's test pattern came on, signaling the end of the television shows.

But that would have to wait. It was almost noon and he had a busy day ahead of him. No time to get into a long discussion with Stella. First, he was going to call Frankie West to see if he wanted to play basketball in the gym at Pinecrest. Then he was going over to Jacob Garrard's house. Theo Jeannsonne, the man who Jake worked for and who owned Magnolia Park, wanted to show off the new erotic art books he'd picked up in New Orleans and Jake wanted Billy to come along with him. Theo's house was near the park, which wasn't far from Pinecrest gym, so Billy could go straight from looking at the dirty pictures to the gym. If Stella asked he'd say he was going to play basketball; if she asked where he'd say school. Don't get her started on Pinecrest or Frankie West or Jake Garrard.

It was at the mention of 'that woman', i.e., Jonnie Vonderheim, Stella's favorite topic of mealtime conversation that Billy tuned out. Adopting his Get Thee Behind Me Satan attitude, he resigned himself to it taking longer than he had hoped to make his getaway. He had heard it all before, many times, knew every look and gesture that went with it. The Vonderheim's, Jonnie and Fred, were on the same telephone party line with the Mayden's; they lived two vacant lots down from the Mayden's on the dirt road that, dead-ending in a sewerage ditch-cum-slaughterhouse sluice, was aptly called Pugh Lane, though it had never been given an official name or number by either Evangline Parish or the State of Louisiana. Billy learned just how much Stella despised the Vonderheim woman when he heard her say to Clinton one day, *That woman* is nothing but a white-trash *slut.* It was the only time he had ever heard Stella say a dirty word. Billy forgave his mother for saying the word, and his father, too, for chuckling.

"She goes to church every Sunday." Clinton Mayden sat at the head of the table. "Plays the piano for the sanging. She even tithes. What else you want her to do? Can't ever body be perfect like you."

"You're always sticking up for her, Clinton." Stella Mayden sat at a right angle to her husband, on his right. Billy sat on her right on the same side of the table, so that she was between her two men, husband and son. Across from Billy and his mother another place, never occupied, was set, plate, silverware, and drinking glass. "You know *why* she joined the church, don't you?"

"Don't start with that again. You ain't got no proof of it. Just because you see his car parked in front of her house once in a blue moon don't mean a thang. He's always visiting people. What else a preacher gonna do with his time? Most of the time his wife is with him."

"He don't never visit us," Stella snapped. "And it ain't never in no blue moon neither. More like ever week."

"No, not no more, he don't visit us." Clinton speared a hunk of pork chop and stuck it in his mouth as if to stop himself from saying more.

"She's going to a big fancy party they're having down at Magnolia Park Monday night. Did you know that? And you know they sell beer and whiskey down there, don't you? And I don't even want to think what'll be going on in those lil'ol shacks they call cabins they got strowed all over them woods."

"How do you know about that? You been ... ?" Clinton stopped talking around the meat in his mouth. Glancing at his prayerful son, he put his fork on his plate and signaled for timeout to finish chewing before saying the rest of what he wanted to say, thereby acknowledging the family rule: No talking with food in your mouth. But, then, seeing the look on his wife's face, he flicked his wrist, opting for the small consolation of waiving the floor before she usurped it. Picking up his fork, he impaled another piece of pork chop and added it to the half-chewed one in his mouth.

"What does it take, Clinton, for you to see that she's up to no good?

She's up all night ever night on the phone. Decent people don't have no reason to be up all night on the phone. It rings so much I can't hardly get any sleep. And it ain't just *his* car I see down there. Ever weekend, as soon as Fred drives off in that awful old beer truck of his … poor man has to have two jobs just to keep her in licker I guess … here they come. It's busy as the Trailways bus station down there. I've seen two different Cadillacs, I've seen cars from both Sheriff's departments. And there's a car with Pinecrest on the side of it just about ever day."

"She's the head of the March a Dimes, Stel. That's howcome she's going to that party and why most of them cars are down there. That's howcome they're having the party in the first place. It's to raise money for all the lil'ol kids that's got polio. She's gotta organize everthang. Get everthang and ever body working together. I reckon she don't drive, so they have to come to her. And probably the reason you seen that Pinecrest car is she *works* at Pinecrest and I reckon somebody from there takes her home ever day after she gets off from work."

"I ain't talking about nobody dropping her off after work, Clinton. This was in the middle of the day and whoever it was was there for hours. How do you know so much about her and her doings, anyway? That's what I'd like to know. How do you know she don't drive? Tell me that."

"Brother Johnson told me. She's always doing stuff like that, organizing thangs, and needs somebody to drive her places, I reckon."

"Yeah, and you know the reason why? So she can be around those men. Any man she thinks is a big shot she goes after and all the rest of 'em go after *her*. She's like a gyp in heat. I can't believe she had the gall to move in next door to us. After what she's done to me."

Both his parents looked at Billy. Billy shot a glance at the empty place setting and then resumed contemplating the food on his plate. Clinton said, "You're bringing that up again? I thought you were over that, Stel. Can't you just let it drop? It's been over twenty years."

"I *know* how long it's been, Clinton." Speaking very deliberately, Stella seemed to be talking to the food on the fork poised halfway between her plate and her mouth. "You thank I don't know how long it's been. Besides I don't care how long it's been. It could be a thousand years and I'd still feel the same way." Turning her head toward her husband, she continued, her voice now plaintive: "I'll never stop being her *mother*. And how *can* I forget it when ever time I look out the window I see that woman's fancy brick house?" She slammed her fork down, sending mashed potatoes and gravy flying onto the side of Billy's face and shoulder, spattering his glasses and the sleeve of his shirt. "That house was built with blood money, I tell you!" Billy didn't move. "Blood money!"

3

"We been over this a thousand times, Stella, hun. It was you that thought they was something wrong. Remember? You kept complaining how she wouldn't hug you the way ... ," Clinton paused, looked again at Billy who remained motionless, ". . . your other one did ... and you couldn't get her to keep her clothes on. Remember, you said the last straw was when she took off her clothes at church in the middle of the invitational and went running around yelling cuss words?"

"I remember, Clinton. I remember lots of thing. I remember who she learned them cuss words from in the first place: you and your fishing buddies. And her just a little girl, barely outa dipers. I remember that she was more interested in lizards and turtles than she was people, even other little kids. I remember how she'd stiffen up if I, her own mother, touched her. Only one she'd let touch her ... ." Cutting her eyes to her right without moving her head, Stella let the sentence trail off. "Do you thank her hiding under the bed ever time I tried to dress her up like a pretty little girl instead of like her ... like a boy ... which was the only way she'd have it ... made it any easier for me to do what I did? Well, it didn't. I also remember how everybody blamed me for the way she was. They even blamed me for her dirty mouth."

"Don't start that bawling again, Stella. You know I can't stand to see a grown woman cry."

"If that woman just hadn't sent her to the Catholic school. And why did she have to give her a new name? You tell me that, Clinton Mayden!"

Billy took off his food-spattered glasses and put them on the table away from the dishes of food. Ever since he could remember, Billy's parents had, from time to time, talked about their other child in his presence. Just as he knew to ignore the empty place setting, he understood implicitly that the conversation was not meant for his ears. By now, places in his body could *feel* it coming like an old wound auguring a downturn in the weather, and he reacted accordingly. Attuned at all times to all aspects of his mother's behavior, he sensed her voice hardening—used to, looking at her mouth, he actually tasted the bitterness—and, intuitively registering his father's resigned and unwonted deference toward the woman, he automatically tuned out before any of the content of their conversation got through to consciousness.

Billy's parents were no more aware than he was of this collective hedging of reality. They knew implicitly they could discuss their lost child as if the one not taken wasn't there. Beyond some vague sentiment that Billy was a 'good boy' (Billy, a baptized believer, had been saved in the higher sense, too), they, no more than Billy, discerned the aberrant nature of the family's intercourse, any more than the air around them felt disturbed by their voices.

The fractured, unfinished sentences and the oblique references still remained. The hard stares and the violent hand signals still flashed between Stella and Clinton. But these were unnecessary, little more than unconscious habits left over from when Billy was little and hadn't yet learned to sign off like Channel 5 at 8:00 pm.

Clinton waited a while, then said, "Okay, what did you hear now? You ain't gonna let me alone till you tell me. So, go ahead and tell me. You'd think a person'd have better things to do than ... ." Clinton's words trailed off, withering away in the glare of Stella's eyes.

"You want to know what I heard? Okay, I'll tell you what I heard," Stella said. She cast a perfunctory glance at Billy—which he took as a signal that the subject hadn't quite changed and he still wasn't there—and proceeded to relate Jonnie's more recent transgressions in her never-ending examination of *that woman*, who, as usual, was sure to be found wanting in ways still ongoing. "Some man ... it's always men she talks to ... was talking about something he *couldn't do without her*. She wanted to know where ... where she was supposed to go, I guess ... and he said he would let her know later. She told him she wasn't sure she wanted to do it *this time*. He told her that she better be there *Sunday night* or there'd be h-word to pay. So whatever it was it was something she musta done before. Sounded like that Dr. Maxwell, the man who runs Pinecrest."

Right after breakfast the phone had rung and Billy watched Stella pick up the receiver, easing it off the hook and putting it to her ear. Her satisfied smile said she had acted skillfully and that Jonnie did not know that a third party was privy to her call. As she listened the smile was replaced by a smirk, but the satisfaction was still there.

It registered in Billy's mind that Stella had done something wrong, but, in the spirit of forgiveness, he let the thought slip away.

"Maxwell? Ain't he got a feeble-minded kid, too."

Looking to her right to make sure her son couldn't see, Stella frantically pounded an invisible shut-off valve with her left hand, telling her husband to shut up. "She's not feeble-minded." The hissing noise she made was meant to be whispering. "She's mentally retarded. And yes, his son *is* mentally retarded, too, but him and his wife think they're too good to put their child in with others like him."

Clinton looked blankly at Billy. Billy remained impassive.

When his wife had stopped glaring at him, Clinton said, "Well, what do you thank he, this Maxwell feller, meant by that? Maybe it's got something to do with her job. He's her boss, I reckon."

"Yes, Clinton, I know he's her boss. I used to see him all the time when

I used to ... ," She glanced at Billy and continued, "... go over there. Linda Garrard, who is his secretary, even introduced me to him one time."

"That could explain howcome you seen that car with Pinecrest on it, too," Clinton said. "Maybe he was dropping something off to her."

Stella continued as if she hadn't heard Clinton's comment. "Linda told me he's not even a psychiatrist, which is what he supposed be, if he's gonna run Pinecrest. Politics, probably. She calls herself a psychiatrist nurse, *her*, I mean." Stella nodded in the direction of the Vonderheim's. "I bet you a hundred dollars she's never seen the inside of no nursing school, let alone have doodlem squat to do with psychiatry. And nurses don't kill people before they are even ... ."

It was Clinton's turn to give Stella a withering look. He nodded toward Billy.

Stella stood up, gathered up a few dishes and went into the kitchen, muttering to herself, "If she's not stealing babies she's killing 'em." The crashing of dishes hitting the bottom of the sink made Billy jump. Coming back into the dining room, Stella said, "Well, anyway, I bet you anything he meant he needed help with you-know-what. What else would they be doing on a Sunday night? If it wasn't something they had no business doing and didn't want to get caught at, why don't they do it during regular working hours on a regular work day?"

"Well, what did she tell him when he said she'd better be there?"

"She said she wanted time to think about it. Said she was thinking of 'passing on this one' is the way she put it."

Billy hadn't meant to say anything. Normally, most of what his mother said was stored in some disconnected, not to say quiet, part of his mind. But today, brought out of his fugue by the crashing dishes, he was momentarily caught off guard, and some inner partition was breeched. Excited by the expectations of the day ahead, he remembered Frankie's saying that Jonnie had let him live at Pinecrest at a time when he had no other place to go. Now she wouldn't let him forget it and made him pay her back over and over by doing the only thing, according to her (according to him), he was good for anymore. And, perhaps, too, Billy was goaded by some sense that Stella needed his support in her never-ending campaign to enlighten Clinton about the danger living next door. At any rate, a vivid (and familiar) image of the two lovers was active in his mind and Billy's tongue sprang into action before he could corral it. "Frankie West said Miss Vonderheim had a scissor-lock on him and he don't think he'll ever get out of it, even if he wanted to."

Clinton gave Stella a look that said, Look what your obsession with that woman has led to. Stella picked up Billy's glasses and shoved them toward him. "Here put these thangs on. We didn't buy 'em just to decorate the dad-blamed table."

2

Pushing his glasses up on his nose—Stella said he needed them on account of his eyes being weak from all the studying he had to do in college—and picking up the phone to call Frankie West, Billy was full of excitement and anticipation. He wanted to call Frankie before Jacob Garrard called *him*. He and Frankie hadn't played basketball since Frankie and the preacher's daughter, Dixie Johnson, got married. There was some sort of dedication ceremony going on at Pinecrest and Billy didn't know when, or if, the gym would be available in the afternoon. He wanted to ask Frankie what he knew about it. And to see if he'd like to play.

He picked up the receiver.

"Come on now, Jonnie, don't clam up on me." Billy recognized the voice. It was Frankie West!

"Hang up the phone, Stella!" Jonnie Vonderheim snarled.

What a coincidence! If it hadn't been Frankie on the line, Billy wouldn't have done what he now did. He pushed down forcefully on the little bar, disconnecting the phone; then he softly lifted it up again. With Jonnie now thinking he was Stella gone away, he was twice removed from detection; doubly free to eavesdrop with impunity. Stella could not have done it better herself.

"Who is Stella?"

"Oh, just a nosey neighbor," Jonnie said.

"Maybe I should come over." Frankie sounded worried.

"Fred's here."

Glancing out the window, Billy didn't see the beer truck in the Vonderheim's driveway.

"Jonnie, I can't afford any more trouble. I've already lost a whole year of my life."

"Trouble? You want trouble? Then let Fred Vonderheim see you over here again. You'll know what trouble is. You'll lose the rest of your life. What there is left to lose. If you're worried about that Mayden bitch's eavesdropping, maybe you should tell her dopey son next time you see him to tell his mother to stop listening in on my phone calls. Otherwise, it's like I told you already: I don't know what you're talking about."

"Her son? Oh yeah, Billy."

"Yeah, Billy *May*den. Good name for the little do-gooder. He's one of your blow-buddies, isn't he?"

It's pronounced *My*-den, Billy wanted to say. Why can't people get it right.

"Come on, Jonnie. Lay off the queer talk, okay. One time doesn't make me a homo. I was drunk, didn't know what I was doing."

"Look, Frankie, you can put that piece of hog-gut anywhere you want to. I couldn't care less. But don't give me that crap about 'one time.' It's *me* you're talking to, Stud. I work for Arty's old man ... ."

"The good doctor M.," Frankie interjected.

"That's right. He has been good to me. To you, too. Hell, he let you *live* at Pinecrest for a while. I know you haven't forgot about that. If you remember, none of your uppity relatives would take you in. That's how come you were able to take advantage of poor old Arthur in the first place. And if you think Dr. M. doesn't know what's going on between you and his son, you got another think coming. *And* he knows you still go over there any time you don't have any better place to go. Like when Dixie kicks your butt out for being so drunk you're no good for her in bed. Or for anything else, far as that goes, except maybe whatever you and Arthur do with each other. Do you think I *like* risking my job by letting you hang around there? Lucky for you and for me Dr. M. looks the other way, at least so far. His own son, for God's sake."

"He don't give a shit about Arthur and you know it. And he's not *about* to fire you. All the dirt you got on him? Besides that'd mess up the good thing you two have going. You're just pissed because I said Arty did it better than you."

"And *way* more than one time."

"Okay, okay. You've made your point. But it's not the way you think."

"I don't think. What about when you were in the 'Marines'? Was that the way you think I think?"

"That's different."

"If you say so. Anyway, I repeat: I don't know what you're talking about."

"Come on, Jonnie! Don't treat me like just any old piece a crap. We've been through a lot, me and you. Used to, you couldn't get enough a me ... and ... you know."

"No I don't know. Tell me."

"You know ... *it* ... *him*."

"I hope for your pitiful sake you're not talking about what I think you are."

"You know what I like you to call him."

"Jesus! You'll never grow up, Frankie. No, I don't remember. I don't *want* to remember."

"His Majesty! Come on Jonnie, say it. Say hello to His Majesty. He has a new crown. He's wearing it right now, just for you. Here I'll put him against the receiver. He'll feel your vibrations."

"Frankie! I know I'm old enough to be your mother, but you don't have to act like a little boy."

"Okay, okay. But can't you do me this one little favor? It's not like you have to *do* anything. Just *don't* do something. Make her *think* you did. By the time she realizes that you didn't it'll be too late."

"Oh, I see. You want me to *fake* it. I thought you had the mistaken idea I could somehow stop it from happening."

"Yeah, fake it. If you really do it she'll leave me for sure. There'll be nothing to keep her. If you don't help me out here, she'll go to some butcher with a coat hanger. She's already made contact with one. I made her think I'd go along with it if she'd go to you. Ever body knows Theo Jeannsonne sends his women to you."

"Who's Theo Jeannsonne?"

"Ha ha. Very funny. Dixie wants to go to Hollywood. Says a kid'll just slow her down."

"Damn straight it will! What woman wants to be stuck raising a snot-nose kid by herself? You know, Frankie, you were singing a different tune the last time this happened. Least from what I heard. I know you're married now, but even if you weren't gonna ... weren't sick ... you still can't afford a family. Besides that, you're a drunk. You'd make a lousy father, just like you've made a lousy husband. She's better off without you, kid or no kid."

"Thought you didn't know what I was talking about!"

"Yeah?"

"Then how did you know about 'the last time'?"

"Word gets around."

"But you *do* know what I'm talking about."

"Nope."

"I can't believe you're being so cold-hearted. I *told* you what the tests showed. Hell, you're supposed to be a nurse. Supposed to have some compassion."

"I *am* a nurse. I *do* have compassion ... in my own way. I have compassion for any woman who doesn't want to be saddled with a kid she never wanted in the first place, for example. And I have compassion for what's happened to you, too. I really do. I'd have more compassion if you hadn't put me and Dixie and every other woman you've been with in danger. There's no telling what you've picked up from Arty over the years. He's worse than you are. He's like a dog in heat, except he's *always* in heat. No telling how many white-trash low-life scum-bags he's been with. I'm not surprised by what the tests show. You've been very careless, Frankie."

"You can't catch leukemia that way."

As always, hearing the word leukemia gave Billy a creepy but not altogether unpleasant feeling. He had heard the disease described as cancer of the blood and that people who had it just wasted away, slowly and painlessly. Wondering how it must feel, his blood would seem to tingle and his eyes would open wide. Thinking it seemed a good way to go, he would imagine himself, with other innocent blank-eyed children, floating up through the ether to heaven.

"I'm not so sure about that, *if* that's what you have. And what about that other problem of yours?"

"What other problem?"

"Look Frankie, I know it must be hell, for you especially, not to be able ..."

"Don't say it!"

"... to get it up."

"Is *that* the reason you're giving me the runaround?"

"Hardly. Didn't you *hear* what I just said? But, since you asked, I put up with that longer than most women would. And let's face it, Frankie. Without *that*, you ain't no good for me or any other woman. That and sports was all you ever had going for you. Now you don't have either one. And you've robbed Dixie of what it is the right of every wife to have. Tell me, Frankie, how did ... I mean, didn't you ever wonder if maybe it's not someone else's? How long's it been since you got it up?"

"Dixie has ways of getting me turned on. She knows tricks that even you don't know."

"Did you get that other test I told you about?"

"Fuck that other test."

"Okay, but I do *not* know what you want from me, Frankie. Even if I did and I did what you want me to do ... or didn't do what you don't want me to do ... I can't see what difference it would make. Once you're gone, a thousand little red-headed Frankie's and Frances's aren't gonna bring you back."

"Jonnie, it makes all the difference in the world. Put yourself in my shoes. What if you couldn't have kids? How would you feel? Leaving nothing of yourself?"

"I'd feel just fine. In fact, I *do* feel just fine. I don't have kids and don't want any. And, like I say, ain't nothing you can leave behind that'll make you any less … . But, okay, Frankie. You've helped me out when I needed it and I've always believed in you scratch my back and I'll scratch yours. I've already talked to him once about it, a couple of hours ago. I gotta tell you he didn't like the idea one little bit. But I'll talk to him one more time, do what I can. But you're gonna have to scratch my back one last time. Okay? It'll involve Crystal and maybe Ralph. They still hang around you all the time?"

Crystal, Billy thought, the alligator lady who lived in one of the cabins at Magnolia Park. And Ralph, the deaf mute, who never grew taller than about four and half feet and still looked like a little boy. Ralph and Billy had been childhood friends before Billy became friends with Jacob Garrard.

"Yeah. Oh Jonnie! You are the greatest! Just tell me what you want and it's yours."

"Okay, but I can't tell you now. Too many ears listening in. Around here and on the party line. (You still there, Stella?) I'll go out and call you later. And Frankie … ."

"Yeah?"

"Get the test done."

"I did."

"What did it show?"

"Don't know yet."

"Don't know or don't want to know?"

3

"I'd rather have you working here, Dixie, close by, in the park." Picking up the bottle on the table at which he sat in a wheelchair and emptying it into his glass, Frankie West thought, So I can keep an eye on you. Ha, that's a laugh.

"Hmm." Dixie put the finishing touches on her blonde wig in the mirror on the back of the front door of their three-room cabin. "Hey, Frankie, think we'll live in a house with a bathroom before we die? Think we'll ever have chairs that don't have wheels on them?"

"Did you hear what I said?" Frankie took a big swallow of 'water.' "Do you have to wear that stupid thing?"

"What? And let all that schooling go down the tubes?" Turning away from her own image in the mirror, Dixie's eyes hardened and she looked at Frankie. "You don't like my wig? Tough!"

"Why do you wear it?"

"Haven't you heard? Blondes have more fun."

"Then you're a natural," Frankie said ambiguously. "Just remember if it hadn't been for me working my ass off driving that stupid pulpwood truck, you couldn't've fucked away all those months in 'beauty school.'"

And you couldna got all those big ideas from those other slut-beauticians you work with, either, Frankie thought, but he knew he was talking nonsense. Dixie had worked as a cocktail waitress at the Magnolia Park bar during the time she was attending the Beauty Institute, commuting to and from New Orleans in the old car she had bought with money she had managed to squirrel away before Frankie could spend it on booze. What Theo Jeannsonne paid Frankie as 'security guard' for the park was less than Dixie had brought home in tips alone.

Frankie hadn't logged since the onset of 'it,' his illness. At least he was pretty sure he had some kind of illness. He had resisted Jonnie V.'s suggestions that he go to the doctor. *Seek and ye shall find.* Isn't that in the Bible somewhere? So, it must also be true: *Don't seek, and ye won't find.* He didn't need no doctor telling him he had leukemia. The very word itself gave him the creeps, made him imagine he could actually *feel* his blood cells dying. The impotence, the weight loss, the fatigue, these were probably caused by the booze. If so, the last thing he wanted was to have some doctor make it official. Not to mention the money he'd have to shell out. Yeah, the swellings in his arm pits and groin he could live without (and hopefully with), but he'd known worse. His year in the 'Marines', for example. He'd just wait and see.

Even if he wasn't really sick he was never going back to logging. That was loser work. Not that his present job was much better. But being able to say he had experience working as a security guard at a 'major amusement park' might help his chances of being picked to fill the next opening in one of the Sheriff's Departments. Plus he had a pistol. It didn't make up for you know what, but at least it was something.

Yeah, Frankie knew that crap about him logging while Dixie lived the life of Riley in New Orleans was absurd. He just wanted his wife to show some kind of emotion and the negative variety was as much as he could hope for these days. Unless he came clean about 'it' but he'd rather die than be pitied. At least by Dixie. "I mean, while you were in the Beauty Institute … I … drove … . While you were in beauty school … ." What the hell am I trying to say, Frankie wondered. No answer came.

"It's a real *school*. Not a *beauty* school. I'm gonna be a *make-up artist*." Back to looking at herself in the mirror, Dixie was upbeat.

Frankie leaned over and fiddled with the wheels on his chair, pushing one wheel back and forth while holding the other one stationary. He enjoyed the mild dizziness caused by the chair's motion which was like that of a hand twisting a screwdriver. "I like these chairs." He had bought four of them cheap from the nearby Hot Springs Sanitarium. Polio victims, allegedly cured by the mineral waters of the springs, had left or donated so many chairs, braces, walkers, canes and other crap, they had run out of room in the Hot Springs Polio Museum. Or so they claimed.

"It's easier to roll than to walk." And the discarded wheelchairs are proof that some people do come out alive on the other side of terrible illnesses, Frankie thought.

"You hear me, Frankie. I'm a *make-up artist*. Not a beautician." Frankie's ramblings, jumping from topic to topic, used to bother Dixie. Not now. In most cases it was easier to just ignore what he said. But she couldn't stand it when he insulted her by refusing to understand what she was trying to do with her life. He didn't *want* to understand. No, he was just too much of a hick, too dumb, to understand. But it still made her mad.

"That what they call you up at Hot Springs? A 'make-up artist'?" The sanitarium was next door to Pinecrest, Frankie's home-away-from-home.

"I'm just working there until I get my break, Frankie. Someday I'll be in Hollywood." With a swipe of her open hand, she created an invisible marquee in the air up near the ceiling and read aloud what it said: "'Dixie West. Make-up artist for the stars.' You wait and see." Dixie was just talking to be talking. Just saying it out loud so she could hang onto her dream. Yes, she'd keep the name West. Who ever heard of anyone, any woman at least, named Johnson having anything to do with Hollywood. His name was the only good thing Frankie ever gave her. "Besides cocktail waitressing don't pay shit."

What's he bitching about, Dixie thought. She had worked it out with Uncle Toe to look the other way when Frankie stole booze from the bar. She had to keep her husband pacified at least until after she left, after she got her big break. She glanced at Frankie. He's a lot easier to live with when he's drunk, she thought. Of course, she wasn't about to let him know she felt that way. Stupid jerk may try to sober up out of spite, and then he really would be a pain in the ass. She knew his little trick of adding water to the vodka bottle to make it look like he drank less than he did; and she knew about the 'secret' blue bottle he kept in the cupboard. She let him have his little secret and ever so often she emptied the 'vodka' into the sink, with him looking, just to make him think she didn't like him drinking so much. And to give him the thrill of getting away with something. One of these days, when she made it big, she would pay her uncle back for every drop of liquor Frankie stole from the bar.

"What will 'Brother Johnson' say? You know what he says about women painting their faces."

"Who cares what that sanctimonious prig would say," Dixie said. "I say 'would' because if you have any bright ideas about telling him I'll drop your ass like a hot potato. Though God knows where I'll *ever* find another palace like this one. I bet there's not a single house on St. Charles Avenue that has a double bunk bed in the living room. And with neon lights no less. Think we can get *Architectural Digest* to do a piece on this place? Maybe we could get your cousin Charlie to take the pictures." She looked in the mirror. She patted her wig and twisted around to check her tight-skirted rear-end. "That's all I need. My old man giving me grief. Telling me I'm going to burn in hell forever and ever and ever. I've heard enough of that crap for *two* lifetimes."

Looking at his wife and her reflections as she aligned the mirrors of her Arcadian boudoir—one on the cabin's front door and one on the wall above the couch—to get a better look at herself, Frankie took in, from the various vistas thus afforded, the smirks of self-satisfaction on her face.

Flinching in the glare of the perfection of her pitiless bottom, he felt a shiver of pride and anger. We used to knock 'em dead, he thought. Stars on and off the court. Homecoming King and Queen. First-team All-State. Two redheads, he thought. The school color. This was enough of a palace a year ago. True, working in the bar meant a buncha hard-legs ogling her every night, undressing her. The smart ones, the city-slickers killing time while their wives looked after their kids with polio at the sanitarium, giving her big tips, sweet-talking her … arousing her. The dumb ones, the redneck hicks and Coon-ass Cajuns smelling of the oil fields and the shrimp boats, telling her they had a big tip for her, wink, wink, asking her if the hair *down there* was red, too. He lit a cigarette, let it dangle from his lips. Yeah, all that is true, but at least she'd be near. Who knew where the job in the sanitarium beauty shop would lead. Or what other big ideas the other women there, most of 'em single, would put into her head.

"What about all your friends … er … customers? Don't you miss them?"

"What are you talking about, Frankie? What customers? You mean those creeps that come to the bar every night?"

"Yeah. Most of 'em come there 'cause a you."

"That's a reason to *stay*?"

"Well, what about Janelle? She's your mother. Don't you care about her?"

"She'll understand. She wanted to be an actress, you know. And I have a hunch she had her fun before she landed the role of Perpetual Baptist Virgin." In the mirror, she saw the cigarette in Frankie's mouth. "What is this, anyway? Why you giving me the third degree?" Walking over to the table, she took a lit cigarette out of the ashtray, dropped it, ground it under the toe her high-heel shoe into the worn linoleum. "How many of those things you intend to smoke at one time?" Reaching across the table, she snatched the freshly-lit weed out of Frankie's mouth and deftly thumped it against the wall. A waterfall of sparks. She inspected her middle finger, front and back.

Was she giving him the finger? Or just making sure she hadn't damaged her nail? "Hey, you gonna burn this fucking place down, you little twat." Frankie jumped up and grabbed her wrist, twisted it.

Showing no sign of pain, Dixie turned to face her husband. Her hooded eyes gave her a look of defiant boredom. Frankie jerked her close, kissed her hard, crushing her lips against her gnashed teeth.

Dixie relaxed her mouth. Let him get a good taste, inside and out. She pushed him away. "Don't start something you can't finish." She turned back to the looking glass. "Now, you've messed up my lipstick."

"Maybe I could finish ... maybe I could do a lot of things ... if you'd ...
." Frankie's words trailed off. He sat down and drained his glass. Fucking watered down crap!

"What? If I'd what? We *tried* that, remember? I'm a beautiful young woman in the prime of my life. If you can't get it up with me, you can't get it up with anyone. With any *woman*, I should say."

"I didn't mean that. And leave him out of this. He can't help the way he is. Just remember it was *your* idea. You're the one wanted to watch. It must have worked. You said you got your rocks off."

"What *did* you mean, then?" Dixie said. Bringing up Arthur was a mistake, she decided. Leave it be. The less her dumb husband, who was drunker than usual at the time, knew or thought he knew about the 'experiment,' the more degrees of freedom for her. "And don't give me that stand-by-your-man crap. No, don't blame your failures on me." Picking up the empty bottle, Dixie pretended to read the label. "Maybe your problem is this stuff. Never known a drunk yet who could ... ." She put the business end of the bottle to her nose. "Still on the vodka? Oh well, this *is* Siberia."

Go ahead and finish your sentence, Frankie wanted to say, *Never known a drunk who could ...* what? But he knew the answer and he was afraid she'd say it if he asked. Why was he always attracted to ball-busters? At least Jonnie gave me blowjobs, he pouted. Not the best he'd ever had, but at least she tried, used to anyway.

Dixie took off her high heels, put them in the big cloth bag she would take to work with her, and put on sneakers for the short drive to the sanitarium. It had been her idea for all the stylists to wear high heels and most of them liked it. The owner, too. Gave the place class.

After she was gone Frankie poured his wife's dirty laundry out on one of the bunk beds in the bedroom. No spots on any of the panties. He looked in her closet, checked her supply of Kotex. Same number as last month. How long ago *had* it been? Frankie couldn't remember now when she said it happened. Besides, thinking about numbers always gave Frankie a headache. Oh, God, let it be ... . Let it be mine.

From a cardboard box in the back of his own closet he took out another bottle of vodka. He was pretty sure she was looking for a mark when she pretended to read the label on the empty bottle. Was it possible that she really did care? Enough to keep track of the 'vodka' and to pour it out sometimes? Did he dare hope for a miracle this late in the game? In the kitchen, he twisted the top off the bottle, breaking the seal. Then he emptied the vodka into his beautiful secret bottle. He loved its dark blue color. It made the vodka actually taste better. He refilled the vodka bottle with water. Put it right here on the table where she'll see it tonight when she comes home. Wait! Better pour some out. She'd never believe he hadn't had *any*. There, go ahead and pour it in the sink if you want to, Dix old girl.

4

"Hey, Billy! Did you fuck her?" Jake Garrard yelled out, loud enough for the whole neighborhood to hear. This was the beginning of their friendship, but Billy's susceptibility to the older boy's charm had been primed by an incident on the school bus a couple of weeks earlier.

Billy had lived in the neighborhood for about two years. During those two years his best friend away from school had been a deaf kid, Ralph, who it seemed didn't have a family or even a last name. He'd show up in the neighborhood from time to time and hang around the Vonderheim house, sleeping on their back porch or with the hounds underneath it. Jonnie didn't seem to mind. Ralph had introduced Billy to sex. Using gestures and drawings and conducting voyeuristic tours that included Jonnie Vonderheim's bedroom and secret places at Pinecrest where according to Ralph the male staff fucked and otherwise abused the patients, and where Billy and Ralph jerked off together, he had contributed to that part of Billy's education that his parents, the church, and school left out. Ralph also stole various items Billy coveted around the neighborhood in exchange for Billy's friendship.

The bus stop was the only place Billy ever came into even minimal contact with Jake who was a grade ahead of him at school. Billy's attitude, in so far as he thought about Jake at all, was that not only was he a bully but he was a snob to boot. The woods is full of them, as Stella would say.

Jake didn't ride the bus often; when he did, as often as not, he showed up just as the bus arrived and broke in front of the other kids waiting to get on. Because the stop was near the end of the run, nearly all the seats would be already taken by kids from the more upscale neighborhoods earlier in the route; but Jake would commandeer a seat in the back of the bus from some smaller kid so he could sit with some older boys he was friendly with at school. He liked to make loud insulting comments about other kids on the bus. His targets included anyone whose looks, clothes, behavior, or social standing he didn't like and anybody else he thought he could insult and get away with it; he was especially nasty to girls and kids from his own neighborhood. He was a grade behind kids his own age and his audience was the older boys at the back of the bus, especially those from affluent families, whom he wanted to impress.

Jake's breaking in line was especially odious on days when it was raining as it was on this day. As usual Jake came running up just as the bus arrived and broke in line, this time right in front of Billy. When he had got on the bus, Jake stopped just past the driver's seat; holding onto the handrails on the back of the seats on either side of where he stood, he blocked the aisle so no one could pass. Fixing his gaze on the girl who, as she did every school day, was saving a seat for her best friend, another girl who got on at the next stop, he said, "That seat taken?"

"Yes, it is," the girl said, not bothering to look at Jake.

"Who for?"

"You know who for."

As this little scenario unfolded, the other kids fell silent in anticipation of a little drama. Outside, in the rain, a strident chorus—children crying out in aggrieved and soggy indignation at their undeserved fate—heightened the tension.

Basking in the attention he was getting, and pausing to increase the effect of his performance, Jake batted his eyelids with exaggerated innocence and mock sincerity. Before he could say anything else, the girl, who was pretty and popular at school and used to being leered at, said, "I hope you're getting your eyes full."

Whereupon Jake said, "Pull up that skirt and pull down those panties and something of yours will be suddenly full."

The edgy silence exploded into laughter, mostly from the older boys in the back of the bus.

In the defensive naivety he always assumed in public, Billy hadn't caught the meaning of Jake's comment; but the laughter was enough to tell him it was dirty, and to crank up another notch the righteous indignation he felt on the behalf of the pestered girl and the kids still outside in the rain, not to mention his own annoyance at having his way obstructed. When he found out that the only reason Jake took the bus that day was to harass the girl, he was even more indignant.

However, after that day on the bus Billy would come to see the world differently. When, after puzzling over it for the rest of the day, he had, in bed that night, finally figured out what Jake said to the girl meant, he felt enlightened, like he had solved a difficult math problem, and was thankful that he had been there. He thought up a new private ritual which both preserved the proscriptive emotions he felt at the time and expressed those aroused later by the images inspired by his delayed appreciation of Jake's brazen proposition; it began with Billy forgiving Jake for his sins and praying for his soul and ended with him masturbating to delicious new fantasies featuring the girl with that 'something' of hers 'suddenly full'.

Thus, by the time Jake yelled out those first words, Hey, Billy! Did you fuck her?, Billy was helpless to resist the older boy's brash and dubious allure and Jake would pick up where Ralph left off with Billy's erotic education.

Billy was coming out of the house across the road from Jake's house when it happened. Jake was standing in his own front yard, his arms draped over the fancy hurricane fence that marked off the Garrard's well-kempt property from the rest of the neighborhood.

The house Billy was coming out of was the new preacher's. (This was before Brother Johnson acquired his ranch.) On an errand for Stella, Billy had gone there to give Brother Johnson Clinton's tithe money. By 'her' Jake meant the preacher's daughter, Dixie.

Crossing the dusty road, his bare feet mincing over the unforgiving gravel, Billy headed over to where Jake was. He kept his head down, hoping Brother Johnson or his wife Janelle or Dixie herself hadn't heard what Jake had yelled out and that none of the neighbors recognized him. If Stella found out that her son had *anything* to do with a boy who had sinful thoughts about the preacher's daughter, she would die.

Although the Johnson's had only recently moved into the neighborhood and Dixie was only in the seventh grade, she had already acquired a certain reputation. It went with the territory of being a P. K. It went double for any girl whose breasts developed early. Triple for a girl from New Orleans, which is where the Johnson's had lived before moving to Tioga. Almost from the start, Dixie played along with the game and eventually it seemed that she reveled in the notoriety. In the meantime she made top grades and when she got to high school she became a star basketball player.

Upon reaching the other side, any remaining scruples Billy might have had regarding Jake's moral character melted in the light of Jake's beaming smile and the shine of his sweaty, naked-to-the-waist body. (Jake had been mowing the lawn, which by local standards hadn't needed it.) He stood out against the bright green background of the Garrard's pampered property like a muscleman posing for the camera. His bulging arms, folded across his chest, framed his sculptured pecs. The upper half of his body, turned by the sun a golden brown, was offset below by starched Levi's and clean white sneakers. The stiff blue jeans were creased like dress pants. He resembled an early-teen movie idol. From that day forward, Billy would insist that Stella starch his jeans the way Jake's mother did his.

Seeing Jake now as if for the first time, Billy was hooked; he had never before been affected this way by another boy. His surrender, preconditioned by the incident on the bus and his own budding pubescence, was as complete as it was innocent, chaste, pure. It wasn't so much that Jake was good-looking and well-built, and he was both, it was that Billy had never before thought of other boys in those terms. His feelings that day were all new and, as of yet, lacked any hint of envy or competitiveness or desire.

"What did you say?" Billy wanted to hear it again.

"I said, 'Did you fuck her?' I didn't stutter, did I? Oh, I see that little smile. You *did*! You fucked that fine hunk of ass. Let me smell your middle finger. Bet there's pussy juice on it, right? You old motherfucker. I been wanting to tap into that ever since she moved in. She is stacked like the proverbial brick shit-house." Jake slapped his hands together, and, laughing, let out a loud, "Ooo weee! Hot damn!" Grinning and wagging his large head like a horse fighting a bridling, he made a slurping sound and said, "Let me at it! Come on in and tell me all about it, you pussy-hound. What grade you in? Seventh, right? I'm in the eighth."

Standing across the fence from the other boy, Billy's eyes made an unconscious survey of Jake's large handsome face. Lips, full and red. Skin, smooth and tan. Nose, straight with big nostrils. Dark, sparkling eyes. Well-proportioned head, jet-black hair, perfect crew cut with widow's peak. His ears, well-formed, not too large and not too small, did not stick out.

Smiling smugly as if confident of the effect of his good looks, Jake said, "Hear they're gonna dunk your ass in Flagon Creek. Cajuns call it Cold Bayou. Bet you didn't know that. " When Billy, not understanding, hardly hearing, shook his head, Jake continued, "You're gonna be baptized, right? Soul-cleansing blood of the lamb? All that good shit?"

"How'd you know about that?" Billy asked.

"Everybody knows everything about everybody else around here. Gossip flies faster'n shit out a duck's ass. Don't you know that, Old Bean?" Jake picked up his t-shirt that he had draped on the fence. "Come on in out of the heat." Reverting to what Billy would eventually learn was meant to be a British accent, he said, "I dare say, Old Chap, I wager you're neither a mad dog nor an Englishman." Then back to his normal voice, "It's hotter'n a fresh-fucked fox out here. Or a fresh-fucked *fist* is more like it. Ha ha." Jake laughed at his own joke. "I'm sweaty. Smell like a swamp sow in heat. We can talk while I shower. You can shower with me if you want to. Whata you say?"

"No, I probably better be getting on back home," Billy said with a deliberate lack of conviction.

"Balderdash, my good man! Poppycock and fiddlesticks, Old Bean." It was the 'British' Jake speaking. Then back to normal: "Bullshit! You don't have to go home yet. You haven't told me what you were doing in that whorehouse across the street. Ah, so that's it, huh? You want to go home and beat your meat, don't you? I've hit the proverbial nail on its proverbial head, haven't I? I can tell by that shit-eating grin on your face. You can do that later. Nice piece of ass, though, eh? I bet she fucks like a snake."

"How does a snake fuck?" Billy asked, laughing at the bizarre phrase, and feeling not altogether displeased that Jake *had* hit the nail on the head.

"Hell's bells on a Christmas turkey! How should I know? Like anybody else, I guess. With its goddamn dick. Come on, I'll ask Mother if you can have dinner with us."

"Dixie Johnson has a dick? I don't think so." Fully under Jake's spell now, Billy was pleasantly surprised that he was able to handle the give-and-take.

"Touché! Hey! You don't think so, eh? That must mean you done seen that luscious pussy, right? Did it have red hair on it? Whoopee! You've *got* to get your ass in here and *tell* me about it. You *did* fuck her, didn't you, you sly fox? I bet you'd fuck a snake if somebody held it head, wouldn't you? Say, I bet you're a smart motherfucker, too, aren't you? Do you make good grades? *I* do. All A's and B's. Not like the white trash scum over there. And over there." With a wave of his hand, Jake dismissed the neighbors on either side of his house. "Too dumb to pour piss out of a fucking *boot*, even if it had the directions on the heel in neon lights.

"Fuck them and the horse they rode in on. Tell me about Dixie. Who put the dicks in Dixie, eh? Who hasn't is more like it. Ooo weee! Pussy's the greatest thing in the fucking *world*." Lowering his voice to a whisper, Jake said, "You know how I want to die? I want to be out in the woods fucking some girl and have an elephant step on my butt."

"Why!"

"Drive my dick as deep as it can go into that luscious pussy. Speaking of pussy, you've got to meet Uncle Toe. He's not really my uncle, but I call him that. He loves pussy more'n a hog loves slop."

"Toe? His name is Toe?"

"Yeah, it stands for Theo. His brother and my old man were in the war together. He's Cajun like us. His brother is the fucking preacher. But Uncle Toe ain't nothing like *him*. Or any other preacher you ever saw. He owns Magnolia Park. He's the one who taught me the four F's: Find 'em, Fool 'em, Fuck 'em, and Forget 'em."

"Fornication is a sin. Says so in the Bible."

"Fuck the Bible! I'm gonna get all the pussy I can and go to Hell happy."

"What preacher?"

"The one whose house you just came out of, motherfucker. That's what preacher. That luscious pussy's old man. The one who's gonna drown your ass in Flagon Creek if you're not careful. Uncle Toe said he changed his name. What's he call himself now?"

"Brother Johnson."

"Not *my* fucking brother. One's plenty. 'Johnson', huh? That's Cracker for 'Jeannsonne', right? Fucker's ashamed of being a Cajun, I guess. I'd rather be a Cajun any day than a Cracker."

"You're a Cajun? You don't talk like one."

"Yeah, on my old man's side. I don't talk like one because of my mother. She won't put up with it. She's Jewish. That makes me Jewish. Don't tell anybody."

Inside the yard, following Jake to the house, Billy got a good look at his new friend from behind. It was only then that he realized how short Jake was, half-a-head shorter than himself. Putting on his t-shirt as he walked, thrusting his arms into the tight-fitting garment, Jake seemed to move through the air like a swimmer through water. Billy noticed the muscles rippling all over Jake's back from his narrow waist to his broad shoulders and thick neck.

Talking over his shoulder, Jake suggested again that they shower together. "I smell like a hog that's been wallowing in shit for a couple of days."

Just then a man and an older boy came around from behind the house, headed across the lawn toward the front gate.

"Hey, Pop. This is Billy, my new friend."

"Not now," the older boy said and he and the man got in the blue pickup truck parked in the driveway and drove away.

(Billy would eventually learn that the pickup was a 'sore spot' with Jake, as he expressed it; he thought it marked his family as poor, if not out-and-out low class, and he hated being seen in it. Although he would have preferred taking the bus, he usually rode to school with his parents and his brother, all four crowded into the cab—Mr. Garrard dropped the boys off at school and his wife at Pinecrest, where she was secretary to the Director—because that way he could sleep a bit longer.)

"That's Pop. Name's Vincent. And my asshole brother. Jimmy. He's one year older'n me, but five years dumber."

A short woman, well-groomed and smelling of lilac and garlic, opened the door just as they reached the front steps. "You boys take your shoes off. I just polished this floor. Oh! He's not wearing shoes!" Billy looked down at his feet. Embarrassed, he kept his head bowed. "Wait here. I'll bring a pan of warm water and some soap. He can wash up. Can't have those dirty feet on my clean floor." Returning with the soap and water, she handed the pan and a towel to Jake. "My goodness, your friend doesn't wear shoes, Jakey? Hasn't he ever heard of hookworms?" Although Billy didn't look up, it seemed to him that Jake's mother could hardly make herself look at his offending feet. From her tone of voice and stiff posture he imagined her expression to be like that of a person seeing their first case of leprosy. What did hookworms have to do with not wearing shoes?

Drying his feet with the soft towel, Billy thought of Jesus getting his feet washed by Mary Magdalene.

The living room was the cleanest, tidiest room Billy ever saw. A sofa and two arm chairs with clear plastic covers. On a curvy-legged table with a crocheted coverlet, a large radio layered with highly-polished inlaid wood. On a glass-top coffee table, reflecting the fancy light fixture overhead, a big picture book of plantation homes along the Mississippi. Underneath the table, on the highly-polished mahogany-colored hardwood floor—clean enough to eat off of, as Jake would later brag—a small thick rug with abstract patterns of dark muted colors. The rug was Persian, it would turn out, and cost 'an arm and a fucking leg'.

"What is your friend's name, Jake?"

"Billy."

"Billy what?"

Billy told her his last name, pronouncing it *My*den. "I think you may know my mother, Stella Mayden". Looking at her face for the first time, Billy noted that Linda Garrard was a short, trim woman whose clean apron and stern expression said: In this house I am boss and all business. He was pleased she had referred to him as Jake's 'friend' and he could see why she didn't want dirty feet in her house. He forgave her for the fuss she made about his feet and the way it made him feel.

The boys followed Mrs. Garrard into her kitchen. "Janelle, I think you probably know Jake's new friend, Billy Mayden. His family goes to your church, if I recall."

Janelle Johnson! Brother Johnson's wife! She was sitting at the kitchen table breast-feeding her new baby. Had she heard Jake's *Did you fuck her*? How could he have forgotten about that?

Billy had been mesmerized by Janelle Johnson's pregnancy. Most every Sunday morning Mrs. Johnson sang a solo just before her husband began preaching his sermon. With Jonnie Vonderheim at the piano. Sometimes Dixie Johnson joined her mother in a duet. Seeing the preacher's wife at the two Sunday services and at Wednesday night Prayer Meetings, and at other times in the neighborhood, he had watched her grow imperceptibly larger and larger. He had often tried, without much success, to envision the preacher and his wife together making a baby. None of the images he could muster were very erotic. It was like trying to picture his parents doing it.

Dixie and Jonnie Vonderheim were another story. Seeing one of them in her Sunday best, Billy couldn't always keep his mind on Brother Johnson's sermon. Images of it being done to *them* came unbidden. But not unwelcome. Except, perhaps, at church, where it was sometimes hard to hide the effects of certain naughty thoughts which could be all too evident in the loose dress pants that Stella made him wear. (Maybe she'd let him wear starched jeans to church … ?)

"Oh, yes. Hi, Billy." Janelle Johnson moved the pink fuzzy blanket away from the face of the baby she was holding.

"Hi, Sister Johnson." Billy studied her face. Nothing. Could it be a trap? Would she act like nothing had happened, let him think she hadn't heard, and then tell Stella the next time she saw her at church? Maybe she was too embarrassed to say anything around Mrs. Garrard. Maybe she felt Mrs. Garrard should be the one to say something.

"Oh, don't call me Sister, Billy. I'm not one of those silly old nuns. Come look at the baby. I know how you love babies."

Bending down, Billy saw a breast lolling outside the unbuttoned dress. The baby was nursing. Straightening up, he said, "Hey, Jake, come look at this cute baby."

Jake came over and looked. His face turned red and he backed away.

"Here, Billy, you want to hold her?" Janelle Johnson said. "It's okay, just be very careful. She won't mind. She likes to be held. Her name is Tommy Sue." Handing Billy the baby and buttoning her dress, she stood up. She ran her hand through Billy's hair. "That is a beautiful head of hair you're got, Billy. And, Linda, just look at the baby blue eyes this boy has. He's gonna be baptized soon. You're a good boy, Billy." Smiling, she said to the other woman, "He's so good with babies. You should see him at church, playing with the little ones. They run to him like he was the Pied Piper."

Linda mumbled, "And look how that turned out." She didn't return Janelle's smile.

No way she would be smiling and letting me hold her baby if she had heard Jake's crude question, Billy decided. Thank you, Jesus. But what did Mrs. Garrard mean, how *what* turned out? Did she not want him and Jake to be friends?

Billy took the baby and rocked it side to side. He reached under the baby's little shirt and felt the smooth skin of her back and belly. Looking around he saw Jake hanging from the top of the door between the living room and the kitchen. Bobbing up and down like a toy monkey on a rubber string, Jake was chinning himself.

"One, two, three, four, five, six, seven … ." When he got to twenty, Jake dropped to the floor. "I bet you can't do that." Facing toward the living room, he tucked in his t-shirt, twisting right and left, making sure it was neatly tucked all around.

"I don't even know how you did it. What were you holding on to?"

"Come here and I'll show you."

Still holding the baby, Billy walked over to where Jake was.

"See that board? Part of the door frame? It's less than an inch thick. I hang from that with just my fingertips. You try it."

"Maybe some other time." Billy tickled the baby's chin. "Wook at dat wi-uh cute face."

"Jake, you need to shower. And your new friend's mother must be wondering where he is." Mrs. Garrard wiped her hands on a dish towel. Done wiping, she folded the towel and put it on the kitchen counter.

"Aw, Mom. Can't Billy stay? Please, let him stay for dinner, Mom. Please." Rushing past Billy toward the side kitchen door, Jake whispered, "Come on out back." Then, over his shoulder to Mrs. Garrard: "We'll wash the dishes and clean up the kitchen. Won't we, Billy?" He tugged on Billy's shirt and went outside.

"You were gonna do that anyway." Mrs. Garrard's remark caused Janelle Johnson to chuckle her approval.

"He means supper, doesn't he?" Billy said, rubbing noses with the baby.

"Dinner is the evening meal." Mrs. Garrard picked up the dish towel and wiped her hands some more. "Only in the South do people say dinner when they mean lunch. And supper when they mean dinner."

"But we're *in* the South." Janelle Johnson cocked her head and smiled her good will. "Can't get more Southern than this." Her open-handed gesture took in the whole state.

"When in Rome, eh? Not for me, thank you." More hand wiping. "I think using words wrongly shows a lack of proper breeding, no matter where you are. But, dinner … supper … call it what you will, it's time for me to start cooking it." This time the towel got thrown unfolded into the sink.

What's Rome got to do with it? Billy thought. He put the baby against his chest, her chin resting on his shoulder, and patted her back.

Jake poked his head back inside the kitchen. "Can Billy eat with us?"

"We'll just have to wait and see. Your father and your brother will be coming back from the hospital soon and they may be pretty hungry. If there's enough, okay, but if not … . And they'll be wanting a shower, too.

So, you go ahead and get yours so they won't have to wait. You know how Jimmy is."

"I'd better get on back across the road myself." Janelle Johnson began gathering up all the baby stuff.

"Thanks for bringing that beautiful baby over. She has such beautiful blue eyes. Just like her mother's." Mrs. Garrard's face seemed to brighten at the prospect of resuming dominion over her kitchen.

"Thank you and you're welcome. John and I are just so happy. We had tried for years to have another baby when we lived in New Orleans. Then, we moved here and it happened. Just like that! Must be the clean, fresh air. John wanted a boy. That's why she ended up with the name Tommy Sue. But he'd be the first to say that God has truly been good to us."

"Well, now we know for sure you're not one of those silly nuns."

"Oh! My Gosh! You're Catholic, aren't you? I'm so sorry, Linda. How insensitive of me! I wasn't thinking when I said … when I told Billy I wasn't … I meant no offense."

"None taken, Janelle. Vincent, my husband, was raised Catholic, but he hasn't been to mass, let alone confession, since before we met."

"You and he might want to drop in on one of our services one of these Sundays."

"I don't think so, but thanks anyway."

After helping Janelle Johnson put the baby in its stroller, Billy went around to the back of the house where he saw Jake poke his head out of a small wooden building painted white to match the main house.

"Pssst!" Jake motioned Billy over and put his finger to his lips for silence.

Inside the little house, Billy saw that Jake had his jeans unzipped and was masturbating.

"I *had* to get out here and jack off, man. My balls were about to explode. Look, the motherfuckers are blue!"

"Why?"

"Why what?'

Billy nodded toward Jake's busy hand.

"*Why!* The motherfucker wants to know why I jacking off?" Jake gestured mock incredulity to an invisible third party. "I cannot *believe* you don't know why! Didn't you see that goddamn luscious-assed *titty?* That great big old delicious titty that fucking baby was sucking on! Why do you think I was chinning myself like that?"

"Let's see … ." Billy pretended to ponder. "Were you were showing-off because you were jealous that Sister Johnson said I had nice hair and pretty blues eyes?" He liked Jake more every minute.

"Ha ha. Very funny. No! It was because I had a fucking erection."

"What's that?"

"A boner. A hard-on. My fucking dick was stiff as a fucking *board*, man. Don't tell me you don't masturbate! I'll call you a bald-faced fucking liar if you do."

"Master what?"

"It's *this*, you asshole." Jake looked down at himself, still pumping away.

"What's that got to do with chinning yourself?"

"I was trying ... ." Jake paused and looked to one side, as if reminding himself that he talking to a small child. "I was trying to ... get the blood ... from here ... ." Using his free hand he pointed at the operative hand. "To here." He slapped the biceps of his hard-working arm.

"What's blood got to do with your thing?"

"It was *hard*, you asshole, from looking at that woman's goddamn titty. And it's not my 'thing,' it's my goddamn pecker."

"Okay, let me put it this way: What's blood got to do with your blankety-blank *pecker*?"

"Jesus, man! Don't you know any fucking thing about the anatomy and physiology of sex? Haven't you ever seen *Gray's Anatomy*?"

"Whose what?"

"Blood is what makes your pecker get hard. It goes down there and fills the son-of-a-bitch up. Like a balloon full of fucking water."

"A balloon full of water isn't hard."

"Good God! There is so much I have to teach you."

"Why did you want blood to go to your arms?"

"So my mother and the goddamn preacher's wife wouldn't see the big-assed bulge in my fucking pants. Why do you think I hauled ass to the living room and why do you think I was facing away from everybody when I chinned myself?"

"I didn't know you guys knew the Johnson's." How come Sister Johnson never visits *my* mother, Billy wondered. He pictured Dixie Johnson in his bedroom.

"Jakey! Get back in here and get a towel and some clean clothes." It was Mrs. Garrard.

"Coming!" Jake winked at Billy and pumped faster.

In his room, Jake put on a record. The bedroom, which he shared with his brother Jimmy, was divided down the middle by a strip of white adhesive tape. "That's Montevonni's new album. Would you like to hear the Mormon Tabernacle Choir? I'm gonna try out for the chorus next year." He put his hand on his chest like he was pledging allegiance. He stuck his chin in the air and looked down his nose at Billy. "Ah seh Old Chap, do you loik to sing?"

"Why are you talking like that?"

"Hahv you nevah hud a British accent, my good fellow," Jake said in the same funny way. Continuing in his normal voice, "That reminds me of the Englishman who is watching his first baseball game. You hear that one? The first batter up hits one on the ground and hauls ass to first, but he's thrown out. Then the second batter draws a walk. Limey say, 'Oi seh, my good man, what is 'appening? Why isn't that chap running like the first bloke?' 'He has four balls,' someone tells him. 'Oi see. That would make it *rah*ther difficult to run.'"

Billy waited for Jake to stop laughing. "No, I've never heard anyone talk like that." He was intrigued with Jake's large mouth and the exaggerated mobility of his lips as he spoke 'British'. "But anyway, yeah, I guess I like to sing. Only place I sing is in church."

"Why don't you try out for chorus, too? We can practice singing together. Maybe we'll both be in the boy's quartet. Wouldn't *that* be something?"

"What's your daddy and brother going to the hospital for?"

"Pop's sick. He was in the war. He came back with some kind of bad-assed Jap lung disease. Doctors over at the V.A. can't figure out what the fuck it is. He has some crazy stories about the war. One time him and a bunch of other grunts ... that's what the soldiers called themselves ... paid five dollars to watch a Jap eat a plate of shit. Another time, they peed in some empty beer bottles and sold it to some stupid fucking Germans for the real thing. After we bombed Japan off the fucking map his division was sent to Germany. He brought back a German luger, but it went missing. He's a great guy. He was in college when the war started. Mom was putting him through. He said after the war he didn't want to go to college any more. He's a smart motherfucker, though. Always teaching me new words. You can bet your sweet ass *I'm* going to college."

"Like what new words?"

"Okay, let me think. You know what the prongs of a fork are called?"

"Prongs?"

"Ha ha. Funny man. They're called *tynes*. Spelled with a *y*. Okay, here's another: *hirsute*. Do you know what that means?"

"Hair suit? Let's see ... anything like what the saints used to wear? You know, a hair shirt with pants to match?"

"No, but you're close. It means 'hairy,' and it's *hir*sute, not *hair* suit. Hey! Time for the three S's. You wanna shower with me?"

"I'll watch. What are the other two S's?"

"Shit and shave."

The shower was in the same little house Jake had masturbated in earlier. Opposite the shower there was a flush-toilet. Jake closed the lid and Billy sat on it. (It would be another couple of years before the Mayden's got an *indoor* flush-toilet, let alone one in an outbuilding.)

Jake spread soapy water all over his body and struck muscleman poses, admiring tautened muscles in his arms and his left leg. After shaving his underarms with a razor kept on a shelf next to the showerhead and rinsing his body clean, he began to masturbate.

"You doing that again?"

"Yeah, I didn't finish yet."

"What did you do that for, shaving under your arms?"

"I have to. Otherwise, I stink like a pig in heat. Something in my blood makes my sweat smell like buzzard puke."

"Never smelled the stuff myself."

"Hey, Billy. Take your clothes off and come on in. We can jack-off together."

Billy demurred. He loved the word 'jack-off'. Saying it over and over in his mind made his throat constrict. It was a pleasant feeling, a vestige of his recent first orgasm. He wanted to jack-off. But he didn't want Jake to see him naked. Stella said it was a sin to be seen naked by other people. Besides, having often looked at himself naked in Stella's full-length mirror—when she wasn't around, of course—he wasn't eager to have his body compared with Jake's.

As he peered at Jake's body, Billy sensed something odd about the way Jake was positioning himself in the shower. Invariably standing sideways, he seemed to be avoiding showing his right side.

Then their eyes met. Billy felt like he had been caught looking.

Jake turned, giving Billy a front view. Billy looked first at the other boy's penis. Then, his eyes were pulled toward Jake's right thigh and he almost fainted at the sight. The shriveled and disfigured thing was about half as big as the massively muscled left thigh and was marred by a dark ugly-colored scar running from just below the hip to the knee, a couple of inches wide at mid-thigh. Another smaller scar on the inside part of the thigh, opposite the larger scar, gave the impression that the limb had been penetrated by a big jagged object.

"Pretty ugly sight, isn't it?" Jake said. He lifted the mangled leg, holding the thigh in his hands like a butcher showing a housewife a cut of meat. "Can't stand for anybody to touch it. Sends electricity ... feels like fucking lightening ... all through it. I can always tell if it's gonna rain, fucker starts hurting. Like a war wound. I *hate* thunderstorms. Lightning scares the shit out of me. It makes me feel all over like the way my leg feels when anybody touches it when I'm not expecting it."

"How'd ... what ... ?" Inwardly wincing and nauseous, Billy couldn't tear his eyes away from the monstrous display.

"Missed a whole year of school because of that cocksucker. They said I would probably be partially crippled and would most likely walk with a limp. But when I got out of the hospital, I *swore* I wasn't gonna be no fucking cripple. I *swore* I'd be stronger than I was before. That's where this ... ." Jake slapped his fist against his chest ... "and this ... ." cocking his arm, he made a muscle ... "came from. Feel how hard it is."

Glad to have his attention redirected, Billy felt Jake's biceps. It was rock-hard.

"I can run faster than just about any boy in my class. And let me show you something." Jake squatted down on the concrete floor of the shower-house. "Watch this." Extending his good leg and holding it suspended out in front of him, he started doing deep knee-bends using his damaged leg. "Bet you can't do that. There's a lot of fuckers with normal legs can't do that. Hey! Get your ass in here."

Recovering from the shock, Billy felt less bashful about his own body. As the initial horror brought on by the spectacle of Jake's injury subsided, it was replaced by deep sympathy for Jake's misfortune, and a narcissistic balance was struck somewhere in his psyche. What started with the realization that he was taller than the older Jake; and was helped along by his noting that, although Jake had more pubic hair than he did, Jake's erect penis wasn't as big as his own got when he masturbated; was brought to completion by the encounter with Jake's atrophied leg. Awash now with a familiar and pleasant sensation of compassion, he wanted to hug his new buddy, make him feel better.

Taking off his clothes, he got under the stream of water.

"Another good thing came out of my being in the hospital for so long. I did a lot of reading. I love to fucking read. How about you? You like to read?"

"I read a book on the geography of South America one time."

"Anything else?"

"That's about it."

"I bet *that* was interesting. Jesus, man, couldn't you find anything better than that to read?"

"What do you read?"

"Everything. Anything. Books. Magazines. Hardy boys. Shit like that. Hell, man, if there's nothing else around I'll even read a Nancy Drew book. I think about fucking her. Makes it more fun. Lots of stories. I read one every time I take a shit."

"What kind of stories? What's your favorite story?"

"Okay, my favorite is a story called 'Hop Frog'. About this court jester who's real short and crippled. But he builds up his arms so the fucker's strong as hell. All the lords and ladies make fun of him, of the way he looked and the way he walked. Called him Hop Frog. Made his life miserable, but he had to take it. Wasn't anything he could do. (Here, put some soap on it. Feels good.) Except make them laugh. That was the only way he could have any control over them.

"The ones he hated the most were these really fat motherfuckers, the king's buddies that hung around the king all the time. The king was a fat bastard, too. One night at a big fancy masquerade ball, the king and his buddies ask Hop Frog to help them come up with some really great costumes for them. So, he talks them into dressing up as orangutans, you know, like apes. He tells them they'll be able to scare the shit out of everybody there.

"First he has them put on something like long-johns. Then he covers them with tar. Then he puts black flax on 'em for hair."

"What's flax?"

"I'm not sure. Something that looks like hair and burns real easy. That's all you need to know. Then he chains them together so it'd look like they had escaped from the circus or something.

"At the height of the festivities, these 'orangutans' come into the big ballroom. Scares the shit out of everybody. But Hop Frog hooks their chain to this hook at the end of another chain that goes up to the ceiling. Then he signals someone to pull the chain and raise the fuckers up, or maybe he has some kind of counterweight or something. Doesn't matter. The fat fuckers are suspended in the air like a big-assed chandelier. Then he sets fire to 'em with a torch. The tar, the flax, their fat bodies, everything burns like crazy. Everybody watches as the bastards are burned alive in a big fiery ball.

"Meanwhile, Hop Frog climbs up the chain and goes through a hole in the roof. Fucker's so strong he can climb using just his arms. Hauls ass out of the country. Gets his revenge and makes his getaway. Like that story?"

"Yeah. What happened to your leg?"

"Watch this." Jake reached up and took the shower head off. Now the water came down in one thick stream, like a rope of water. Jake cupped his penis in his hand and let the water-rope pound it like a sparrow trapped under a down-spout during a heavy rain.

"Jesus, doesn't that hurt?"

"Nah. Try it. I can make myself reach a climax this way."

"Reach a what?"

"You're kidding, right? You're not? The motherfucker doesn't know what climax means! It's when you come. When you have an orgasm. You know about coming, don't you? When sticky white stuff comes out of the end of your dick?"

"Oh, that. I'd rather do it the regular way. So, you're two years older than me, then." Billy eyes shifted from his own dick to Jake's and back. "'Climax'. 'Orgasm'. Are those words your old man taught you?"

"Yeah. He says there's nothing wrong with sex. It's natural. According to Kinsey, everybody fucks their fist, ninety fucking percent of men, anyhow. Some women do it, too. The slutty ones. You can use your hand or you can do it this way with the water. Here, wanna try it?"

"Some women fuck their fists?"

"Ha ha. You know what I mean, you pedantic moron. They finger-fuck themselves. Turn this way. Let me see your dick. Jesus! You got a big dick!"

"You little queers done in there?" someone said. It was Jimmy, Jake's tall lanky older brother, poking his head into the little bathhouse. Stepping into the room and lifting the toilet seat, he flopped his penis out and started peeing.

"Billy, this is my ass-hole older brother, Jimmy. Jimmy, Billy."

Jimmy pissed for a long time. He looked at his penis with a solemn expression. "I bet I could make Dixie Johnson bleed like a stuck pig with one hard jab," he said when he had finished peeing. His gaze having never strayed from his penis, he pulled the foreskin back, exposing a lot of white pasty-looking gunk coating the shaft. Billy noticed that the business end of Jimmy's penis was bright red. It looked inflamed, like it had poison ivy or something.

"Dream on, you pompous motherfucker," Jake said. "You're hallucinating. What makes you think she'd want to fuck you? A dick that dirty, a fucking sow wouldn't fuck you. And what gives you the idea she's a fucking virgin."

"A 'fucking virgin'? Isn't that a contradiction in terms?" Jimmy said.

"She's going to be a missionary," Billy said.

"How do you know that?" Jimmy looked at Billy for the first time.

"She goes to my church ... or ... I go to her daddy's church."

"Well, all I've got to say is, So what?" Jimmy retracted his penis and zipped his pants. "Her going to be a missionary don't mean shit. Take my word for it, Dixie Johnson's like all the rest. They all want it as bad as we do. I don't care if she *is* the preacher's daughter. In fact, being the preacher's daughter just makes her think about it more than other girls. That's all preachers ever talk about. All they ever think about. Sex!"

"Then you'd make a good one, motherfucker. Hell, we *all* would. Show me a motherfucker who doesn't think about pussy all the fucking time and

I'll show you a motherfucking queer. But you're wrong about girls. They're not like us. Not all of them. Not the good ones." Jake winked at Billy. "Let's go listen to some more Montevonni. Want to?"

Back in his room, Jake said, "Look at that fucking mess," indicating his brother's side of the room. "Motherfucker's the biggest slob on the face of the fucking earth. You think his *dick* is dirty, take a whiff of that mattress. Motherfucker jacks-off every night by dry-fucking the bed. Sleeps in a puddle of his own come. Can you imagine anything more fucking disgusting?"

Billy's contempt for Jimmy was diluted by the fact that he masturbated that same way every night just before falling asleep. It helped him fall asleep and he believed that way, when Stella came into his room unexpectedly, she was less likely to figure out what he was doing than if she caught sight of a tell-tale sheet-tent. It freed his hands to caress his pillow, to press it against his face; kissing it, he imagined it was Dixie or some other girl. The hands-off mattress-method of masturbation seemed to him to be closer than the other to what he imagined real fucking was like. I'll have to stop doing that, he thought, remembering the sticky fluid his recent orgasms had yielded.

He'd still pray for Jimmy's soul, though. Jesus loves even the most unlovable of sinners.

In contrast to Jimmy's bed, which was unmade and piled with clothes, Jake's bed was neatly made, with the unwrinkled bedspread tucked under and over the fluffed-up pillow in the proper manner. Side by side at the head of the beds, in the space between them, were two identical phonograph record players. Jimmy's was piled high with school books draped with dirty socks and drawers.

"Cocksucker never listens to a fucking thing. Only reason he has a record player is because he has to have every-fucking-thing I have. Hey! Do you like Robert Shaw?"

"Who's Robert Shaw? He go to Tioga?"

"You mean ... . Oh, you sly fox. You're pulling my fucking leg. You're not as dumb as you let on, are you? I bet you make good grades in school, don't you? Yeah? I thought so. Me, too. All A's and B's. Here's a good album. You'll like this one. It's called *Songs of the South*."

Jake took a t-shirt out of his chest-of-drawers. He sniffed the underarm of the garment. "Pee yoo," he said. "Would you take a whiff a that fucking shit?"

Billy couldn't smell anything and said so.

Jake threw the offending object into a hamper and took out another t-shirt. "I can't *stand* dirty fucking underwear. Especially t-shirts. Particularly dirty armpits.

"Oh, that reminds me. I want to show you this book Uncle Toe gave me." Jake got on hands and knees, took a book from under the bed. "He has more fucking books that you ever saw. He let me borrow this one. The best parts are in Latin but he had a priest at Loyola translate them. Don't let my shit-head brother know it's here, okay?"

"Why did armpits remind you of it?"

"I'll show you." Jake located the page he wanted. "Listen to this: *'I learned from a sensual young peasant that he had excited many a chaste girl sexually, and easily gained his end,'* ... means he fucked her ass ... *'by carrying his handkerchief in his axilla'* ... means armpit ... *'for a time, while dancing and then wiping his partner's perspiring face with it'.*"

"Disgusting." Billy's throat constricted.

"Oh, while I've got it out, let me read you something else. Proves that fucking Jimmy doesn't know his ass from a hole in the ground. Jesus, is that bastard arrogant. He's more than arrogant. He's ate up with hubris."

"What's hubris?"

"*Supreme* arrogance. I can't *stand* that in a person. Jimmy has it worse than just about anyone I know ... . Where is it? Here it is. It's talking about the difference between men and women. Listen: *'Man has beyond doubt the stronger sexual appetite of the two. From the period of pubescence'* ... means when you get hair around your dick and girls' tittys get big ... *'he is instinctively drawn toward woman. His love is sensual, and his choice is strongly prejudiced in favour of physical attractions. A mighty impulse of nature makes him aggressive and impet ... '* something ... *'in his courtship'*. Then, next paragraph: *'Woman, however, if physically and mentally normal, and properly educated, has but little sensual desire. If it were otherwise, marriage and family life would be empty words. As yet the man who avoids women, and the woman who seeks men are sheer anomalies'* ... means freaks.

"Pop says you should always marry a virgin. My Mom was. Was yours?"

"I guess. What did Jimmy mean he could make Dixie Johnson bleed like a stuck pig?"

"Stupid fucker thinks she's virgin."

"What's that mean? That like the Virgin Mary?"

"Means she's never been fucked. Virgins still have their hymen. When you stick your dick in 'em it breaks and they bleed."

"I guess your old man told you that, too, right? Okay if I sit on the bed?" Billy had no idea what his friend was talking about, but had heard all he wanted for now.

The perfectly made bed reminded Billy of hospital rooms. He thought of Jake being in bed for many months. He saw Mrs. Garrard sitting by the bed.

"Better not. You'll mess it up." Jake sat down on a straight-back chair and began putting on socks; rolling them part-way down, he was careful to get them just so. "It's great to have a friend like you, Billy. Someone who isn't ate up with the dumb-ass like my brother and most of the people in this fucking neighborhood." Then suddenly he started laughing and slapping his thigh. The good one, Billy noticed.

"Did you hear that screaming across the road a couple a days ago?" Jake's laughing grew louder. He slapped his hands on his knees. "Oh, you *must* have. Fucking woman dropped her fucking baby in the outdoor toilet. I mean right down in the shit, man. With all the fucking maggots. How in the *fuck* can a woman drop her goddamn baby in the goddamn toilet?"

"You don't mean Sister Johnson, do you?"

"No, no. I'm talking about the bitch that lives next door to her."

Holding his shoes up, Jake examined them closely, tracing over the surface with his finger. "Mother-chicken-shit-fucker, would you look at these fucking goddamn shoes."

"They look great to me. They look heavy. Why is the sole on that one so thick?"

As soon as he said it, Billy wished he hadn't.

"They're special shoes. I had to start wearing them after I hurt my leg. Bad leg is shorter than the other one." Jake began polishing his shoes. Then, he started laughing again. "Another time, same fucking woman … . You're not gonna believe this one. Stupid bitch got her fucking tit caught in the wringer of her fucking washing machine. You talk about *screaming*."

"Hey, Jake. What's a nun? Sister Johnson said she wasn't a nun. What did she mean?"

"A woman who never has sex. That's why they call 'em nuns. They don't never get none."

Just then the record player started playing *Old Black Joe*. Jake jumped up and started conducting. "This is my favorite. *I'm coming, I'm coming, for my head is bended low.*"

5

The girl caused something of a stir among the boys, at least for a while, until the holidays were over and they got a close look at her. It was her first public appearance at Tioga High School; Billy was in the ninth grade. The Eighth Grade Girl's Chorus came over at Christmas time and gave a concert for the high school student body. Up on the stage, in the center of the back row, she drew every eye. From the highest point in the closed little world of the auditorium, she, in her robe of angel's white, looked down on everyone in the house.

Up there, she was beautiful, even though she wore her dark brown hair pulled back in a bun on the back of her head. The austere look imparted to her face by the severely restrained hair, and by the way the stage was lit, seduced the Stella in Billy. This left the barn-door unguarded, and the billy goat in Billy—Stella's figure for the Devil and for the ubiquitous evil of lust—flew the coop and careened around the auditorium.

Tall, slender and athletic, the girl would become a great rebounder and rank second only to Dixie Johnson in scoring; on the court she and Dixie played so well together their bodies seemed to work as a unit, as the twin agents of one mind. But that was later when the girl got to high school.

After the holidays that freshman year, Billy and some other boys went over to the eighth-grade building to check her out. They saw what wasn't apparent on stage. She was stoop-shouldered, as tall girls often are, and wore no make-up. More disconcerting, she had a scar on her face. Half an X-stroke, it ran diagonally and down, a back-slash across her left cheek, bisecting the right angle formed by her eye and her nose.

At that point the other boys lost interest.

Billy fell in love.

Working it out in his head, Billy imagined the scene. Under attack, she had turned her head to the right, to escape the blade's slicing open her eye. The knife, wielded by someone taller than she—a left-handed assailant, her father, as Billy imagined it—had found its mark in the soft flesh of her cheek. There had been lots of blood and the wound had been incompetently stitched up.

Even without the scar, the girl would never have had a chance at THS, if she hadn't hooked up with Dixie. To start with there was her family. They were Pentecostal, which explained the hair-do and the lack of face paint. The family was large and moved at least once a year to whichever Army base her father's low rank and disciplinary problems doomed them. The family name was Faustpool, which meant that in every new school, there was a kid or two in every grade from her on down, who got greeted with gibes of 'Cesspool, Cesspool, Cesspool'.

But the scar was her albatross. It was the symbol, the embodiment, of all that sullied her self-image. When the little ones huddled around her at school for shelter from the storm of invective, the scar was the focus of the vicious taunting, the rod that drew the bolts of bullying belligerence. Which only isolated her all the more from kids her own age, even as it added fuel to her smoldering self-hatred. Where Hester Prynne's burden was only an abstract letter, hers was the icon, the very picture, of Mother Eve's shame and her own. It could not be shed even at night any more than it could be washed away by the strongest soap or by a river of tears. Nor could it be transformed by fancy needlework into a badge of defiance.

So, is it any wonder that the scar would be the thing Billy loved most about her? Far more than had been the case with Jacob and his gimpy leg, her damaged cheek was his point of spiritual contact with her. Answering to the gash on her ruined face, a thorn of sacred lust was forever lodged in his heart, and he made room in his own soul for her tarnished soul.

In the years to come Billy would think: no scar up there, no Billy at the sisterly site down there on That Night, that summer night following her senior year, when—a few days before she left, first the state, and then the world—in his initial bowing down before the altar of Sex, he tasted Paradise. If it hadn't been for the scar lots of other boys, maybe even Frankie West himself, would probably have courted her and she wouldn't have given Billy a second look. As it was, he was more than grateful that it was he who enjoyed the privilege of punctuating the five years she lived in Tioga, the longest time she would ever stay in any one place. From That Night on, and even more so after her then-imminent death, when he thought about her, whenever something reminded him of her, usually some cloacal odor, he remembered the scar and his heart ached with every beat.

One cold day in his sophomore year, she and the two others he loved the most inflicted on him his own scar, no less damaging (and precious) for being figurative—preparing the ground, perhaps, for That Night, three years later, when he would kneel for the first time before his divinely designated deity.

It happened at the annual choral competition. During a break in the action, Billy went back to the Trailways bus for some reason and found Frankie West on the back seat flanked by two girls. It was freezing cold in the bus and a coat was draped across the trio's laps. One of the girls was Dixie Johnson, the other was the scar-faced girl of Billy's dreams.

The crushing pain of what followed was made all the more cruel by the fact that both Frankie and Dixie *knew* how much Billy liked the Faustpool girl. The element of deliberate betrayal redoubled the torment of his jealousy, even while it bound him all the more closely to his tormentors.

"Hey, Bill, my man!" Frankie said, holding up an open bottle of beer. "Get on back here and join us. His majesty is helping us choose up sides. We need one more to make 'em even."

Billy and Frankie became friends when they were both twelve and on the same Little League baseball team. Billy knew a lot about Frankie even before that. They were in the same grade but in different classes. Frankie's pimply cousin, Charlie West, the smartest boy in Billy's grade, was in Billy's class. Charlie was always telling stories about his cousin's exploits. When Frankie's father died and his mother couldn't take care of him and his siblings, Charlie's well-to-do family took Frankie in.

When that didn't work out and after Frankie had stayed a few months in Pinecrest, Jonnie Vonderheim talked Brother Johnson into letting Frankie come to live and work on his ranch with him, his wife Janelle, and two daughters Dixie and Tommy Sue. But that was later, after that initial baseball season was over.

Meanwhile, from Little League on, Billy made a special effort to become best friends with Frankie. When they got to high school, Frankie talked Billy into trying out for the basketball team. For a time Billy resisted the idea, but the two boys would go to the gym at Pinecrest Asylum just about every Saturday and Sunday afternoon, often just the two of them, to play basketball, practicing their shooting and perfecting their form. Billy knew his mother wouldn't go along with his even being around so many boys and girls wearing those skimpy little basketball uniforms in a gym full of people—many of whom Stella somehow knew got lickered-up for the games—much less would she go along with the only child she had left wearing the Devil's livery himself. Billy couldn't even wear jockey shorts (or Levi's, only over-sized Penny's Foremost were allowed) because Stella said they showed the shape of his butt.

On the bus, when Billy came near, Frankie pushed the coat to the floor. Each girl had a hand around Frankie's erect penis. They appeared to be holding hands with each other behind Frankie's back, their arms a ring of flesh, Billy thought, bejeweled by Frankie's phallus.

"Give us a hand. There's room for one more." Frankie laughed. He balanced the little metal cap off a beer bottle on the head of his dick. "There you are, Your Majesty. Your *High*ness." The girls giggled. "There's a crown for you. Anybody want a swig?" More giggling.

Billy would never forget the sight of the three of them sitting there. With time, and forgiveness, he came to think of the trio as King Solomon and the two women disputing ownership of the infant, that part played by His Majesty. At some prior and deeply-felt level they were a tribunal of his superiors. And he was found wanting.

And so the stage was set for Billy's initiation.

It happened near the end of the summer after Billy's freshman year in college. It began with what Frankie meant as a cruel prank, though it didn't turn out that way. In fact Billy wouldn't know that he had been tricked until much later when history would repeat itself, so to speak; when the final shape of his character would be sculpted, the final touches given to that secret portrait that would remain forever young and uncorrupted for the rest of his life. (See back cover.)

During that last summer, behind Stella's back, Billy and the Faustpool girl double-dated a lot with Frankie and Dixie. Billy had long since forgiven the girl for what he caught her, red-handed, doing on the back seat of the Trailways. How could he condemn her for that? Given half a chance, what girl wouldn't give her right arm to wield Frankie West's royal scepter?

Vowing to get as far away from Tioga as she could, the girl planned to leave for college in the fall. She and Billy had never had sex and Billy wondered, and talked a lot with Frankie and Dixie, about how things would end between them. Like most other guys, he believed a man's sex appeal, not to mention his overall social worth, could be measured by how far his girl would let him go. The girl understood this. She said she *wanted* to have sex in the worst way, which Billy took to mean she wanted to have sex with *him*, though he hoped that, in the event, it wouldn't be in the worst way. Knowing the choice was not his to make, he was prepared to continue begging until the cows came home. More than anything else she could imagine, she said, she was *deathly* afraid of getting pregnant out of wedlock, a fate she considered, she said, *worse* than death. She was, she said, 'saving herself for God'. Which meant, she said, she would make love only to her husband, *if* she ever got married, and then only to have children.

Billy understood her point of view, or so he said. He wanted to believe she was a virgin, but down deep he believed that if Frankie *hadn't* fucked her it was only because he didn't want to, or was afraid of what Dixie would do if she found out. Anyone could tell from the way the girl acted around Frankie that she was a poster-child for the Biblical pronouncement that (with the appropriate change in gender) stated: *I say unto you, That whosoever looketh on a man to lust after him has committed adultery with him already in her heart.* It was from the Gospel According to Stella—a. k. a. GAS when he was with Frankie or Jake—that Billy knew it worked both ways. Taking a step beyond that august authority, he forgave the girl. All the girls acted that way around Frankie, and Billy forgave them, too. (As for his own frequent solitary yielding to the *coarse, animal desire for sexual satisfaction*; well, that was a pre-marital, stop-gap, equivalent of the Apostle Paul's decree that it was better to marry than to burn.)

A few days before what would be their last date, Frankie told Billy that he, Frankie, had eaten Dixie's pussy. Frankie said it had been great, he loved it, couldn't wait to do it again and again. Frankie said Dixie had told the Faustpool girl that having her pussy eaten had been *fantastic*, the cat's meow; but it wasn't the cat that meowed, Frankie said, it was Dixie. Billy should a heard her! It was better than straight sex.

"Dixie said your woman was really turned on just hearing about it. Dixie thinks if you want to she'll probably let you eat *her* pussy." Frankie put his arm around Billy's shoulders and poked him in the ribs. "Worth a try, if you have the stomach for it. Nothing to lose but your supper."

Billy, innately precocious in such matters, knew all about cunnilingus by now from cherry-picking the sex book Jacob Garrard had. He lied and said he couldn't believe, *didn't* believe, Frankie had done such a disgusting thing. When Frankie proceeded to say that it was done all the time, Billy played dumb and let Frankie continue to try to talk him into something that he would, as Jake would say, give his left nut for. Frankie said Dixie read somewhere that the *mouth* was the dirtiest part of the human body, much dirtier than a pussy. What about the asshole? Frankie wasn't sure, he was just saying what Dixie said. When Frankie told him about a chart he had seen in a very scientific-looking book he had stolen out of the library at the college where the choral competition had taken place one year showing that fifty-five percent of all married men had eaten their wives' pussies, Billy acted surprised and disgusted. Ditto for what the book said about nearly all upper-class men having eaten pussy at least one time.

Frankie said, according to Dixie, who was the one who found the chart in the first place and who had actually read parts of the book, it said that when women jack off they usually don't finger-fuck themselves. She showed him a place at the top of her pussy that she said was the most fun to be touched. Dixie told him the name of it, which Frankie couldn't remember, and Billy refrained from telling him, but it was like a tiny little pecker, except it had all the feeling of a regular-sized pecker.

Long before this, Billy had done his homework and once the idea and his first tentative images of oral sex were in his head there would be no getting them out. Ever. So, when Frankie said the girl might let him do it to her, he was more excited than he had ever been. He read again what Jake's sex book said. It carried a lot more weight with Billy than the books Frankie talked about. *Cunnilingus has not thus far been shown to depend upon psychopathological conditions.* Even though the book then seemed to contradict itself in the very next sentence—*This horrible sexual act seems to be committed only by sensual men who have become satiated or impotent from excessive indulgence in a normal way*—the contradiction only stimulated his imagination all the more. After thinking about it long and hard, he convinced himself that what he knew he would do if the chance arose was okay; if a 'sensual' man was what was described by the second quote, he wasn't one, so this second sentence didn't really even apply to him. He would be a special case. Case 239. What finally did it for him was the phrase 'horrible act'. Far from discouraging him, these two words made what was unimaginable for his peers irresistible to Billy.

The pure prove their purity by wallowing in filth and emerging unspotted.

The way it happened, the way it came out of nowhere—in a car in the driveway of her family's hovel of a house, in the middle of a thunderstorm that shielded them from the eyes of the outside world—at the last moment, just before her curfew, made it seem like a miracle; having already broken 'in his heart' the taboo, Billy was primed to do the unspeakable and to be transformed by his act of transgression, by his interface with the sacred flesh of Womanhood, into the man he was meant to be.

Suddenly he had a new, a *clean*, non-sinful sex organ, his mouth, Dixie's contrary dictum notwithstanding. With his mouth he could go *way* beyond the paltry animal satisfactions of jacking-off. At the same time he could avoid the dangers, metaphysical-theological and social-biological, of sexual intercourse, of what Jake's father called *coitus*.

The girl could have gotten any old guy to fuck her, but how many would have done *this*? After *this* she needn't feel the self-loathing of a fallen woman because she wouldn't be one.

Let her try and forget him after *this*! *This* would always be in the present tense. *This* is his way of showing her—and Everywoman—how much he loves her. *This* is *beyond* fucking. *This* is of the essence of love between a man and a woman. *This* allows Billy and her, the girl-soon-to-be-woman, to give free reign to that *aesthetic, ideal, pure and free impulse that draws the opposite sexes together,* as Jake's sex book put it so well.

To the extent that Billy had thought about what sex might be like outside his own head, beyond the self-inflicted sensations of his own body, it *had* been for him a lot like religion, more or less the way Jake's sex book said: *Both will in certain pathological states degenerate into cruelty.* Sex was a secret thing, an adult thing. A thing adults reserved for themselves and took very seriously or pretended to. Sex and religion (the adults said) unless governed by rules and rituals, private in the one case, public in the other, could screw you up. So, yes, Billy was willing to concede, without understanding just what he was conceding, that religion and sex, that kind of sex, *base* sex, could screw you up. Just look at Jimmy Garrard, for a religious example. At Theo Jeannsonne or Arthur Maxwell for a couple of sexual ones. What was with people like that? Just as he never believed, in spite of Stella, in his heart of hearts, that things he could not see or otherwise apprehend—such things as the supernatural entities of religion—really existed in the way his body and its sensations, say, did, in some part of his mind, at one level of his psyche, he never really believed (in spite of his fantasies, in spite of what in some sense he knew *had* to be to be the case) that sexual intercourse as it had been described to him ever really happened. Or if he did it was like believing that China existed, a belief devoid of any relevance.

This was no doubt due to inexperience, making Billy unable to imagine *fucking* in a vivid or veridical way. The sound of the word itself was more arousing that anything he could call to mind. After all, what did he have to go on? Just as in the case of religion where all he had to go on were the few paltry images in Sunday School books of angels floating in and out of antebellum mansions in the heavenly clouds, and Jesus feeding the multitude (okay, some scenes of the crucifixion was exciting, but if Stella ever found out she would die), in the case of sex all he had to go on were pictures in the ladies lingerie section of the Sears and Roebuck catalogs that turned outhouses all over the South into a poor boy's brothel and the thin veins of gold his imagination could mine from the granite prose of Jake's sex book. And, yes, there were movies. And just as in the love scenes in the kind of movies Stella liked—and had to take him to because there was nobody for him to stay with—in which there were gaps, fadeouts, at crucial points, so too were there gaps in the sequences of images he masturbated to, and at the climax he was thrown back on the only thing he could believe in. Surrendering to automatic workings of the various erogenous zones of his body, orgasm was little more than a really good shit. Dirty and private, but pleasurable enough.

What was missing, of course, was some sort of connection between him and the thing his paltry images stood for. Without that spark of connection the vital affective qualities necessary for an other-directed and mutual *sensuality* were impossible. And without *that* there could be no sustained and sustaining *faith*. It was the difference between the epiphanies of St. Teresa of Avila surrendering to the fiery arrows of divine ecstasy and the dry reasoning of the theological scholar poring over his dusty volumes.

Empirically, before his enlightening—in lightning!—connection, as he saw or imagined sex at work in real life, in the lives of the adult men and women he knew personally, it seemed a poor candidate for the Greatest Pleasure in Life. And the stories told about it—if they weren't dirty, designed more to denigrate and deny than to dignify—made it seem little more than one in that long line of 'white' lies that began with Santa Claus and ended up in the sky somewhere. After all, married people could have all the sex their hearts desired, but the married people Billy knew didn't really seem all that happy.

The biggest gap of all, naturally, was the gap that engulfed that most fundamental essence: the female genitalia. Where boys had a dick, girls had a hole, a negation. And what did negations do if not negate?

Hardly the thing dreams are made of.

Everything changed That Night, as Billy would forever remember that night. Freed of guilt and using the secret key of the clitoris, Billy entered a sacred realm That Night. That Night he knew what female sexuality *felt* like, what it *smelt* like, and all the rest. Sex now had the aura, the *glow*, that true religion is said to have.

He found confirmation of his new doctrine in Jake's sex book:

Man puts himself at once on a level with the beast if he seeks to gratify lust alone, but he elevates his superior position when by curbing the animal desire, he combines with the sexual functions ideas of morality, of the sublime, and the beautiful.

Sexual feeling is really the root of all ethics, and no doubt of aestheticism and religion. Religion as well as sexual love is mystical and transcendental. Both are metaphysical processes which give unlimited scope to imagination. They converge in a similar focus; for the gratification of the sensual appetite promises a boon which far surpasses all other conceivable pleasures, and faith has in store a bliss that endures for ever. Religious and sexual hyperaesthesia at the zenith of development show the same volume of intensity and the same quality of excitement, and may therefore, under given circumstance, interchange.

From then on, (finally having found uses for the high-falutin' but empty phrases of his native religion), Billy would encounter, in the most unlikely places, the Truth and the Beauty of what he discovered That Night. Breaking through the veil of secrecy and deceitful appearances, he connected with the Real Thing. Written before in a code that he could not read, the Meaning of Life was now his unmediated, as, on his knees, in the dark, in the storms, inner and outer, before the altar—in the manger, Clinton's Chevrolet—he became one with the Divine Source, the heretofore *deus absconditus*. At the Center of the Universe, the Origin of the World, he at last perceived the Thing Itself and knew what it meant to be Born Again.

Years later, when the stream of his libido has reached at last that last stretch of level ground, just before emptying into the Sea of Dissolution, he would find in two other books, both older even than Jake's sex book, the bare bones of the truth of That Night spelled out in its most basic terms.

First: *Every man feels that perception gives him an invincible belief of the existence of that which he perceives; and that this belief is not the effect of reasoning, but the immediate consequence of perception.*

When philosophers have wearied themselves and their readers with their speculations upon this subject, they can neither strengthen this belief, nor weaken it; nor can they show how it is produced. It puts the philosopher and the peasant upon a level; and neither of them can give any other reason for believing his senses, than that he finds it impossible for him to do otherwise.

Cunnilingus was unmediated sensual perception of Truth, a sixth sense.

Second: *Now everyone recognizes that the emotional state for which we make this 'Love' responsible rises in souls aspiring to be knit in the closest union with some beautiful object, and that this aspiration takes two different forms, that of the good whose devotion is for beauty itself, and that other which seeks its consummation in some vile act.*

Those who love beauty of person without carnal desire love for beauty's sake; those that have—for women, of course—the copulative love, have the further purpose of self-perpetuation: as long as they are led by those motives, both are on the right path, though the first have taken the nobler way.

His love was not 'copulative love'; he had taken the nobler way.

Everything had gone down so quickly, over almost before it got started, that, as he was driving home from the girl's house, Billy was unable to quell the tumult inside his head, let alone focus his thoughts on what had happened. As soon as wet met wet, her thighs must have closed around his head, like a catcher's mitt taking in a fast ball. (*His own high hard one, so reliable in his solitude, was never in evidence even in afterthought, but was rather more like the ceremonial first pitch of a season that would be cancelled before any balls could be put into play.*) Yes, her whole body *did* convulse, he was sure of that, and she *did* thrash about for a few seconds on the car seat like someone undergoing ECT, because he remembered three sharp pelvic thrusts into his face and he remembered wondering, even as it happened, how there could be so much movement in the small space of the front seat of a car, where—without a word being spoken, so she must have known as surely as he—-the whole thing had to be *now*. Yes, their lips did ignite, in a split second, a world-ending burst of orange light, in and around his head. Was that the reason she grabbed her tormentor with both hands by the hair of the head, pulling it out of there like she was birthing Satan's invading fire? Was that why she slammed her thighs shut, why she curled up in a foetal knot, shaking, sobbing, gasping for air, as if she were in a maelstrom of profound post-partum despair, as if she were lamenting the loss of her very soul?

Had this apparent eruption of long-suppressed (displaced) passion been quelled by a case of cold feet? Or had the fear that her father might be able to see through the deluge, to hear over the din of the storm, been the cause of her cutting him off? Or had the pain of being torn apart by two great conflicting interior forces been more than flesh-and-blood could bear? At any rate, in the years to come Billy's valuation of transcendence would owe a lot to his believing that, for one brief moment, he had been face-to-face with The Greatest, Most Sacred Mystery: Womankind.

Many, many years later, all that he would retain by way of actual memories was meager to the extreme and utterly concrete; but it would always be enough. Paltry as it was, it was for him a plethora of undiminished and imperishable wonder. It never failed to arouse him. Withdrawing into himself, he relives that first contact: he seems to be entering an underground passageway, which veers slightly to the left and is lit by a radiance coming from an unseen source around the bend—this visual eyes-closed image is accompanied by the strong strange scent of something slick slipping and sliding, wet, wet, wet against his lips and cheeks, and by the tickling touch her pubic hair that nested his nose like a baby chick.

For the next couple of days, Billy puzzled over why, after four or five years of resistance, she had gone along with it. (Okay, he admitted to himself, according to conventional standards, they hadn't gone all the way—more like a run-down between third and home—but Moses himself never made it all the way to the Promised Land.) Was it some sort of animal contagion powered by proximity to the heat Dixie and Frankie were giving off? Had she been on the razor's edge of her lust for Frankie for so long that she was exhausted so that all it took to tip the balance was a slight nudge of sisterly permission? Was cunnilingus the compromise, an open-ended ritual of closure, that would allow her to gather herself up, to get her shit together, in preparation for her flight toward independent womanhood?

She may have done it out of simple gratitude for his loyalty, the affection a lady feels for her faithful lapdog.

Three days after she left, Billy learned that the girl had died in a car crash. On her way to some small college in the Great Northwest, her car ran off a mountainous road at high speed and plunged into a deep crevasse. The police report said death was probably instantaneous.

One rumor was that it was an accident: She had gone to sleep at the wheel. Another rumor had it that it was murder: Her father had rigged the brakes on the old car he gave her because he was the father of her unborn child. It did seem odd that a man so poor could afford to give his kid a car, even an old one. The most widely believed rumor was that it was suicide, brought on by a broken heart: She was pregnant by Frankie West and took her life when it became clear that he would marry Dixie Johnson. A corollary to the pregnancy-rumors had her dying from a botched abortion. (How her body ended up in the crevasse was easy enough to imagine.)

It wouldn't be until just before the naturally red-haired Dixie left the Deep South that the pubic hair of the archetypal iconic pussy in Billy's mind—around which Frankie's phallus always lurked like the serpent in the Garden of Eden—would be any other color than black.

Beyond Billy's memories, the best thing to come out of the whole thing was Billy and *Dixie* became good friends. Though neither of them ever talked about the incident—Frankie's 'trick' that culminated in That Night—it seemed to Billy that Dixie understood that what he had done was an act of true love and she liked him better, respected him more, for his having done it. From then on Dixie talked to Billy about things that bothered her, including the many things about Frankie that she came to hate after they were married.

A sort of precursor to this more substantial relationship—something that, for a while, threatened to go beyond the anemic friendship growing out of their both loving Frankie—was a sequence of events (that didn't quite add up to an *episode*) during their senior year. Billy was sure of the essential reality of it, though nothing was ever said about it by either one of them. It, whatever 'it' was, had been possible—Billy was sure of this, too—only because Frankie had dropped out of school after junior year and was nowhere to be seen for almost a whole year after that.

One cold day in January, Billy was sitting on the steps of the science building waiting for the bell to ring when he became aware of Dixie looking down at him from the second story window of a nearby building where she had English. Their eyes were locked together for what seemed like an eternity. When the eye contact was finally broken by the ringing of the bell, Billy looked around to see who else she might have been looking at. There was no one it could have been but he, himself. The next day, the same thing, and for many days after. Then they discovered other places where they could look at each other. Passing in the hall they exchanged meaningful glances. During chorus practice, they gazed at each other across the room. At basketball games, she searched Billy out in the stands as she warmed up for the game.

In vain, though, did Billy wait for Dixie to give a sign, a signal for the next step in their 'relationship'. (There had been one disastrous incident at a party when something should have happened between them but didn't; they were both drunk and Billy had managed, sort of, to lay the blame for his failure off on the booze). One night just before graduation, Billy worked up the courage to approach Dixie. Going to the skating rink where she, an accomplished skater, was something of a star, he discovered her and Frankie West wowing the crowd with a flashy routine they had obviously practiced. The next day on the phone she told Billy that Frankie had asked her to marry him.

"Do you love him?"

"He *needs* me. He makes me feel needed."

And that was that.

After coming back from wherever he had been, Frankie was his old self toward Billy, only more so. After Frankie and Dixie got married, they fixed Billy up with some girls and they double-dated. If one of these girls showed signs of liking Billy, Frankie would flirt with her and make fun of Billy in front of her. The ridicule usually took the form of disparaging Billy's masculinity. "Ain't nothing short about Billy ... but his dick." "Billy pulled out a thread and pissed in his pants." "Billy says once you get past the smell, you got it licked."

Later, after That Night, Billy would wonder if Dixie—remembering how close, as he wanted to believe, the two of them came to being lovers—hadn't somehow brought about, through the Faustpool girl, what she would have liked to have happened between herself and Billy. And the time would come when dreams came true.

6

A man in a cream-colored suit and two-toned shoes rolled into the Tres Beau Dame beauty shop where Dixie sat in a barber chair smoking a cigarette. Acts like he owns the place, Dixie thought, as she watched the man looking around the room. The man looked at himself in one of the many mirrors, approving of what he saw, or so it seemed to Dixie. How's a man in a wheelchair get to be so cocky? Taking a colorful tie out of his suit jacket pocket, the man turned up his collar and began putting the tie on. Attractive in a debauched sort of way, Dixie thought. Rich, too, she could tell from his clothes and his haircut and his manicure. It takes more than money to give a man the kind of self-confidence this old rooster has, though. Hairline is receding, I'd put him somewhere between forty and fifty.

Dixie put her hand in her uniform pocket and slipped off her wedding ring.

"Can I help you, *sir*," Dixie said, still sitting, still smoking, not making any welcoming motions.

"Let's go somewhere and get a drink." The man looked at Dixie in the mirror. Turning around, he rolled over toward where she sat.

He's coming too fast, Dixie thought, He's going to ram into me! She raised her legs just before the wheelchair bumped into the barber chair.

"Oh, I beg your pardon." The man grinned like he'd just made a hole-in-one without getting out of his golf cart. "Did I scare you? I am *so* sorry. I shoulda said fore."

Okay, he's got me back for the way I said 'sir'. And got a look up my dress in the bargain. Eat your heart out, you old coot.

"Let me introduce myself. I'm Lester LeBeaux. Friends call me Bo."

"Okay, Bo. Hope you don't mind if I call you Bo. But I can't go. With you. To have a drink. Don't get off till six." Dixie took a drag and blew smoke at the man.

"I'm giving you the rest of the day off."

"Oh, you are? And what do you think my boss will say to that?"

"I think he'll say what I just said."

"Maybe you better go let *her* know."

"*He* knows already."

Dixie grinned and pointed at LeBeaux. "*You!*" Stubbing out her cigarette, she offered her hand. "I recognize you. You're a ... . "

"A humble civil servant." LeBeaux took Dixie's hand in both his and kissed it.

"No really, what are you?" My, what big soft hands you have, Grandpa.

"A State Senator. At your service." LeBeaux turned Dixie's hand over and traced circles on her palm like a connoisseur of fine silk.

"There've been rumors that we were gonna be getting a new owner. Congratulations. I think." As Dixie withdrew her hand, LeBeaux closed his hands around it and watched it slide out of his grip like the fish that got away.

"Igor goes with you everywhere, I take it." Dixie gestured through one of the big windows of the Mardi Gras bar at Magnolia Park where she and 'Bo' were having a drink, toward the uniformed bodyguard who, draped over the rail of an outside walkway, was smoking a cigarette. "Does he have a name?"

"That's it! Igor. How did you know?"

Igor had rolled LeBeaux down the hill from the beauty salon to the high-ceilinged bar that straddled Flagon Creek, a.k.a., Cold Bayou, like a large converted covered bridge, high and wide, its erstwhile wooden walls replaced with huge plate-glass windows framing views, upstream and down, of the tributary moving imperceptibly beneath them on its way to the Mississippi River and the Gulf of Mexico.

"He's not house-broken?"

"State Police. Not allowed to drink while on duty."

"Pretty cushy duty, I'd say. Couldn't he go swimming or something while he waits?" Dixie gestured out the window toward the swimming pool below them; the pool was a wide place in the creek, formed by a dam flush with the upstream wall of the bar.

"He's okay. Tell me about yourself."

"What do you want to know?"

"Tell me your dreams, what you want to be when you grow up. Girl like you doesn't want to work in a beauty salon all her life. Not even one as fancy as the Tres Beau Dame at the Hot Springs Sanitarium. I don't know if you're married or not … . No, don't tell me. I don't want to know. But, if you don't mind my saying so, you don't look like the marrying kind."

"I'll take that as a compliment. The salon, this job, is just the first step."

"To what? If you don't mind my asking."

"I want to be an artist. A make-up artist. I want to go to Hollywood."

"If you're going to Hollywood, why not go all the way and become an actress? You've got the looks. You may have the talent. Won't know unless you try."

"I've thought about that. I think maybe I do. Have the talent, I mean." Should she show him the nude art photos cousin Charlie had taken? Frankie ever finds out about those … . Thank God for Crystal and her cabin.

"What makes you think so? Have you ever acted? High school play? Local theater? Maybe I can be of some help. We'll have to talk more about it later. Right now I want you to accompany me. To be my accompanist … my accomplice … to go somewhere with me."

"Where's that?"

"Bogalusa. I'm giving a speech tomorrow and I want you to be with me. They're dedicating a new wing to the hospital. Expecting a big crowd. Television cameras already set up. You can be with me on the stage. I'll give Igor the day off. He can go swimming like you said. I'll make a better impression on television with a future starlet standing behind me than a big old dumb state trooper. Ever drive a Cadillac?"

"I'm looking at the most beautiful girl I have ever seen."

Lester LeBeaux's voice filled to bursting the dimly-lit little room, already full of heat and steam and the scent of Dixie Johnson West, who, naked, was sitting on the edge of a large tile-lined whirlpool spa bath, soaking her feet in the hot rust-colored water. It was the day after the senator's Bogalusa speech. So far, so good, Dixie thought. Assuming an expression she hoped would convey the idea that big men in a wheelchairs bestowing superlatives rolled soundlessly into her life every day, she looked up. When her eyes met his, LeBeaux lifted her bikini and, dangling it to one side of their line of sight, cocked his head as if to say, Look what I found. Surprise, surprise, Dixie thought. Someone must have dropped it just inside the door so some rich old bastard could see it. And look who's taken the bait. When she looked at the tiny garment, LeBeaux lifted it over his head, and gazed at it as if examining it in the light. He pressed it against his cheek and gave Dixie a pouting look. Holding it in both hands, he buried his face in it and moved his head side-to-side.

Like a dog sniffing a candy wrapper, Dixie thought. She needed to slow herself, brace herself for this old walrus's inevitable charge, and then, when he's within range, I'll stop him in his tracks. She lit a cigarette and thought of Uncle Theo's stratagem: Stretch it to the breaking point.

"I have always thought the color of that water was ugly at best. Now that I see it juxtaposed to your hair my mind is changed. *I* am changed. You have added beauty to its reputed powers to heal. Did you come up out of the ground? Are you the spirit of the Hot Springs? If you leave does the magic go with you?"

"Sure. Why not?" Looking down, Dixie shaped the hot end of her cigarette in the ashtray beside her naked hip. She hoped her demeanor conveyed the message that, even if by some remote chance LeBeaux should someday get lucky, it was much too early in the game for any serious hanky-panky.

"I notice that you make no effort to hide your beautiful body." LeBeaux was still holding the bikini a few inches from his face. Wary of tender feelings welling in her, Dixie clung to the security of her protective cynicism. Fido likes the smell of D. J.'s nether parts, she thought.

Looking at Dixie, LeBeaux smiled. "You have no idea how exciting … how erotic … it is for an old geezer like me to be this close to such beauty." Looking back at the bikini, he said, "And this … ." He draped the crotch of the tiny thing over his thumb and sucked on it. "This is mother's milk, the fountain of youth, and the elixir of life all rolled into one."

"You forgot Spanish fly, Bo. You sure you wanna put that thing in your mouth. You don't know where it's been." Any minute now he's going to eat the damn thing, Dixie thought, and, imagining it, she suddenly shivered and felt beads of sweat forming on her face and back. Stabbing the ashtray, she snuffed her cigarette.

"*Au contraire.* What's the old joke: What's next to the best thing?" the man said. "Say, how did you know my name, Pretty Girl?"

"Saw you on the television yesterday. Dedicating the new wing over at Bogalusa General." Two can play this game, Dixie thought. Can he be serious? Do I look so different in that stupid uniform and that ridiculous wig that he doesn't even recognize me? She congratulated herself on a quick recovery. But she was taken aback by how much it hurt for LeBeaux to joke around like that, if that was what he was doing. Less certain now of the impression she had made the day before, she couldn't shake the thought: Maybe he isn't joking. Maybe I'm just what's next. She had been so *sure* that, unlike Frankie, the older man had seen that she was something special, a lot more than just a pretty face with a body to die for.

Her eyes fell on the large sensual lips mouthing the tiny swimsuit like a baby at the breast. Then their eyes met and, her doubts receding into the background, the caressing sounds of his voice and the ravenous look of his gaze resumed their spell. Intuiting the longing lurking in his fancy words, she was momentarily staggered by an image of her hands framing his face like a nest holding a wounded bird. Then, reining herself in, she crossed her thighs tight enough to make it feel like a fist down there. Putting on her game face, she readied herself to return serve.

"Yeah, this *is* a classy joint, isn't it? Not only does it have miraculous waters, it has *T.V.*! Best of all, it has naked dancing girls. You will dance for me, won't you, my salacious Salome?"

"You're pretty classy yourself, Ahab." Straightening up and locking her hands behind her head, Dixie flexed forward, and wondered, too late, if there was enough light for LeBeaux to see the aroused state of her double-crossing nipples.

"I notice you didn't answer my question, my little Jezebel. I have thrown myself on your mercy. Life as I know it depends on your answer. Is it dance or death?"

"Maybe when I get to know you better. I *am* married, you know." Lighting another cigarette, Dixie brandished her ring, a warning to herself, a talisman thrust into the face of a fast-closing adversary. Afraid of losing the only thing of real value she owned, she hadn't taken the ring off as she had the day before. Now it seemed a straw in the furious and electrifying storm of LeBeaux's advance.

"I noticed the diamond. It's true what they say. Diamonds *are* a girl's best friend. Must've cost your little prince half his kingdom."

"You notice a lot." He *is* serious. The sorry bastard does not remember me! If he did, he'd know that I didn't have the ring on yesterday. Must be too vain to wear glasses, too, Dixie thought, remembering the trouble LeBeaux went to at the hospital in Bogalusa to hide his affliction and his wheelchair from the television camera. Just like a lousy politician.

"I notice everything."

"I notice a lot of bullshit." Dixie caressed her shoulder and flashed a come-hither smile. I spy, said the spider.

"I love a woman who is hard to get."

"I'll try to remember that. Demand some prophet's head. Speaking of princes and dancing slave girls, I can't help noticing your throne. I *was* gonna ask if you were a real king or if you ruled in name only." Dixie nodded toward the towel covering his lap. "But lo and behold the royal scepter. Looks like *your* little prince is erecting a tent. Must be a revival going on down in the lowlands." Now forget me, you old buzzard. That ought to teach him to dismiss her so soon and so easily.

Lester LeBeaux wound the bikini around his neck and put his hands on his thighs on either side of the towel-tent. "Salvation is at hand. After forty years in the dessert. Give me a hand?"

Dixie stood up and snatched away her bikini. "Let me get dressed. Don't want anyone to get the wrong idea." She tried to make the retrieval of the token of her modesty a playful gesture, but, in the execution, it felt a tad too bitchy. Such a fine line, especially when she didn't know whether she wanted to fall or not.

"I think I already have. You tell me: I was thinking of you on my lap in the hot, steamy water. Is that such a wrong idea?"

"Dream on. There's a rumor going around this place has been sold. Don't want to get off on the wrong foot." How long can this charade go on? Sooner or later the other shoe had to fall and when it did, what would it mean—end or beginning?

"I've never tried it with either foot, but I'm willing to give it a shot if you are."

Her bikini on, Dixie, despondent and feeling fat, called for help getting the invalid into the whirlpool. After the attendant left, she felt the full weight of disappointment for her dashed dreams.

As she turned to leave the room, LeBeaux, in the water, said, "You look a lot better without that blond wig, Dixie."

At the sound of her name, the other shoe hit the floor, and Dixie jumped into the water. Laughing like the happy little girl that she was, she hugged Lester LeBeaux. "Oh Bo! Where have you been all my life!"

They kissed and she gave him a hand job. She was prepared to resist any further below-the-waist activity, and was glad when it didn't prove necessary.

Uncle Theo's technique had worked perfectly … on *her*.

LeBeaux gave Dixie the next day off on the condition she spend it with him. On the veranda overlooking the sanitarium grounds, he alluded to an earlier topic of conversation: "You're pretty quick on your feet. An actor needs to be able to improvise."

"You mean in the bath yesterday, I take it. Is that the way it seemed to you or is that just more of your bullshit?" Dixie lit a cigarette. "I thought that you hadn't recognized me without my wig ... and the uniform, of course. Think it'd be okay, if us stylists stop wearing those stupid things and switched to civvies? Great, thanks." Dixie put the cigarette out. "Then when it turned out you had recognized me even without the wig ... well ... you reaped the benefits of my gratitude. I have to hand it to you, you had me going there for a while."

"But that's my point. You were able to keep the inside and the outside separate. That's what actors *do*. Are *able* to do. Control their *appearance*. Control what is *public*. What is private remains just that, private. And, if they are good, and if they are properly trained, actors can *create* any appearance or *illusion* they want to. What is a play or a movie if not an elaborate seductive *illusion* that takes us away from the mundane world of reality? All we have to do is to agree to sit in the dark for a couple of hours."

"But a make-up artist does the same thing. She creates something out of nothing, almost. You ever see pictures of famous movie stars before they became movie stars? Many of them are as ordinary-looking as you or me."

"Leave yourself out of that, sweetheart. There's nothing ordinary about you."

"Yeah, yeah. You know something? Politicians go actors one better: They manipulate people into believing their crap for years. Election after election." Maybe I *will* show him those photos of me nude, Dixie thought.

"Touché. Okay, okay. I have an idea. It's a little test. Are you game?"

"Depends. Tell me what you have in mind."

LeBeaux reached under his wheelchair for a thin briefcase, opened it, and took out a large photograph. "See this? Can you make yourself look like this?"

"She's a flapper, right? Looks like Zelda what's-her-name. Sure, why not? I'll need a dark wig."

LeBeaux gestured to his bodyguard who was sitting as unobtrusively as he could in the shade of the veranda's awnings. "My car. In the trunk. A black suitcase. Get it for me."

When the man had gone, LeBeaux answered Dixie's questioning look. "Everything you need, Doll. Everything you need."

✳   ✳   ✳

"Ladies and Gentlemen, thank you for coming out today as we dedicate this beautiful new facility. It is fitting that you are here today, because it is you who have made this dream come true. I want to preface my brief remarks today by reminding you of something that you don't need reminding of, but that many in our radio and *television* audience seem sometimes to forget."

It was a few weeks later, on Saturday of the Labor Day weekend. Lester LeBeaux was dedicating a new wing to the hospital at Pinecrest.

"This great country of ours was built by people who were appalled by the idea that some people are more equal than others.

"By people who would *not* be subservient to snobbish and decadent British aristocrats.

"By people who would rather brave storm-tossed *seas* than live in bondage.

"By people who founded the first and greatest *democracy* this world has ever known.

"And ever since, we, as a nation, have recoiled from the idea of second-class citizenship, the elitist notion that some people are better than others.

"This morning, as I stand before this very special audience and look into the faces of the parents and siblings and friends of Pinecrest residents, what do I see?

"I see the face of compassion.

"I see the face of understanding wrought by personal hardships and suffering.

"I see the face of triumph over never-ending adversity.

"I see love for very special children. Children that the rest of society would turn its back on and walk away from.

"I see a love that stood up and said, 'No! We won't let you discard our children.'

"I see a love that is deeper than the love of money and the craven desire for social status. A love that is stronger than hatred and cynicism and apathy. Stronger than discrimination. Stronger than bigotry.

"I see a love that does not look the other way when a child needs a helping hand to walk. A love that does not turn deaf ears to a child who is confused and cannot learn as quickly as others more privileged, more blessed, more gifted. A love born of a deep, spiritual realization that a world where it is every man for himself can never be a home, but is hell itself.

"And above all, I see a love that will not abandon the hope that some day we will all have the strength and grace to live up to the greatest of all Jesus's teachings: Do unto others as you would have them do unto you.

"We the people of the great Southland and of this great state stand at a crossroads. We have a momentous choice. A choice that will determine the economic and political health not only of ourselves, but of our children, and *their* children. We can choose to be the masters of our own fate. We can heed history's terrible lessons and refuse to repeat them. Or we can choose to be victims of a heartless leviathan that cares not one whit for the things we hold most dear. A juggernaut that will roll over us and leave us for dead, like road-kill on the highway to prosperity. We can continue to fight a war that was lost nearly one-hundred years ago or we can shed our shameful sheets, cast off our childish and cowardly costumes, and join the twentieth century.

"I have referred to you as a special audience. How are you special? And how can that specialness help our state and our region in its hour of desperate need? Its hour of decision, to quote the great Billy Graham. Well, first of all, you are special as parents of Pinecrest residents. You have spanned the great divide between what others have chosen to call the 'normal' and the 'abnormal' and made them see that there is no 'normal' and 'abnormal' but that we are all the same in the eyes of a loving God.

"Second, you are special as people who live along the border between the two great sub-regions of our state, Acadiana and the Bible Belt. Yes, I say 'Bible Belt'. I say it proudly. And I say to whoever the Yankee sociologist is who first called us that, 'Thank you for calling us the Bible Belt.' I say to all Yankees, 'You should wear a bible belt yourself sometimes. It can save you a world of shame and embarrassment, not to mention your marriages, your families, and, most of all, your immortal souls.'

"You, we, the people on the border have built bridges connecting the many and various cultures that make our state unique among the forty-eight. Cajun, French, Spanish, Indian, Creole and the descendants of the largest slave culture the world has ever known live together here in harmony, in peace, and in fellowship. If America is the melting pot of the world, we are the Gumbo Bowl of America.

"Being special in these two very special ways you can set the standard. You can be the model. You can lead the way for the rest of us as we struggle and suffer and pray our way through this great trial that God has seen fit to test us with. And as the new owner of the Hot Springs Sanitarium, I pledge to work together with you, the parents and staff of Pinecrest, who I am proud to be next-door neighbors with, to continue to bring together people of all creeds, nationalities, dialects, and conditions of mental and physical health in one big happy family that will be a shining beacon on the shores of tolerance for those lost on the stormy seas of hatred, animosity, and violence as we sail the ship of state into the uncertain waters of the second half of the twentieth century. Thank you."

7

The tall, coffee-with-cream-colored young Negro man in the back seat of Lester LeBeaux's Cadillac closed his eyes and savored an air-conditioned respite from the summer heat. The car was idling in the shadeless parking lot of Hot Springs Sanitarium. Picturing himself caressed by sea breezes and native hands under a palm tree on a South Pacific island, the young man hummed a tune, *The evening breeze caressed the trees, tenderly*. I could steal this big old boat, he thought, and be in New Orleans before they knew I was gone. He had driven Theo Jeannsonne's Cadillac many times.

Me and 'Uncle Toe' sho do loves being in Sin City. Especially up on the stage of the My Oh My Club.

Hearing the sound of voices outside the car and thinking it was LeBeaux and his bodyguard, the young man sat up and opened his eyes. Seeing instead that it was his two Pinecrest bosses—Dr. Maxwell and Jonnie Vonderheim, the director and his foxy head nurse—he became frightened. Then he remembered he was hidden inside the car by the heavily-tinted windows. He watched the two people get into a white Chevy with the Pinecrest logo on the door, Jonnie behind the wheel. He followed the car with his eyes all the way to Pinecrest, a distance of less than a quarter-mile. Seeing the car turn into the Pinecrest parking lot, and watching the doctor and his nurse enter the side door of the hospital building, he wondered why they were working on a Sunday.

Doc M. got that gumbo all heated up, now he's gonna cop him a mess of it. Not a bad rear-end for a white woman. Wonder how that cute nurse's uniform would look on me. Bet your sweet ass it'd show my butt off at least as good as hers.

Still looking across the field between the sanitarium and the home for the feeble-minded, the young black man recalled the day before: "Dat sho' was some fine speechifying, Senator LeBeaux, suh." He had waited until the white people who had crowded around LeBeaux following his speech at Pinecrest had scattered before approaching the great man.

"Glad you liked it, son."

"I sho do wish you coulda sayed what you wus really meanin,' suh."
Teejay and LeBeaux played this game every time they met; it started out
as a way to hide the nature, the very existence, of LeBeaux's more or less
paternal relationship to the young black man whose college education the
older man helped pay for.

Knowing that voices carried well in the cavernous gym, Teejay looked
around to see if any of the people still hanging around (all white, he
noticed) had turned their heads toward him. An aspiring actor, he enjoyed
attention, even, and in certain moods, *especially*, the negative kind; as long
as he could control it; could play with the minds of the yokels and get away
with it. Nimble of tongue, of mind and body, as he believed he was, he
was resigned, sometimes bitterly, to the limits placed on men of his race.
Taking the prevailing rules of inter-racial comportment as stage directions,
he used as best he could the few degrees of freedom that were his in his
restless search for the discerning eye of his next benefactor, whoever that
may be.

"Oh, you do, do you? I like a man who reads between the lines. Well,
let me tell you, my boy, that day's acoming. You young people will live to
see some great changes." LeBeaux inserted a cigarette into a long cigarette
holder. "Do you know Dixie … ?" He turned his head to one side. "What's
your last name, honey?" Dixie who was standing behind LeBeaux's
wheelchair told him her last name. "Do you know Dixie West?"

"Yessir, I sho does." Teejay looked down at his shoes. God, I hate this
Uncle Tom crap, he thought, wishing he were in New Orleans. LeBeaux
knows only too well that I 'know' that white girl.

"And what is your name, *boy*?" Winking, LeBeaux spoke the offensive
word softly, savoring his little in-joke.

"Teejay, suh." Come on, Lester, enough of the minstrel show already.

"What does T. J. stand for, if I may be so bold as to inquire?"

"Nuttin, suh. Stands fo itself. Dat bees my name, not my nishus." You
can be so bold to kiss my ass.

"And your last name?"

"Just Teejay, suh." The old fart's been doing this so long he *likes* it,
Teejay thought. Subterfuge has devolved into theater, a comedy of Southern
manners. He could see that LeBeaux got a kick out of their shtick, playing
it even if there weren't other white people around. Teejay had to go along
with it. For now.

"No last name?"

"No suh. My great-grand-pappy's massa was a man named Vuhvuh,
but my grand-pappy sayed he don't cotton to no slave name."

"Verver? The Verver's of Plaquemines Parish?"

"Yassah, dat's de berry same ones, sah." Bending at the waist, Teejay executed a jerky series of comic bows.

"And why didn't he choose some other name?" LeBeaux grinned and looked up at Dixie, who, looking toward the far end of the gym, seemed not to be following the conversation between the two men.

"He done sayed he ain't have no use fo no nuther name." Teejay wondered how this was playing with the people still left in the gym. Rednecks eat this shit up, he thought. Cajuns, he wasn't sure about.

"Well, mercy me." LeBeaux spoke loudly and looked around the gym. "It's not often I have the privilege of meeting two such very attractive young people both on the same day. That is what I'd call a red-banner day, wouldn't you?" He turned and smiled up at Dixie and back around and winked again at the young black man. Both young people mumbled assent.

"Let's see if we can scare up a basketball game." The Senator reached into his suit coat pocket and took out a gold lighter which he handed to Teejay. When Teejay had lit his cigarette, LeBeaux winked and whispered, his words wreathed with smoke, "Teach some of these white boys how the game is played and the lighter is yours."

Inside the cool Cadillac cocoon Teejay lay back and closed his eyes again. Like I was his house nigger or something, he thought. What do I need with a lighter? Hope that white girl ain't gone and told her cracker husband about me cozying up like some kind of Uncle Tom to *that* white man. If there is anything Frankie West hates more than niggers its nigger-*lovers*, especially nigger-lovers that cut in on his pussy. No telling what fool thing he is liable to do if he finds out about me and LeBeaux. I don't even want to *think* what he'd do if he knew how far back me and his wife Dixie go; and, Jesus help me if he finds out about this latest gig LeBeaux cooked up for the two of us. Shoulda run the other way when that little split-tail first started in on me.

Before yesterday, Teejay had counted on his and Frankie's having the same boss, Theo Jeannsonne, who Teejay worked for part-time, to minimize Frankie's making too much trouble for him. Now, after yesterday—after the shellacking, the 'lesson' as Lester called it, Teejay gave Frankie on the basketball court—Mr. Theo's being Frankie's boss probably wouldn't count for much. In fact, it could make things worse; it could set Frankie to brooding about being on the same payroll as a nigger.

I better watch my back from now on like never before. There is *way* more than enough already to push the crazy red-headed bastard over the edge.

Just then the door across from him opened. "Wake up, boy. Can't sleep your life away. There're things to do. Places to go. Miles to go before we sleep." LeBeaux was back.

After being helped into the back seat by his bodyguard, LeBeaux looked over at Teejay and slapped him on the leg. "Hope you've been having some good dreams. Some a that Pickaninny Pussy, eh?"

"Yassa Massa." Here we go again. Have to put on a show for the bodyguard. Why is it white people can't stand the idea of a black man having an education?

"Okay! I like a man who doesn't take himself too seriously. Can take a joke. Laugh at himself." LeBeaux winked and gave the bodyguard the finger surreptitiously.

"I hopes you don't mind my asking, suh, but how long is dissheeah little trip gywna take? I's gotta be to wuk in a few hours. Wukin the three o'clock shift today. I's only askin cause I didn't know just what you all had in mind. You didn't say yestidday. You just … ."

"Just said I'd pick you up. Yeah, that was your first test and you passed it with flying colors, Teejay. I like a man who can sense when opportunity is knocking. That grabs the main chance by the horns and runs with it." LeBeaux looked in the big rearview mirror at his bodyguard. "Take us down to the dock, Joe. We're going to N-town." Then to Teejay: "How you like that mirror? See how it works? It's got two panels. Joe can see what's behind us on the road in one panel and when I sit on this side he can see me in the other panel. That way I can give him signals without having to say anything."

"Non-vubal cah muni kayshun."

"Yeah, that's it. You're quick-witted, aren't you? I like that in a man. Anyhow, mirror comes in handy sometimes. Like when I have a lady friend with me and I don't want to break the flow of our conversation. Say, I don't want her to know where we're going. I just wink, once for this place, twice for another place. Hand to my left eye for 'speed up'. To my right eye for 'slow down'. You get the idea."

"I sho does. What we's gwyna be doing over at Darktown? If you don't minds me asking, suh." This is getting old, Teejay thought. But I can't complain too much. Mr. LeBeaux and Mr. Theo have been more than good to me. Of course, they've used me, too. I better be careful. White men are all alike. I really shouldn't trust any of them. Not even Mr. Theo. *Especially* Mr. Theo. The more they do for you, the more gratitude they expect. There's always strings with white people.

"You sound like an educated fella, for a … country boy."

"Thank you, suh. It's white mens like yoself done seen to it I gots me some decent learnin." You're laying in on rather thick, Teejay thought. We both are. At least Lester caught himself and didn't say 'for a nigger'. I wonder what this is really all about.

"Like myself? Whata you mean? Like myself?" LeBeaux frowned and nodded toward his bodyguard.

"No offense intended, suh. It's just that you reminds me of dis yeh udder white man what hepped me gets some gubment money, das all. I guess it's cause you bof's got Cadillacs." And wear too many rings. And use too much perfume.

I shouldna said that about the Cadillacs, Teejay thought. LeBeaux probably doesn't want there to be any public connection between him and Mr. Theo. Like knowing the same nigger. Not that many Cadillacs around.

At the dock the bodyguard helped LeBeaux into a big motorboat. He then took a smaller, folded wheelchair out of the trunk of the car and loaded it into the boat. With all three aboard they sped up the creek toward the cluster of shanties on stilts the whites called Niggertown.

"You are about to be given your second test, Teejay." LeBeaux fitted a cigarette into his cigarette-holder; when Teejay lit it for him the older man winked and complemented him on his lighter to which younger man said thanks.

"We're in the midst of a revolution down here in the South. A revolution that's gonna change everything. Do you know what I'm talking about?"

"I thinks I does, suh." And so soon. It's only been ninety-something years since the Emancipation Proclamation.

"Yeah, I thought you might. What you said yesterday about saying what I really meant. That told me you were hep to what's going on."

"Yassa. I's … whas dat word you done used? Hep?" Where'd this spook pick up a word like hep? Maybe he's got some reefer … ?

"Means you're in the groove, man. That you dig what's going down."

Oh brother, now he really is laying it on too thick. "Thank you, suh. I trys to keep abreast … I means I trys to keep up wif whas happnin."

"You're joshing me, aren't you? You're pulling my leg. That's okay. I like a man who plays his cards close to his chest. Here's what I have in mind for today. I want to get to know as many of the good people in … Darktown … as I can. And I need someone who knows the place to be my guide, so to speak. You up for that? Think you can handle that?"

"Das my second test, suh?" LeBeaux nodded. "Yassa, I's up to it, I reckons. It sho be helpful, tho, if I knowed *why* you wants to makes the acquaintance of these excellent people." I'm losing it, Teejay thought. Hard to keep up the shucking and jiving routine for that long.

"You something else, you know that? Me and you gonna be a great team. Yeah, okay, fair enough. I want to register voters. The key to the revolution is voter registration."

Gonna take more than one day of ass-kissing to get those niggers into the white man's court house or wherever it is that voters are registered, Teejay thought, but hey, it's your nickel. If that's what you're *really* up to.

When they got there, Joe the bodyguard pushed LeBeaux up the zig-zag ramp onto the wharf that ran along the creek for a couple of hundred feet. Hand-painted signs on the buildings that faced the water, with crude drawings supplementing the words, indicated what was to be had inside. Fried fish, bait, fishing tackle, hunting supplies, food, booze, dancing and music.

Drawn by the mournful sound of a lone saxophone, they went inside an unlit saloon, passing hand-drawn pictures on either side of the door; on one side a woman dancing, on the other a man playing a trumpet. The artist had put the woman inside a double set of nested parentheses meant to impart the illusion of swaying hips. Musical notes that could have been flying insects hovered around the horn player. Inside LeBeaux gestured Joe to roll him to the far end of the narrow dark room where a man playing the sax sat on a small stage with his back to the entrance. A hand-rolled cigarette burning on the edge of a chair in front of the man sent an intricate swirl of smoke up through the shaft of light seeping through a dirty skylight overhead.

They listened to the music. LeBeaux began tapping his foot but switched quickly to drumming his fingers on the arm of his wheelchair. What's he doing, Teejay thought, trying to keep time with the music? Try again, old man. After several minutes, LeBeaux cleared his throat loudly. The man stopped playing and looked around, glancing at each intruder in turn. Turning back around, he picked up the cigarette, took a drag and waited. His demeanor, insofar as it could be deciphered from behind, seemed to say he didn't have the energy to deal face-to-face with the nonsense behind him.

Don't look back, something may be gaining on you, Teejay thought.

"Where can a man get a drink around here, my good man?" LeBeaux said. "You thirsty? Playing makes a man thirsty, right? Let me buy you a drink. What's your poison?"

The man stood up, put his sax on his chair, descended the stage, and went behind the bar. Without removing the cigarette hanging out of his mouth or looking at his customers, he said, "Washawlwant?"

When LeBeaux and Joe had been served beers and Teejay a coke, LeBeaux said to the musician-cum-bartender, "We're here to see about getting some of you people registered to vote. Election coming up, you know."

"One dalla." The black man was looking down, absently wiping the bar, his hand moving the dirty rag across the shiny plastic surface in desultory fashion.

Joe put a dollar bill on the bar.

"What kind of tobacco is that you're smoking?" LeBeaux smiled knowingly at Teejay. "Got any more of that?"

Pocketing the dollar, the black man put the rag down and exited through a door behind the bar.

"Well, we're off to a rousing good start, wouldn't you say?" LeBeaux wheeled his chair around and waited for Joe to roll him out the way they came in.

From there they proceeded on walkways made of thick oaken planks connecting all the buildings, mostly shacks, in the little collection of dwellings.

Eventually, a small group of people was assembled inside the church, mostly children who had followed the wheelchair in growing numbers as the three visitors made the rounds. LeBeaux delivered a short speech full of promises of what he was going to do for the good people of Darktown. Chiefly, he was going to see to it that a seawall was built so that Darktown wouldn't be flooded anymore. That in place, Darktown could, with some money from the state and maybe with proceeds from church-sponsored activities like bingo and bake sales, build a school with a football field. Then, who knew, maybe a gym for basketball. But nothing was going to happen unless and until everybody registered to vote.

"Any questions?" LeBeaux asked when he was done.

Without a word people began filing out of the church past LeBeaux's bodyguard who stood at attention by the door offering registration forms. Wearing that State Trooper's uniform, he might as well be passing out little bags of dog shit, Teejay thought. A couple of men took forms, though. Sitting on the back pews, they began slowly filling in the spaces.

"You gentlemen take your time filling out those forms." As LeBeaux rolled past the two men, he put his finger on the side of his nose and winked. "No hurry." Reaching the church entrance, he raised his hand, signaling his bodyguard to stop. "Wait here, Joe, for these gentlemen's forms. We'll be back in a jiffy. Teejay, you wanna give me a hand with the chair?"

LeBeaux and Teejay went to home of the saxophone player who opened the door when LeBeaux knocked.

In the front room of the small house a beautiful woman, a 'high-yellow', sat knitting and watching television with the sound off. When LeBeaux entered she glanced at him long enough to recognize him and then back at the small screen. Then, seeing Teejay, she smiled and motioned him for a hug.

"Hi, mama," Teejay said. "Sorry, I haven't been to see you. But you know how it is."

"Yeah, I know how it is, son. But after tomorrow that'll all change. Thanks to Mr. Lester LeBeaux. I guess it's time to tell you the big secret. This man ... ," she nodded toward LeBeaux, ". . . still thinks he's your Daddy. Mr. Theo does, too. They both claimed you. I never would tell which one was your real Daddy. They've been trying to outdo each other ever since you were born. They couldn't do enough for you. I'm thankful for it. And I hope you are, too."

"Oh, yeah." Teejay was hardly surprised by his mother's revelation. There had to be some reason for the way the two men had taken care of him over the years and she had dropped some hints during his last visit. But if she was thinking what he thought she was thinking she had another think coming. He had a pretty good idea what she and LeBeaux had cooked up and he would be having none of it. He had plans of his own. It was *north* he was heading, not further south.

"We can't take much time," LeBeaux said. "We don't wanna give Joe any reason to suspect the real reason we are here. I'm pretty sure he's swallowing the voter registration shtick. Is the boat ready?"

"All set. Food and water for the passengers and a two-man crew for a week, just like you said," the saxophone player said.

"Good. Gas tanks all full?"

"Enough to get you well outside the twelve-mile zone. After that you'll have to hoist the sails."

"What about the crew?"

"The best. They don't know you from Adam's off ox. They be the ones filling out your papers like you said."

"Okay, we'll be here tomorrow night at midnight, after the big party. Everybody'll be so drunk they won't notice us leaving. The rest of the money's in the bank. The one we talked about. It'll be available to you one week from tomorrow. Okay? You trust me?"

"I don't have to trust you. I know where you're going."

"You okay with all this, Teeje? Okay, let's get back to Joe."

LeBeaux and Teejay returned to where Joe was waiting in the church. "Ready to get back, Joe? What time is it?" Joe showed him his watch. "Oh yeah, got plenty a time. Plenty a time."

Just as they started down the ramp to their boat, the saxophone-playing bartender called out for them to wait. He came over to where they were and handed Joe a small brown paper bag. "Ten dollah."

66

Joe took a bill out of his wallet and gave it to the man. "Thanks, Boss," he said, as they headed down the ramp.

8

The derelict old car was Billy and Jake's favorite place to talk and masturbate. It was permanently parked in the locked garage of an abandoned mansion in an isolated part of the neighborhood. In the glove compartment was a cloth measuring-tape which Jake used to keep track of any changes in the dimensions of his erections. Sometimes Jake read aloud passages from the sex book that, he said, Theo Jeannsonne gave him. He kept the book hidden under the driver's-side seat of the old car to keep 'that fucking Jimmy' from finding it and burning it.

"Why would he do that?" Billy asked.

"Because it's mine."

Jake always sat behind the wheel. Billy rode shotgun.

"What do you want to do when you grow up?" Jake tightened his grip on the steering wheel and scanned the road ahead that only he could see.

"Don't know. My mama wants me to be a preacher." Spot-lighted in the vast, packed amphitheater, Billy, in dark suit and tie, welcomes sinners with open arms like Billy Graham. In this habitual fantasy, exhausted but standing tall, his face streaming with sweat and tears, he descends into the hushed congregation; he is mobbed by newly born-again believers who, stirred by his rousing sermon, want only to touch his person.

"I want to be an FBI agent." Jake steered the souped-up cop-car through heavy imaginary traffic in pursuit of future villains.

Jake liked to talk about how he wanted to be just like Uncle Toe. "Rich and chasing pussy in a big, long Cadillac."

"Jesus loves all sinners." From the first Billy would be fascinated by Jake's wish to be like Theo Jeannsonne. It just didn't make sense to him that someone as good-looking and well-built as Jake would pick as his idol this pear-shaped old man. The allure of this man, for Jake and for alleged legions of sexy women—this man with his chin-wattle, his big hook-nose, and his darting reptilian eyes—would become an ever more engrossing puzzle for Billy, much more so than the vague mysteries alluded to in church. Long after these halcyon days with Jake and long after the Baptist religion became for him just another amalgam of far-fetched hedges against the uncertainty of personal continuity on the yonder side of death would Billy Mayden be possessed by and obsessed with the elusive enigma whose first avatar was Theo Jeannsonne.

Thus would the serpent enter the garden and thus would Jake play Eve to Billy's Adam.

"You pious asshole! Did you fuck Dixie yet?"

"No! When are you gonna stop asking me?"

"Well, tell me what happened that day I saw you coming out of her house."

"Okay. I go over to her house to bring Daddy's tithe. I knock on the door. Dixie opens the door. Brother Johnson and Mrs. Johnson are gone somewhere."

Assuming poetic license, Billy commenced to relate a highly-adapted incident which had happened, if it happened at all, not to himself but to Ralph the deaf boy long before the day Jake shouted *Did you fuck her?* for the whole world to hear; before the Johnson's ever left New Orleans. It featured a little girl in the neighborhood with whom Ralph claimed to have often played show-me-yours-and-I'll-show-you-mine.

"So it was just the two of you there?" Jake unbuttoned his fly.

"Yeah. She says, 'Come in. Have a seat on the couch.' Then she goes into her parents' bedroom. I don't have any idea what she's up to."

Jake slipped his hand into his shorts.

"I sit on the couch. I wait a minute or two. Then I get up and look for her. I get to her parents' bedroom and she's not there. But I see the dress she was wearing on the bed, so I know I've got her treed. Pretty soon she comes out of the closet."

"Out of the closet!"

"Yeah, it's big one. You can walk into it like a little room. Even has its own light." The closet Billy had in mind matched Ralph's pantomimed description of the one in Dixie's parents' bedroom, which Billy understood Ralph to say had more lady's dresses and men's suits in it than you could shake a stick at. "Anyhow, she comes walking out and you're not gonna believe what she has done."

"Tell me, anyhow." To keep his starched jeans from getting wrinkled, Jake took them off, folded them, and put them on the back seat. Then he pushed his jockey shorts down to his knees.

"Her panties … that's all she has on … are rolled down and she's put a whole bunch of her daddy's ties in 'em. They're hanging down like a hula-hula skirt. She comes over to where I am and wiggles her hips. Like she's a hula dancer."

"Now that's more like it." Jake looked down at his hard-on and gave it several quick strokes. He looked over at Billy. "Did she put that luscious pussy right up in your face? Did you see it?"

"*See* it? I could *smell* it, it was so close." Encouraged by the feigned intensity of Jake's curiosity—they were both trying to get themselves worked up—Billy was embellishing. "Her panties were rolled down ... ."

"What do you mean, 'her panties were rolled down'?"

"Here, I'll show you." Sliding his hips forward, Billy undid his belt. Raising his hips off the seat, he pushed his pants down. Keeping his hips elevated, he folded the elastic band of his boxer shorts like he was rolling up the sleeve of a shirt, stopping just short of revealing his penis. "Like a sock. You know how you roll down your socks? Well, that's how she did it. It would be easier if I was wearing panties."

"If you were wearing panties, I'd be on you like stink on shit." Jake looked down at his little wand, gauged its power and savored its magic. "What did you do then?"

"About that time we heard her parents drive up."

"Let me see your pecker."

Billy pushed his underwear and pants down to mid-thigh. He let Jake look at his erection.

"Hey! You've got a big one. Let me measure it."

Fending off Jake's hand with his elbow, Billy put both hands over his crotch and blushed.

One day Jake caught Billy staring at his damaged leg. Billy's curiosity, unabated from the time they showered together on that first day, had got the best of him.

"Yeah, I know, not a pretty sight. Wanna know what happened?"

Billy nodded yes.

"I was on a horse ... ." Jake put his hands on the steering wheel and gazed through the grimy windshield, through the back wall of the fusty garage, and into the distance beyond. He spoke in solemn tones. Billy just listened, forced himself not to interrupt. "And that asshole brother of mine popped a whip right up close to its fucking head. Made it rear up and I fell off. Fucking horse fell right on top of me. Freak accident.

"Fucking bone was broke so bad that the jagged end of it tore right through the leg muscles and punctured the skin. Like a knife through a side of beef. Looked like a bunch of white splinters sticking out. Took forever to get the bone set. I was in the operating room for over *eight hours*. What really made it bad was the fucking doctor ... son-of-a-bitch must a been drunk as a fucking skunk ... he put the plaster right on top of the fucking wound." Jake applied a double handful of imaginary plaster-of-Paris to the large scar on his thigh. "No gauze, no pads, no nothing. Not even a fucking band-aid. Just wet fucking plaster. Of *course* it got infected. That night the pain was *out of this fucking world.* For a while it looked like they were gonna have to amputate my leg, for sure, at the fucking hip. Had to have three separate operations to scrape the infection out of the inside of the fucking bone. Altogether I was in the fucking *hospital* for six months.

"My parents tried to sue the motherfucking doctor, but this slick-assed lawyer fucked them over. I *hate* that motherfucker. If it hadn't been for him we would have a big fine car and a big fine house. I wouldn't feel so bad about what I put my parents through."

"What did he do, the lawyer?"

"Fucker was getting ready to go into politics so he didn't have time to mess with us. He talked the old man into settling for about one-tenth as much as he could have got. Just to get rid of us. Or maybe he got a kick-back from the insurance company. I wouldn't put it past him. Old man got really sick at the time, probably from worrying about me. Didn't know what the fuck he was doing. They had him on some strong-assed medicine that made him not even know where he was half the time. If I ever get the chance I swear I'll kill that cocksucker. So help me God, I will. Jimmy, too. We took an oath together. That's just about the only time we ever agreed with each other. Fucking shark got polio right after that. Serves his ass right.

"Mom had to go to work. Right around that time the doctor, Maxwell's his name, fucking quack, took over at Pinecrest. Mom went to him and told him if he didn't hire her ... the old man was sick and out of work ... fucking VA was taking forever with the paperwork. She had to do something ... . She told the son-of-a-bitch if he didn't hire her, she'd go to the newspaper and tell them what he did to our family. She was bluffing, but it worked. He said he felt bad about what happened. He gave her some cock-and-bull story about how at the time he and his wife were fighting over what to do with his own son. Said she ran off with another man and left him with the fucking kid, Arthur. Fucker's feeble-minded and queer to boot.

"Old man Maxwell got my mom classified as professional staff, so she earns a lot more that she would as just a secretary, which is what she really is. Me and Jimmy both think he's got the hots for Mom and that's the only reason he hired her. Even with her working, the old man still had to work when he could ... when he wasn't in the fucking hospital and too sick to work. And him getting sicker every day. Shit, if it hadn't been for that sorry-assed cocksucker of a lawyer, he could have retired and lived his last years in comfort. And Mom wouldn't have to work for the sorry bastard that fucked up my leg.

"I couldn't go to school for two whole years. Mom worked with my teachers while I was out though. She picked up the assignments and turned in my homework. I took the same tests the other kids took. So I only missed one year of school.

"But it nearly destroyed our family. We're just now paying off all the medical bills, hospital and rehab. Fucking VA wouldn't pay a goddamn dime."

"Didn't mean to bring you down. Maybe I shouldn't have brought it up."

Now that Jake had finally told Billy the story of the broken leg, Billy felt like their friendship was sealed forever.

"That's okay. I've been thinking about it anyway. Man, do I have the bots! Every time we come here … just sitting in this old car … I start thinking about what kind of car we might have now if we'd a got that money. Don't you see? If it hadn't been for that fucking shyster, I wouldn't have to be so embarrassed about asking girls out."

"No, I'm not following you."

"If you were a girl would you want to be seen riding around in a stupid-assed pickup truck?"

"Have you ever asked a girl out?"

"Hell no! I know what they'd say. And I wouldn't blame 'em."

Billy wondered what a date with Jake would be like. An image flashed through his mind of a girl sitting on the seat between them in the old car. The faceless girl was wearing a white formal and a wrist corsage and smelled of perfume like the girls at church. Looking past the girl, he and Jake, both wearing suits and ties, looked at each other and smiled, both remembering the girl on the school bus.

Suddenly, Jake's face lit up. "Wouldn't it be something if we could get this old buggy up and running?"

"I was just thinking the same thing."

"We could get more pussy than Clark fucking Gable. Wanna see my dick?"

One hot summer day Billy noticed Jake rubbing his right thigh, the bad one.

"What's the matter? Your leg hurt?"

"No, motherfucker. It feels great. I rub it like this to make myself come."

Billy didn't say anything.

"I'm sorry," Jake said after a pause. "Sometimes it just starts hurting. Like before a thunderstorm. Even after all this time. But I'm used to that.

I'm in a lousy mood because of something else."

"You wanna go home? It's pretty dark out there. And I think I heard some thunder a few minutes ago."

"Nah, I'm alright. Besides I've got to be tough. If I can live through this," Jake touched his bum leg, "I should be able to live through a stupid-assed thunderstorm, right?"

"Then why *are* you in a bad mood?"

"I think I may have really fucked myself up. Used to, right after the accident, my fucking leg would hurt so bad that I'd jack off ten times a day just to get my mind off the pain. It was so bad I couldn't do anything else, like read or anything. And, of course, I had to stay in bed, at least at first. And after that I couldn't go outside. So what else was I gonna do?

"I think all that masturbation may have really fucked me up. I'm afraid if I don't stop doing it I may wear my fucking dick out. Sometimes it feels like an old worn-out shoe or a piece of sugar cane that's had all the juice squeezed out of it."

Jake pulled the sex book out from under the seat of the car. Finding the place he wanted he said, "Listen to this: *'Nothing is so prone to contaminate—under certain circumstances, even to exhaust—the source of all noble and ideal sentiments, which arise of themselves from a normally developing sexual instinct, as the practice of masturbation in early years. It despoils the unfolding bud of perfume and beauty, and leaves behind only the coarse, animal desire for sexual satisfaction. If an individual, thus depraved, reaches the age of maturity, there is a wanting in him of that aesthetic, ideal, pure and free impulse which draws the opposite sexes together. The glow of sensual sensibility wanes, and the inclination toward the opposite sex is weakened. This defect influences the morals, the character, fancy, feeling and instinct of the youthful masturbator, male or female, in an unfavorable manner, even causing, under certain circumstances, the desire for the opposite sex to sink to* <u>nil</u>*; so that masturbation is preferred to the natural mode of satisfaction. Every masturbator is more or less timid and cowardly. If the youthful sinner at last comes to make an attempt at coitus ... '*, that's a fancy word for fucking, *' ... he is either disappointed because enjoyment is wanting, on account of defective sensual feeling, or he is lacking in the physical strength necessary to accomplish the act. This fiasco has a fatal effect, and leads to psychical impotence,'* that means you can't get a hard-on. *'A bad conscience and the memory of past failures prevent the success in any further attempts. The ever present* <u>libido sex</u> *... <u>u</u> ... <u>alis</u>,'* ... means sex drive, *'... however, demands satisfaction, and this moral and mental perversion separates further and further from woman. At times, under such circumstances, bestiality ... '*, that's having sex with animals ... , *'is resorted to. Sexual aberration reaches this*

degree in the <u>normally</u> constituted, <u>untainted</u>, mentally healthy individual.'
That means it can happen to regular people, like you and me."

"Guess what I did one time," Billy said.

"It means you don't have to be a freak like Arthur Maxwell for it to happen to you."

"Don't you want to know what I did?"

"Okay, what did you do?"

"I let a dog lick my dick. It was one of my old man's hunting dogs. Happened in McMannaman's slaughterhouse."

"What did it feel like?"

"It was great! Best thing I ever felt. That same day I got a bad case of poison ivy. Ever take a hot bath when you had poison ivy?"

"No. What about it?"

"It feels fantastic! The hotter the water, the better it feels. I had poison ivy on my dick when the dog licked it. I wanted to feel that hot dog spit on it. That's why I let him lick it. He'd already licked my hands. That's how I knew it'd feel so good."

It felt just as good later when Stella put white salve on all the affected areas. Billy became afraid the dog would betray him, would do something—like trying to lick his crotch in front of the preacher—that would suggest to Stella's suspicious mind what had happened in the slaughterhouse. So Billy killed the dog—the mutt was called Buster which is how Billy's twin sister pronounced Mustard, the name given it as a puppy by Clinton because of its color—and buried it behind his house in the pit inside the outdoor toilet made obsolete by recently-installed indoor fixtures.

"How'd you get poison ivy on your dick?"

"Had it on my hands and took a piss."

"'Took a piss', my ass. I bet you were jerking off."

"Coulda been."

"So, you let a dog lick your dick? I don't know. Sounds pretty perverted to me. Did you ever do it again?"

"No, just that one time. I've never told anyone else about it."

"Why not?"

"Too ashamed. Too afraid people'd think I was … you know."

"Queer?"

"Something like that. You said it sounded … what was the word you used?"

"'Perverted.' Perverted doesn't mean queer. Being queer is perverted, but there are other kinds of perversions."

"Like beasty … . What was that word, the one in the book?"

"Bestiality. Yeah, that's a perversion, but don't worry about it. I'm not going to tell anybody. You only did it that one time, right? If you did it a lot, it'd be a perversion, I think. If you *only* wanted to do that or if you couldn't fuck a girl unless you did that first. . . like guys who can only come if they sniff a woman's shoe or panties or only want to suck somebody's toes … then I think you'd qualify. You ever think about it when you're jacking off?"

Just then lightning struck nearby. Jake's eyes widened in fear. He opened the car door and ran toward the garage entrance. Another bolt of lightning struck, this time even closer. Thunder shook the old garage, dust fell from the ceiling. Jake fell to his knees, then toppled over and balled up into a knot on the oil-caked dirt floor.

Billy got out of the car. He took Jake's hand and urged him slowly to his feet. He put his arms around him. Clutching his trembling friend to his chest, Billy was overcome with a sense of deja vu and sadness. It seemed like he had done this before. Long ago, he had often held someone he loved to calm their fears. Now, today, he felt a sharp pang of grief for the loss of this person who he was not even sure was real.

"It is always best for the mentally retarded child to be placed. It is not only in *their* best interest, but it is *essential* for the emotional-mental-social health of their normal siblings." The woman's clothes were all white, even her shoes and stockings and the funny little cootie-catcher of a hat on top of the big black pile of hair. She flicked her cigarette ashes in the general direction of an ashtray atop some documents on a low table in front of the couch she and Stella Mayden were sitting on. The two women were in the Director's office at Pinecrest. Billy and his sister Sibil sat on the floor near the door playing together.

Sibil played with the screw-on part of a Mason jar-lid; with her palm flat on the floor, the circular lid was propped on her thumb, so that it wobbled like a tiny see-saw when she struck it lightly with her finger. Bent over with her ear only inches away from the grooved metal ring, she listened to the teensy tinny sound it made on the polished floor. It was her favorite toy, the only inanimate object she could be induced to play with. Left alone, she played with it for hours on end, stopping only when the little makeshift toy was taken from her.

Out of the corner of his eye, Billy watched the cigarette ashes drifting down, some falling into the nurse's coffee cup. She didn't seem to notice.

"Placement is even more imperative in the case of twins, where one is spared. And now that Billy is talking and is beginning to understand adult speech, you can expect to see your problems multiply, if you haven't already. Especially in the area of *social* development." The nurse jabbed her cigarette toward Stella on the stressed word. Glancing at Billy and Sibil, she frowned and shook her head. "Sibil really should have been placed at birth. I just hope it's not too late for her brother. He's such a bright child, it's hard to say. It could go either way. Sometimes the bright ones are the ones most affected."

"Will I get to see her?" Stella asked.

"Yes, but we recommend that you not visit for the first year or so. We need to give Sibil time to bond with our staff. After that, we can talk about visits."

"Can she ever come home?"

"Mrs. ... Stella, once a patient has accommodated to dormitory life, it is very hard on him to be taken back into the domicile-of-origin. The transition would be traumatic for all involved, but especially for the retardate."

"What makes you say it may be too late?"

"Well, Stella, I can tell already, just from the little I've been able to observe this morning, that your son seems to be somewhat passive for a boy his age ... even *feminine*." The nurse looked over at Billy. Hearing the emphasis in her voice, he had looked over at her and their eyes met. "This often happens with twins where one is retarded. The normal child misses out on a lot of attention that he would have otherwise received under normal circumstances. This is especially detrimental for male children. Often they are recruited into helping take care of ... sometimes they even learn to actually *mother* ... the retardate. This can be devastating to a boy's sense of masculinity. Have you noticed anything like that?"

"Well, yes. Billy hugs Sibil all the time. If there's a thunderstorm and a bunch a thunder and lightning ... she gets scared. At Christmas and on the Fourth of July ... there's fireworks which is loud and Clinton's dogs start to barking, which they are liable to do even when there ain't no reason for it that anybody can see. Stuff like that makes her start shaking all over."

"And Billy hugs her, you say, when she is frightened?"

"Yeah. He loves her more than anything."

"That's the kind of thing I'm talking about. It is not appropriate for a boy to do that. And there are other harmful ways a boy in his situation might learn to win his mother's approval or, if not approval, attention."

"What other ways?"

Billy stopped playing with his sister and looked again at the woman in all-white clothes, but this time she didn't look back.

"Good question, Stella." The nurse glanced at her watch. Dropping her cigarette into her coffee cup, she sat up straight and blew smoke toward Stella. "Okay, they can accomplish this end by, number one," she stuck her thumb out like a hitch-hiker, "holding back, not asserting themselves. And two," her index finger shot out—it looked to Billy like she was pointing a make-believe pistol at his mother. Frowning under the weight of what she was thinking, the nurse let her hand fall into her lap. "Well, frankly, there is no number two. Unless … ." She reached for another cigarette. Finding the pack empty, she crushed it in her fist and flung it toward the wastebasket in the corner of the small room. Missed, Billy noted. Snatching up her purse, she peered in and rooted around for a fresh pack. Dropping her purse on the couch between herself and Stella, she ripped open the new pack and lit a cigarette with a kitchen match which she struck on the underside of the table. Blowing out the smoke, she closed her eyes and fell back on the couch, the match, on which Billy's eyes were glued, still lit in her hand. Pinching the bridge of her nose with the thumb and ring finger of the hand that held her cigarette, the woman sighed, as if the very *idea* of what she was required to say unnerved even her. Sitting up, she dutifully resumed. "Unless it is to *rebel* … ." Pausing and discovering it still lit in her hand, she shook the match out and dropped it into her cup, giving Stella time to absorb the impact of the momentous word. Now out of danger of having her fingers burnt, thus forfeiting Billy's direct attention, she continued, "In which case, it is almost inevitable that, eventually, they will *lose* … not only the mother's love but a whole lot more, such as the father's approval which is *so* vital for boys. Without those, they can never be what they really want, namely, to be normal, like other boys. They can only become habitual losers, to put it bluntly.

"Everything will be multiplied in Billy's case, of course, because of the his father's long absences from the home. (Your husband works for the railroad, does he not?) In cases like this, the male child's identity is all wrapped up in being a 'good little boy' or 'mother's little helper'. The very fact that your son is *here*," she looked over at Billy, "on such a beautiful day and not outside, playing with other boys his age, is evidence that this pernicious process is pretty well along. By the way, did he *want* to be here?"

"Yeah, he loves his sister, besides … I couldn't just leave him at home by hisself. He's not even four years old yet."

"He's *such* a good boy," Sibil said, not looking up from her jar-lid toy, "A *good* boy."

"See! Sibil, of all people, proves my point," the nurse said. "She doesn't know what she's saying, of course. She can't express any original ideas. She is *incapable* of original ideas. She can only repeat what she has heard.

"Yet she senses the truth. Remarkable! You talk about out of the mouths of babes! She must have heard you express many times, in many different ways, your hope, your wish, your desperate implicit *demand*, that her brother be a good boy. Which means that you must be picking up from Billy, unconsciously of course, hints, signs, and signals that make you fear that he may be capable of *rebelling*."

Stella blinked, sat back in her chair. Billy looked up and listened. "He *used* to be a good boy. He's not such a good boy anymore. I try to keep him from ... touching ... ."

Blushing and cringing, Billy turned away from the two talking women. Sliding his butt on the floor, he got next to his sister, close enough that their bodies were touching.

"All the more reason to remove the *root* of the problem from the home. To remove the weeds from your garden so your flowers ... or your fruits ... or vegetables ... can grow and reach their full potential and be productive members of society."

"You're saying Sibil is a *weed*!"

Hearing her name, Sibil looked up. Billy looked at Stella's face and tried to get his sister to return to her Mason jar-lid.

"Oh, no, no. You're taking it the wrong way, Mrs. ... . Listen, Stella ... may I call you Stella ... . I feel I know you well enough. Listen, Stella, I know how you feel. It's perfectly natural. But you shouldn't blame yourself. I believe that most psychological problems begin, if not at the moment of conception, pretty soon after. Long before birth, let me put it that way. Now, you said Sibil is the older twin, did you not, by a few minutes? It is entirely possible that, *in vitro*, in the womb, Billy sensed that there was something wrong. That there were going to be problems. So, he may have wanted to *remain* in the safe environment of the womb. And that could have been the *beginning* of his passivity."

"What's so bad about ... ?"

"Passivity? Well, in a nutshell, the passive person is one who, in an attempt to bolster his sagging self-esteem, and again this is *so* much more important for male children, may feign an air of superiority. But it is a pseudo-superiority, a *false* feeling of self-worth that will crumble in the face of the *least* adversity. In reality, the passive person puts himself down. So far down that the only other person with whom they can form an emotional attachment is ... ." The nurse looked in the direction of the framed diplomas on the wall behind the Director's desk and then back at Stella. "I tell you frankly, the only real attachment would be ... an *unhealthy* attachment. With someone he *perceives* is on his same level. The kind of person who will participate in rituals of mutual self-degradation."

"Like who?"

"Well, the worst case scenario would be ... an *unhealthy* ... alliance with a retarded twin."

"What about Sibil? Don't she have feelings, too? Why ain't *her* feelings important?"

Billy took his sister's hands which appeared to be trembling.

"Mrs. ... ," moving the ashtray, the nurse looked at the papers underneath. Unable to spot Stella's last name, she started over. "Stella ... , let me tell you a little about these pe ... the mentally retarded. Let me start by saying, yes, they *do* have feelings. But they're not the kind of feelings you and I, say, or Billy, have. Basically, here's the situation with Sibil ... with most all retardates: Because of her arrested brain development, it's the *higher* human functions that she doesn't have or that have been impaired. Things like cognition, language ability, *moral* judgment."

"But Sibil can *talk*, she can sing. She knows all the hymns they sing at church by heart."

Sibil began to sing *Standing on the Promises*. Glancing at Stella and seeing that she was looking at Sibil, Billy put his arms around his sister and patted her to shush her.

"Let me finish, Stella. Now, the lower, *animalistic* functions, the ones that develop during early gestation, the ones that depend on the *lower* brain centers, *are* intact in Sibil. In fact, they are, in effect, *amplified*, owing to the absence or weakness of the higher, *inhibitory*, brain functions."

"Animal what?"

"Animal*istic*." Leaning over close to Stella, the nurse whispered, "Sex."

Hearing the change in the woman's voice, Billy's ears perked up. Sibil began whispering the forbidden word. Billy put his hand over her mouth. (In conversations with Clinton, Stella always whispered words the twins weren't supposed to hear.)

"I thought that's what it meant," Stella said, looking resigned, "Okay, I guess I better let you take her."

"I think you've made the right decision, Stella."

"What did you say your name is?"

"Miss Lopez. Juanita Lopez. My friends call me Jonnie. You may call me Nurse Lopez."

Just then Billy noticed a puddle forming on the floor around Sibil. He moved between her and the two women.

The last time Billy and Jake were in the old car together was late in the summer before Billy started high school. Billy had met and begun cultivating Frankie West in Little League and by now they were good friends, getting together often to play basketball. Already he sensed that the new friendship with Frankie was going to affect the old one with Jake.

From the start Billy had mixed feelings being, and *about* being, with Jake like this inside the car inside the dark moldy garage. When they first started doing it, the feelings of erotic excitement, in his throat and in his groin, had been tolerable and tolerated by his Baptist guilt. Gradually imagination and hormones combined, increasing the lust, and Billy's conscience began doing the job it was designed for: Making sexual pleasure seem abhorrent, but without diminishing in the least the pace and power, the mystery and magic, of its ineluctable and incandescent flowering. Hearing Jake read the passage on masturbation from the sex book had complicated the process and enhanced its myriad effects. The clash between the internal and external prohibitions and Billy's lustful feelings seemed at times headed toward an almost chemical resolution, either an explosion or a new synthesis.

Now on the threshold of high school, Billy, anticipating spending more time with Frankie than with Jake, at least at school, was searching, groping, for a way to extricate himself from his entanglement with Jake.

A short time before this day, Billy had gone alone to the old car and re-read the passage on masturbation. He discovered that Jake had skipped over one crucial sentence: *'Intercourse with the same sex is then near at hand,— as the result of seduction or of the feelings of friendship which, on the level of pathological sexuality, easily associate themselves with sexual feelings.'*

Now, today, in the car with Jake, the tension was almost unbearable.

Jake must have sensed that something was different and decided to push it. He toed off his shoes and pulled his jeans and shorts off. Maneuvering around the gear shift, he moved over next to Billy. "Look at my dick. Son-of-a-bitch is hard as a fucking rock."

"Not worn out after all?" Billy's mouth was dry.

"No, never felt better. Can I touch yours?"

Billy took his hand away from his crotch. Jake undid Billy's pants and freed the mindlessly eager occupant.

"Motherfucker! You have *got* a big dick. Fucker just keeps getting bigger and bigger. Why won't you let me measure it?" Holding his own pecker in one hand and gripping Billy's with the other, Jake shifted his hips forward and tilted his body so that he was facing Billy. "Here, take mine."

Billy reached over Jake's arm and Jake thrust his penis forward into Billy's hand. (Billy's mind was racing; a thought intruded: It is like we're passing batons in a relay race. But there's only *one* baton in a relay race. It seemed like these thoughts weren't his own, like he was observing someone else's thoughts.) Jake's cheek brushed against Billy's shoulder.

"Feel how hard it is?" Jake whispered, his voice hoarse, into Billy's ear.

A moment of silence and stillness ensued.

Then, in the electric calm, holding and being held this way, with his arm x'ed with Jake's, Billy was overcome by an uncanny sensation. He felt dizzy. He had masturbated with other boys before, but no one had ever touched his penis when it was hard. Except himself, of course. Nor had he ever touched another person's penis. At first it was hard for him to focus his attention. He was distracted by the unfamiliar lack of correlation between the movement of his hand on Jake's penis and the sensations Jake's hand were causing in his own penis. Jake's dick, apprehended by touch alone, seemed small and oddly shaped, large in the middle, small on both ends.

But then he and Jake got in sync and Billy began to feel excited, aroused like never before.

And scared. Something unknown, unthought, inconceivable, was coming into being. A sense came over him that something dreaded and dangerous was about to happen. Something strongly forbidden and, in equal measure, powerfully attractive, too. (*'Intercourse with the same sex.'* What did that *mean* exactly?) A closed and familiar and secret space was about to open up and when it did, he would be exquisitely profaned, deliciously polluted. Poised on the brink of a precipice, a bug on a leaf on the crest of Niagara, he was almost delirious with lust.

Struggling to draw away, he was aware of these words: *No! Stop!* *** *don't want to do this.* Did he say that or just think it? Was it 'I' don't want to do this or 'you' don't want to do this? Was he talking to Jake or to himself?

Jake stroked Billy's dick.

You left out a sentence the last time you read out of that book.

"Mmmm." Jake rubbed his cheek against Billy's shoulder.

Billy had memorized the sentence. He recited the sentence. Or did he just think it? He hadn't heard himself speak, but that didn't mean anything because he couldn't hear anything over the roaring in his ears.

Still holding the shaft of Billy's dick in one hand, Jake reached over with his other hand and caressed the head of it with his fingertips. This caused simultaneous contractions in Billy's throat and anus. There was so much going on in his throat Billy couldn't tell whether his vocal cords was making coherent sounds or he was merely moaning.

Don't you understand what that means, Jake? Speaking, if he *was* speaking, caused painfully erotic sensations in his throat, otherwise Billy might have surrendered to the all-devouring silence. *Listen to me:* *'Intercourse with the same sex is then near at hand.'* What do you think we've *been doing? It's called mutual masturbation. 'The feelings of friendship ... easily associate themselves with sexual feelings.' This doesn't bother you?*

I say if it feels good, it is good. Jake cupped Billy's balls in his hand. *That book's bullshit. What's the difference between us jacking off together and our jacking each other off?*

Who said that? Jake or that part of Billy's mind ruled over, over-ruled, by the Devil?

Then, suddenly, Billy began to feel choked and panicky. The scales of his ambiguity lurched toward horror. A deep, almost spiritual revulsion ripped through him. Two images, one tangible, one mental, dominated his thoughts:

Jake's right thigh, withered and scarred, dark against his own lily-white thigh (which by contrast seemed soft, vulnerable, feminine), slipped into his awareness like a log floating out of shadows, half rotted-away, just under the surface of black water. Jake's mutilated limb was a bigger, more revolting version of his worn-out penis! Billy remembered the story of Hop Frog Jake had told him the day they became friends. Jake was Hop Frog! A vengeful incinerator sent by the Devil to snatch Billy's soul away!

Equally powerful was the other image: Frankie West's smirking face. What if *he* saw what I am doing?

No longer beguiled, Billy became aware of his surrounding. Jake's body rubbing against his own suddenly seemed an unbearable intrusion. Like a mother whose screaming baby is in danger, he was awash with concern for the safety of his penis. It was as if Jake had reached into his body and commandeered an internal organ, his kidney or his heart, and was fondling it.

"Didn't you say you couldn't stand for anyone to touch your leg?" Billy jiggled his own leg to draw Jake's attention to their thighs touching.

"That's only ... if I'm not ... expecting it," Jake croaked. His eyes were closed and his lips were dry. He looked like some reptilian creature warming in the sun. He thrust back and forth in Billy's hand.

Just then a sharp rapping filled the inside of the old car. It was Jake's brother, Jimmy, knocking against the back window of the car with a stick. The spell was broken.

$$* \qquad * \qquad *$$

Later that same day at the Garrard's after lunch Billy and Jake were doing the dishes when Jimmy came into the kitchen.

"Careful! You're gonna *drop it*!" Jimmy told Billy, who was drying. "Hold it with both hands. If you held on to those glasses the way you hold on to my brother's reproductive organ, I wouldn't worry." Then he said to Jake, "I've seen you with your nose in that disgusting book you got from Theo. I hope it tells you what kind of moral monster you're turning yourself into. Better yet, take a good look at your 'friend' here. That ought to tell you more than any book. Hereditary degeneracy, I think is the proper term. That's just a fancy way to say white-trash. It's in his *nature* to wallow in filth. But, Jesus, Jacob, *you* don't have to be that way. I pray to God every day that you will come to your senses. Won't you try to do *something* to save your miserable soul? Please don't tell me that I have hoped in vain for you to wake up and see the light. "

Billy braced himself. He knew what was coming. He had witnessed many confrontations between the two brothers. Run-ins that began with the older brother instructing the younger one, for his own good, on the finer points of proper conduct were the most common and the most likely to become violent. Now that Jimmy was born-again, his harangues more and more resembled Brother Johnson's preaching style, which made it easier for Billy to tune out their content. That and the fact that he, Billy Mayden, had been saved and baptized. Once saved, always saved.

Billy felt Jake's elbow nudge his own. Out of the corner of his eye, he saw his friend glance his way and bow his head, as if in shame.

Jimmy wasn't done. "You ever dry dishes before? If you can't do it without breaking them, just leave 'em. I'll put them away after they've dried."

"Get your *ass* out of here," Jake commanded without lifting his bowed head. His hands, submerged in the dishwater in the sink, were motionless, waiting. "We don't need your fucking ... goddam ... motherfucking ... dicklicking ... chickenshit help. We sure as shit don't need your cocksucking supervision. And you can take your moral instruction and shove it up your tight ass."

Unfazed, Jimmy said to Billy, "You hang around with that deaf kid, don't you? What's his name?"

"Ralph."

"That's the one. He's the worst kind of white-trash. A perfect example of what you find any time there is incestuous interbreeding. Needless to say he was born out of wedlock."

"Leave us the fuck *alone*, Jimmy!" Jake said.

"I've seen you hanging out with Frankie West," Jimmy said to Billy, ignoring Jake. "He's illegitimate. Did you know that? Born out of wedlock."

"Who made you chairman of the House Un-American Activities

Committee?" Jake demanded. "What cocksucking business is it of yours who the fuck Billy is friends with? He can be friends with fucking-ass Hitler if he wants to, and it's no skin off your sorry ass."

"Take it easy, Little Brother. We're having a civilized discussion. I'm just trying to show this young man that, bad as he is, there are worse things he could have been. No need for you to get all bent out of shape."

Up until now, it seemed, Jake had struggled to maintain a show of patience. But now his voice had the hiss of a lit fuse in it. "I'm *warning* you, you holier-than-thou motherfucker!"

"I'm just stating facts. And, Willy, do you know Arthur Maxwell? Do you know he was born out of wedlock? Had to be, someone as degenerate as he is."

Whirling around, Jake bellied up to the taller boy. "His chickenshit name is Billy, not Willy. I've told you a thousand times. And I told you to *leave us the fuck alone.* I'm not going to tell you again."

"Want to try and make me?" Jimmy sneered down at his younger brother, not giving an inch.

Jake immediately drew his arms back, and stepping forward like he was passing a basketball, unleashed a swift two-handed shove into Jimmy's chest, slamming him against the refrigerator and sending a half-full bottle of red wine crashing to the floor.

Regaining his footing, Jimmy pinched the front of his shirt with two fingers and held it away from his body. "Now look what you've done. You got dirty dishwater on my clean shirt."

Billy looked around and saw a red puddle of wine on the floor with slivers of glass in it. The sharp odor of wine filled the room. Billy thought: It is a sin to drink wine. I wonder what it tastes like.

When Jimmy looked up from examining his shirt, Jake moved in close. The broken glass crunched under his heavy-soled shoes.

"Okay, okay. Don't push it." Jimmy held up his hands like a man who, knowing the gun pointed at him isn't loaded, is willing—for the sake of decorum and minimizing the damage to the furniture—to humor his lesser adversary and give him time to cool off. There was no fight in his voice, but no fear either. While it was true that whatever respect he had for his younger brother was not for Jake himself, but for his capacity for violence, it was the kind of respect an experienced dog-trainer would afford a vicious maltreated mastiff; the situation required an extra measure of caution, but posed no real problem. Looking down at the broken glass on the floor, he backed away. Jake advanced with clenched fists, pressing his advantage. Jimmy said, "Look what you've done. You better clean that up." Turning and walking out of the room, he said over his shoulder, "See you later," and chortled to himself.

"Prick!" Jake began cleaning up the mess on the floor. "Why does he have to be such an asshole? I can't *wait* to get the fuck *away* from that bastard. You would not believe how many times I have been embarrassed by that son-of-a-bitch. It's such a burden trying to stay popular when you have a prick like that for an older brother. Everybody expects me to be like him, so I have all his shit to overcome just to be where everybody else *starts*.

"He spies on us. I guess you know that after what happened a while ago. He wouldn't have known we were in that old car if he hadn't been following us around, spying on us. It's nothing new, though. Fucker won't leave me the fuck alone! It started when I got hurt. Naturally, I got all Mom and Pop's attention for a long time after it happened. And, of course, Jimmy felt guilty because he's the one who caused the accident. But Billy," Jake assumed the hand-on-heart posture of oath-taking, "I swear to God, I never did anything to make him feel that way. I've always said it was just a freak accident."

"When did all this 'born out of wedlock' stuff start?"

"Oh, you don't know? He's a big-assed Christian now."

"I knew he joined our church not too long ago."

"I think maybe it's his latest attempt to get Mom and Pop's approval. I guess he thinks they're still mad at him for causing the accident. Wants to do something to show them he's as good as me. Or more likely he just wants to piss them off. He knows they don't believe in that crap. Or at least he should know it."

"What do you think he meant by, 'See you later'?" Billy wondered how much Jimmy had seen of what he and Jake were doing in the old car. Permitted by the relief of a narrow escape and motivated by suppressed regret for unspeakable allurements snatched away, he tried to remember what had actually happened; and to imagine (now giddily immune from any actual consequences) what might have happened if Jimmy hadn't shown up when he did.

"Fuck if I know ... or care. Motherfucker gives me a supreme case of the red ass."

"Why does he do it? Follow you around, I mean. Spy on you?"

"I don't know. I mean, I kinda know, but it's hard to explain. He *says* it's because he wants to protect me. Don't ask me what *from*. The Devil, I guess. After I started back to school, I had to walk on crutches for a while. There were some kids that were pretty cruel. And Jimmy wouldn't let any of 'em mess with me. Which made my parents, especially my old man, proud of him. For being such a good big brother, you know. But, hell, Billy, he *knows* I don't need him taking care of me *now.* You saw what happened just now .... I can lick *his* ass any day of the week and twice on Sunday. So, why would I need *him* to protect me?"

"You can lick his ass?"

"Ha ha. You know what I mean. It's like if he can't be mean to me ... you know ... get even with me for getting all Mom and Pop's attention ... for stealing them from him ... then nobody else better be mean to me, either."

"That makes sense, I guess."

"You don't hang around with Frankie West, do you?"

"Not really."

9

Billy was in high school before he finally had a chance to observe Theo Jeannsonne up close.

"You remember the one I was telling you about, J. G.?" The man behind the wheel glanced over at Jacob Garrard.

Jake was riding shotgun. Billy was in back, sitting on the edge of the back seat, his chin resting on his arms which were folded on the top of the front seat. It was the first time Billy had been in the big baby-blue Cadillac. With Theo's proud approval, Jake had named it—'christened' was the word Jake used the day Theo gave them fifty-cents each to wash and polish the car—The Pussy Wagon.

They were racing north on Highway 165. Theo was taking them for a spin.

The air-conditioner was on. It blew the sweet scent of Theo's cologne into the back seat. Peering over Theo's shoulder, Billy's eyes shifted from the gaudy rings on the hand gripping the knob attached to the steering wheel to the man himself. He found it easy to believe that Theo was Brother Johnson's *adopted* brother. For one thing, there was his big hooked nose; no such aberration marred the preacher's face. For another, his starched *pink* dress shirt and his flashy tie. Most of all, he wasn't built like Brother Johnson. He was fat and his shoulders were narrow, his hips wide.

"You mean the fat one?" Jake smiled and winked at Billy. "How you like this air-*cunt*-ditioning, eh, Billy? Can you feel it back there?" Billy said he could. "Ain't this *something*? Oh, oh, oh! Uncle Toe, tell Billy about the heater. And, oh yeah! Show him how you shift gears when you're ... ."

"Trying to score?" Theo glanced over at Jake. "Don't you want to know what happened with the 'fat one' as you call her? What gave you the idea she was fat, anyway?"

"Fuck, I don't know. And fuck yeah, I want to hear all about her. But first show Billy what you do with the heater and the gear stick to get a bitch to give you a piece of that voluptuous pussy."

Theo put his hand on the knob of the gear shift lever, which, like the knob on the steering wheel, was of transparent blue plastic and had a naked woman inside. "Okay, slide over this way." He gave the seat a pat. Jake moved over to the middle of the front seat. "First, you have to get the gal to snuggle up nice and close." With a prurient purr in his voice, he said, "Don't you want to move over a little bit, baby," and reached across Jake's lap and gently hooked Jake's right leg with his right hand.

"Don't touch my leg!" Jake blushed and scrambled away. "Gives me the heebie-jeebies. I don't need to be that close. Just tell it. Let the son-of-a-bitch use his fucking imagination."

Billy's imagination was fully engaged: He couldn't take his eyes off Theo. The man, apparently unable keep his hands to himself or his eyes on the highway, seemed bursting with dangerous wild energy.

"It's just a demon*stra*tion, J. G." Theo chuckled. "*You*'re the one who brought it up. Don't worry, I'm not gonna pop your cherry. I wouldn't fuck you with *his* dick." He motioned with his head to indicate Billy's dick, which was primed and in sync with his imagination.

"I'm not a fucking virgin," Jake said.

By definition Jimmy would say, Billy thought. Jake was lying, he was pretty sure. If he ever did get a piece, I'd know almost before the girl did.

After a little more coaxing Jake agreed to sit next to Theo.

"Now put your knees together, like a proper young lady." Theo put his hand on the gear shift knob. Looking straight ahead, he said, "Okay, you're driving along like this." He reached down and lightly touched Jake's knees. "Her knees'll be right here, right? The heater is here." He turned the heater fan on. "Now, I got the blower aimed right here." He again tapped Jake's knees with his fingertips. "That hot air blows right up her dress. Gets that pussy all heated up for you, like a hot pie in the oven."

"Cool," Billy said. He felt uneasy. He thought, He's the kind of man Stella is always talking about, the kind who sniff around Jonnie Vonderheim. At the same time, he was mesmerized by the man. Jesus loves sinners as much as anybody else, he reminded himself.

"No. *Hot!*" Jake slid back across the seat to the shotgun position. "Now show him what happens when you change gears."

"Okay, come on back over here." Theo turned the heater fan off.

Jake moved cautiously back across the seat.

"Okay, you're tooling along, right? And you go to change gears." Theo put his hand on the gear knob. "Look what happens." He clutched and took his foot off the gas pedal. "You're just coasting along, right?" Shifting out of third gear, he said, "You push it forward ... move it over. The car's in neutral. So are you. You're cool. You're not thinking about her. At least you don't show it. You're busy driving. Just coasting along. You look around." Theo looked around, right, left, his double-chin uplifted, its wattle flapping with the motion of his head. "You feel the heel of your hand or your shirt sleeve maybe rubbing against her knees, barely touching them, but that's okay, you're still cool. Then … youpullitbacklikethis!" He pulled the gear lever back towards the seat, putting the car into first gear. Holding the blue plastic knob with just his fingertips, he was able to force Jake's knees apart with the heel of his hand. In the lower gear, the car decelerated as if it had been braked. In mid-lurch, Theo released the knob and forced his hand between Jake's thighs all the way up to the crotch.

Jake scrambled away like a spooked kitten. "Hands off the gonads!" He blushed and tried to smile.

Theo chuckled. Turning his head to the right and speaking out of the corner of his mouth to Billy, he said, "Before she knows what's happening, you're inside her panties, getting your finger dirty. You do that half a dozen times and she's hot to trot." Then he laughed.

Billy couldn't tell if he was joking or not. Watching the two demonstrations of cocksmanship, he had felt like an outsider, like a kid peering over a barrier at something Stella would say a boy his age had no business seeing. Seeing Uncle Toe touching Jake that way was unnerving in a strange way. Strange in both senses, unfamiliar and *weird*.

"Anyway … the one I was telling you about … I wouldn't call her *fat* exactly." Theo looked over at Jake with a crooked smile on his face. "You wanna hear this or not? Or are you still mad?" Seeing Theo's lower lip bulging out, Billy thought, so that's where Jake picked up that habit. Imitating Theo to see how it would feel, he pressed his own tongue against the inside surface of his own lower lip. When Jake did it, it meant what he just said was a joke, literally 'tongue-in-cheek'. For Theo it seemed to be a sign of self-satisfied amusement at Jake's expense.

"Yeah, fuck yes, I wanna hear it." Jake's smile looked strained and painful.

"Did I say she was fat?"

"Hell, I don't know," Jake said. "Something you said gave me that idea. I don't remember what."

"I may have used the word *embonpoint*." Theo said, "I think I remember you asking what it meant. It's French for 'pleasantly plump'. It doesn't matter what you call 'em. I like 'em like that. Gives you something to hang onto and just because a woman is big doesn't mean her pussy is. It's the same with men; big men don't necessarily have big dicks. Besides, the fat packed *inside* a woman's body makes her actually *tighter*; it's like a pillow packed full as you can get it; gives you more friction than a skinny woman."

Looking around and satisfying himself that his audience was still with him, he continued, "Anyhow, she showed up at the park a couple a days ago. Early, before the bar was open." Theo ran his heavily-ringed fingers through his black wavy oily hair which was combed straight back, not parted. (See back cover.) Reaching for the lit cigarette in the car ashtray, he took a drag and blew smoke out his big nostrils. His nails were closely and evenly trimmed. "Guess what happened."

"You fucked her!"

"Better! *Much* better!"

"What could be better than sliding your dick into a big ole luscious hairy pussy?"

"I'm gonna tell you. Listen to this: She says ... ," Theo drawled in falsetto, mimicking the woman's voice ... , "'There is something I have been wanting to do ever since I first laid eyes on you, Theo Jeannsonne.'"

"Hot damn! I got a hard on just listening to this." Jake squirmed and glanced back at Billy.

"No, wait. Need a little build-up. She starts telling me this story. Says she's laying in bed, can't sleep. Decides what the hell. Gets up. Takes a bath. Gets dressed.

"I interrupt her, tell her, 'Look Jay, I'm busy'." Theo chuckled. "'Gotta get the bar ready for business', I says. Nothing drives a woman wild like a dude who acts like he don't want it when she's hot to trot. She comes around behind the counter where I'm acting like I'm working, right? She looks down at my crotch. I'm out to here." He indicated with his hand how far out he wanted them to believe was. "She says, 'Oh! I *see* you're working hard, alright. *Real* hard'. She takes my earlobe in her teeth and unzips my pants real slow. Then she's giving me this look. Like she's a naughty little girl or something. She takes Sir Winston out. And ... . It okay for him to hear this? Can he keep his mouth shut?" He gestured with his head toward the backseat.

No longer peering over the barrier, Billy was slumped back in the seat, rearranging himself, dealing with his excitement.

"Yeah! Yeah! Come on! Don't stop now, goddamn it," Jake said breathlessly.

"This gets around, her old man might blow my ass off with a fucking shotgun. Fucker is *jealous* with a capital J."

"He's cool. He's okay. Tell him, Billy. You aint gonna tell ... . Hell, Toe, who's he gonna tell? His fucking *mother*?"

"Okay, like I say, she pulls him out. By this time, I'm hot to trot myself. I mean let me *tell* you. Somebitch is harder'n a rock. I'm still acting like it's not a big deal, though. I say, 'Wuh ell, I guess it won't hurt if the bar opens a few minutes late', and I turn away like this … ," he shifted his narrow shoulders away from Jake as if Jake was the one who had hold Sir Winston, "... without moving my hips, you know. There's no way I want her to turn loose of old Winny. I reach over and get a rag like I'm gonna wipe my hands. This drives her out of her fucking *mind*, I can tell. She's huffing and puffing like a fucking freight train, kinda bouncing up and down like she's got ants in her fucking drawers. And she's holding onto my dick like it's a lease on a dog that might run away or something, you know. Whata ya think happened next?"

"Oh, you son-of-a-bitch! Don't tease me like that. Tell me, you motherfucker!" Jake squirmed as if the car seat were painfully hot.

"Okay. Get this: The lady kneels down on the fucking floor and starts sucking my dick. I mean like her life depended on it. You've seen a young calf nursing on its mamma? That's the way she was. She was squirming around … her head was going this way and that, like the head of my dick is a lug-nut and she's taking it off with her mouth … she was moaning and groaning, even with her mouth full … made my dick vibrate like one of them electric clippers barbers use to give flat-tops. Best fucking blowjob I've had since I can't remember when. Better'n a nigger queer from the French Quarter."

"Ooo weee! *Son of a motherfucking bitch*, Toe. That's got to have felt *so* fucking good*!*" Jake was now bouncing up and down on the seat in seeming excitement.

"You bet your sweet ass it did. It's the best, man. And it's so easy. Don't even have to take your pants off, or anything. Just unzip your fly and there it is." Theo held his half-fisted hand above his crotch, the negative space an exaggerated stand-in for his quiescent and trouser-bound penis. "Don't leave any smell on you, either, 'cause spit don't stink like pussy juice. Not that I don't like the smell of pussy, you understand." Theo chuckled. "Anyhow, she looked up at me with those baby blues like she was sucking Jesus Himself. I started to come, I grabbed two fistfuls of that long black hair and held on like a rodeo rider on a bucking bramer bull. She's swallowing my jizm like it was mother's milk."

Squirming on the seat and pulling at the crotch of his pants, Billy wondered how anyone could do such a digusting thing and what it must have been like for Theo and for the woman.

Theo sighed, dropped his hand to the seat and looked around at Billy and then at Jake. "Listen, fellows, you gotta keep this under your hat. She lives around here somewhere. Your old man or old lady finds out, Jake, that could throw a monkey wrench in our plan. You do still wanna come work for me after you start to business school, right? Like we talked about?" Jake said hell yes he did. "Good. God knows I need someone who's up on the latest in how to run a business, and I'd rather it be you than some stranger I can't trust."

"I thought you wanted to be in the FBI," Billy said to Jake.

Jake acted like he hadn't heard Billy. After a moment he draped his left arm over the back of the car seat and motioned with his hand for Billy to be quiet.

"Speaking of people I don't trust," Theo said, "You see Jimmy this morning? He was supposed to come down and help me out. Big weekend coming up. I'm gonna need all the help I can get."

"Jonnie Vonderheim gave Dr. Maxwell a blowjob," Billy said, thinking out loud.

During the long silence that ensued, Jake watched Theo's face, waiting for his reaction.

"Who's Dr. Maxwell?" Theo patted his shirt pocket for his cigarettes.

"The guy who runs Pinecrest," Jake said. He looked around at Billy and gave him a questioning look. "Mom's his secretary. He's the fucker who fucked my leg up."

"*Your* mom?" Theo shook a cigarette half-way out of the pack and put it in his mouth. "She know about this?" He motioned with his head toward the back seat. As he spoke the unlit cigarette bounced up and down in cadence with the movement of his thick dry lips.

"She hasn't said anything to me about it." Jake grinned. Turning toward Billy, he asked, "Where'd this alleg-ed blowjob take place?"

"At Pinecrest, in his office. Ralph saw it. He used to be at Pinecrest, but Dr. Maxwell kicked him out."

"You say *Vonderheim*?" Theo took the cigarette out of his mouth and twisted around to look at Billy. "Married to *Fred* Vonderheim?"

"Uh huh."

"Skinny, mopey-looking bastard?" Theo turned around again. "Fred, I mean, not his wife." He licked his lips. "Drives a Jax beer truck? Uniform always dirty and sweaty? Smokes those nasty little cigars that look like dog turds?"

"That's him," Billy said. He wished Uncle Toe would look more at the road and less at him. He didn't like the man's eyes boring into him like that, his big nose aimed like a pistol. It was as if he was looking for something in Billy's face and meant to take it, by force if necessary. "I mean, I guess. I don't know what he smokes."

Theo lit the cigarette and blew smoke out his nostrils. "Okay, you little ass-wipes. I gotta head back now. Gotta stop off at the park before I take you home. That okay?"

Headed back the way they came, Theo chuckled, nervously, without mirth. "You talk about a pussy-whipped motherfucker. Talking about Fred Vonderheim. Somebitch comes in the bar ever morning pissing and moaning about how his old lady spends all his fucking money on clothes and booze. Says she hates that sister-in-law a mine, John's broad. He don't know John is my brother. Seems the two of 'em … John and Janelle … J&J, I call 'em … came by Fred's house one day, you know … 'witnessing to sinners'." He wiggled his right index finger to indicate quotation marks. "And Janelle turned up her nose at the way Freddy's Mexican Fraulein kept house. Or at least Fred thought she did. Which is apparently a sore spot with old Fred and after J&J left he said something about it to her. But J. V., she was waiting for him. Her, she could care less what some snotty bitch thinks about her house. Least that's what I heard. But she used it as an excuse to get back at the poor bastard Fred by making him buy her a whole shitload of new furniture. On credit. Now he's working his ass off just to pay the fucking interest. Maybe that's why he's got himself mixed up with the Foster brothers. Hauling their moonshine in his fucking beer truck, distributing their hooch for 'em, to get a little extra money. They even gave him a pistol to keep in his truck, case some really thirsty motherfucker tries to rob his ass. They got a still somewhere way back in the swamp … up the creek from the park. Just before you get to Darktown, on the other side a the creek. Good whiskey, though. I keep some at the bar for special customers. Some of 'em need it. Lot of the ones with kids with polio come in the bar from the sanitarium. Don't take much to get you drunker'na skunk. Can't beat the price, either."

Theo was talking fast now, like he was nervous. He reached for the cigarette in the ashtray, saw it had burned out, lit another one, and took a deep drag. "It's illegal, but what the hell. No skin off my nose. Besides no need to get on the wrong side of dudes like that." Smoke came out of his mouth as he spoke, like he had forgotten to exhale it. "I'm surprised she's fucking around on him, though. Somebitch has one hell of a big dick on him." He pulled at his lower lip with his ring-laden fingers, like it was numb and he was trying to put some feeling back into it.

"How do you know *that*, Uncle Toe?" Jake laughed nervously.

Theo didn't answer at first. He just stared straight ahead. Then, his head jerked toward Jake. "Huh? Oh! Because I can see the motherfucker bulging out. That's how I know. Hangs halfway down his leg." Then he laughed. A forced laugh, Billy thought. "Just like that so-called brother of mine, the Good Reverend. I wouldn't fuck any woman either one of them had fucked."

"Why not?" Jake asked.

"Cunt would be too stretched out. It'd be like trying to wind a lady's wrist watch with a Monkey wrench. Woman ain't gonna wanna mess around with a normal-sized dick after she's had something like that rammed up in her a time or two."

"You mean there's actually two women you wouldn't fuck, Uncle Toe!" Jake said. "You're slipping!"

"Huh? What'da you mean?" Theo's mind seemed elsewhere.

"You've always said, 'Fuck anything that'll fuck you back'. Now you're telling me you wouldn't fuck Jonnie Vonderheim and you wouldn't fuck the preacher's wife."

"Yeah, I guess."

"I thought you said women don't care how big a man's dick is," Jake said. "Remember? You said, it's not the wand, it's the magician."

"Did I say that? Yeah, I guess I did. 'Not the meat, but the motion'. That's what us little-dicked guys have to keep telling ourselves, anyway, right?" Theo let out a strained laugh. He looked back at Billy, with the same intense scrutiny as before. "You *see* her give … this fellow … a blowjob?"

"No, but Ralph did. *Said* he did, anyways."

"Who's Ralph?"

"He's a deaf mute Billy used to hang around with," Jake said.

Theo turned off onto a gravel road. After a short while they came to Magnolia Park.

"Anyhow, as I was saying … ," Theo said after they had come to a stop, squirming around on the leather seat, rearranging his big butt. They were parked in the shade of the tall pines surrounding the parking lot of Magnolia Park.

"Oh yeah. You come in her mouth?" Jake asked.

"Hell yes, man. She wouldn't turn me loose till she had every last drop."

"Good to the last drop, eh? Like Maxwell House?" Jake laughed loudly. He looked back at Billy. "Good to the last fucking drop." Billy could tell Jake was greatly pleased with himself, as if by making what he thought was a really funny joke he had somehow participated in Theo's exploit.

Theo put his cigarette out and got out of the car. The heat of the day and the smell of the pines flooded into the car, mingling with the smoky artificially-cooled air and the odor of Theo's perfume.

Sticking his head back into the car, Theo said, "Or good to the last *drip*," and laughed at his own joke.

10

Theo said good night to the last customer and locked the door. He had announced an early last call; early for a Saturday night, at any rate. His barmaid-waitress, the widow woman he had recently re-hired, W. W. as he called her, had left early and he didn't feel like messing with the usual stragglers who would stay there all night if you let them. They don't so much nurse their drinks as try to raise them from the dead. Where had he heard that? He went behind the bar, poured himself another glass of whiskey, took a sip. *My* turn now. How many's that make? he wondered. Four or five, but who's counting. I can sleep late tomorrow. Really shouldn't drink when I'm working, though. Already drunk enough some fucker with a gun try to hold me up I'd shit my pants.

He began washing the dirty glasses that had accumulated in the hour since W. W. left. She was catching on quickly this time, thanks to her having cut way back on her drinking, or maybe she was just learning to hold her liquor. "By the ears," he said out loud, the punch line of an old joke. She'd soon be just what he needed. Someone who could wait tables *and* tend bar. He couldn't wait to tell his holier-than-thou brother about Dixie's going to work in a beauty salon and about hiring the widow of a Pentecostal preacher to replace her. Pentecost is as bad as a Catholic to a Baptist preacher. I'm gonna cut back on W.W.'s hours, I think. Not enough customers on week nights to justify keeping her past nine o'clock. Not that he needed the money, thank God. Taking the operation out of the city was a good move. The park is a good front. "*Some*body's got to carry on the Devil's work," he said out loud. Most of the polio customers, mostly dads, drank to sleep, not to party or dick around, so they did their drinking early. Instead of supper, Theo suspected. "All he ever did is fuck that girl up. What kid with any gumption wouldn't rebel?"

Glancing up, he saw endless reflections of reflections of himself in the huge windows in front and back of him. "I go on forever," he said. "Upstream and downstream ... and never the twain shall meet." Finishing as many of the glasses as he was going to, he dried his hands, reached under the bar, and flipped a switch, turning off all but a couple of night-lights. As his eyes adjusted to the dim light, he lit a cigarette. Hello, loneliness, he thought. You're right on time. Like clockwork. "Maybe I'll give J. V. a call," he said. Scratch that, he thought. Fred's home this time of night. I'll call her in the morning. If it still seems like a good idea.

What's that scent? Must be Jonnie's ghost. Summoned by the sound of her name. Or her initials, rather. "*Rah*ther .... You can call me Bominishous and my nishous be T. J."

J. V. says smell is the most important ingredient of sex. She says it's the fuse, the muse. The spark that drives the piston. The pilot light that keeps the oven ready for quick action. The appetizer that gets the juices flowing. In other words, Theo thought, Perfume and pussy. "*Go together like a horse and carriage*," he squeaked. He was trying to sing, but self-pity and its twin, late-night lust, had him by the throat. "Get past the smell, you got it licked," he said, loudly, as if to take back control of his voice. "Dat woman sho do likes me to eat dat dar pussy a huz."

There it is again! You're picking up something, Toe Ole Boy. Besides the smell of booze and cigarettes, that is. "Probably the clap." Yes, I'm definitely getting it now, he thought. Closing his eyes, he intoned, "I smell you ... come out, come out ... wherever you are," remembering the game he played in childhood of talking out loud to the monsters that plagued him when he was alone and scared. Were there any women here earlier tonight? Other than W. W., that is. It sure as hell wasn't *her* he was smelling.

"It's the scent of a *woman*." Certain sex-related words, repeating themselves in his mind, *woman ... woman ... woman*, often worked as aphrodisiacs. He mouthed, *wuh mun ... wuh mun ... wuh ... wuh ... wuh*, paying attention to the pursing of his lips. Like they were closing around a nipple, he thought. "Or a *clit* ... or something *lie kit*." Sniffing his hand to see if it was clean, he put his fingers to his lips to feel the breath expelled as he spoke. Like a lady excusing a burp, he thought. "*Puh ... see. Puh ... see*," he whispered. It was his favorite word. He imagined little puffs of air, *puh see, puh see, puh see* .... "Coming in pairs" ... released into his ear canal ... . "Tickling, titillating, torturing." It was J. V.'s sure-fire way of getting him to go down on her. "Whispering pussy in my ear. Put your ear to a seashell and you can hear the ocean. Put your nose to a pussy and you can smell it. Hey, that's good! Ought to write it down."

Everything happens very quickly. A surprise attack of rough touch and sibilant sound freezes him in his tracks. Something, someone, presses against his back and something, a hand, is forced into the crack of his butt. At the same time, wet warm lips brush against his ear. A blast of hot breath, laden with words whispered hurriedly, fervently, intrudes into his ear: "*It's an uncanny smell* … ." The words build quickly to a climax, "*Familiar yet strange … more than a smell* … ." The hand increases its pressure and scope; rapidly ranging over the whole expanse of Theo's big ass, it commandeers one fat cheek and then the other; now back into the crack, swiping up and down, like a tongue, big as a cow's. "*You are enveloped … all your senses are excited … you are on* … ." Suddenly, the last word is shouted, " … **_fire!_** … ," and his pants and underwear are jammed into the breach of his butt.

Theo gasps. He feels his body begin to revolve, tilting backwards as he turns. From behind him, a figure sweeps around in front of him and grabs his long oily hair and pulls hard on it, straightening him up, propelling his head forward. Braced for a head-butting collision, he is stopped short, his nose one inch from another nose.

A disturbing uncertainty floods his mind: This close *he couldn't tell if it was a woman's or a man's face!* What woman would be doing this?

Johnnie Vonderheim used to be fond of sneaking up behind him and stroking his ass. She had perfected the timing and the execution of the maneuver and it never failed to surprise and arouse him. (He had made the mistake of telling her about certain prison experiences.) She would hang around outside or inside his house and ambush him on his way out or in. She would jump him in his bedroom, in the shower, while he was bent over brushing his teeth. Slipping her hand into his crack, she would press her fingers against his anus. Sometimes, if he wasn't wearing underwear, she'd stick her finger up his ass and then make him smell it. Next she would grab his hair and pull his head down between her legs. Ride him like a bike, his upturned face the seat. One night she stalked him among the big pines in the moonlight and he sucked her off right there on the pine-needled path, her moans a doleful duet with the breeze in the boughs overhead—wafting resinous scents.

Theo knew that kind of sex wasn't exactly normal, but most of the time it was all he could do for a woman. Unlike other women who often just laid back and enjoyed it—at least until they realized that was all he wanted—J. V. went after it, did what it took to make it happen. She *liked* it. Liked it as much as the other. Or so she said. The more she seemed to like it, the better it was for Theo, at the time and later when he was alone.

He hated that he still liked being touched on the ass so much. It cast serious doubt on his masculinity. He resisted calling it a perversion, but, surely, only queers liked that sort of thing. He hated even more that another person knew how much he liked it. Did he know that he still had this … abnormality … undiminished … before Jonnie reactivated it? He couldn't remember, or rather, didn't want to remember. It left him vulnerable to shameful invasions, humiliating seductions.

In the very midst of the currently ongoing *coup de arse*, as he was wont to think of it, he was desperately trying to assess it, comparing it to the way J.V. did it.

This was different, more forceful.

Did that mean his attacker was a man?

Finding nothing that would dispel the fast-becoming-terrible uncertainty, his mind began to flail, far from the shores of sobriety and the safety of his already-compromised sexual identity.

In the grip of vertigo brought on by the rough ass-handling and too much booze; not knowing if he was gonna be seduced, raped, killed, or all of the above; he becomes hyper-aware of his astonishingly intense erection. Fearfully, blissfully set to surrender to a desire buried so deep that it has till now seemed not to be his own, but infused into him by some subterranean force, by some inner demon taunting him to wager his soul in an ultimate game with two divergent outcomes—a homoerotic snuff-version of the lady and the tiger, or a satyric enticement to relax and enjoy a fate-worse-than-death (wink, wink, sneer, sneer)—he is spiraling down, collapsing in on himself. The beast is gnawing on him, he *is* the beast, gnawing on himself. His swollen lust-strangled windpipe is rigid as his hard-on, his mouth is gushing saliva; swallowing is exquisitely, excruciatingly painful, each swallow adding torque to the downward twist of his excremental demise.

On the point of surrender, in a moment of crystalline clarity, Theo's heart stops. The world stops. Everything stops.

A miracle has happened.

Standing before him in a jacket made of alligator skin and a short dress of basic black is a dark-haired green-eyed angel.

Chaos becomes perfect order, the roaring in his ears a melody. In that improbable moment of revelation, all the formidable, formerly frightening things are broken down and re-assembled, crystallizing into a sublime pattern, a profound understanding worthy of minds far greater than his.

Theo is able to appreciate the miracle, *as it is happening, second by second*—that's part of the miracle—the *beauty* of it, the *form* of it, as it unfolds. From being Isaac under the knife, brought down, humbled, made ready to surrender to death like a sacrificial animal, he is now lifted up and out of himself and *revealed* to himself. He *is* Theo Jeannsonne. Theo Jeannsonne *knows* Theo Jeannsonne. Knows him in his entirety. And knowing himself he knows everything.

It is as if he has zoomed up to Heaven and he, too, has become an angel, a worthy companion to the celestial being in front of him.

Literally unable to speak, Theo's lips mouth the angel's name, *Janelle*, sending a shiver of anticipation down his spine and beyond.

As the raven-maned woman (her eyes now lapis lazuli) lets her alligator jacket slip off her shoulders and fall to the floor, she whispers, *Theo*, and a cold invisible hand squeezes the scruff of his neck.

The apparition's ruby lips, wet and glistening, retract, revealing dazzling pearly teeth, and emit a soundless growl, that, humming in Theo's ears, shut out everything but the two of them, Theo and the Angel. Her black dress is sleeveless. The skin of her smooth white shoulders seems to shine with its own light in the dimly-lit bar.

The miracle, the angel, the woman, *is* Janelle, *has* to be, Theo wills it. They have a past; he is saturated with it; *that* is the scent permeating the air, filling the room, infiltrating his very being. Theo and this woman are as unblemished here-now as they were there-then, not a day older, not a hair's difference.

And now the miracle becomes even more miraculous, more complex; it unfolds along two time tracks, *then* and *now*. Theo is in two worlds simultaneously. The past and the present. Both are real.

Then the angels were, and *now* they *are*: two eighteen-year olds, Theo and the only person he has ever passionately loved. Heaven *then* was that first moment of baptismal bliss in the backseat of a borrowed car. A time-stopping moment that Theo has never stopped living, a seismic moment that restructured his very existence. Heaven *now* is the certainty of what is going to happen; his knowledge of the immediate future is so certain, it might as well have been predestined; he can already taste the outcome.

Now Janelle stands before him. *In the flesh*, he thinks, the words dancing in his head with pristine clarity and beauty. *And* she is the beautiful young woman she will always be in his heart of hearts. Theo is the life-chastened man he has become *and* the innocent young man he was when their union was consummated in the most blessed way possible. (Think: When summer's in the meadow.)

He takes the woman's hand and leads her around the end of the bar. Guiding her into a chair, he floats, a mote in the light of her eyes, into the chair next to her. After a long airless pause, he starts to light a cigarette.

"Here try one of mine," the woman says. She opens her purse, roots around, hands Theo a slender cigarette.

"What kind of cigarette is this?" With newly-restored innocence, Theo holds it up against the light to get a better look at it.

"You'll see. Put it in your mouth." Amidst the aura of her words, the woman's eyes and smiling lips sing, in the ineffable mother-tongue of hijacked procreation, a silent diddy of love-and-lust.

Theo lights the cigarette.

"Take a big puff and hold it in as long as you can," the woman, a callow girl, says, and now a sultry seductress, "Then put it in *my* mouth."

The cigarette is traded back and forth a few times and Theo says. "You snuck up on me." He is aware of tiny clouds of smoke shooting out of his mouth with each word. The smoke is his breath restored, made visible. But the words are not his. The words are someone else's. "What are you doing here?" It is his grown-up self speaking, his practical self, on automatic pilot. This other dissociated self, perceiving and responding to the mundane world around him, is like an unobtrusive shadow, a disembodied observer, disemboweled, without feelings or expectations.

"I need your help, Theo," the woman says.

Then for a moment the grown-up Theo sees what is happening, or thinks he does, and it threatens to crush him, to undo the miracle. Some kind of trick is being played on him. He just doesn't know what kind of trick it is. Is it being played *on* him or is it more like a game he is meant to go along with to their mutual benefit? He forces himself not to panic, or even show doubt and disappointment. If the woman sees any wavering, the spell will be broken and all will be lost.

If he can trust his instinctive self to keep putting one foot in front of the other; if he can keep his eyes on hers and keep them looking back at his or maintain some skin-on-skin contact; if he can just let the words automatically perform their function, unnoticed, like strings on a puppet; if he can trust this other collateral entity, his front-man, his pimp, his partner in crime, to do its part; if he can do all these things, maybe together he and she can get past this obstacle. Maybe they can carry each other over the threshold, keep the world out, and save the miracle. "Where were you? How did you get in here without me noticing?" He takes the woman's hand into his own.

"You always ask so many questions?"

"You are taking a big risk, *Janelle*. Must be something big to get you to come down here," the practical voice says. As he hears this, Theo experiences a kind of double vision, and he knows the magic has been saved: "Down here" had two meanings. Down here to the park from a few miles away where Automatic Theo knows that Real Janelle lives. And down to earth like a spirit or emissary sent from Heaven or from wherever in the Universe idealized memories and unattainable desires are closeted.

"It's big alright." The woman slips her hand out of Theo's and touches his knee. "I like to *come ... down*," she moved her hand up his thigh, "*... here.*"

"That's my line." Theo begins laughing and can't stop for what seems a long time. He begins to panic, thinking that he might never be able to stop laughing.

Sensing his panic the woman takes her hand away. "Oh, Theo. This is no time to be joking around." She brings her hands together and, closing her eyes, touches her fingertips to her lips like she is praying.

Just like that Theo quits laughing. Tears are running down his cheeks. It is like he has never been laughing. Have I been crying, he wonders. Time is fractured, full of gaps.

Seeing Theo's tears, the woman says, "I'm glad to see that you understand." She takes his head between her hands. "Close your eyes." She wipes the tears off his face with her thumbs and kisses his closed eyes.

Theo is soothed, the child of a loving mother, and is reassured that the lines of this play will come to him and his partner as they are needed and will win for them a standing ovation.

Waiting for Theo to open his eyes, she sits back in her chair. She closes her eyes, tilts her head back, and runs her red-nailed fingers through her long black hair. Opening his eyes, Theo sees her expression clearly in the dim light. Her face says, I am weary, I am suffering. "I couldn't sleep. So, I got up and came down here."

"Awfully dark down here," Theo says. "How did you know the way?" His sense that something wonderful is going to happen, or happen again, is acute.

"I've made the trip a thousand times in my mind. Lying awake ... thinking ... tossing and turning."

"What was wrong? Why couldn't you sleep?" Theo's heart is melting with tenderness.

"It has to do ... with ... Dixie. She doesn't know I know it, but I think she may be pregnant. Again."

Once more the miracle evolves. Janelle is Mother Janelle ... . Good Janelle ... . Real Janelle ... .

"Dixie, huh? Well, she's married now." Still not quite certain of the rules of the game being played, but somehow even more certain of the outcome, Theo can only play along.

"But, Theo, don't you see. She'll have to quit work. Even as it is, that job at Les Beau Dames hardly pays enough to keep Frankie in booze. How's she gonna be able to raise a family?"

"Oh, that poor child. Breaks your heart, doesn't it?" Theo summons up as much generalized sympathy as he can. "Actually, she and I have talked about it."

"Yes, I know."

"She made me promise not to tell you that we talked. She should have known you would know. A mother's intuition. She said you didn't care what happened to her. I told her that wasn't true." This last was a probably lie— he couldn't recall whether he had contradicted the daughter's assessment of her mother's love or not—but the lie, if it was one, seemed needed and so he said it. Besides that was a long time ago. He marvels at how the old words from a conversation years ago reconfigure themselves and the new ones find their place in the flow; it is as if some third mind, not his, not hers, but some alloy of the two of them is supplying the words, as naturally and unconsciously as two lungs breathe air for one body.

. . . and she is also the more-than-real Janelle . . .

"Really? She didn't want me to know? I didn't think she cared *what* her dear old mother thought. What about John?"

"I don't think she gives a good one what Johnnie Boy thinks."

. . . Janelle-of-the-Mind . . . Janelle made flesh . . .

"You never did like him, did you, Theo?"

"That is a beautiful dress you're wearing, Janelle."

. . . Janelle Incarnate . . . here, now.

"Basic black, Theo."

"Not the kind of dress wives of Baptist preachers normally wear. What kind of fabric is that?"

"It's silk. Would you like to feel it?"

"Yes, I would," Theo says. "But let's sit over by the window. On the couch." He stands up and leads the woman across the room, weaving them through the maze of tables and chairs like two birds zigzagging through Peek-a-Boo Canyon. After they are both seated, he says, "So much more comfortable over here."

The woman takes Theo's hand and puts it on her knee.

"Frankie's gonna be such a proud father," the woman says.

By now Theo is twenty years in the past. His eighteen-year old girlfriend is saying to the eighteen-year old Theo: "I am going to be a mother."

Without moving his hand off the woman's knee, Theo sinks to the floor. Sitting in front of her, he slithers forward on his butt; and by jamming his legs, spread-eagle, under the couch, he has his face directly in front of her knees; he can feel the tapered toes of her high-heeled shoes rubbing against his scrotum and balls. Not yet where he wants to be, though, it is a place to catch his breath, a base camp from which he will launch the final assault on the summit.

Putting his other hand on her other knee, he moves them apart, making just enough room for his face in the open end of the V-shaped Avenue of Eros. Pressing her knees to his cheeks, he looks up past the hem of her dress and meets her eyes gazing down at him like a child peering into a magic well.

"You need a shave, you dirty old man." The woman's voice is choked with lust.

"I love you, Janelle. I have never stopped loving you and I never will." As he speaks he feels his cheeks rubbing against the silken harness bridling his face.

Removing her high-heels and shackling the woman's ankles with his hands, Theo moves her legs apart. Shouldering himself forward into the enchanted zone this creates, he fits his hands into the crooks of her knees—smoothly interlocking ancillary body parts presaging a sublime interfacing—he lifts her legs and drags her forward until her buttocks rest on the edge of the couch.

Then the woman takes the initiative. Good thing, too, because, seeing that she is not wearing panties, Theo is stricken, Paul on the road to Damascus.

When she gets his attention, she smiles and opens her thighs wide; then she playfully cradles his cheeks and ears with the soles of her feet, holding him in that affectionate way a mother cups her baby's head in her hands and rubs noses with it. He kisses the cool dry skin of one her arches. He sucks her big toe. He fills his mouth with her smaller toes. She rubs his cheek and neck with the sole of her other foot; then, wrapping the top of this same foot around the back of his head, she wags it side-to-side, like a wind-shield wiper, messing up his hair. Then they switch feet and do the same on the other side.

To his tongue, moving unhurriedly from toe to toe, the salty gaps in between are multiple miniature versions, each one a prelude, of what is foremost in his mind—each nasty niche is an upstream eddy of the meandering river of which he is a part and through whose mouth he will pass into the ocean of self-oblivion.

Does the spider thrill to the waves of motion coming from the fly struggling among the frets of her artful trap? Imagine the awe of the fly in its final moment.

Sliding his palms along the outside curves of her thighs, Theo feels the flesh softening and burgeoning bigger in his hands. Reaching her hips, he cups her panty-less buttocks in his hands. Lowering his parched lips, he laps the ambrosial moisture issuing up out of her in the rosy center of her mossy forest.

Grabbing fistfuls of his hair and digging her heels into his back, she guides him deeper into the wet portal of darkness from whence we come and into which he would-but-he-could return.

Imagine a tete-a-tete with a tarantula as big as your face. Surrender to your metamorphosis and the frenzy of mutual devouring.

$$*\qquad *\qquad *$$

"Don't you want to … ?" The woman said some while later, pulling her dress down.

Theo willed himself up off the floor, into a painful crouch; unable to straighten up any further, he spun around, and collapsed on the couch beside her.

"Couldn't possibly." Theo was sated. "Any more would be like eating a fourth helping of dessert. That was perfect. Even better than before. You're a mature woman, in your prime." Remembering the sour taste and meager bush of her unripe pussy when she was thirteen or fourteen, he thought: It was as sweet tonight as a juicy-ripe persimmon, complete with a pelt of matching color. Lighting a cigarette, he asked, "Where did you get that dress? Is it hers?"

He was sober now. The miracle was over. Only ordinary bliss remained.

"Yeah, she gave it to me," Dixie said, taking off the black wig and gesturing for a cigarette.

Some while later, after Dixie had left, Theo knew that Dixie really was pregnant again and that Janelle had been, too, that night twenty years ago when he ate her pussy for the first time. He didn't *know* he knew, though. It was a timeless, sensual knowledge, comprised entirely of the smells and tastes he had taken in of the two women, mother and daughter, and the new life inside them. It would not pass away or diminish or change in any way like ordinary memory, but would gestate inside him, a growing figurative fetus that may one day burst forth in some miraculous creation. All Theo knew tonight was that he was stronger and more alive than he had been in twenty years.

11

On Memorial Day of that year, 1957, Jake and Billy were in Theo Jeannsonne's fancy house on Flagon Creek, a short distance downstream from Magnolia Park. Billy would remember a lot that day.

From time to time, he went with Jake to Theo's house to look at his art books and listen to jazz and classical music on his expensive record player. (Theo didn't like rock 'n' roll and he loathed country music.) They just had be careful not to scratch his records and put them back where they found them. Theo kept a house-key under a lawn ornament, which he called his 'artificial nigger', and didn't mind Jake letting himself in.

The time before this Billy was not with Jake; he was with someone else; she also knew where to find the key.

Theo's was the only house on a white-shell road. At the end of the road, beyond the turn-around, in among tall pine trees, was a place, just big enough to park a car, where Dixie Johnson and Frankie West went a lot, before they were married, to neck and lots more. The best time to go there was Saturday night, when Theo would be watching over things at the Mardi Gras bar. Dixie suggested to the Faustpool girl that she have Billy take her there for their last date. When they had parked, the girl jumped out of the car and motioned for him to follow. She went straight to where the house-key was, snatched it up, and they hurried inside. Indoors, with a flashlight she got from somewhere, she looked for a particular book; turning to a particular page, she showed Billy a picture of an octopus with terrifying eyes performing its version of oral sex on a Japanese woman whose ecstatic expression and the way she was laid out on her back reminded him of St. Teresa's chiseled ecstasy. The picture was called *The Dream of the Fisherman's Wife*.

In the backseat, in the light of the full moon, the girl's naked thighs and hips were silver. Ten days later Billy was a pallbearer at her funeral.

The first time Billy was in Theo's house was some years before, on the day Theo gave him and Jake a ride in his new Cadillac. As Theo was getting out of the car that day, Jake asked if he and Billy could stay in the car a while with the air-conditioner on.

Theo could do them one better: Why didn't they hang out in Theo's house, right down the lane? Jake knew where the key was, right? He tossed Jake the car keys and said for him to take the Caddy, just move the seat up so he could reach the pedals.

When they were in Theo's house, Jake said Billy never told him about Jonnie Vonderheim giving that fucking Dr. Maxwell a blowjob. He wanted to know when Ralph the deaf kid Billy used to be friends with had told him about it.

Can't remember, long time ago, Billy said, he hangs around her house, spies on her. He used to be in Pinecrest where she works.

Yeah, you said that before, Jake said. He asked why the motherfucker kicked Ralph out. Was it for spying on him and Jonnie?

Billy said probably, but Ralph said Dr. Maxwell said it was because Ralph wasn't retarded, just deaf. Pissed Ralph off. He hates him now.

Jake said Ralph should join the club and how could a deaf motherfucker tell Billy all that stuff anyway. He couldn't talk, could he?

Signing ... you know ... you make words with your hands? Billy signed something and said Ralph was good at it and had taught Billy a little. Enough for him and Billy to say most of what they wanted to say to each other. You hang around a deaf person very long, Billy said, you pick it up pretty quick. Ralph could draw pretty good, so sometimes he drew pictures to tell Billy stuff.

Jake wanted to know what Billy had said with my hands just then.

For God so loved the world, Billy said, looking around the big living room. Hey! Nice house! You been here before?

Yeah, Jake had been there a bunch a times. He bet that fucking Toe had fucked a lot a fucking women in that fucking place.

The living room was large, high-ceilinged, with a skylight. Books lined the walls on three sides and in front of the bookshelves were built-in velvet-cushioned benches. Jake said Uncle Toe didn't like books left laying around or put back where they didn't belong. He pointed out that a person wouldn't have to stand while looking at a book to see if it was the one they wanted. They could sit right there on that soft-ass cushion and when they were ready to put the book back they could just put the motherfucker in the crack where it was before. That way the book wouldn't be left laying around or be put back in the wrong place. Jake said Theo said a book was like a woman's pussy; you could open it up and put your nose in it and you could keep your finger in it to hold your place until you were ready to give it your 'full' attention.

Billy said the furniture was fancy, everything was. He picked up a gold-plated sculpture that was on the glass-top coffee table in the middle of the room. What was it? Holding it in both hands, he turned it, inspected it like the winners do their Oscars on TV. It looked to him like there were wings on the side. Whole thing looks like a baby with no arms or legs or face. He did a couple of curls, lifting it up to his chin and feeling his muscle with his other hand. A person could lift weights with that thing. It's heavy enough.

Jake said Uncle Toe said it was supposed to be a dick and balls and could Billy guess what it was called.

Billy said it looked like a dick with wings. Was it called *A Dick with Wings*? That was what he would call it. He did some curls with his other arm and put it back on the table.

It was called *Princess X*, Jake said. Uncle Toe had all kinds of great sex stuff. Books, movies, you name it. Did Billy want Jake to see if Uncle Toe would show them some movies of people fucking sometime?

Billy said he didn't know, he guessed he did.

Another time there was something at Theo's house that Jake said Billy just *had* to see. When they got there, Jake ran a finger along a bookshelf until he found the book he was looking for. Finding the page he wanted, he pointed to a picture. Look at that! Had Billy ever see anything so luscious?

To Billy the picture looked like a bunch of boulders. That right there, he said, pointing, looks like some bushes growing around the top of that crack between those two rocks. Looks like there may be a cave back in there somewhere behind those bushes.

Hell man, Jake said, was Billy fucking blind? That was a big old luscious pussy they were looking at.

Oh yeah! Wow! What's it called?

Origin of the World, Jake said, did Billy get it?

No, Billy didn't get it. Why was it called that?

Because that's where we all come from, Jake said. From a goddamn pussy!

On that Memorial Day, Jake and Billy were sitting in the living room of Theo's house looking at art books when Theo came in through the front door. Jake gestured toward Billy, who was sitting in a wing-back chair with a big book open on his lap, and said, Uncle Toe you remember Billy, don't you? He reminded Theo that he had taken the boys for a ride a while back in his new car.

Theo sat on the couch next to Jake. Jake slid away from him. Theo looked down at the expanse of couch now open between them and put his hand where Jake's butt had been, like he was checking, Billy thought, to see if it was still warm there. Looking up at Jake, Theo grinned but didn't say anything.

Billy could tell that Jake didn't like to look at Theo's face, either, when he was grinning like that.

Jake asked Billy to help him out. What did Billy remember about that day Theo gave them a ride?

Crossing his legs, Theo took a gold cigarette case out of the inside pocket of his sports jacket and began tamping a Lucky against the back of it.

Jake said, What was some of the shit we talked about, Billy?

When Billy didn't respond—he was still more than a little afraid of Theo—Theo paused and looked up at him, cigarette suspended in mid-stroke, as if he would if he must hear what Billy might say, but his eyes showed little interest. It was as if he had looked up from something he was writing and was thinking about what to write next. When Billy still didn't say anything, Theo resumed the tamping.

Billy looked at Jake and back at Theo and said all he could remember was Theo talking about the time some woman had given him a blowjob. Billy closed the book in his lap and placed it on the coffee table. Picking it up again, he stood up and looked around the room. Unable to find the gap where the book belonged, he sat again, holding the book in his lap. He said Jake had said the woman was fat and Uncle Toe had said she was pleasingly plump.

Not looking at Billy, Theo grunted, shook his head. He looked at his watch and put the gold case back inside his jacket. He put the cigarette in his mouth. The cigarette, dangling, almost perpendicular, looked small in comparison to Theo's big thick purple lips.

Impatient with the older man's lack of interest, Jake sat forward and turned toward Theo. He said, I remember, Uncle Toe. He made a snapping motion with his fingers that didn't make any sound. It had been early one morning .... She hadn't been able sleep .... She had come down to the bar .... Did Uncle Toe remember? They had laughed about her not wanting to let go of Theo's dick until she had sucked out the last drop ... ?

Again Theo shook his head no. He didn't remember. He made two fists and looked at his rings.

Like Maxwell House Coffee ... ? Jake prompted.

Oh yeah, Theo thought he remembered, maybe. But that reminded him. Whatever he was thinking put a leer on his lips. Talking about dripping, he said, and good to the last drop, he had a good one to tell Jake. Jake *had* to hear this one. The unlit cigarette in Theo's mouth moved up and down in time with his speech. Funniest fucking thing. Did Jake remember that widow woman? Pentecostal preacher's wife? Wanted to come work for

Uncle Toe? He lit the cigarette with a gold lighter. Holding his head back to keep the smoke out of his eyes, he chuckled.

Jake remembered. She was an *old* motherfucker, wasn't she? Had Uncle Toe hired her?

Yeah. She had worked about a week. Theo had had to fire her. Bitch drank too much. And yeah, she was kinda old, but that was all right. She wasn't *that* old. Fifty-something. She looked pretty fucking good, if anybody wanted Theo's opinion. She bleached her hair, fixed it up like Marilyn Monroe. Bought some sexy new clothes. Musta got some insurance money or something.

Theo straightened his leg and looked at the toe of his highly-polished shoe. Uncrossing his legs, he pinched the fabric of his pants, taking the pressure off the creases. Leaning forward and catching Billy's eye, he pointed at the ashtray on the coffee table, the cigarette lighter still in his hand. Billy accommodated.

Listen, my man, you take pussy where you find it, Theo said to the young man who called him Uncle. That was the number one rule of the pussy-hound. Besides, the old ones were *so* grateful. They knew … . Theo paused, then asked if Jake wanted his fucking advice or not.

Fuck yes, Jake wanted his fucking advice. Just because he wasn't looking right at him didn't mean he wasn't listening.

Theo put the lighter in his pants pocket and continued. Old women know every time somebody fucks 'em may be the last dick they ever get. They can't get knocked up so they can let themselves go. Fuck without fear. And Theo could tell Jake another thing: The ass and pussy are the last to go. What he meant was a woman can be really fucking old … face all wrinkly … fucking skin hanging down on her arms … lost almost all her hair and, if you're lucky, all her teeth, because there's nothing quite like the blowjob a toothless old horny-assed bitch can give you … mind shot to hell … but she'll still have a young-looking ass and her pussy'll still be juicy and have a big bush of hair around it. May be white as fucking snow, but it'll be there, and it ain't like you're gonna spend a lot of time looking at it, anyway, so who cares what fucking color it was.

Hell, Theo was gonna be old himself someday and he just hoped … you know. Theo shook his head and for several seconds seemed to be looking out a high window across the room, as if he had noticed something of interest in one of the tall pine trees shading his house. Snapping out of his reverie, he continued: Anyway, you talk about funny. He wagged his head and laughed. Bitch was working the bar one night. When it came time to close, she said her car wouldn't start … would Theo take her home. Theo hadn't thought anything about it. Bitch hadn't said three words all night. Drinking bourbon all night, straight up, ever chance she got. You know, between customers. Theo had told her no drinking on the job, but he hadn't had the heart to crawl her ass about it then. He said yeah he'd take her home, but first let him see if he could get her car started. Son-of-a-bitch started right up, which told Theo that either she was too drunk to know what she was doing or she was wanting some dick; either way Theo made up his mind right then and there he was gonna get him a piece of that. He told her she probably shouldn't be driving anyhow, much as she had been drinking. She said she could hold her liquor good as any man. He told her she could stay here in the park if she wanted. Plenty of empty cabins at the time. She said show her one.

To make a long story short, one thing led to another, and let me tell you, Theo said, that fucking woman couldn't get enough. Screaming and pissing and moaning. You coulda heard her all over the fucking park. Theo was afraid someone was gonna call the cops or something. Sounded like somebody was being killed. She hadn't had any in so long, Theo guessed, it was like the very first time or something. She even made him give it to her in the ass.

Ooo weee! You cockhound you! Jake laughed. That *was* funny. Theo *was* shitting him, wasn't he?

Hell no, Theo wasn't fucking shitting him. But wait. Fucking her in the ass wasn't the funny part. He said, I'm taking her home, see? I think she was a little embarrassed by all the noise she made. Wanted to go home. Rather than stay in a cabin or something. Anyways, in the car, Theo noticed she was squirming around a lot on the seat. Kinda pulling at her crotch. He hadn't thought much about it at first. He figured she was just straightening her clothes or some such shit. You know how women are, he said to Jake.

Jake said damned straight, he knew how women were! He had the best teacher in the world. Jake grinned and winked at Billy, like something about the whole business was a secret just between the two of them.

Theo did not acknowledge Jake's flattery but said the woman started reaching around and doing something to her ass. Like her panties was stuck up in there and she was trying to pull 'em out or something, you know. That's when Theo really started noticing her. Getting curious, you know. Then he noticed she's got the smell of her own shit all over her. From the corn-holing he gave her. Later he realized that smell was all inside his car. In fact, stayed in it for days. He had to spray some shit in it to keep the smell down, so people wouldn't think he had done shit his pants or something. It hadn't done much good, just made it smell like cherry-flavored shit.

Of course, at the time, you know, when he was giving it to her, Theo couldn't have cared less. He said, I mean a woman's shit don't smell all that bad when you got your dick up to the hilt in her ass ... in fact, that stink could make you that much hotter. But later, when it was all over ... . Well, you know how you feel right after you come, right? I mean, that's just the way a man is. A woman, all she wants to do is *cuddle and talk*—Theo pooched-out his lips, wagged his head, and spoke in a high-pitched mocking tone—but a man, it don't matter how much he wants that pussy *before* he shoots his wad, *after* is a whole nuther story. A man, he don't want to even be *touched* right after he gets his rocks off. Well, add to that Theo's having to smell this old cunt's shit and Jake would know about how he was feeling. After he dropped his load bitch smelled worse'n a fucking shit-house.

Theo winced and gave his head a hard shake, causing his fleshy, rubbery face to flop like a loose-fitting Halloween mask. Anyways, he continued, she was wearing slacks that night. By now, though, they were all wrinkled and dirty from being on the floor behind the bar. Theo glanced over both shoulders out the window behind him; then, as if satisfied no spies were lurking about, he tittered. See, she had put her elbows up on the bar, you know, waiting for Theo to turn some lights out or some such shit. Theo said he likes to stop just when the woman thinks he's about to stick it in her ... likes to pretend there's one last thing he just *has* to do first before he pokes it to her. That drives 'em crazy. The woman kept looking over her shoulder, trying to see what was taking Theo so long. He waited till she looked away and wham! He took her. Now she was holding on like she was in a storm at sea ... squealing and grunting like a bunch a pigs. Pretty soon she was pushing that ass back at him so hard she almost knocked him over.

Theo sighed and smiled at his fingernails. Looking up and blinking like he was waking from a nap, he smacked and ran his tongue over his lips. He wanted to know where he was in his story. Oh yeah, he remembered. Anyhow, the woman had just let her slacks and drawers fall down on that grimy floor behind the bar ... they were all wet and dirty by the time Theo was done with her. He and the woman had both stomped all over 'em. Looked like a herd of cows had come through there, Theo was telling Jake and Billy.

Her hair was all messed up. I mean she looked like shit, Theo said. Smelled like shit and looked like shit. She kept squirming and wiggling, squirming and wiggling, like the car seat was burning her ass or something. Theo hadn't been able at the time to figure out what the *fuck* was the matter with her. He dragged the back of the hand holding the cigarette across his face. He asked, You know what it was? He looked at Jake, then at Billy.

Neither one of them knew what it was.

It was come dripping out of her, Theo said. Jizm, spunk, oozing back out of her cunt and ass. Kinda like a runny nose, when you have a bad cold, Theo guessed. He reckoned it must a been tickling her or something. He hit the couch beside him with his fist and laughed, a kind of forced and fitful yelp. He nearly shit. Son-of-a-bitch, he laughed till he cried. He couldn't help it. The bitch started crying, calling Theo a heartless prick. You know how women are, Theo reminded Jake. This woman's tears had just made Theo laugh harder. The harder he laughed the madder she must a got. Before he knew it she took one of them little derringers outa her purse and poked it in his face, threatening to shoot his ass.

It took Theo an hour to calm her down. He had ended up fucking her again before he went home. Her pulling that pistol on him got him excited all over again, he guessed. He fucked her in the shower. Then he told her she was fired. He had unloaded that little pistol first, though. Grinning, Theo he took a bullet out of his pants pocket and held it up for Jake and Billy to see. Fucking pistol held two of those. Theo keeps it for a souvenir.

It looked to Billy like Jake was laughing too loud. It wasn't *that* funny. When Theo said that about sex and the smell of shit, Billy remembered jacking off in his grandmother's outdoor toilet and he had to pull at the crotch of his pants to keep it from hurting down there. He made a mental note to check and see if he could smell the stink of the widow woman's shit the next time he was in Theo's Cadillac.

Then Theo showed Jake and Billy some dirty comic books. He called them 'eight-page bibles'. One of them showed Goofy and Minnie Mouse on a park bench. Goofy first ate Minnie's pussy and then he fucked her. In the ecstasy of cunnilingus, Minnie sprawled out on the bench like she was tanning on the beach. She hooked her neck over the top of the bench like you would a coat-hanger so she could grab Goofy's ears with both hands. She pulled him down between her legs. When his slobbering tongue made an amphibious landing on her sloshing pussy, she wrapped her thighs around his head. There were little lines floating in the air around her hips that showed that she was hunching him in the face. In the balloon over her head were the words, *Oh Jesus! Jesus! Jesus!* Goofy's dick was huge and when he stuck it in Minnie's pussy, big drops of liquid spilled out of her pussy. In the balloon: *Yes! Yes! Yes! Give me all of it!*

Looking at the pictures made Billy so aroused he almost threw up. He thought about his last date with the Faustpool girl. Her hips had moved around like that, too. At first, the rhythm was slow and easy, but then she caught fire. With his head locked in the vise of her thighs and his nose and mouth jammed hard into her pussy, he couldn't catch his breath. Which was probably good, because, like at the start of taking peyote, he almost vomited and what with all the new and various smells she was giving off, not breathing-in may have been what got him over the hump and put him on the path to Shangri-La. What started out like having his face crammed into a toilet turned into something more like being baptized in the soothing mineral-rich waters bubbling up out of a hot-springs well. At any rate, the nausea soon went away and by the time she started to reach her climax, she was bucking like an abused bull and rubbing his face against her greedy pussy. In the end Billy's mind and her body joined together and it was like they were one person and there wasn't anything dirty about it.

At first, he was in a dark moldering tomb; but, in time, rooting around, scooping and scoping, he dug out the lodestone oystered in the folds around the entrance of her (by-now-fatally-wounded) womb; when he kissed the cold stone it came to life, like a celestial beacon, lighting up like the polestar at the top of the world, illuminating the Rosy Way all the way to the black hole and touching off the super-nova of her resurrection. Drawn deeper and deeper into the sepulcher by her hot spoor, then hurled higher and higher into the incandescent sphere by the heady storms of her blissful shrieks and her pitching pelvis, he spiraled homeward in a headlong flight through space-time toward the mutual insemination of their souls and the spiritual union that would establish the eventual tenor of his mental life, determine the ultimate texture of his bodily existence, and write in stone the truth of his being.

At the peak of her discharge, he felt like he was being deliquesced by some sublimely slimy alien solvent; embedded head-first between her thighs, he was a tick, a leech, feeding off the placenta inside the uterus of some divine creature come down from out of the wild blue yonder to wreak his re-birth.

Later, when he realized that at the eternal moment of her crisis she had farted—with his ears flattened by her thighs against the side of his head and in the crescendo of her orgasm, it had not make a separate impression, but it had registered in his brain and in time, when he <u>was</u> able to hear it and feel it and smell it, it would be like a cherry bomb going off underwater, marked by the ascendant odor of gunpowder escaping the roiling perturbation miraculously cradled in the humble confines of his hands, his hands brimming over with the blessed burden of her bare buttocks, Oh Heavenly Handful!—he knew that this unclassifiable, profoundly disgusting experience was a mystery he would spend the rest of his life trying to understand, knowing full well that to attempt even to describe it, let alone express what it was like, would be to alienate him from the rest of normal society forever.

Now when he masturbated, the cloacal blend was enriched by echoes of the gagging in her lust-strangled throat and the vertiginous sensations of being engulfed, painlessly smothered, re-enwombed, and ecstatically entombed by her smooth soft flesh at the ever-recurring and defining moment of his life.

The thing Billy thought about most, without coming up with anything close to an answer, is what it was like for her and he wondered if she had time to remember him before she died. They say that when all of sudden a person knows they are about to die they see a movie of their whole life flashing before their eyes. Billy wondered if he was in the Faustpool girl's movie even for a second or two.

The mental trace of the fart was connected in Billy's mind to the memory of another very special time in another very special place. It was on a hot summer day in that concupiscent crucible, that caldron of childhood carnality: his Grandmother Woody's ancient outhouse. Bent over like a mother bird tending her chick—*improvising on the one-stringed lyre*—a couple of feet above the layered leavings of several generations of his extended family, in the company of spiders and wasps, he achieved or, as it seemed then, was granted, his first taste of the Holy. With one eye on the knot hole in the door of the outhouse, on the look-out for intruders who might interrupt his solitary pleasure; with his lungs full of the stench of the steamy miasmal vapors by which he seemed kept aloft, levitating like the ashes of burnt leaves or paper over a bonfire; his throat had begun to gag and his esophagus had begun to spasm. In an agitated eternity of ecstasy, there occurred in him an impossible fusion of appetite and nausea, of desire and disgust, of lust and loathing. This divine synthesis of contradictory sensations and emotions had been his first orgasm.

Theo tossed his car keys to Jake and said, Here, J.G., you guys can take the Caddy for a spin if you want to. He had to get back down to the bar. Had to get ready for tonight. Saturday night was always a mob scene, not to mention it was a holiday to boot. Theo's ass was gonna be in a crack if he didn't get someone to help Jimmy. Could Jako lend him a hand, if he couldn't round up some help? Jake said no problem. Theo would bring them back some lunch if him and Billy wanted it. They did.

Jake drove them to Camp Livingston, an old Army base that had been demolished after the war. On the way, remembering the story of the widow woman, Billy sniffed the air; he was pretty sure he could smell her shit still lingering in Theo's car. Taking two flashlights with them, they went to an underground room, entering it through a gaping hole in the ground where the steel trapdoor at the top of the descending staircase had been ripped away by looters and no doubt sold for scrap-iron. The room had been a prison cell for a German prisoner-of-war who had drawn a picture of a naked woman on the wall. It was a place Jake and Billy sometimes went to masturbate, an alternative to the old car in the garage by the abandoned mansion. Shining his flashlight on the drawing and imagining the prisoner jacking off while looking at his sweetheart was an erotic thrill for Billy. Other people obviously knew about the place as there were fresh piles of shit in two corners of the room.

In response no doubt to his immediate surroundings, Billy's mind took him back again to Woody's toilet, this time to an even more primitive memory, to an unhappy incident at the very beginning of his sexual life. He was just a little boy but had already learned the primitive mechanics of sex while masturbating with his cousin and other older boys and from watching farm animals. At best, the incident was a lesson in humility, at worst the next thing to castration. Afraid to go inside the outhouse, because it was dark in there and full of creepy-crawly things, he piled some boards in front of the door. Standing on the boards, he made his dick hard and stuck it through the knot hole in the door into the hot dark dangerous interior of the little kingdom of wasps and spiders. Then, looking over his shoulder, he saw Stella coming down the path toward the toilet. He could tell, perhaps from the purposeful pace of her stride—and the stern look on her face, no mistaking the meaning of *that*—that she didn't approve of what her son was doing, to say the least. In his haste to put away the evidence of his crime, he got his scrotum caught in the zipper of his pants. (They were his first long pants and he wasn't used to zippers.) Worse than the pain and shame of being extricated from his own blood-stained pants by his own mother; worse than the anxiety of wondering for several days what his father would to him when he returned home from working on the railroad; even worse than the helpless feeling of being held by one arm and dangled in the air, as his father, with no more empathy than he would afford a dead squirrel he meant to skin, raised welts on his only son's naked butt with a switch that must surely have been taken from a thorn bush—call him Isaac-betrayed-by-Sarah; worse by far than all these lesser humiliations was the absolute mortification he suffered when Stella told Clinton about the double-crossing, scrotum-feeding zipper—Billy thought his father would never stop laughing.

Jake's asking if he had noticed Uncle Toe's fingernails snapped Billy out of his dark reverie. Jake was leaning against the wall, just his back touching, looking at his dick in the light of his flashlight; as was often the case, he seemed to be talking to his dick. Fucker gets them *manicured* every week. In the Bentley Hotel. By the sweetest piece of ass he, Billy, was ever gonna fucking see. She has a little setup in the corner of the hotel barber shop. Theo took Jake there one time. Fucking Theo gets his nails done *before* he fucks her. Theo says by the time she's done with his fingers his dick is about to fucking explode. Theo says if he didn't take a cold shower he'd come all over the carpet of the hotel room before he could even get it in her. And, get this: *She* pays for the room!

He do it when you were there? Billy asked.

Nah. Didn't have time. Probably had some other bitch waiting for him to come fuck her was Jake's guess.

Billy undid my jeans. Shining the flashlight on the Nazi drawing, he remembered with an erotic jolt Jimmy's incredibly dirty dick in the shower-house behind the Garrard's. He said, Your brother wants to be a missionary, Jake, I guess you know that.

Yeah. Fucker's on my ass all the time to join the church. Jake shined his light on Billy's dick and back on his own. He's a royal pain in the ass, he said. Not that they ever got along very well. But ever since he started this religious kick, Jimmy keeps getting worse and worse. It has got to where Jake can't stand to even be in the same room with the bastard. He thinks maybe his brother Jimmy figures if he says he wants to be a missionary Dixie Johnson'll like his sorry ass.

When, back at Theo's house, Theo came back with lunch, consisting of sandwiches and Nehi's, he said, sure, Jake could work for him all summer long if he liked. Perfect timing, in fact. Theo said, That brother of yours didn't show up this morning and he wasn't down there just now.

You're better off without him, Uncle Toe. Jake said he probably could only work until August. He was hoping to get in the FBI training program. Wilderness camp begins in August.

Is that a fact? Theo's mind seemed to be on something else. He paced slowly around the coffee table a couple of times. Then, reversing his direction he swung by and looked into the next room. Apparently not seeing anything of interest there, he turned and said, That's like boot camp, right? Gonna be hot.

Gotta be tough. Jake took a swig of red soda and unwrapped a sandwich, offering half to Theo.

Theo waved off the offer and lit a cigarette. Jake and Billy weren't going believe the shit Theo just saw. Fucking moron, he said. He's talking about a real *moron*. Never seen anything like it in his whole fucking life. Theo paced the room, puffing on his cigarette, mildly agitated.

Who? What? Jake motioned for Billy to eat.

Big fucking ... . I don't know what to call the son-of-a-bitch. Theo stopped pacing long enough to tap ashes into the ashtray on the coffee table. He *guessed* the fucker was a male, but he couldn't be sure. First of all, he ... she ... or it ... had a big wide ass like some fat-ass housewife that's let herself go to pot, you know. And long fucking hair. Theo means dirty, *filthy* fucking hair. Make you sick. And he, it, whatever it was, had these disgusting kinky-ass whiskers on his neck and under his chin. Scraggy like the pubic hair you see on a young pussy that's just starting to get ripe. You know, when it's just about to lose that pissy-smell. Face like Baby Huey. You know. Stupid, like a fucking clown. Big fucking nigger lips. Fat-ass cheeks and big ugly-ass nose … fucking nose like a goddamn potato … covered with the biggest bunch of blackheads Theo ever saw. Shit-load of big-ass pimples all over his face, all red and full of pus. Looked like they're about to pop all by themselves.

Oh! Jake bet he knew who Theo was talking about. Was he wearing old worn-out dress pants? Expensive shoes? Shot to hell, but expensive?

Yeah, that's him alright.

That's Arthur Maxwell, Jake said. Gotta be. What the hell's that freak doing here?

It looked to Theo like Arthur was hanging around with that fucker West, Theo's alleged security guard. That's who he was talking to just now. This freaky bastard … Arthur, is that his fucking name? … was something else. Theo sat backwards on a straight chair, resting his chin on folded arms. He wished Jake and Billy could have seen it. Acting like a fucking woman, but crazy, man. Theo means he was prancing around, swishing his fat ass from side to side, fluttering his eyes, hands all floppy, like some kind of fucking queer. Like he was trying to *flirt* with the motherfucker. West, Theo means. But *exaggerated*, you know.

What happened? Jake asked. He wanted to know what Theo did.

Theo told West he didn't want the freaky bastard around the park.

What'd he say? Frankie West, Jake meant.

Frankie claimed he never saw the fucker in his life before today, but Theo doesn't believe him. All kind of weirdoes hang around that bastard. And Theo's not even talking about those hoods with their imitation black leather jackets. He's talking about really *strange* ones.

Strange ones? Jake prompted.

Well, okay, first, Theo stuck out his thumb for number one, there's that deaf mute. Short. Dick-high to a midget. Creepy little fucker.

Ralph. Billy felt a tiny bit disloyal saying Ralph's name, but he was anxious to know Theo's point-of-view.

Theo wants to know if the bastard has a last name.

If he did Billy didn't know it.

Then, Theo says, sticking out his index finger for number two, there's this Crystal something. Wears sunglasses all the time, even indoors and at night. Eyes must be sensitive to light. They're a faded light-blue, like bird eggs that have been out in the sun. Used to be in Pinecrest. That right there tells Theo she's wacko. J. V. talked him into letting the freaky bitch look after his alligators. She, this Crystal cunt, stays in one of Theo's cabins. He sees her and West sitting together … at the same table, at least … in the bar sometimes. Always during the day, when West's wife is at work. They don't say much to each other, though, it don't look like. West drinks himself into oblivion and Crystal plays the juke box. She listens to the same two fucking records, *Born to Lose*, and *Your Cheating Heart*, over and over.

Bitch just sits there, J. G., Theo said. She just rocks back and forth, staring off into space. She never speaks to anyone, even when they speak to her. It's like people don't exist for her. Or, if they do, they're no more than a tree or a chair or something like that. It's weird, it gives Theo a creepy feeling. Hard to explain. Theo tried to strike up a conversation with her a time or two. She wouldn't look at his face. Least he doesn't think she did. Who can tell with those sunglasses, but she never even turned her head toward him. She loves those fucking gators, though. Takes good fucking care of 'em, Theo had to give her that. Theo doesn't know what Crystal did to make it happen, but the alligators are breeding like crazy. He's gonna have to build a bigger pen soon, way things are going.

Crystal has short hair, Theo continued. Not bad looking actually. Pretty blue eyes. Good ass, real good.

When Theo added that Crystal always wore boots and khaki pants and flannel shirts, and a hunting knife on her belt, he started laughing, apparently because the way she dressed reminded him of something funny, which turned out to be that stupid fucker—Theo thought his last name was Wade—that thinks he's a deputy Sheriff. (Theo's thumb and index finger were still sticking out—*one*, Ralph, *two*, Crystal; Billy expected Theo to stick out his middle finger: *three*, the stupid fucker Wade; but he didn't.) Theo doesn't know where Wade got that fucking uniform. Thinks one of the other deputies musta gave him one of their old ones. Fucker wears them thick coke-bottle glasses. Anyhow, Theo said, the asshole thinks this freaky Crystal woman is a man. Fucker can't see shit. Wade's always telling her those dumb fucking jokes of his. She never laughs. It ain't 'cause she ain't smart enough to get 'em, Theo doesn't think. It's just her sense of humor is for shit. Of course, Wade's jokes are, too, but Theo's never seen her laugh. Or even crack a smile, for that matter. J.V. says she was put in Pinecrest when she was just a little kid, but they found out she's a fucking genius. At least in some things. She's got book-smarts. J. V. told Theo Crystal's already finished college.

But the one Theo saw today is the weirdest one yet. He told West to chase Arthur's ass off before tonight. Theo doesn't want such shit as that bugging his customers.

They say he's a hermaphrodite, Jake said. He turned and snapped his fingers at Billy and said, Oh, that reminds me of something I heard. Arthur used to hang around the dumps at school ... probably still does, when school's in session. Anyway, Jake heard that a bunch of the hoods that hang out down there had a bet going about whether Arthur had a pussy or not. They made Arthur pull his fucking pants down.

And? This was something Billy had wondered about ever since he first saw Arthur.

Person telling it to Jake wasn't sure, said the fucker was so fat who could tell. But the next thing you know the hoods were betting on who could keep a hard-on the longest while looking at his fat ass. Crazy bastards!

Billy asked Theo: Uncle Toe, this guy, West … is his first name Frankie? Billy didn't think Theo liked him very much, so addressing him directly— and especially calling him Uncle Toe—made him feel a little self-conscious. But he wanted to stay on the good side of this man who knew so many things that he wasn't likely to learn about any place else. Then Billy realized that Theo might have already said Frankie's first name and he felt even more embarrassed.

Yeah, why? Theo didn't look at Billy.

Just wondering, Billy said, relieved that Theo hadn't already mentioned Frankie's first name or, if he had, had forgotten having done so.

Useless fucker, Theo, said, still not looking at Billy. Shiftless bastard's only claim to fame is he used to play basketball for the high school.

Jake said, He did more than just play, Uncle Toe. Jake couldn't stand the motherfucker either, but Frankie West was *still a* legend at that fucking school. Fucker was so popular that when he joined the chorus at school, all the guys wanted to be in it. Even the hoods that used to hang out down at the dumps and smoke during lunch hour. Jake said, I mean those fuckers never did anything but take shop and there they were up there singing *Hymn to Music, The Happy Wanderer*, shit like that and all kinds of fucking religious songs and shit.

Ever body says he's good-looking, but Jake couldn't see it. Frankie's fucking head was too small. To top it off, wouldn't you know, the fucker could sing like Perry-fucking-Como. Made boy's quartet *and* mixed quartet. Not many guys do that. Fact, Jake thinks he's the only one who ever did. Jake also thinks Old Lady Love, the choir director, that's her fucking name, Love, musta had the hots for Frankie.

Jake who didn't make chorus until his sophomore didn't even make boy's ensemble.

Oh, yeah. It was all coming back to Theo now. He hadn't made the connection. Was Frankie the one Theo's brother John 'saved'? Theo put the word in quotes by wiggling his index finger.

Same one, Billy said when Jake didn't answer. He didn't say that preachers didn't save people, Jesus did.

Theo, pulling his chins in and wagging his head and speaking out of the corner of his mouth in a sing-song ridiculing manner, said, *He had the most beautiful jump shot you ever fucking saw.* Except that stupid fucking alleged brother of his would never use the word fucking. Theo stubbed out a still-long cigarette, lit a fresh one, and resumed speaking in the mocking tone, *Ball would't hit nothing but the bottom of the net. Make the most beautiful sound you ever heard.* Switching back to his normal voice, Theo continued, If you don't count the sound a woman makes when she's about to come. Theo laughed, barked, at his own joke. He grinned at Jake. He said he got so fucking tired of hearing his sanctimonious brother talk about that somebitch West, he thought he was gonna shit. But Theo guessed the fucker musta been pretty good. He wiggled his finger and said 'Brother John' said Frankie was even better than he was himself and it took a lot for that conceited fucking brother of Theo's to admit that anyone was better than him at *any*thing.

Fucker ain't much good now, Theo could tell Jake and Billy that right now. He had agreed to put the fucker Frankie on the payroll at the park, though. Security guard. Even let the bastard live in one of his cabins. Theo *had* to hire *some*body. There had been some stuff stolen and neither one of the fucking sheriffs would do anything about it. One of 'em was a self-righteous bastard who'd like to close Theo down if he could. Only trouble is, he couldn't. Theo's bar was on the wrong side of the Parish line. Sheriff was in Evangeline, which was dry. But the bar was in Acadia, which was wet and out of his jurisdiction. Flagon Creek, or as the Cajuns called it, Cold Bayou, was the Parish line. Actually the creek was in Acadia, all of it. Theo meant the line didn't go down the middle of the creek, like a person might expect. It went along the north bank. That was why the bar was put *over* the creek, so it would be in the wet Parish. Which is the *other* Sheriff's territory. Theo let out a self-satisfied chortle. Of course *that* fucker wanted a payoff for every little thing he did. It was cheaper to hire the drunk.

Theo felt sorry for the poor bastard, really. This West feller, he meant, not the fucking sheriffs. West would do anything for 'Brother John'. And now that John has got tired of fucking with him, Theo gets him. That was the way it had always gone. Theo gets his brother's hand-me-downs. And Theo's *older* than him! Should be the other way round. Anything John has outgrown or got tired of or has just got to be too goddamn good for, Theo gets. Maybe *that*'s why he hired the worthless fucker. Good Old Toe: The end of the line, the bottom of the barrel, morally speaking.

Jonnie told Theo, Theo said, Frankie's old man left the family high and dry when Frankie was just a kid and the fucker had lived hand-to-mouth ever since. Till he married the preacher's daughter, that is. Now he lived off her. J. V. let him stay over at Pinecrest when he didn't have any place else to go. Hell, for a while John was letting him stay in his own fucking house. John had 'borrowed' money from Theo to buy that ranch he has. Did Jake know that? He has never paid Theo one fucking red cent of that money back.

Anyhow, this guy West was supposed to be helping Theo's sorry-ass brother raise cattle. Theo *knew* that dog would bite. Put this young stud in the same house with that adopted step-daughter of his … . Theo looked over at Jake. Janelle's kid … ? Jake, wake up! The one they say she had by some another man … ? I heard John adopted her after they got married … ? What's her name … ?

You don't mean Dixie, do you? Billy said. He didn't say it, but he couldn't believe Theo didn't know his own niece's name. So, Sister Johnson had Dixie by another man, he thought. Wonder if she was married to him. Stella could have a field day with this, if she ever found out.

Yeah, Dixie, Theo said. Her and that fucker West ended up running off one time when they were still in high school. Theo heard he knocked her up. She stayed away about long enough for her to have a baby. Missed half a year of school. She didn't come back with no 'bundle of joy', though. So Theo didn't know. Somebody told him *he*, meaning Frankie, was in jail during that time.

No, that was later, Billy thought.

Jimmy's in love with her, Jake said. He's been obsessed with her for years. Nearly killed him when she got married. Could Theo *believe*: that Jimmy thought Dixie was a sweet little virgin bride! Jake hoped his stupid brother doesn't find out she's adopted.

Now you talk about a wild li'l ole thing, Theo said, that Dixie's wild. She's a redhead. Redheads are always wild. Just like that worthless West. They're two of a kind, Theo guessed. John didn't get her outa New Orleans soon enough, if you ask him. He knew because he used to see her flirting with men all the time. And he meant men, not just boys. Used to hang out at the park all the time. It's a wonder the little twat didn't get knocked up 'fore she did, if in fact she did. The ass she's got on her … man alive! Uncle Toe shook his head in apparent disbelief at the ass Dixie had on her. Howcome Jake hoped Jimmy doesn't find out Dixie was adopted? Theo asked.

Jake said he thought Jimmy had got the idea that *he*, Jimmy that is, was adopted. Jimmy has never come right out and said it, but Jake has picked it up from some of the things he has heard his brother say. Jimmy spends a lot of time at the courthouse, going through records … birth certificates and shit. Fucker thinks anybody who's adopted is got to be a bastard. This is all since he got religion. He thinks bastards are bad because they are …

'born in sin' … is the way he puts it. Theo wouldn't believe how *devout* he has become.

Hmmm. Theo's eyes narrowed. He wondered if that's why he … .

Whata you mean? Jake studied Theo's face.

Oh, nothing. It's just Theo was talking to somebody yesterday and the topic came up. Might have been Charlie West, whats-his-face's cousin. Nothing like him, though. Theo can't even remember what he and Charlie started out talking about, but he knows one of them said something about John's kid … Dixie? … being adopted, and Jimmy might have heard it. Jimmy's always slinking around, poking his nose where it don't belong. Spying on people in the cabins. Listening in on other people's conversations.

Jake gave Billy a knowing look.

Theo didn't know Jimmy was that touchy on the subject. He didn't know Jimmy had the hots for the little cunt, either.

Oh, he doesn't have the *hots* for her, Uncle Toe. It's much more *exalted* than that. Ask Billy, he knows what I'm talking about.

'Exalted', 'devout'? Theo liked that. (Apparently, Billy's corroboration wasn't necessary.) Theo liked those fifty-dollar college words Jake used. But he knew what Jake meant. Her shit don't stink. Theo knew the feeling. Used to, anyways. It happened to him one time. He had it bad, and that ain't good, as the song says. Won't happen again, though. Not anymore. They're all cunts to Theo.

Well her shit will stink now, Jake said, if his brother did hear Uncle Toe talking. To Jimmy, anybody 'born out of wedlock' is no better than a syphilitic whore.

Theo wondered if that had anything to do with Jimmy's not showing up at Magnolia Park this morning. He lit another cigarette and nothing was said for a while. Oh well, fuck him. Last thing Theo needed was some motherfucker slinking around, listening in on his conversations. Like Jake said, Theo was better off without him. He slapped his knee, an indication of insight. He bet he knew why that fucker Maxwell was down there! He must a been fucking around with the Foster brothers. They are the most degenerate motherfuckers you can imagine. Fuck cows, dogs, chickens, you name it. Compared to some of the stuff they've fucked that ugly bastard Arthur Maxwell looks like goddamn Marilyn Monroe.

*   *   *

Like everybody else at Tioga High School, Billy knew who Arthur Maxwell was. He had seen him flirting with Frankie West many times, just the way Theo described it. The time he remembered best was early in his and Frankie's freshman year in high school. Arthur really put on a show that day.

The incident resulted in a big boost in Billy's popularity, just the kind of payoff he had counted on when he began courting Frankie as a friend. The incident and the events that followed it had the added benefit of showing him just where Jacob Garrard fit into the social hierarchy of Tioga High School. He learned that day that Jake's reputation was not what Jake had led him to believe. For a while after that day Billy was careful of how he acted toward Jake when there were other kids around. It wasn't always easy to distance himself from Jake, even at school, but it had to be done, especially at school. Otherwise, the stain would have rubbed off on him.

Arthur's timing was perfect. His audience was practically the entire student body. It was during lunch break on the day all the clubs and various other organizations were having their year-book pictures taken in front of the main building of the school. While one group, standing on the wide steps, posed for the camera, the other groups and spectators waited on the grassy lawn near the flagpole—some were sitting, eating lunches brought from home—or milled around on the large shady porch of the school building.

Thronged around the periphery of the high school students were dozens of younger kids from the grade school across the road from the high school, come to watch the fun.

The usual delays of picture-taking and the hot noonday sun reflecting off the columns of the building's facade added tension to the drama of the scene, tension that was about to be released in an explosion of laughter and disorder.

Arthur, wearing a form-fitting knit dress and lots of jewelry, came up to Frankie and Billy, who were standing behind the photographer and the camera. Plopping his big pudgy hand on his pimply cheek, his elbow in the palm of his hand, ala Jack Benny, he fluttered his eyes at Frankie. Then, placing his hands on either side of his hairy neck, his long thick fingers adorned with several rings, he smiled coyly with downcast eyes. He was a delicate flower of modesty.

By now the group on the steps were laughing and pointing; the photographer turned around to see what was going on.

Then, his lips pursed, feigning huffiness, Arthur put his hands on his broad hips and flung his head back and looked haughtily down his nose. Turning his back on Frankie, he pranced away, twisting his enormous butt, a caricature of some movie goddess. Mae West uncorseted. A pirouette, and back towards Frankie, all the while pointedly not looking at the one whose attention he so obviously and exuberantly sought. Stopping suddenly and acting as if he was surprised to see him, Arthur blew Frankie a kiss.

At this a roar of laughter filled the air and a large circle of people formed around the three of them: Arthur, Frankie, and Billy.

Acting as if Frankie had responded in kind, Arthur put both hands on his cheeks and opened his huge mouth wide, making a big O of mock surprise and indignation. With a lazy downward swipe at the air to shoo Frankie away, he turned his face aside. A travesty of feminine shyness.

So precise was the sequence of Arthur's extravagant gestures that it appeared automatic, like some bizarre mating dance, or a performance practiced in front of a mirror.

Mesmerized, Billy couldn't take his eyes off the freak show. He was so busy watching and Arthur was so busy performing that neither of them noticed Frankie walk away and slip into the cheering, jeering crowd. This made it look like Arthur was now flirting with Billy.

Just then a pack of grade-school boys broke through the circle of spectators and flooded out onto the lawn. Stepping back, Billy watched as the little boys converged on Arthur. Swarming and chirping like a clamorous hoard of tumblebugs assailing a cow-pile, the little rowdies surrounded Frankie's bejeweled suitor, bombarding him with their high-pitched taunts and insults.

"Hey! Fatso! You want to play tackle?"

"Hey! Lard-ass, your dress is dirty."

"Hey! Morpho! You stink like a pig!"

"Pull up your dress, Fatty, let us see your pussy."

"Let me see your bra, Dumbo."

"Pretty rings, you big sissy."

The spell broken, Billy looked around; order was being restored. He saw Jake standing among the other spectators who were now turning away and going, receding like water after the storm is past, back to what they were doing before the impromptu entertainment began. Jake, though, was not moving. His expression was dark with envy and rage. He was a shaded boulder in a swift sunlit stream, impervious to the motion around him.

Arthur ignored the verbal abuse and the pack of boys started hitting and kicking him. He ran across the school yard and into the gym, the caterwauling boys in pursuit. Seeing Jake among the pursuers, Billy followed the stampede to the boy's locker room where the tormentors cornered their prey between two banks of lockers. When their fists and feet failed to faze Arthur, they shoved him and tried to trip him. He went down, more or less voluntarily, and curled up on the wet tile floor. Their cruelty stymied for the moment, the tormentors stepped back. Arthur rolled over on his back and smiled at the ceiling.

Just then, Jake, pushing and shoving and cursing, elbowed his way through the clot of bodies into the clear area where the downed behemoth lay motionless. Casually noting that Jake wasn't much taller than many of the much younger grade school kids, Billy wondered what Jake meant to do. Forced to guess he would have said Jake was stepping in to stop the abuse. Which is why what happened next shocked Billy so much.

Jake walked up to Arthur. He bent over and spit in his face. Stepping back and lifting his damaged leg, he took aim and kicked the floored figure hard in the side of the head. The sound of the heavy shoe hitting its target—a muffled crack like the breaking of a stick wrapped in wet towels—seemed to linger on in the awed silence like an unfamiliar odor.

Billy flinched, as if *he* had been kicked. But the downed creature made no sign of being in pain. He didn't cry out. He didn't make a face. He made no effort to touch the bloody patch, just in front of his ear, marking the point of impact; which, Billy thought, had to be devastating. Arthur just lay there on his back like a corpse in a coffin, his hands at his sides, his eyes closed and a beatific look on his face. The only sign of life he showed was to make a fist when one of the little boys tried to take one of his rings.

As the silence, which seemed to last forever, was replaced by a din of surprised wonder, the still air seemed to thicken with the sour odor of Arthur's corpse-like body.

Turning to leave, Billy saw Frankie's cousin Charlie West standing in the door, popping a pimple on the back of his neck. Charlie must have seen Jake going toward the gym and followed him. Shaking his head in disgust, Charlie headed toward the front of the gym. Billy followed.

Can you believe that! That guy is a nut-case, Charlie said when they were outside. Reaching over his shoulder, he stuck his hand inside the collar of his shirt, and popped a pimple on his back.

Who is that fucker? Billy asked, pulling at the crotch of his pants, still too stunned to notice that he had an erection.

You know him, Charlie said, sniffing the pus on his fingers. I've seen you hanging out with him.

Oh, I thought you were talking about that .... Billy's head seemed too full and he didn't know what was safe to let out. *Is* that fucker ... a *guy*? He acts like a fucking girl. What the shit is wrong with that stupid cocksucking son-of-a-bitch? Billy used the curse words like a paddle, to swat away, or to accelerate himself away from, a swarm of disturbing thoughts and emotions.

No, I'm talking about Jake Garrard. Everybody in this whole school thinks he's a complete idiot.

What's he do ... done ... that's so bad? The implications of Jake's amazing attack were part of what Billy couldn't assimilate but there was more to his confusion, something else even more formless—and much more threatening.

You *saw* what he did in there! Charlie's look said he couldn't believe the attitude Billy was taking.

Yeah, that was ... pretty bad, wasn't it. Billy was becoming aware that he was sexually aroused, adding to his bewilderment and fragmenting his attention.

He's a complete bully, Charlie said, and a real garbage mouth. Charlie has noticed that Billy has become a garbage mouth, too, by the way. Another thing is Jake's always claiming that girls are looking at him. Wanting to have sex with him and stuff. And, really, Charlie said, they can't stand the little twerp.

To Charlie, it didn't seem like Jake even *liked* girls. He said, for Jake, it was like talking dirty around girls and *about* girls was a way to build himself up. Jake's always wanting to 'fuck the dogshit' out of somebody. Or get a 'luscious titty' in his mouth. Some 'bitch' is always wanting to 'suck his big dick'. It was never—as Charlie implied would be his own much smoother, more sophisticated, and ultimately more successful way— 'She has a good figure'. No, Jake had to say, 'Would you look at the *ass* on that woman. She is built like a brick shit-house', or, 'Look at that luscious pussy'.

Under the cover of random thoughts—Jake's dick isn't all that big—what does it mean to be built like a brick shit-house—Charlie seems to be getting off on saying the curse words he attributes to Jake—Billy was mentally ducking ideas and images zooming around in his head like squadrons of wasps in a dog-fight.

Not that I don't think about stuff like that, Charlie continued, adding a touch of personal honesty to his instruction to Billy on the etiquette of heterosexual relations. I do. But you don't have to use cuss words to talk about girls. You can say: 'We really made out'. Or: 'She's hot for my bod'. Or: 'That girl has a really good-looking face'. Or: 'I like the way she looks in that tight skirt'. You'll never hear *Frankie* talking dirty around girls.

Everybody laughs at Jake behind his back, Charlie confided to his obviously clueless interlocutor, especially the way he sings in chorus. He opens his mouth real wide when he's singing. Closes his eyes, like he's carried away by the music. Even the religious songs and he doesn't even believe in God.

Billy felt grateful for Charlie's being there. The conversation was giving him something to latch onto. Unable nor inclined to muster much of a defense of his friend, he said, Jake's okay. He's been through a lot. He acts like that because of his brother Jimmy. He's trying to show everybody he's not like him.

What's so bad about Jimmy? Charlie stopped walking; his look said, This, I've got to hear.

Oh, you know. Always asking people if they're a Christian. Telling couples they're going to hell for holding hands. Stuff like that.

Yeah, okay, Charlie knew what Billy meant. He would give Billy that one. He would even admit that his cousin Frankie hated Jimmy. It was because Jimmy was always bringing up the fact that Frankie's mother wasn't married when he was born. Jimmy didn't bother *Charlie* that much, though: Believe me, he said, people put up with Jimmy better than they do Jake. A religious fanatic is better than an atheist. Charlie's advice to Billy was to avoid Jake like the plague. It didn't matter *why* Jake was the way he was and it was not like he was gonna change in the near future.

Jake says he's a Jew, Billy said. He was in no mood to defend Jake, even without Charlie's high-minded calumny.

Jew's same as an atheist, Charlie said, worse. He bet Jake had a small dick, too. Jews supposed to be smart but Jake wasn't near as smart as he thought he was. Billy was a lot smarter that Jake will ever be.

And my dick is bigger, Billy thought, as well he might, given its size at that moment.

After that Billy didn't exactly avoid Jake at school. He just didn't seek him out. When he did run into him in the halls or outside during breaks, he was more cordial than friendly, shortening, postponing, or diverting their encounters with promises to go over to Jake's house after school.

Billy thanked his lucky stars he had been there that day when Arthur confronted Frankie. That was pure luck. After what happened that day he was sure to be seen by the other students as being close to Frankie. Although he knew better, he let himself imagine that Arthur had been flirting with the two of them, not just Frankie. Billy even believed that he enjoyed a vicarious popularity stemming from his association with Frankie; and this seemed to be confirmed when Arthur, apparently picking up on Billy's new status, flirted with *him* a time or two. Which pleased Billy more than he cared to think about.

More subjectively and more enigmatically, Arthur's performance and what happened in the locker room afterwards had a strange effect on Billy. What to others apparently seemed absurd or merely comical was disturbing to him.

Part of Billy's reaction had been envy. The targets of Arthur's flirtations were not chosen at random. He had picked Frankie West to flirt with that day because Frankie was already one of the most popular kids in school, even though he was only in the ninth grade. The cheers, and even the jeers, that had greeted Arthur's little show proved that, grotesque as it was, the performance constituted a kind of twisted homage to Frankie and it did nothing to diminish Frankie's already considerable reputation.

Billy eventually accepted that he was envious of Frankie and asked God's forgiveness. Other more troubling aspects, though, of Billy's reaction to the events of that day were harder for him to deal with.

For one thing, Arthur's display had been, at a conscious level, a strange puzzle that Billy felt both compelled and helpless to solve. Lacking the necessary mental categories to make sense of it, he went over and over in his mind what he had seen that day. On the one hand, there was the enormous body with its hairy arms and legs, big hands and feet. There was the abundant chest hair that went up the thick neck, all the way to the line of the jawbone. There was the stubble on the fat cheeks. Billy was thoroughly disgusted by Arthur. On the other hand, there was the feminine attire, the affected demeanor, the seductive mannerisms. Although Arthur's behavior toward Frankie was a caricature, a ludicrous imitation, unintentionally farcical, of a girl in her early teens trying to be sexy, they affected Billy like the real thing. This mixture of male and female, confusing on a conscious level, stuck a deep chord in Billy's psyche.

For another thing, during the ordeal in the locker room, Billy had felt not only deep *sympathy* for Arthur. He had *empathized* with him as well. He felt what Arthur felt. He was sure of it. But not just the physical blows. He shared with Arthur the *sexual pleasure* of pain, more reminiscent than anything since of the thrilling, choking, paradoxical sensations of his first orgasm, when he was cheerfully certain he would surely die. Death, if it had come then—there in his grandmother's outdoor toilet—would have found him with a smile on his face. However, the suspected meanings and imagined consequences of what he now thought and felt with regard to Arthur were no cause for mirth.

A third thing, related, perhaps, to the other two, but even more disturbing: he had responded *in kind* to Arthur's ritual and would again when they were repeated. It was as if there had been some sort of affinity, unspoken and unspeakable, between him and Arthur. As if something had passed between creatures of similar natures. As if some deep pattern of innate tendencies, hidden from himself, had been activated in Billy. As if emotions associated with some forbidden content, had been brought to awareness, but not the content itself.

The composite impact of all these puzzling and frightening things and the end result of the whole affair—the flirting in the school yard and later, the beating in the locker room—was that Billy had *continued* to be sexually aroused by the memory of it. The feelings of lust and pain grew stronger for a while until, even when he wasn't masturbating, Billy sometimes found himself, to his horror and self-disgust, having intrusive thoughts about Arthur.

Thankfully, he met and fell in love with the Faustpool girl soon after that and the disturbing thoughts and feelings receded into the background.

Now, in Theo's house on Memorial Day, Billy recalled the incident. He remembered something he had read in Jake's sex book: *The individual being must also itself pass through these grades of evolution; it is originally bisexual, but in the struggle between the male and female elements either one or the other is conquered, and a monosexual being is evolved which corresponds with the type of the present stage of evolution. But traces of the conquered sexuality remain. Under certain circumstances, these latent sexual characteristics may provoke manifestations of inverted sexuality.*

12

"Uncle Toe, you've got to help me. I'm pregnant."

"Are you sure, Dixie?"

"I'm sure. I didn't get my period two times in a row."

"Didn't you just start having your period? Have they been ... you know ... regular? Okay, take it easy. Who told you to come to me?"

"Teddy."

"Teddy! Who's Teddy!"

"What are you so mad about?"

"I hate that name."

"I know you do, but I'm not calling *you* that. It's somebody else. I can't tell you who. Look, are you going to help me or not?"

"Okay, okay, I said okay. I'll help you. Who's the father? That boy your daddy let live out back of your house?"

"No, it's not Frankie's. What difference does it make? I'm going to get rid of it. One way or another. If you don't help me, I'll find somebody who will."

"What, and get yourself killed? I want to know who the father is. It makes a difference. If it's ... Frankie's ... I think you should have it. You can always give it to your parents. You said they've always wanted to have more kids. If it's a boy, the Good Reverend .... Wait! Where are you going? What's the matter?"

"Nothing. Let go of me. You're hurting my arm."

"You're being overly dramatic. I'm not hurting you and you know it. Now just calm down and let's talk this thing over. I won't say 'like two adults', because, you may be what ... ? Thirteen? Fourteen? But you're acting like a baby. Now, tell me: What has got you so upset?"

"He's *not* the Good Reverend! Don't call him that."

"Okay, I was just being sarcastic. I know you two have your differences, but you've heard me call him that a thousand times. Why does it upset you so much now?"

"He's *not good!*"

"Yeah, okay. He's no hero of mine either. But what are you saying?"

"Nothing. Just forget I ever came here."

"Jesus, Dixie! You're shaking like a leaf. And why are you crying? What in the hell is going on? Come here. Lay your head on my shoulder. Now, just relax and tell me what's wrong."

"You won't help me unless I tell you who the father is? Okay, it's *him!* It's the 'Good Reverend'. Now, you happy? You forced me to tell you and I did. *Now* will you help me?"

"That motherfucker!"

"No, *daughter*fucker."

"When did this happen?"

"You mean the *last* time? The last time was last weekend. I was taking a nap. Janelle was at the grocery store. Came right into my room. Before I knew what was happening, he ... ."

"There, there. Here let me dry your tears. What does your mother say? Have you talked to her?"

"She doesn't give a hoot what happens to me. Hmmm. Feels good here with you, Uncle Toe. Is that a gun in your pocket or are you just glad to see me?"

"That was a quick recovery. Oh Dixie! I didn't know better I'd think you were my own daughter. Same deliciously dirty one-track mind. Yeah, it does feel good holding you like this. You're developing into quite a woman. Mae West *wishes* she was as good-looking as you. I've always thought you were the prettiest girl that ever went to that school. That's why I made sure you made Homecoming Queen."

"So, it was *you* that bought all them votes. A hundred dollars! Put me way over the top. And me only a freshman. Thank you, Uncle Toe. Now, let me do something nice for you. I'm already pregnant and I've heard you say once you get pregnant, you can't do any more harm than's already been done. I can't get any more pregnant than I already am, right?"

"When did you hear me say that? You haven't been spying on me, have you?"

"Frankie says you say it to all those women that come up here from New Orleans to get rid of their babies."

"Jesus, Dixie, please ... don't do that. Oh ... oh!"

"You know you like it, Uncle Toe. Frankie says that's what Miss Vonderheim's always doing to you? If she can do it, why can't I? Give me your hand, I'll let you do it to me. See, I don't even have panties on."

"My God but you're beautiful, Dix. You already have a perfect body. You're not showing yet. Not that I can tell."

"Wait! You've got to promise me ... ."

"Yeah, okay, okay. I promise. I'll take you to New Orleans. To a real doctor. He's safe and clean ... and not too expensive."

"So, if I let you ... do it ... to me, you'll pay for ... you know ... 'it' ... what the doctor does?"

"The state you've got me in right now, I'd promise anything. But, yeah, seriously, I'll take care of it. We'll go tomorrow night. Come by after the bar is closed."

"And one other thing?"

"What's that?"

"Promise me you'll tell the doctor you're the one who got me pregnant. I can't stand the idea of anyone knowing *he* ... did that to me."

"You got it. Let's go sit over there by the window. I want you to tell me who told you to come see me? You said his name was Teddy?"

"It was Frankie. Miss Vonderheim told him."

"Frankie! Dixie, don't you lie to me!"

"I'm not! Sometimes I call Frankie Teddy. You know that song, *I just want to be your teddy bear?*"

"Cute. I want to show you something that I think you'll love. There ... now ... that's better. How do you like my new couch? Isn't this nice and comfy? I wanted to have a nice place where special customers could sit and talk. Now ... you just relax."

✳   ✳   ✳

"That was quite a scene there, Big Brother Theo."

"You spy on me and you call *me* Big Brother? You're running up quite a list of mortal sins, aren't you, Good Reverend? First incest and now voyeurism."

"She carried out her stupid little threat then, huh?"

"You mean you couldn't *hear*, too? Next time I'll let you hide behind the couch. I don't know about any threats, but she did tell me some *very* interesting things. Tell me, did you come in your pious preacherly pants watching old Toe slurping up that delicious little oyster?"

"Good old Theo. Always the silver tongue."

"Don't give me that holier-than-thou routine. Everybody knows about you and your little 'home prayer meetings' ... about how you like to get the 'whole family' involved."

"Don't always believe everything you hear."

"I don't. Not always. But your snooping around here, hiding in the shadows, is pretty good evidence, albeit circumstantial, that what I heard tonight is the gospel truth. And you call yourself John the Baptist! What would Our Lord say? Better yet I wonder what you-know-who would say. She'd have your head on a platter faster'n you can say 'Salome', if you get my reference. It's one thing to diddle other people's daughters, but this is a whole different kettle of fish. Which reminds me, did you hear the one about Eve taking a swim in the Garden of Eden?"

"Look, Theo. After what I just saw, you of all people must understand what I've been subjected to. The little bitch is as seductive as Satan himself, but I swear I didn't give in and the baby's not mine. Look, I don't care about her. Or you. And I don't care that you … took your pleasure … with her. All I want is the baby."

"The baby? Why's that?"

"Murder is a sin and it's my calling to prevent sin."

"And incest isn't! Bullshit! You'll have to do better than that."

"I've been … we've … Janelle and I … have been trying for years to have another baby. But she's apparently become barren. Probably a result of … the way she lived before she met me … something you know all about. We'll love it, give it a good home."

"You didn't do so well by the one you did have. Why should anybody believe it will be any different the next time around?"

"This one will be … is … a boy. I'll do better with a boy."

"What makes you think it's a boy?"

"I've prayed and I know my prayer will be answered."

"Jesus, John. You really are full of yourself, aren't you? You've always thought if you wanted something bad enough that it must be ordained and right … or *righteous* … that you should get it. I know what's going on inside that sanctimonious skull of yours. You want a boy so you can make him into the great athlete that you never were, never could be. You had the muscle, you just didn't have the moves. Two left feet and all thumbs. I'd hate to be that kid, if it ever does get born, especially if it turns out to be a boy. You'd fuck him up something awful. Tell you what I'll do, though. I promised Dixie I'd take her to New Orleans to a real doctor. And I'm gonna keep that promise, but I won't tell anyone what I *heard* tonight, *if* you'll promise you won't tell anyone what you *saw*. That fair?"

"Theo, you destroy that baby and I'll kill you."

"My! What white knuckles you have, Grandma!"

"Maybe not right away. I'll let you live in fear for a few years. But I'll do it. I swear I will!"

$$* \qquad * \qquad *$$

"Janelle! What are you doing here? How long you been out there?"

"Long enough, Theo. I saw you and John talking and I have a pretty good idea what you were talking about."

"You're white as a sheet."

"I was afraid John was gonna catch me following him. He can be pretty brutal when he's upset. I guess I shouldn't have worried. He was so upset tonight he wouldn't have noticed a freight train about to run him over."

"That bastard beat you?"

"Oh, Theo! That's not why I'm pale. Seeing you brought back old memories."

"Of you and me?"

"Yes."

"Remember that first time? In the back seat of Lester's car?"

"Yes! How could I ever forget!"

"Well, the couch is right over there. We could pretend the last ... how long *has* it been, ten, fifteen years? ... never happened ... ."

"No, Theo. I wish it could be that easy, but, we have to talk. There are things you don't know. ... Theo! Stop that. We can talk about us later. Right now I need you to listen. I'm almost certain that Dixie told you she was pregnant ... . Theo! Now, *you're* the one turning white. What's wrong with you?"

"Nothing, I don't know. I just remembered something."

"What?"

"Uh ... nothing ... I mean ... us, you and me ... that first time, by the lake. Here, let me sit down. I'll be okay. What were you saying?"

"I said I know that Dixie told you she was pregnant. You're not denying it ... ? So, here's what I've come to say. She's *not* pregnant. I took her to the doctor myself."

"Which doctor?"

"A Dr. Maxwell. Frankie got his name from Jonnie Vanderheim."

"When?"

"What do mean 'when'?"

"When did you take her to the doctor?"

"Why is that so important? A few days ago. Let me have one of those."

"I didn't know you smoked. I know you used to, back in the day, but I figured you'd a given it up once you became a preacher's wife."

"I don't ... I did ... give it up, but being here with you brings back old times."

"Which day exactly did you take Dixie to see this Maxwell fellow? Was it before or after the weekend?"

"It was after ... Monday ... but what difference does it make? Look, what I came to tell you is John thinks she *is* pregnant, *believes* she is. He *wants* it to be true. If he finds out ... *when* he finds out that she's not, he's going to think you helped her get rid of it ... and he may try ... ."

"Boy! Is she good, or what? She had me absolutely *convinced*."

"She was here tonight? When?"

"Just before John. He must a been following her."

"And you ... ? Theo! Did you ... . Oh! *That's* why you're white as a sheet. No, I refuse to believe you'd do ... . Please, tell me you didn't."

"Hell, Janelle, I'm only human. Haven't you noticed? She's a beautiful *woman*. Show me the man who can resist something like that ... ."

"Oh, I get it. Now you're afraid you may have ... . You wouldn't have done it otherwise? If you hadn't thought she was ... ?"

"Yeah. I mean, no, I wouldn't have done it. Probably *couldn't* have done it. There's something about pregnant women ... that turns me on. Just the *idea* turns me on like nothing else can."

"Yeah, it usually takes something pretty quirky to get you ... aroused. Well, okay, let me think. I have to say, if you did get her pregnant, that makes me feel pretty jealous ... but then, maybe it's okay. I don't like the idea of ... killing ... your baby. John already thinks it's his ... probably ... so he'll be happy ... and he won't think you got rid of his baby, right? And if she's not pregnant, there's nothing to worry about."

"Okay, but there's only one problem: I promised Dixie I'd take her to a doctor in New Orleans for an abortion."

"Just tell him to tell her that she's not pregnant and by the time she realizes she is, it'll be too late to do anything about it. You know, Theo, I can think of another quirky possibility that ought to appeal to you."

"What's that?"

"How quirky is this? A mother and her daughter ... both on the same day ... the same night ... on the same couch ... . That *is* where you ... 'took' her, isn't it? *That* ought to turn you on."

"That would do it, alright."

"You *were* saying something about a couch ... weren't you? That one over there by the window? And ... . Oh, my God! Wouldn't it be something if you got us *both* pregnant? How did Dixie know to come to you?"

"She said Frankie told her to come see me."

13

After Dixie restored her make-up and put her black wig back on and left, Theo turned off the lights, locked the doors, and went up the hill to his car. A full moon lit up Magnolia Park. Instead of starting the car, he sat behind the wheel, masturbating. Thinking about what had just happened with Dixie aroused him as nothing had for a long time.

Just then, someone in the back seat says his name. A woman's voice. Startled, Theo wheels around and what he sees nearly causes his already overwrought heart to stop. The residual effects of being with Dixie blaze up, engulf him, start his head swirling again. Listing like a wind-driven keel-less vessel, he spins away from what he fears may be just a mirage and grabs the steering wheel, a life raft in rough seas. After who knows how long, he gets out of the car and sits on the back seat opposite the woman, two car doors and his fly wide open.

"Well, aren't you going to say something, Theo?" The woman's voice is tremulous with anxiety. She is wearing a black sleeveless dress, just like the one Dixie had on earlier. She picks up the white sweater on the seat beside her and spreads it over her arms and chest.

Perfume, wafted by the motion of the sweater and mixing in his mind with Dixie's lingering flavors, promises a new, more fabulous feast. It is as if the scenario that Dixie had merely evoked, however artfully, is now a manifest and realistic potentiality, the stage now set, complete down to the last detail—the scent, the sweater, the dress, the shallow breathing, the lucky car seat eager to conform to the shape of her body—for Theo's re-entry into Paradise. Could it possibily be that Dixie's play-acting, flawless as it was, would now become the real thing, the thing itself? Would the back seat of a car once again be the whole Universe for two virtual virgins on their first night alone together, again, for the very first time?

Theo reached up and turned the inside light off. He could think better in the dark. Some of Dixie's aura remained like a ghostly curtain circumscribing—a backdrop informing and coloring—this new scenario.

The timing of the two visits—first by a young woman pretending to be an older one when the older one was about the same age as the pretender, and now by an older woman looking young and beautiful enough to be the one the first one was pretending to be—was as suspicious as the plot was convoluted. What were the odds that she would show up less than ... he glanced down to check the time, but it was too dark now to see his watch and his eyes wouldn't focus anyway.

With Dixie, Theo thought, he had been playing from behind. The aptness of the image amused Theo and he gave free reign to a sudden facility for sports metaphors he hadn't known he had: With the younger woman he had had to drive to the basket: he had blown by the screen, penetrated off the dribble, and streaked to the hole for the game winning lay-in just before time ran out. What was needed now with this older woman was to play within himself; to let the game come to him; to look for the screens and dribble around behind them, running time off the clock.

Not now to be the heat-seeking missile; but like water, to glide, to dampen the life-giving earth, to etch grooves in the bed-rock, to seek the lowest level, to meander to the sea.

Theo looked at the woman's face, which was wide-eyed and pale in the dim light, then straight ahead, through the windshield, at the tall moonlit pine trees surrounding the parking lot of the Mardi Gras bar. He whispered, "I'm seeing you everywhere tonight. Do I dare believe my eyes? Do you really exist? If I look at you again, will you be gone? If I reached out to touch you, would my hand go right through?" He lit a cigarette. After one deep drag he put it in the ashtray behind the front seat, holding the smoke in, making himself dizzy. Folding his right leg on the seat between them, he turned and faced her, tracking her eyes in the smoky swirl of his vertigo.

"Theo, I meant to call you after that night, but so much was happening ... well ... I just couldn't."

"'That night'," Theo whispered. "Yeah, that's the way I think of it, too. *That night.*" With his hands, he framed an imaginary marquee in the space between them. "In capital letters: THAT NIGHT." Then, not whispering, without the dreamy quality in his voice, "That night was a busy night. Dixie, John, and Janelle. A regular parade of Johnsons. Then, not a word ... for how many years ... no closure." Everything left open and raw like an exit wound, Theo thought and, smiling inwardly at the image, he flashed again on Dixie. What was he to make of all these repetitions. Everything was all set up for a possible repetition of the scene with Dixie, which was a repetition of 'that night', which was a repetition of the scene by the lake twenty years ago. Frantically trying to imagine possible motives for her being here, and hardly daring to hope that one of them would be what he had never given up hoping for, he said, "So, what brings you down here tonight?"

"Something has come up that I thought you needed to know."

Trying without success to gauge the emotional quality in her voice, Theo waited.

"Your brother John is sterile."

Theo shook his head as if to unscramble a kaleidoscope in his brain. Like a pilot looking for a break in the clouds, he scanned the past twenty-odd years, trying to think his way past the sound of Janelle's words to their meaning. Instead, the rhythm of her speech won out over the reference of her remark and the punch-line of an old joke about a singing telegram, popped into his head: *Your sister Rose is dead.*

"Theo ... did you hear what I said?"

"How do you know ... I mean ... when ... how long ... who?" Images of Dixie at various ages flashed through Theo's mind like snapshots in a photo album and he remembered a time under a bridge when his younger brother John won a contest with Theo and some older boys to see which one of them could ejaculate their semen the furtherest.

"Jonnie Vonderheim told Linda Garrard and Linda told me. Seems John went to Dr. Maxwell ... my guess is she, Jonnie I mean, convinced him that Dr. Maxwell could be trusted to keep a secret. I'm a little surprised that she told Linda, though ... I wouldn't have thought they were that close."

"I hate to tell you but he couldn't have made a worse choice." The mention of the doctor's name brought Theo's thoughts into focus a bit. He wondered if that fucking Jimmy Garrard might not have been snooping around in the records department at Pinecrest where his mother worked. Did Linda Garrard, for God knows what reason, sisterly solidarity, malice, just-for-the-fun-of-it, pass on her son's ill-gotten information to where she imagined it would have maximum effect? "That man doesn't know his ass from a hole in the ground when it comes to things like that ... or anything else, as far as that goes." Theo suspected not only was the doctor wrong about John being sterile; he also suspected the doctor had been wrong about Dixie not being pregnant, way back when. Which, he thought, Janelle had to know that by now.

"Yes, but you don't know the half of it," Janelle said, strengthening Theo's suspicion that she knew more than she was saying.

"Really? Why don't you fill me in?"

"Maybe later, but right now there are more pressing things we have to talk about."

"Um." The words 'pressing things' triggered a sharp increase in the undischarged tension built up in Theo's loins over the past couple of hours, and he emitted a little chuckle.

"I don't want to be alarmist, Theo, but there's nothing funny in any of this." Janelle lifted the sweater off her chest, folded it, and put it on the seat beside her. "Both our lives might be in danger."

"How's that?" Theo reached for his cigarette. It had burned up to the notch in the ash tray and gone out.

"Well, okay, that's why ... I'm here ... why I came to see you. We have to think this thing out. You remember, I hope, what happened that night I was down here before ... . After Dixie and then John left ... we ... , you know, ... did ... it."

"Not likely to forget *that*, now am I?" Or the time before by the lake, Theo thought, and then, jolted by a randy sensation that would have staggered a goat, recalled the choicest moments with Dixie on the couch in the bar. As the visceral effects of these more recent images subsided like the fake flakes in a snow-globe, he wondered if Janelle had picked up Dixie's smell on his face and marveled at the way three encounters, two past and one (the ultimate one?) still ongoing, formed a bridge that spanned and effaced all the years in between. He put his hand next to his nose and mouth and sniffed, trying to get a whiff of his upper lip. Does she know, did she actually *see*, and does she care what he had done with Dixie tonight? She hadn't cared before, 'that night'. Was he being set up, used? Now? Had he been a pawn *then* by the lake, and again 'that night'? For what?

"Okay, here's the thing. Right after that I learned that I was pregnant."

"That would a been ... what did you name her ... Tommie Sue?"

"Yeah. Now, you see what this means? Can't you see that if John puts two-and-two together ... ?"

Two-and-two together. Another upsurge of pleasurable tension in Theo's blood-rich loins.

"Are you paying attention, Theo?"

"Are you telling me you think *I* ... . ?"

"No, I don't *think*, I *know*! Who else could it have been, Theo! If John is sterile, it *had* to be you. But it's not what *I* think that's important, it's what *John* thinks. There's no telling what he might do."

Theo was trying his hardest to focus on what Janelle was saying. He closed his eyes to shut out the sight of her and chewed on her words like a canine connoisseur gnawing on a bone of questionable quality: *There's no telling what he might do* ... . *It's what* John *thinks* ... . "Why would he think it was me? Yeah, I know, *you* know it had to be me." Theo bit down on, *Or so you say*, because he was remembering ... .

*   *   *

When the couple stepped out onto the dance floor, set up outdoors in Audubon Park for some sort of high society charity function, Theo saw the woman's face first. If she had been with someone else that night; if his eyes had not been drawn so quickly and so forcefully to her escort's prominent face; if her hair had been bobbed and blonde instead of long and brunette; if he hadn't sunk to such a level that he didn't feel worthy to kiss the dirty drawers of any decent woman; if he had seen her, say, sitting alone in one of the cheap dives where he used to hang out after he dropped out of college; if one or some of these things had been true, his vague sense that he recognized her might have stuck in his brain, and he might have been tempted to ask her, Haven't I seen you somewhere before, and not meant it as a pick-up line; because, for one thing, Theo was not one, not yet, to go sniffing around trying to pick up women, and, for another thing, this woman was so classy and beautiful there was no way she would ever be alone, and certainly not in the places Theo used to frequent when he was between lousy jobs, each one more demeaning, of more marginal legality, than the last.

At any rate, when a second later, he saw who she was with and recognized his old college roommate whom he hadn't seen since he dropped out of school, he was overcome with such strong emotions that the brief sense of having recognized the woman Lester LeBeaux was with went out the window, so to speak. And, if that hadn't been enough, the panache with which the couple danced—it was as if Fred and Ginger had stepped off the silver screen into the midst of the Podunk High School prom, slowing the other dancers to a shuffle and turning them into onlookers—would have disabused Theo of any notion that he had seen her before. Outside movie houses he had never seen any two people as dazzling as these.

Theo had no intention of approaching Lester that night or at any other time. Quite the opposite. He was part of the crew that set up the dance floor and the tents and tables and the rest; and he had been asked to stick around to see that the party wasn't crashed by any undesirables. Like me, he thought at the time.

But Lester had recognized Theo and treated him like a long-lost friend, even introducing him to the angel he was with. (Theo later learned that it was on Lester's recommendation he had been hired to work the job he was on that night.)

No, Theo would not remember thinking that he recognized the woman with Lester, certainly not after hearing her classy name: Janelle Littlepage.

By the next day, after being close enough to her to smell her perfumes, man-made and natural, after seeing in her eyes all that he could never have but would forever pine for, he would have said that his first impression of her was one of falling hopelessly in love. Over the ensuing days, he and Lester renewed their old friendship and Theo learned that Janelle had recently moved to the city; that she had plans of making it big either as a singer with one of the better jazz bands in the French Quarter or as a dancer-singer in musical theater or, if she was lucky and good enough, with maybe a light-opera company, if there were any in the city. It was the easiest thing in the world for Theo to imagine, without even thinking about it, that she was as attracted to Lester as he himself had always been. Even after Lester hired him as a kind of bodyguard-personal manager and he got to know her better and where he, she, and the others fit in—who were the spiders and who the flies in the web of intrigue and ambition connecting Lester and his associates—it never occurred to him that Janelle was anything but Lester's current favorite. He automatically took for granted that she was as helpless as all the many other women in Lester's prestigious, high-visibility social circle to resist the urbane charm of the young up-and-coming attorney and man-about-town.

If, while watching Janelle surrender, as it seemed obvious that she did, to Lester's intense erotic sway—naturally assuming that she would end up, like so many others he had heard about, as one of Lester's conquests—Theo entertained dreams of inheriting her when Lester was done with her, he confined his illusions to moments of solitary sex. It was a long step down from Lester to Theo, and a dame like Janelle would surely have many better, intermediate options open to her when the end came. Publicly, overtly, in the real world, Theo stuck to maintaining his own status in Lester's circle, showing his sincere gratitude to Lester for allowing him to be in the near vicinity of this glittering, ambitious young Creole beauty, by treating Janelle, who was as beautiful and alluring as Rappaccinni's daughter, as if she were also as poisonous and deadly to the touch.

Theo and Lester had met in college. Theo dropped out after a few semesters of lackluster scholarship. Lester graduated and went on to law school. After the two reconnected Theo learned that Lester often helped the young unmarried daughters, wives, mistresses—and other human chattel (Lester was the soul of discretion)—of his rich clients avoid the legal consequences of the 'mistakes' and 'accidents' of their love lives—and 'professions'. Theo, a lapsed Catholic had seen the ruined lives of many women, including that of his own mother, laid waste by the Church's rigid rules, and, believing himself to be a true lover of women, was glad to become a part of what he saw as a worthy cause. Theo acted as go-between, making sure that the doctor and the damsel-in-distress arrived, anonymously, at the right (remote) location at the same time. Theo made a study of the process and the practitioners, personally seeing to it that high standards of cleanliness and safety, during and after the surgery, were met. He spent a lot of time with the women, calming their fears, hearing their stories, and shepherding them back into their normal lives. He was pleasantly surprised to learn that women in the situation these women were in, for reasons of being away from the usual strictures of father, husband, and pimp; of not knowing exactly when and in what circumstances their immediate post-surgery love-life might be resumed; of having already suffered the most dreaded penalty of their waywardness, and thus seeing no reason for further restraint; were often very highly-sexed and in excruciating need of certain obvious remedies. In most cases, Theo was able and more-than-willing to accommodate in his own special way, having worked out a complicated, i.e., not fully conscious, compromise with himself and the considerable post-lapse residue of his Catholic conscience. The unforeseen, and, as it turned out, mostly unlamented result of all this was that Theo came, first to prefer and then to be limited, both interpersonally and in his masturbatory fantasies, to oral over genital sex, cunnilingus over coitus, the latter eventually, perhaps for having been forgone for too long, seeming to fade away as a real possibility, with only a couple of future exceptions.

As expected Janelle liked Lester a lot. Who didn't? And why not? He took her many places with him, restaurants, movies, plays, museums, parties, weddings and funerals of friends, enemies, and members of his large Catholic family. At first, her demeanor around Lester seemed to Theo to be that of a girlfriend or even a mistress, his perception perhaps being a function of his own (repressed, erotic) attraction to Lester. But then, with time, Theo wasn't so sure. For one thing, to give a trivial example, unlike most of the other women in Lester's circle, Janelle didn't laugh at jokes, including Lester's, she didn't think were funny. For another thing, not so trivial, Theo was almost always with Janelle and Lester wherever they went and Lester always took her home before Theo—the two men often stayed up late drinking and talking—and, at times she seemed to like *him*, Theo that is, as much as she liked Lester. (She and Theo had even once gone, on a lark, to his hometown to attend the funeral of his mother's common-law husband.) Or was he just hoping she did? Did he *want* her to like him that way, as a lover? Could he handle that? He was a long way from being comfortable with the whole idea. How would Lester feel about it? To deal with the uncertainty, he increased the guard on his affections and tightened the constraints on his imagination; and cursed himself for his inexperience and ineptitude around with women in high-profile social situations.

So much did he wish it, that, with time, he came to believe that Janelle had never slept with anyone, even Lester. (After all, wasn't it true, that Lester didn't keep seeing women once he had fucked them and wasn't it most unlikely that a playboy of Lester's caliber would ever let himself fall in love and risk the danger of being led around by the nose by a *woman*?) So, to that extent at least it appeared that Janelle remained a good Catholic girl. That didn't mean she didn't have fun, though, didn't enjoy the excitement of city life. Through long nights of singing and partying in some of the hottest clubs (according to Lester) in the Quarter, she pranced and danced, her supple body erotically charged, like a footloose diva among the hoi polloi; her laughter rising above the din, and her eyes flashing in the dark, of crowded sweaty rooms like fifes and flares over a battlefield; the otherworldly glow of her skin—arms, neck, back, and shoulders—enhanced by the elegant attire of her calling, giving *a tantalizing foretaste of the divine splendor of some future Eden where she will reign, like some amoral Hindu goddess, taking her pleasure in taking life from and giving life to everything she touches.*

Then it seemed that Janelle became more and more anxious, edgy, even afraid. One night she called Theo and told him to pick her up at her apartment. He borrowed a car and she had him drive them out to a deserted spot by Lake Pontchartrain where Negro Voo-Doo ceremonies were once staged in bygone times; a circumstance that Theo later came to appreciate as deliciously ironic, given the resemblance to ritual sacrifice—in Theo's mind they were both virgins-at-heart—of what would happen that night in the light of a full moon.

The moment the car engine was turned off, Janelle was all over Theo and he was almost certain he knew why. He fully expected that sometime in the turbulent course of the evening—they were tumbling around in the backseat of the car like dice in a croupier's cup—she would reveal that she was pregnant and that Lester had told her to put herself in Theo's hands for the purpose of making her otherwise. None of which diminished in the least the splendor of what took place between them that night.

Later, in the sleepless ensuing hours, he would tell himself that he failed because he was terrified of what Lester would do when he found out; because he was angry that Lester hadn't had someone else take her through this ordeal or done it himself; because he preferred cunnilingus over coitus; but, most of all, because, ambushed by its precipitate unveiling, pixilated by its perfume, he was unmanned by the naked awesomeness of her secret essence.

In the eye of the storm, it had all came together in complete and celestial harmony. Old ship-wrecked Theo had made landfall on the shores of the continent that Lester's phallus had colonized; by the time it was over he had become *that august organ, taking it in and taking its place; absorbing its power and acquiring all the beauty of it in Janelle's eyes and all the love for it in her heart.*

A blinding bolt of hope, *conceived in the vertiginous vortex of his rapture,* sprang up—*a rogue phallus flying him to the moon, leaving the Milky Way in its wake*—that he had been wrong about her.

But then how did she know about this place? How many times had she been here with Lester? Did she think that giving herself to a nonentity like Theo didn't really count for anything? Did she think it would quell the fierce fires of her lust? That it would damp down the fumy furnace and keep her mind clear for the battle being waged in the main arena of her life? That throwing good old schleppy Theo a bone was of no more consequence than tossing a bum on the street a few coins for a bottle of cheap wine?

Even aside from the fact that, from that night on, all Janelle had to do to make him do her bidding was to threaten to tell Lester that he had eaten her pussy, Theo was now Janelle's sexual slave; her anointed, baptized acolyte; her groveling lackey; her abject body-stewart. Even before they got back to the city, any sense of sexual failure on Theo's part had given way to a child-like born-again feeling of blessedness and invulnerability that would never diminish in the years to come.

When Janelle failed to bring up the question of abortion, Theo figured that maybe she wasn't pregnant and that Lester, having finally fucked her, was just passing damaged goods on to his chief underling, and for some reason she was going along with it, at least for now. Among other things this made Theo very happy. Over the next couple of weeks, every chance he got, he went down on Janelle, a bee in her blossom, imbibing her nectar in backseats of strangers' cars left overnight in parking lots, in bathrooms of gas stations, in empty rooms at schools or churches, on midnight back-seat bus rides, on blankets under bridges, on marble slabs in graveyards. Long after she abruptly left town without even saying good-bye, he re-lived their encounters, in his head, face-down, between her thighs, encounters that proliferated in fantasy like some impossible Escher creation into a countless number of replays and refinements, reenactments and embellishments, that would be a bottomless wellspring of enchantment during the long years of his exile.

It was when the invitation to the wedding ('Dear Theo . . .') caught up to him two weeks after the event that Theo learned of Janelle's marriage to his brother John.

*   *   *

"But why do you assume that he would automatically think it was me? There must have been others stiff-legs sniffing around you at the time, sexy young preacher's wife. What about that Mayden feller?"

"Clinton Mayden! Don't be ridiculous!"

"Well, anyway, John was already gone by the time you … I mean, you waited until after he was gone before you came into the bar that night, remember?"

"Yeah, but maybe he came back … . He wasn't home when I got back home that night. At the time, I thought he had gone to what he took to calling 'choir practice' … but now I don't know. What if he *did* come back, Theo? What if he saw *everything*?"

"Don't you think he would have done something, at least said something, at the time?" 'Everything' flashed before Theo's eyes and the hope, the possibility, rose up in him of a second reenactment; or had Dixie been the second reenactment? Would the drama of the one miracle in his life turn out to be a four-act play?

"Not necessarily … probably not. First of all, he had already started up with Jonnie by that time … that's still going on, you know … so he may have figured that … you know, what's good for the goose is good for the gander or some such thing."

"Yeah, but this wasn't just any old gander … ."

"Then there was the fact that he knew that Dixie had told me that he had … molested her. Not that I necessary believe that even now … but who knows … I've seen her … you know?"

"Coming on to him?"

"Yeah, and he knew that she claimed that he had got her pregnant. So, he may have figured that he had better remain on my good side, in case it ever came to a showdown between him and her."

"In that case, why did he try to bully me into not helping Dixie get rid of her baby?"

"Did he? I didn't know he had."

"Yeah, he did. Wouldn't you think he would a wanted it out of the way … I mean … if he was worried about Dixie causing him trouble?"

"Okay, I see what you mean. Maybe he did molest her and maybe he *did* think it was his. God knows he wanted a son in the worst way."

"I'd say incest is the worst way, alright."

"Or maybe he thought it was Frankie's. He still liked Frankie at that time. Or maybe the thought he could bully Frankie into saying it was his."

"Didn't the question ever come up of why it took ... what? Eight, ten years for you to conceive?"

"The official explanation is I was finally able to conceive because I was away from the stress of trying to raise a wild child like Dixie in New Orleans. And then when he thought he had got me pregnant ... and if he believed he got Dixie pregnant ... he would have had no reason to believe there was anything wrong with him."

"Makes sense."

"Jeez, if he believed he got us *both* pregnant, he must have thought he was ... ."

"Some kind of a bad-assed stud."

"Exactly. Actually, that's what I wanted him to think. I remember being pretty sure Tommie Sue was yours ... call it woman's intuition ... turns out I was right ... so I wanted to give him ample reason to think she was his. I made him think I couldn't get enough of him. This went on for weeks ... I was scared and I pulled out all the stops, let me tell you."

"I wish you hadn't." In vain did Theo try to block out images of the 'this' that went on for weeks. "Told me, that is."

Janelle put her hand on Theo's knee.

Theo wanted to put his hand on Janelle's hand, but his arm wouldn't move. With 'this' still before his eyes, he remembered how passionately Janelle had come onto him in the car by the lake, and he wanted to put both hands all over her. But, imagining Janelle fucking Lester, a man Theo loved and emulated, was one thing; even if it hurt, *because* it hurt the way it did, it had the benefit of being intensely erotic. Imagining her fucking John, a man Theo despised and who was everything Theo was not, was something else again; it went beyond hurt, it was a palpable horror.

Yet, his opinion of and his feelings for Janelle, *qua* Janelle, was untouched by any of this, at least for the moment. The reason he didn't reach out and put his hand on hers was not that he didn't want to; nor was it that he felt animosity or resentment toward her for what she had done to him—he didn't at the moment feel that she had done anything 'to' him. His paralysis had more to do with some profound sense of unworthiness, specific to her, at the center of his being; with the condition of his being so far, and for so long, from the center of *her* being, which, of course, hadn't been the case when he had been the third point in the triangle with her and Lester.

As if she felt helpless to ease the misery she read on Theo's face, Janelle removed her hand from his knee.

"He still denies that he ever ... did anything with Dixie."

"Which is what you'd expect."

"But I have reason to believe him."

"And what might that be?"

"Well, for one thing, I ... we ... know now that he couldn't have got her pregnant."

And now 'we' know that he never got you pregnant, either, Theo thought, sullen and dejected, and yet you fucked his brains every night after that night for God knows how long and probably loved every minute of it. Not to mention that that fucker Maxwell is probably wrong about John's being sterile. Recalling this latter possibility caught Theo off guard, surprised him; it hurt more than he expected; it hurt more than the (after all, old) idea of Janelle's enjoying sex with his brother. Suddenly it sunk in how much the (new, but dubious) possibility that, in spite of everything, he was more of a man, at least in this one respect, than his brother, meant to him. "What was he like after he found out that he was shooting blanks? Was he ... pissed? Did he say anything about ... you know ... Tommy Sue's ... 'origins'?"

"He wasn't too happy about being sterile, as you can imagine. The way I see it, by now he is in no position to complain about my being unfaithful. If it was just me, I doubt he'd much care ... I mean, if he believed it was anyone else but you ... and if I agree not to say anything, which I'm not about to ... say anything, that is."

"Yeah, but if he realizes that he has been raising not just another man's child, but one fathered by me ... Son of Satan ... well ... that may be a different story."

"What do you think he'd do if he convinced himself that it was you?"

"Who knows? He may see it as an excuse to settle a lot of old scores with his wicked older brother. And he may think harming you is a good way to get back at me, or vice versa." The level of tension Theo was feeling had come way down from what it had been a few moments earlier. "Oh well, I'm not going to let it bother me too much. The business I'm in you get used to people wanting to do you in. I say, when your time comes ... ." Theo shrugged. "You'll keep an eye on him and let me know if he's up to something, won't you?"

"Of course!" Janelle started putting her sweater on. "It's getting chilly, don't you think? You cold?"

"No, I'm okay. When you say he is in no position to complain, you mean ... Jonnie Vonderheim ... right? Is that what you meant by 'choir practice'? I heard about that. In fact Jonnie told me herself."

"Tell me what she said."

"You sure you want to know?"

"Couldn't be surer."

"She said what really turned her on was the fact that he was so *good*, by which she meant sexually naive, I think. A case of innocence being the best aphrodisiac, I guess you could say, except it's usually the man that needs that kind of help. That and him wanting her *so* bad. Said she could *see* him craving her. Could see it in his eyes. All over his face. Said he was practically drooling at the mouth. He couldn't stay away. He was like a kid in a candy store. Or, more like it, a dog smelling a bitch in heat. I think it was the *combination* that turned her on. The *tension* between his 'goodness' and his randiness. Jonnie's had many men ... it takes something a little quirky ... a little twisted ... to turn her on at this stage of the game." And, of course, there was the size factor. Jonnie made no secret of it, she was mad for size. The bigger, the better. Luckily, she liked other things as well. "How'd you find out about them?" When Janelle didn't answer right away, Theo leaned toward her and asked, "Are you blushing? It's too dark for me tell. Am I embarrassing you?" Or are you reminiscing about John's big dick. "Don't suppose you and Johnny Boy ever talk about such things." Oh, how he would have liked to hear Janelle *say* that it didn't matter to her how big a man is!

"No, we don't, but that's okay. You don't have to watch your tongue with me."

"I love it when you talk dirty."

"Shut up! How did I find out? It was like Jonnie said: You could see it on his face. From the first time he saw her he was unable to control his ... himself. Or unwilling. Which amounts to the same thing. What is it about her, Theo, that make all you men go wild for her? Is it her hot Mexican blood? She joined the church. I'm sure you must have heard about that. Even in church he couldn't keep his hands off her. I caught them one night ... it was while an ice cream social was going on in the back part of the church. I was sitting in the auditorium. Taking a break from all those people. You have no idea how hard it is being a preacher's wife. The inane things you have to put up with from people. Anyway, it was dark in the auditorium. They came in."

"Jonnie and Johnny. J and J."

"Right. They didn't see me and I didn't let them know I was there. He tried to kiss her, but she wouldn't let him. She went and sat at the piano. She's the pianist at church. She tell you that? Not too bad, really. Just about every Sunday she accompanies me and Dixie when we sing a solo or do a duet. Anyhow, she began to play. *The Old Rugged Cross*, I think it was. Must be some sort of in-joke between them. John sat beside her and forced his hand up her dress. She didn't resist this time. I kinda like her, though. She knows what she wants and takes it. There's a certain honesty in that."

"What happened?"

"You mean on the piano bench? Not too much. When she started moaning, I started laughing ... I couldn't help it. I wish you could have seen it. It was actually funny. The two of them going at each other on that little old piano bench. I could actually *smell* her ... , you know. That's the way it is with those Mexican women, I guess. I was sure they were going to fall off onto the floor at any minute."

"What did they do when you laughed? Did they hear you? Did they know it was you?"

"*He* did, for sure. They jumped up and ran back to where the others were."

"And so you think this'll keep him from doing anything too drastic?"

"I think the fact that he has sinned too will make it harder for him to work up too much righteous indignation. That's the way his mind works. He's much harder to deal with when he thinks he has God on his side."

"Why am I getting the feeling that none of this has anything with why you came down here tonight?" The possibility that Janelle may have seen him and Dixie together, or that she had something to do with it, was lurking around in Theo's mind, but he didn't want to think about it until he had to.

"Okay, you're right. That's not the main reason I'm here. But I did want to remind you, to warn you, if you didn't already know: John's planning to go to your March of Dimes party Monday night. And even if he didn't see anything that night ... or any other time as far as that goes ... he's had time by now to think things over and ... you're ... ."

"The usual suspect."

"Yes, I don't think he was ever convinced that you and I hadn't been lovers before he and I met."

"Are *you* gonna be at my party?"

"Wild horses ... ."

"Good. What *is* the main reason you're here?"

"I need your help, Theo."

"And here I was, beginning to let myself believe that the real reason you were here was for the company. What kind of help you talking about?"

"You already know what it is, right? It's *him*. You know he's here, don't you?"

"You mean the good Senator, the 'Caring Cajun', Lester LeBeaux. Yeah, I hear he's on the television a lot. Claims to have polio. Did you know that? They say he always stands when he's giving a speech. Like he doesn't want anyone to know that he's a gimp. Just like his hero."

"FDR?"

"Yeah. I wouldn't put it past the basta ... muh ... son-of-a-gun ... ."

"Go ahead and swear all you want to. I told you I don't care about that kind of stuff. Did you hear what I said? He's *here*."

"Really! You don't mind if I cuss? There's an old joke about a boy talking dirty to his girlfriend I'll have to tell you sometime. How do you know he's here? Maybe you saw him on one of his trips to Hot Springs. I hear he comes here a lot for the cure ... in disguise, so nobody'll know it's him. But he always manages somehow to make himself conspicuous. He *wants* to be seen, but he wants it to *look* like he doesn't, like he's *above* using his 'ailment' to get the sympathy vote."

"No, that wasn't it. What is it you wouldn't put past him?"

"I wouldn't put it past him to fake having polio for political ... and *tactical* ... purposes. I mean, here's a man who probably doesn't have polio 'bravely' pretending that he doesn't have polio so people will 'admire his courage in the face of over*whelming* adversity.'" Theo wiggled his finger to reinforce the derision in his voice. "What do you mean, that wasn't it? What are you so afraid of, anyway? What makes you think he's gonna give you or ... us ... trouble?"

"I saw him in his car, parked across the road from my house one day. It aroused my curiosity. I thought at first it might be you."

"Why's that?"

"It was a Cadillac. You're the only person I know who drives one."

"What was it that seeing me aroused?"

"My curiosity, Theo."

"That's all? Just your curiosity? Nothing else?"

Janelle lowered her head, hiding her moonlit smile. She seemed to be having trouble gathering her thoughts. Blowing a big breath of air out of inflated cheeks, she waved her hand like she was clearing away the smoke— and dissipating the heat—between them.

"Go ahead with your story," Theo said. He noticed that his fly was undone.

"This is no story, Theo. I'm telling you the truth." Janelle sat up and reached across the seat. She put her hand on Theo's. "You've got to promise you will believe me, Theo." When Theo didn't withdraw his hand, she continued. "I got John's binoculars and hid behind the curtain so he couldn't see me. Mr. LeBeaux was in the back seat of the car. The car windows were tinted, but his was rolled down. I think he wanted me to see him. I couldn't see the driver too well. I think he was colored. Probably some kind of bodyguard, if I know our Mr. Bo. No mistaking *his* face. It's in the papers enough. And now, like you say, on television. Someone who saw him on television said he claimed to have bought the sanitarium."

"Yeah, Lester LeBeaux. Biggest nigger-lover south of the Mason-Dixon." Your hand is cold, Theo thought. That still mean what it used to mean? "You still call him 'Mister'?"

"Force of habit, I guess. Lester is such a dreadful name. And he wasn't the kind of man you'd call Les."

"You mean 'more' is more like it."

"You didn't exactly hate him, Theo. How'd he come to have such a hold over you?"

"It's a long story. Happened a long time ago."

"Tell me, Theo." Janelle moved closer, sliding across the seat in the dark.

"Well, okay, if you insist." Janelle put her hand on his thigh, as if to say, yes, she did insist. "As you know we met my freshman year in college. It was a case of a naive Cajun boy from the swamps falling under the spell of a slick city boy. He kinda took me under his wing. Made me feel incredibly special."

"Yeah, he had a way of doing that ... making you feel special."

"I didn't even know what I was doing in college. I just went because I didn't know what else to do. I took the same courses as he did. I hung out in his dorm room. We did everything together. For a while. We'd stay up till all hours of the night. Arguing about the meaning of life, that kind of thing. Then, second semester we roomed together. And, as you might expect, things started to cool between us."

"Honeymoon was over."

"Yeah. Sharing a room like that ... being around him nearly all the time ... I began to see things I hadn't seen before. Lester had lots of friends who were queer. Me and some of the other guys who hung around with Lester began to wonder if *he* wasn't queer. He was always saying, 'I never discuss my sex life', which, of course, made you wonder what his sex life was like. Which was, of course, just what he wanted. I don't know how he manipulated us, it was subtle, but to this day when I think of Lester the first thing that comes to mind is: Is he queer or straight or both?"

"Yeah, I know what you mean, I think."

"'Polymorphous perverse' is a phrase that comes to mind." Of course, it applies more to me than it does to Lester, Theo thought. "Anyway, he was drawn to anyone who had anything unusual about them, good or bad. He knew all the really cool people on campus and he was always taking in losers of one kind or another."

"Which were you?"

"Good question. Good luck on finding the answer. I don't think he made that distinction. With him it was, were you interesting or not. Of course, at first I thought the only reason he liked me was because he thought I was a loser and felt sorry for me or something. I asked him about it one time. He convinced me that I was special. And I do mean *convinced*. I *still* feel that way. I mean, if I ever feel at all out-of-the-ordinary, it's because of Lester LeBeaux.

"Of course, I still didn't know what he *thought* about me, or anything else for that matter. Still don't. He was, is, a complicated man. I knew he liked me, though. The reason I *think* he liked me, at least at first, was he thought I was weird. I remember, right after I met him, there were a bunch of guys in my dorm room looking at dirty pictures Lester had taken of some whores he knew. I said something about wishing I could stick a banana up in ... there was this short-haired blond one who was drop-dead gorgeous ... . You sure you want to hear this? Yeah? Okay. I said I would like to eat the banana as it slid back out of this ... I think I said ... goddess. I noticed Lester looking at me. I think he was really surprised by a dumb-ass Cajun saying ... thinking such a thing. Right after that he found out that I was an atheist, and he began saying I was a 'free thinker'. At that time he thought that was the best thing you could be: A free thinker."

"You were saying things began to cool."

"Yeah, we had a third roommate. A little weasel from Mamou. Erd was his name, I swear it. He had this buddy, a kid from Thibodeaux. The two of them were always in the room. During the week at any rate. Erd went home to be with his girlfriend every weekend. So, when Lester started finding other things to do more interesting than being with me, I fell into listening to Erd tell his buddy what he did with his girlfriend on the weekend. It was like a serial. Each week I'd learn how much closer he got to porking her. He'd go into the most minute detail. Eventually, it got to be fairly interesting. As interesting as vicarious sex can get. Which is pretty damn interesting, actually. Especially when you aren't getting any yourself. Hint, hint."

"What do you mean, 'hint, hint'?"

"I'm talking about the last thousand years without you."

"I wanted to, Theo. I really did. But ... . Besides it's not like you have lived a monk's life all these years."

"Don't worry about it. I was just kidding. Anyway that was a long time ago. Where was I? Oh yeah, Erd and his girlfriend. Eventually ... after Erd finally lost his cherry, I guess ... and he didn't have any more stories to tell ... I began telling him and his buddy from Thibodeaux about Lester. Naturally, I didn't paint a pretty picture. I was an ignorant Cajun, for Christ's sake. The subtleties of human relationships weren't my strong point."

"I know."

"Touché. Anyhow, Erd and his buddy came up with the idea that I should take Lester on. You know, egging me on to start a fight or something. I was pretty screwed up at that point in my life. I didn't know why I was in college. My mother was married to ... actually they *were*n't married ... she was living with this son-of-a-bitch drunk that beat her. He was threatening to kick her out, to tell everybody they weren't married. (The only reason she stayed, she said, was the old bastard had a daughter who was living with them at the time ... hiding out from her pimp ... and Mom felt like she couldn't leave her to the mercy of the old lech ... and I was 'indisposed' at the time and couldn't go home to rescue them.) In other words, I was fucked-up. My life was fucked up. How else can I put it? To make a long story short: One weekend I followed Lester to see what ... who ... . Hell, I don't know what I was thinking. Anyway, I followed him. He went to this queer bar. I waited outside. After a while he came out with someone. A little guy. Looked like a queer to me. I followed them back to our room. I waited for a while just outside the door, trying to decide what to do. Then, I just busted in. This little queer was kneeling on a pillow in front of Lester who was sitting in a straight chair. Lester was wearing a t-shirt. Nothing else. You get the picture. The queer jumped up and ran out of the room. Lester just cocked his head as if to say, now what? I don't remember what I said. All I remember is we began to wrassle and then to ... I won't say 'exchange blows' ... . We started fighting. With our fists."

"Well, let me tell you, Lester beat the shit out of me."

"Okay, slow down. This story started out you were gonna tell me how Lester came to have such a hold over you. And now you're telling me how he beat you up."

"I'm getting to that. In fact, I'm there now. By the time he got through with me, I was on the floor, too tired and humiliated to get up. Lester, who still had on nothing but his t-shirt, sat down on my chest. You know, straddled my chest. He was actually *aroused*. He put a pillow under my head ... the same one the queer had been kneeling on, and he forced ... himself ... into my mouth." Theo lit another cigarette.

"Theo, that's terrible. What did you do?"

"You mean, did I fight him? Did I resist him? Did I try to bite it off? No, I didn't. I know this will sound crazy, but he did it in the most loving way possible. In fact, it seemed at the time that there was nothing he could have done that would have ... that could have ... been more loving. I felt like a child, lost and hungry, whose mother had just showed up and was letting it breast-feed. I can't put it any other way. I was crying, I was humiliated by the beating he had given me. And here he was in my mouth. My lips were bloody and hurting. Sucking was unbelievably painful, but at the same time it was the most pleasure I have *ever* had. *The* most *erotic* pleasure."

What made it so erotic for Theo, aside from the perfect balance of concentrated pain and pleasure in his mouth, was the <u>innocence</u> of their merging. No only was he was a child, soothing himself and at the same time pleasing his mother by accepting her gift, her most precious treasure; he was also a loving mother to Lester's phallus, treating it as a mother-cat treats her new-born kitten, grooming it and keeping it frisky.

"Can you even begin to understand, Janelle?"

Janelle laughed nervously. "I think so. Maybe. Probably not. What happened after that?"

Theo thought Janelle seemed surprised—and embarrassed—by the unwonted depth of his sincerity and by her own reaction to his confession of homosexual love. He imagined that every detail of the story of him and Lester added fuel to the fire of her mounting lust. Could it be that what had started out as merely an expedient—or at worst fear-management—on her part was becoming not only imperative, but justified, even sanctified, by the mutually redemptive benefits it would have for her ravaged lover and herself?

"Well, you know what happened. I quit school. Got an apartment in the Quarter. He went on to Law School. That was the only explicitly sexual thing that ever happened between Lester and me. But he *owned* me after that. I was a *treasured* possession, but a possession nonetheless. I became his ... ."

"I think I know what you mean. I mean, I felt the same way."

"Yeah, I figured you did . . ." Theo paused. It felt like he was crying. In the rearview mirror, he thought he saw tears in his eyes, but they were dry to the touch. Turning back to face Janelle, he said, "Now, don't get me wrong, Janelle ... . Do you realize I haven't said your name out loud in ... what? twenty years ...? Well, except for that one night ... . Let me repeat it, savor the way it feels on my tongue. *Jan ... nelle.* I'm thrilled beyond words to see you here, to be this close to you again. To *smell* you. God, you smell good. I never thought I'd ever get to talk to you again."

"You're the one who ran away, Theo ... , *Thh-ee oh.*"

"That's not the way I remember it."

"How do you remember it?"

"The only woman I ever loved, ever *could* love, dumps me for my stepbrother."

"You didn't do anything to stop it."

"That's not the same thing as running away. By the time I figured out where you had gone, it was too late. What was I supposed to do? You were already married. I guess you had a big church wedding, right? You wear white?"

Janelle smiled sheepishly.

"You *did*, didn't you?"

"Off-white."

"Off-*color* white, you mean. So, John-John has no clue about your past?"

"Oh, Theo! I *had* to get out. I mean, once I realized what Mr. Le ... Lester ... wanted me to do and why he wanted me to do it. I'll always be grateful for what your mother did for me. Taking me into her home like that. Letting me get away from LeBeaux ... and New Orleans. I had no idea you were so hurt by my leaving, but then, when you didn't come to the wedding, I realized how much I wanted to see you again, how much I had been missing you. I think I must have sent you the invitation, hoping that you would come home. If you had, I would have done anything in my power to make it up to you."

"Anything in your power? I don't think so. It would've taken a lot to make it up to me. I don't think you'd have been willing to go that far. Wouldn't have been morally compatible with being the preacher's wife. No sarcasm intended. I was hurt pretty bad. I don't guess you ever told John about you and LeBeaux."

"Nothing to tell."

"Nothing to tell!"

"I swear it. To me it was just 'business', you know, and, I thought, for Lester, too."

"*Swear*? That's not a Baptist word."

"Swear it on the Bible."

"Swear it on the *Bible*? I wish I had one on me." Theo freed his wrist from the grip of Janelle's cold hand. "You mean you were just an ornament?"

"What do you mean?"

"What did you mean by 'business'?"

"Let me tell you how it was with me and Lester. At first I took him at his word that he just wanted to help me in my career. But then the pursuit heated up, so to speak, and when I let it be known that I didn't want to play, he started spelling out the rules, I guess you could say, and letting me know I was in the game whether I wanted to be or not. He made it crystal clear the ways he could help or hurt me. He reminded me that he knew people in high places."

"Were you in love with him ... I mean before he started trying to intimidate you?"

"No, and he wasn't in love with me, either, I'm sure of it. I believe the way he saw himself ... to be the kind of man he wanted to be ... he thought he should never settle for just one woman and should never consent to being just one among many suitors of the same woman. But it was more than that: It wasn't his style to be *refused* by a woman, *any* woman."

"His style?"

"Yes. And he wouldn't settle for my just pretending that he had ... ."

"Fucked you?"

"Right. It went deeper than just a social thing. I believe he was trying to be true to himself, as they say, I grant him that. Well, anyway, I wasn't so much worried about any harm to myself, not monetary harm, or harm to my 'career', at any rate. My main concern was more one of ... decorum, I guess you could say ... of what it would look like ... of what people would think. About me ... and about Lester, too ... . I just didn't want that kind of attention ... and blame ... directed at me. You have to realize I was still very naïve.

"I don't know what people I was worried about ... just 'people'. I could see, we all could see, that is, all the members of the little society that swirled around Lester could see ... except maybe for you, Theo ... you were so loyal to him ... and with good reason, I know that, and I not *blaming* you or anything ... but everybody else could see that things would eventually, sooner than later, come to a head and Lester's ... I won't say heart ... his pride, I guess, was going to be ... I don't want to say broken ... was going to be ... affected, and it would be my fault."

"No, it wasn't his heart that was in jeopardy. It was something lower down and much more precious to him."

"Anyway, it was clear that the situation was going to turn ugly, and it was my anticipation of this ugliness ... and how it was going to affect other people ... that made me afraid. No ... I have to admit it ... I was afraid for myself, too ... of how Lester was going to handle it ... of what he might do to me."

After three glorious seductions, two for real, and one make-believe, and a fourth one in the making—Please, God!—Theo wanted to believe what he was hearing, but he still wondered what could make someone like Janelle sink to his level. Why had she practically raped him that night by the lake? Why had she given herself to him so freely in the weeks that followed? Was she trying to turn herself into something so low, so degraded, that Lester could walk away from her with his pride intact? Why, *really*, had she taken the risk of coming down to Magnolia Park tonight? Why was she here now in his car? What did she *really* want?

(After Janelle left Theo had been in a very low state. Around that time he had been arrested in connection with the abortion business, and he had spent some time in prison, essentially taking the fall for Lester, who promised Theo he'd get him out after only a short time, which he did, but not before Theo went through some pretty rough times. After that Lester had put a lot of pressure on him to be in a pornographic movie that he and some of his friends were making. In prison Theo had developed certain erotic tastes that led to his doing things that he would never have dreamed of doing before that; things that none of the other 'actors' would do, not well at any rate, but which Lester had sensed that Theo, in the self-punishing state he was in, not only wouldn't mind doing in front of the camera, but would do with the kind of unfeigned relish any director, even at this lowest level of the 'film arts', loved to see. It was this that Lester wanted in his movie.)

Janelle took Theo's cigarette out of the ashtray, took a long drag. "Did you call John your *step*-brother? I thought you were *half*-brothers."

"No, Mom is not my real mother. I came with Old Man Jeannsonne when they 'married'. Turns out he was already married. He may actually be my real father, I don't really know. I should say she's not my biological mother, because she did the best she could to be a good mother to me, under the circumstances. I mean, when the old bastard died, she could have kicked me out, sent me to an orphanage or something, but she didn't. As for my real mother, I haven't a clue who she may be. John is by Mom's second 'husband' … some hobo that came around one day looking for a handout and she took him in for what was supposed to be a couple of days … lucky fu … bas … fellow must have thought he'd died and gone to heaven … but the couple of days became a week or two … you get the picture."

Janelle took another drag, put the cigarette back in the ashtray, and looked out the window.

Theo took her hand. Why was she so distracted? "You look frightened."

"Theo, I *am*. I'm scared to death."

"Of what?"

"Of *him*."

"You think he's still mad … even after all these years. He a big *solon* now. He has to be careful what he does, don't you think?"

"*Theo*. He's a *State Senator*. Those guys can do just about anything they want to and get away with it. It's not like I have a lot of money. I'm in no position to fight back."

Theo released her hand. "I don't know. I think you're just being paranoid. Get back over on your side of the car." Back on her side, Janelle crossed her arms across her chest, a pouting gesture. She slouched down on the car seat, pushing her dress up and exposing her thighs. Looking at Janelle's thighs, ghostly white in the dark inside the car, Theo was finding it hard to think. "You come waltzing back into my life after, what, twenty years? ... well, not counting that one lousy night ... and now you want me to help you. I'm having a little trouble getting my mind around all this."

"It's *Dixie*. I want you to help Dixie."

At the mention of her name, Theo felt and smelt again Dixie's slick wet labial membranes on his lips and cheeks. He lit another cigarette. "She seems to be doing just fine on her on."

"Okay, moment of truth. Theo, I've never told another soul what I'm about to tell you. You have to promise not to tell anyone else."

"How can I promise ... ?"

Janelle slid back across the seat and snuggled up next to Theo. She put her hand on his lips to shush him. Her dress was still hiked up, almost to her panties.

"I was pregnant when John and I were married." Theo tried to say something, but Janelle shushed him again. "I was so far along that there was no way anybody was gonna believe otherwise. So, John signed up to do the last year of his divinity training in Nashville. That's where Dixie was born. When we got back to New Orleans we told everybody the baby was my sister's. Then, when we moved here, we just let everyone assume that Dixie was ours, which is true ... well, partly true."

"You have a sister? You never said anything about having a sister. I always thought you were an only child."

"We didn't know each other very well. She was a lot older than me. She left home when I was little and never came back. Hardly ever wrote. A Christmas card maybe, nothing more. Not a word about her life. She was my dad's favorite. Broke his heart. Things were never the same after she left. I always blamed her for our parents' breakup. I wrote and told her so. After that even the Christmas cards stopped."

"And so you figured she'd never know the difference if you told everybody back home that Dixie was hers? Weren't you taking a risk that she'd find out? Your sister, I mean." *Alleged* sister Theo was thinking.

"She knew what we were doing. What our story was ... . What we would tell people about Dixie. She had somehow heard about my ... us ... John and me ... getting married and tracked me down. She came to Nashville. She was sick at the time ... terminally ill, as they say ... and she wanted to make amends. She said she always loved me. Never blamed me for how things were. We actually became friends. I 'forgave' her for what I thought she had done to the family. I mean, after I heard her side of the story. Understood why she had to leave. When I told her I was pregnant, we cooked up the plan to say the baby was hers."

"That's a lot to take in at one time." Theo pushed Janelle's hand away. "Pull your dress down!" He got out of the car, opened the front door, got behind the wheel, got a bottle out of the glove compartment, and took a gulp. "Let me see if I have this straight .... What you told me before was a lie?"

"No! What?"

"About you and Lester?"

"Yes! I mean *no*! What I said is true. He never .... You think *he's* Dixie's father?"

"Who, then?"

"I'll get to that. The point is that at the time I *thought* John was the one."

"You're trying to tell me that rather than admit that Dixie was yours, you and John told everybody, including Dixie, that she was .... Who did you tell her was her father?"

"Oh, Theo. I know it's crazy. I know that now. At the time ... John was trying to protect *me*. Don't you see? He was afraid ... we were afraid ... that if some trouble-maker ever started nosing around .... "

"Did the math."

"Yeah, and if word got around that ... Dixie .... " Janelle began to cry. "Then added to that if someone in his congregation got wind of my background .... I mean just the fact that I lived in New Orleans for a while as a single woman would've been enough to .... See, they all thought I was from somewhere else, not New Orleans. You're Catholic, Theo, you don't understand the Baptist mentality."

"But you and John *lived* there for ... how many years?"

"Yes, but by that time we were married. It's different when you're a single woman. And besides, John and I were like missionaries in some heathen land. And a lot of the congregation, the ones that mattered, the ones that tithed, felt the same way, like they were living in the very shadow of the enemy. And, too, we were thinking, I was thinking, that if any kind of scandal did get stirred up LeBeaux might find out where I was and come after me ... and do what he could to make things even worse for me."

"Weren't you afraid he'd find out you were living in New Orleans?"

"Not too much. I never came in contact with any of the old crowd ... anyone who might tell him that they had seen me. Besides he was Catholic and Catholics and Baptists live in completely separate worlds."

"So, there you were, right under his nose. Kinda like the purloined letter."

"I don't know what you're talking about ... purloined letter?"

"Never mind."

"Anyway, this way John's career was not jeopardized and ... ."

"And you got to grow up to be Snow White. I get it. What I don't get is: Where in all your schemes was Dixie?"

"Oh, Theo ... we ... I ... did what I thought was in the best interests of everyone at the time. Yes, looking back on it ... . It's easy for someone on the outside, like yourself, to see clearly, especially in hindsight ... but at the time ... . Come to think of it, you're hardly one to talk. After all, it wasn't exactly in her best interests what you did to her that night, now was it? She was only fourteen ... you could have gone to prison for that."

"It didn't seem so bad at the time." Theo had thought a lot about what he had done to Dixie that night, especially in moments of guilty lust. He took another swig and, as if to close off further discussion of any wrong-doing on his part and to signal that he was, nonetheless, ready and capable of defending himself against all charges, even to level counter-charges, if need be, he sat up straight and did some perfunctory self-grooming. When Janelle didn't say anything, Theo said, "So you let your own daughter grow up thinking her 'real' parents, her 'real' mother, didn't want her ... that the two people who really *are* her parents ... well, her mother, any way ... are her adoptive parents ... . Did it ever occur to you how all those lies would affect your own daughter?" He wanted to but didn't say that he had always loved Dixie and that at fourteen she was anything but a child. As for what had happened earlier tonight, well, he just couldn't see the harm. After all, she and he weren't *blood* relatives, and he hadn't actually fucked her either time. "And what if she somehow finds out the truth?"

"We *told* her the truth!"

"When?"

"When we thought she was old enough to understand."

The *truth*? You told her the *truth*? What exactly is the truth? Theo wondered. He emptied his bottle with one gulp. Wiping his mouth with the back of his hand, he made a windshield-wiping motion in front of his face as if to shoo away a swarm of pesky questions. "What do you want me to do, then, exactly?"

"I want you to come back here with me." Janelle was sitting on the edge of the back seat. She slid over to Theo's side of the car. Leaning forward, she put her head next to his and together, cheek to cheek, they contemplated the moonlight and the shadows. Then, tenderly cupping his left ear in her hand, she kissed his other ear. Licking the external part of his ear, her tongue traced the intricate whorls and, insinuating its way deeper into the tangy opening, thrust suggestively, wetly, in and out.

"Just like old times, eh?" Theo's voice was full of surrender.

Theo returned to the back seat and asked again what Janelle wanted him to do.

"Find out if Dixie's involved with him."

"Involved? With Lester? What makes you think … ?"

"I can just *feel* it."

"Feel it?"

"Yes, and a friend of mine said she thought she saw Dixie standing behind him when he was giving that speech in Bogalusa. On television. She said if it wasn't her, it was someone who looks just like her. It's not so far fetched, Theo. Think about it. He's now her boss. You know what he's like. How much he likes to manipulate people. Look how he tried to manipulate you and me. And you know what *she* is like. How ambitious she is. They're two a kind. She's already threatening to leave Frankie. She's not gonna want to keep on working as a hairdresser forever. She'd see Lester as just what she needs to make her escape."

"Then, why not let her go? You lost control of her years ago, anyway."

"But what if she tells him about … ."

"About what?"

"Well, I don't know … what we've been talking about."

Theo shook his head. "I don't understand."

"Well, okay, you tell *me*: what's he doing here, anyway, Theo? Do you think it's a coincidence that he has showed up here now? That he just happened to buy the sanitarium that just happens to be right next to the park that you own? That just happens to be in the town where I live? He's up to something. I can feel it."

"Yeah, you're probably right. He's always up to something."

"He could make all kinds of trouble, and he'd do it just for the fun of doing it."

Janelle began to cry. She groped at Theo's fly and, finding it already open, glanced up pleadingly at him and, bowing to the task, rummaged around in his drawers, until she had extracted what she was after. Holding on and taking a big breath, like diver going under, she slumped down onto the floor of the car. When she surfaced she wiped her mouth on the sleeve of her white sweater.

Theo patted the car seat where he wanted her to sit.

*   *   *

W. A. Moltinghorne

ENTER LEWD
O'd

Locked in the limbo of libido, captive of concupiscence, his heart is a storehouse of unsublimated sentimentality. The fissures of his brain are sluices spiced with the super-savored slush of the juices, flavors, and vapors and vestiges of various floods and flows—full, frequent, faint, deferred for 40-4, or finished forever—from the private parts of a parade of partners whose fecundity was a to-be-forestalled fait acompli. Lost limp-lingamed lamb, his soul is a depository of salacious silt—layer-upon-layer—from a lifetime of licking labia and lots more, of lascivious longing and licentious looking; from looting the literature and lore of lust for all he can learn of lesbian love-making techniques.

Kneeling in abject obeisance before the Altar for the Altered, auto-erotically erected to his febrile, infantile fixation on, his dogged determination to be the horny handmaiden of, his obsequious obsession with, the occulted orgasms of Her Otherness, he neighs, he brays and bawls, he bellows and barks, hollers and howls, spewing a brazen shower, a douche of devotional doggerel—a lap-puppy's paean: 'O, wee, be-pearled portal (by pubes parenthesized), I pucker-up and push past the pisci-scent of the loose juicy puce lips, pardoning the periodic pollution, postponing the perpetual perdition, partially playing the priestly part, not pious per se, passing up all patriarchal privileges of partnering for the paternal purpose of propagating, co-populating, and perpetuating posterity. It's Thou-and-I, twixt-thigh-and-thigh. Mouths of-a-piece in mute mutual loose-lipped lip-service, we vent and voice the sibilant and sonorous sounds, the laryngeal lyrics, of libidinous love.'

Kow-towing to the utterly Other (O+her), the infirm worm, in the interior castle, squirms, turns in the blink of an eye; stooping not just to propitiate, praise, and please; not just to applaud and appease and appreciate; but to appropriate, apprehend, and appraise; not just to pray but to pry; to pry apart the double doors. Dangling his diminished divining-rod, dribbling drops of amber rain, he dowses the divine delta for molten gold.

Fervently cavorting down the slippery slope of the cloven, covertly vaginate and convoluted, deep-delved diluvial declivity, he comes across the crux in the cranny; cornering the kernel of carnality in the nectared nest, he nuzzles the Gnostic nub, noshes the Hobbit-knob, nicks the niched node of nymph-nerves.

Questing the quick in the quarry, he uncovers a diamond in the hOly ground: Eve's secretly-enfolded jewel, her verboten grape—smuggled by Sophia, the Serpent-Goddess, out of the griffin-guarded Garden—a gratuitous gift of grace for girls.

Untenting and tasting the petite teat, he tests the temperature and turgidity of the tongue-stroked touchstone.

Forging his tongue in the rectal smithy, he flutes the fleecy-furry furrow from anus to clit, lickety-split, without halt, up and down the ass-fault.

He is a lowly galley slave, fettered in the hold; he rides out passion-storms, with one hand on Onan's oar. Coveting a blessing from eyes of lapis lazuli blue, harbors of heaven's hue, he glimpses—through the tangled rigging of pubic hair—signs of things to come, flitting across the sun-tongued decks of faces forgone for further down. Buffeted and soaked by silky thrusts brought to bear by oft-hoisted world-girding thighs, he absorbs the seismic tremors of protracted orgasms reverberating in the bilge of pitching, bucking, bug-bitten buttocks.

Enough! You ewe, you eunuch, you euphemism; you jerk-off junky, you joy-stick jockey!

EXIT

*　　　　*　　　　*

Afterward, Theo said he would have Teejay snoop around and see what he could find out about Lester's designs, if any, on Dixie.

"Theo … ?"

Theo waited.

"I know you're never gonna believe what I am about to tell you. I don't expect you to. But I have kept this secret so long it's got to where *I* don't believe it sometimes. But the time has come to set it free."

Theo waited.

"Dixie is yours. *You* are her father."

Theo had a vague memory of what Janelle might be talking about. After that first night by the lake, he and Janelle had returned a second time to the same place and Janelle gave him the first of the three blow-jobs she had given him to this point. At the time he was sure it was Lester's cock she really wanted to suck, Lester's cock that was in her mind. At any rate, Theo had achieved a good-enough erection and, egged-on by Janelle, he had managed to penetrate and ejaculate into the canonical orifice—she was, after all already pregnant by Lester, so where was the harm?—which was pleasurable enough, but it didn't come close to altering his preference for cunnilingus.

"And while I'm at it," Janelle continued, "You *did* get Dixie pregnant 'that night'."

Theo knew this wasn't possible, but he didn't say anything.

"We sent her off to 'boarding school', Janelle continued, "A place where unwed mothers can go to have their babies. Our babies were born on the same exact day. That's why we ... John and I ... were able to make people believe that I had twins and that one of them was born dead."

"So, you didn't make her get rid of it?"

"That's right, I didn't."

"Why not? You told me that night that if she *was* pregnant you were gonna make her get rid of it. Remember? You said you were jealous."

"Yes, I remember saying that and I *was* jealous. But I guess when I realized it might be yours I decided I'd let it live. That sounds so horrible! Like I was God, or something. 'Tah, tah, I decided I'd let it live'. I do know ... I remember ... that when I realized I was pregnant, too, I wasn't so jealous anymore. That was quite a day. Two babies born. A boy and a girl. Conceived on the same day, born on the same day."

"What happened to the male child?"

"It was still-born."

"Which one did you have? Boy or girl?"

"A girl has to have some secrets."

"You're a mystery wrapped in an enigma ... how does that go ... ?"

Theo has plenty of questions to ponder as he tosses and turns and tries to sleep; his post-orgasmic bliss has dissipated, and he is left with the usual enervated insomnia. Why hadn't Dixie come back the day after 'that night' as they had planned? Had she been kidnapped? Abducted by John, maybe with Janelle's help, and taken to the home for unwed mothers? Had Dr. Maxwell really been so incompetent, or had John gotten to him before Janelle and persuaded him to lie and say Dixie wasn't pregnant? What *had* John seen 'that night'? Had he come back down to Magnolia Park that night and seen Theo fucking Janelle? Had he bargained with his wife, telling her he would 'forgive' her, if she'd help him save Dixie's baby? Was he, Theo, Tommy Sue's father, *really*? Would John be out to get revenge now that his sterility was official? How much weight should be given to the fact that Janelle went down on Theo *before* he lied and led her to believe that he might be able to help?

He wanted to believe that he was Dixie's father, but how could he be sure that he was? All he had was Janelle's word for it. Of course, that's all any father ever has, but what if she *had* been pregnant by Lester; and what if she figured Lester was going either to drop her like a hot potato, make her get an abortion, or both? Maybe she thought Theo was her best shot under the circumstances. But then why'd she leave town without even saying goodbye? Maybe she wasn't running *away*; maybe she was running *toward* something … something really, really big.

One question, more of a suspicion than a question, but a strong suspicion, was planted in his mind when Janelle told him that he had got Dixie pregnant that night. He remembered that she had assumed that he had fucked Dixie that night, and that he hadn't told her otherwise. But the fact was he hadn't. John was sterile—so who was the father of the infant boy-child who didn't make it? Why was Janelle still talking like he might be the father; he was almost certain that by now she knew he wasn't? What had sealed the baby's fate? Had he really been still-born? Or had there been something about Dixie's baby, the baby itself, that made it obvious the moment it came out that it wasn't John's?

Theo didn't want to think about this, but couldn't get his mind off it. The fact was he was pretty sure he knew the answer, had *known* the answer, had guessed it correctly 'that night'. He remembered that, when he suddenly realized who Dixie meant when she said 'Teddy' had sent her, he almost fainted. Janelle had said something about his looking pale and he had had to throw her off the scent by leading her to believe that he was upset because he had fucked Dixie, thinking she was already pregnant, only to find out she hadn't been and that he may have knocked her up 'that night'. He also remembered Dixie's saying that she had missed two periods; which meant that she had been pregnant for a couple of months before that night; which meant the two babies probably weren't born on the same day. Unless Tommy Sue was pre-mature and assuming that he really had knocked Janelle up that night.

It was all too complicated. Theo forced himself to stop thinking about all the implications.

Of course, it was too late for anyone to do what Janelle wanted: To save her daughter from LeBeaux. Way too late.

Or was it?

14

On one end of the court in the unlighted gym at Pinecrest, a little boy was heaving an old rubber-soled shoe up at the hoop, trying to get it through the net. On the other end, some older boys were playing an abbreviated version of baseball called work-up. Their bat was a broom handle; waxed Coke cups wadded together, their ball. There were only two bases, home, a dirty t-shirt; and first, the mate to the shoe being used as a basketball at the other end of the court.

There were two batters. If one batter got on base, the other one would try to drive him home. When a batter made an out, he went to left-field and the catcher took a turn batting. At the same time, all the other fielders moved to the next position in a pre-determined order. It was a pointless game. There were no teams. No score was kept. The game was never over, the players just quit playing.

"Hey, you little fuckers!" Jake Garrard yelled. He and Billy were standing on the side-line at midcourt. They had just arrived. "Take off your shoes. You're marking up the floor." Lowering his voice, he said to Billy, "I can't stand that. Fucking black streaks all over that fucking floor." Pointing toward the wall at the back of the gym, he said, "Did you notice? Someone stole the mat under that goal. Bet you anything it was your old blow-buddy, Frankie West."

"Billy! What took you so long?" It was Charlie West coming down onto the court from out of the stands on the opposite side. He was dressed out, ready to play. "Hi, Jake, thought you were in cop school. What's the matter? Not tall enough?"

"Fuck you, Charlie," Jake said.

Charlie grinned and said to Billy, "Hey! New glasses, eh? Let me look through them. Not very strong, are they? Just like regular window glass to me. Must be psychosomatic. Can you play with those on?"

"Gonna try. Where's Frankie?" Billy looked up at the clock on the wall above one of the goals, checking the strength of his glasses for the umpteenth time. They *do* improve my sight, he thought.

"Don't know. Said he was coming," Charlie said. "Guess what. There are no balls! What are we supposed to use for balls?"

"Charlie West has no balls? Tell me something I didn't already know," Jake whispered to Billy.

"What's he doing here?" Charlie said to Billy under his breath. He smelled of acne medicine. "He can't play worth a darn."

"Everyone is equal in God's sight," Billy said aloud so that both could hear.

"Frankie West is coming!" someone yelled. Just then the wide side-door of the gym was flung open. Frankie swaggered in. He seemed borne by the sunlight streaming in with him. Like he owned the place, as Jake remarked under his breath.

Frankie had on new basketball shoes and a new warm-up suit, bright-red top and bottom. But those inside, blinded by the outside light, saw only an array of silhouettes.

Frankie was accompanied by his usual entourage of three or four black leather-jacketed hoods and by a young woman with short hair wearing dark glasses and masculine clothes—blue jeans, flannel shirt, cowboy boots, and a hunting knife on her big-buckled belt.

Then, coming into the gym through one of the end-doors, was a big man in a wheel chair. He was accompanied by Dixie Johnson and a tall young black man whose skin was the color of coffee-with-cream.

A couple of minutes later Jimmy Garrard came in through the same door. He went into the stands and sat down.

When Frankie saw his wife, his mouth dropped open. By the time she had seen him, he had hurried over to where she was. "What the hell are you doing here?"

"She's with me," the man in the wheel chair said. "Is that a problem?"

Ignoring the man, Frankie said, "How come you're not at work?"

"As it happens," said the man in the wheel chair, "I'm her boss and she has been kind enough to indulge my request for the pleasure of her company for a while this afternoon."

"And since when do you hang around with niggers?" Frankie said, still looking at Dixie.

Only then did Dixie look at Frankie. Her face and pitiless hooded eyes conveyed a bloodless reptilian aspect, less sullen than frigidly indifferent.

"The late, great Frankie West, I presume," the man said.

Only then did Frankie look down at the man, who said, "Tell you what, Frankie: Twenty bucks says this young Negro … whose name is Teejay, by the way … can beat you one-on-one. Or, if you prefer, given your apparent lack of conditioning, a round of the child's game Horse."

"I know the fucker's name. I ain't never met a nigger I couldn't beat with one hand tied behind me."

"As you say, but indulge me. Use both hands. You win, the twenty is yours."

"Make it a hundred, big man, and you're on."

"Frankie!" Dixie said, suddenly interested. "You don't have that kind of money."

"Oh well, if you don't have the money, why don't we just play for bragging rights? Unless you're afraid ... ."

Frankie turned around to the leather jackets who had gathered behind him. "Give me all your money."

The hoods dug into the numerous pockets of their jackets and jeans. They came up with thirty-something dollars.

"Gimme your watches."

Frankie put the money and watches into a cap he snatched off the head of a little boy and showed them to the man in the chair.

"Good enough," the man said. "What's it to be? One-on-one or Horse?"

"Hold everything. We don't have a ball to play with," Charlie West said. "But I've got an idea." Addressing the young woman in sunglasses: "Crystal, can you pick the lock on that door?"

In a minute or two the door was open. Charlie went into the equipment room, selected a ball and gave it to Frankie. Dribbling the ball onto the court, Frankie announced, "One-on-one. Military rules. No refs. No fouls. No change of possession after a made basket. First to score twenty baskets wins."

Teejay went over and sat in the first row of the stands to put on his tenny shoes. As he stood up to go back onto the court, Jimmy Garrard gave him a thumbs up.

"Here's a quarter," LeBeaux said when Teejay was back on the court. "Dixie, why don't you toss it to see who has the ball first."

Frankie won the coin toss. He went to mid-court and waited for Teejay.

Billy noticed that Frankie hadn't taken off his sweat-suit, but he didn't think much about it at the time.

By the rules of the game, the man in possession of the ball passed it to the other player who passed it back, putting the ball in play. When Teejay was in position to take Frankie's pass, one of the leather jackets yelled out, "Nigger meat!" Another: "You got a big butt, nigger."

Teejay looked toward the hecklers. Frankie hit him in the chest with a hard two-handed pass. Just as the ball hit Teejay, Frankie said, "Ready?" Taking the ball as it rebounded off Teejay's body, he raced to the basket for an easy lay-up.

The little boys who had been playing work-up cheered. The leather jackets let out shrill whistles. One of them yelled, "Hey! Big butt nigger! Ever hear of dee-fence?"

Frankie tossed the ball to Teejay who passed it back and the game continued. This time Teejay stayed between Frankie and the goal, forcing Frankie to take a long jump shot which he made.

More cheering and whistling. "That's what you call a jump-shot, Nigger boy."

On Frankie's third possession Teejay sprang up and slapped Frankie's jump-shot back beyond the circle. Two quick steps and Teejay had the ball. Two quick dribbles and he was past Frankie, springing up toward the goal. Rather than dunking the ball, he held it with two hands over the rim. Before dropping the ball through, he seemed to float, buoyant like a balloon or kite, for a second or two.

An awed silence filled the gym, underscored by the diminishing pat-pat-pat of the ball on the floor as, its momentum petering out, it rolled to a stop on the side of the court.

"Like putting the baby to bed. Easter eggs in the basket," murmured Lester LeBeaux. He motioned for Dixie to come closer. "His big butt is solid muscle. It's the reason he can jump so high. His ancestors were bred for strength and agility."

After that Frankie never touched the ball again, except to put it in play.

On Teejay's second possession, he took Frankie's in-play pass and was around him and scoring before Frankie got to the foul line. On Teejay's third possession, Frankie aimed his in-play pass at Teejay's feet, but Teejay jumped out of the way before it hit him. The next time he put the ball in play, Frankie threw it at Teejay's crotch, but Teejay caught it before it hit the intended target. "Keep your mind on the *game*, Frankie," LeBeaux murmured with a chuckle.

On subsequent possessions, Frankie tried to foul Teejay. As the black man's score mounted, Frankie's attempts to hurt Teejay became more and more flagrant. But Teejay soon learned to anticipate Frankie's moves and he won by the score of 20-2.

LeBeaux gave Teejay the cash. He wheeled over to where Frankie lay collapsed on the floor, the underarms of the new warm-up suit dark with sweat. Without a word, the man in the wheelchair emptied the watches onto the exhausted and vanquished man's heaving chest. It was clearly a gesture of contempt, like dropping something in the toilet. Smiling, LeBeaux returned the cap to its owner and wheeled over to where Dixie and Teejay were. The three of them headed for the door. None of them looked back.

Gasping for breath, Frankie croaked like a petulant frog, "Hey! ... Dixie ... where ... going ... with ... god ... damn ... nig ... ger?" As he rolled over on his stomach to watch his tormentors exit, the watches spilled onto the gym floor.

Jimmy Garrard came down out of the stands and followed LeBeaux and his two young friends out the door.

"Take it easy with those watches, Franko," one of the leather jackets said.

Frankie gestured to the one who said it to help him up. When he was on his feet, he began stomping on the watches, crushing them on the hard floor. He kicked at what was left of them, sending some of the bigger pieces skidding to the far end of the court. This seemed to re-exhaust him. Bending over and gasping for breath, he said, "There ... moth ... er ... fuck ... er. There ... your ... chicken ... shit ... watch. Too ... stupid ... tell time ... any ... way."

Frankie was helped onto the first row of stands. Waving off his solicitous companions, he lit a cigarette and lay down flat on his back.

Charlie West retrieved the basketball and began shooting baskets. Other balls were taken from the equipment room. For the next quarter hour the gym was full the sounds of leather on the hardwood floor and on the steel backboard and rim as a dozen or so kids flung half as many basketballs at the basket.

"Where's Jake?" Charlie was sitting on a basketball, taking a break. Reaching across his chest and over his shoulder, he popped a pimple.

"He left." Billy squatted beside Charlie. "Had the red ass, he said. Or maybe it was the botts."

"What's the difference between the red ass and the botts?" Charlie sniffed his fingertips, then looked at them thoughtfully.

Billy shrugged. Then he saw Jake leaning against the railing in front of the stands. Jake had taken off his jeans and street shoes and had on swimming trunks and thick-soled tenny shoes. Billy could tell from the black look on Jake's face that he had heard his and Charlie's remarks.

"You notice Jimmy Garrard a while ago?" Charlie asked. "Is he following Dixie? Every time I see her, I see him lurking about."

"Don't know." Billy moved a few steps in Jake's direction, stopped, and looked back at Charlie.

"Hey! You guys, let's choose up sides." Frankie had regained his breath and was on the court.

Every boy stopped dead in his tracks. The dropped basketballs rolled among them like giant pinballs in a tilted pinball machine.

"Okay, you pussies," Frankie said, "We're gonna play full court."

"You sure you wanna play full court, Frankie?" Charlie West whispered, but everyone heard it.

Frankie ignored his cousin's remark. "Charlie, you pick four to be on your team and I'll take four of the ones left. Full court, first team with twenty baskets wins, have to win by two. Okay?"

Billy was hurt that Frankie hadn't let him be the one to choose a team.

Charlie chose Billy first and the three best of those who were left.

Jake wasn't chosen for either team.

Even with inferior teammates, Frankie was able to keep the game competitive, using skill and intimidation and calling frequent timeouts. Camping under the basket on defense, he forced Billy and the others to shoot outside shots. He rebounded the missed shots by elbowing other players aside, climbing over their backs if necessary.

Charlie West was of no help to his team. He seemed to be playing under protest, just going through the motions. Refusing to take a shot of any kind, he was little more than a bystander, always passing the ball to another player when it came his way. He seemed more interested in harvesting his bumper crop of pimples than playing basketball.

Frankie never passed. Leisurely dribbling the ball the length of the court after a basket, or, more often, a miss, by the opposing team, he took every one of his team's shots. Mainly he took long jump shots which no one was tall enough or brave enough to defend. Occasionally he would drive to the basket, flashing through the other players and daring anyone to get in his way, and, after one of the boys on Charlie's team tried to stop him and was knocked to the floor so hard he had to be replaced by another player, no one did.

Following each drive to the basket, Frankie called timeout. Leaning back against the padding on the wall behind the backboard at the front of the gym, he gasped for air like an asthmatic on a vertical bed. By now his warm-up suit was completely soaked with sweat.

Billy was disgusted by Frankie's behavior. He's playing like he's in the State Finals, he thought. Angry at the way Frankie was bullying people around and pissed that none of the other players were fighting back, Billy started taking hopelessly long hook shots from thirty feet out. With the aim of disrupting the game, he dribbled around forever near mid-court, refusing to pass the ball or advance toward the basket. Half-heartedly trying to spin it on his fingertip, he lackadaisically let the ball fall to the floor, stopped it with his foot, and sat on it.

"Come on, goddamn it." Frankie kicked the ball out from under Billy. Landing on his butt on the floor, Billy didn't bother to get up. Then, Frankie, running backward on defense after making a jump shot, came up to where Billy sat and glared at him. Leaning over and keeping his voice down so only Billy could hear, he said, "Play right. I'm warning you, motherfucker."

Angry that none of the other players had followed his lead, Billy got to his feet. "If you don't like the way I'm playing why don't you get Arthur Maxwell out here and you can fiddle around with him all you want to." Unlike Frankie, Billy made no effort to keep his voice down. "You don't have to act like you don't know him here. You're among friends."

Turning away before Frankie could say anything, Billy ran to take the inbound pass. Only then did he notice a large figure in a black leather jacket sitting alone high above the floor on the top row of seats, gazing down at him like a vulture. At first he thought it was just one of the hoods with Frankie, but suddenly it hit him: It was Arthur Maxwell. Suppressing a pang of contrition that he may have hurt the outcast's feelings and turning his head sharply away from the melancholy eyes, he suddenly felt light-headed, almost cavalier.

At mid-court Billy stopped dribbling and held the ball on his hip. "Okay, you guys, listen up," he yelled to the passive herd. Pointing at Frankie, he sneered, "There's your king. Bow down to His Majesty. Do what he tells you. Kiss his ass for all I care."

Frankie stared at Billy through narrow slits. Billy walked toward the sideline, the ball still on his hip. Frankie glanced into the stands, first to where, in a cloud of cigarette smoke, the leather jackets looked on; then he looked up toward Arthur, who waved, opening and closing his hand, like a timid child. Frankie turned back to Billy. "Give me the fucking ball."

Billy flung the ball at the basket. It landed high on the brick wall behind the basket.

Grabbing the ball as it came bouncing away from the wall, Frankie advanced toward Billy.

"Hey! That's walking." Billy motioned for the ball. "Our ball."

When he was three feet from Billy, Frankie stopped. Holding the ball with both hands, he brought it to his chest. In a flash, the sweat-covered ball slammed into Billy's face, sending his new glasses flying across the floor.

In the explosion inside his head, Billy heard what Frankie said as the ball was on its way and after: "You want the ball. I'll give you the ball, you sissy-assed goody-two-shoes bastard!" In a swirl of sweat and flashing lights he saw Frankie's fists coming toward his face. He felt the hammering blows smashing his lips against his teeth, flattening his nose against his skull, ramming his eyeballs against the backs of their sockets.

Suddenly, on his way to flopping on his butt on the polished floor, Billy saw the blur of someone stepping between him and Frankie. Looking up from where he sat on the floor, Billy saw Jake—Jake's big fists were raised and trembling like the heads of two angry but reined-in mastiffs—and heard him say, "Come on motherfucker. Fight someone your own size."

"My own size!" Frankie tried to laugh, but didn't seem to have the breath for it. "Why, you little, sawed-off Jew Boy ... you *must* want your ass ... jacked up. If I was as short as you, I'd sue the city ... for building sidewalks so close to my ass." He bent forward and put his hands on his knees. He bowed his head. Straightening up, he took in a big gulp of air and stared up at the ceiling. Sneering at Jake, he said, "It's gonna be fun ... stomping your pigmy butt." He looked up into the stands where Arthur was sitting and then back at Jake. "Come to think of it ... I owe you one ... you little creep."

Just then Jimmy Garrard broke through the circle of boys surrounding Jake and Frankie.

"Get the fuck out of here, Jimmy," Jake yelled. "I don't need your fucking help."

Jimmy moved back, merging into the crush of onlookers congealing around the two fighters. The bodies of the throng, tightly packed like inflamed tissue around a carbuncle, formed a ring around a small combat-arena with no exits. In a thicket of thighs, Billy was still on the floor. Someone lifted him to his feet. Still woozy and with sirens in his ears, he fought his way to the front row of spectators. Through revolving kaleidoscopes of vertigo, he saw flashes of light in a mix of blurring colors and changing shapes; as his head cleared, this tumult of movement resolved into shiny patches of skin and the motion of elbows and knees, buttocks and shoulders, arms and legs; and the ringing noise gave way to the sounds of flesh slapping and slamming against flesh, bone crunching against bone, and breathy grunts of effort and response. Finally zeroing in on the particulars of fists and faces, he was initially discouraged by what he saw.

Frankie danced in a circle around Jake, dripping sweat on the floor. Hoping to exploit his reach advantage by going over and around the shield of upraised fists and forearms with which Jake tried to ward off the attack, he threw a barrage of punches from all angles.

Forced by Frankie's tactics to adopt a defensive strategy, Jake twisted one way and then the other, confronting his foe like a radar-saucer locked-in on a zigzagging, back-tracking enemy aircraft. His shoes squeaked, hardly ever losing touch with the shiny and ever-wetter floor.

At first most of Frankie's punches found their mark. Cuts opened on Jake's lips; blood flowed from his nose and dripped off his chin. The color of the puffed-up flesh around the swollen slits of his eyes soon matched that of the sweat-diluted blood on his white t-shirt; later the rosy red would darken to purple, turning his eyes into heat-ruptured overripe plums.

Just when it seemed to Billy that his intrepid would-be avenger and erstwhile best friend was beaten, Jake, in a startling blur of movement, water-bug quick, brushed aside Frankie's flagging fists and advanced into the vacated space like a dancer bellying up to an out-of-step partner. The shorter fighter's own fists slammed into Frankie's ribs and abdomen, driving him back staggering and breathless.

The aureole of spectators flowed across the floor, moving with the sweat-drenched pugilists in the nucleus like wind and rain swirling around the eye of a hurricane. Billy struggled to stay upright, to maintain his position on the inside wall of bodies. He held his arms out to the side and leaned back against those behind him, surfing a wave of bodies and preventing anyone from getting in front of him.

"Get back, give them room," Billy shouted.

The leather-jackets came out of the stands. Like vultures, black and grim, waiting to feed on carrion, they looked on from the outer edge of the coagulated mass.

Arthur stayed where he was, high above the fracas, silent and vigilant.

On the face of it, it looked like Jake was losing badly. In reality it was the other way round. As Frankie's blows were all aimed at his shorter opponent's head, the damage he did was visible. Jake's punches were all to Frankie's mid-section, their effects internal and otherwise hidden by Frankie's wet sweat-shirt.

After a while Frankie's dancing slowed to a shuffle. Absorbing attack after attack to his mid-section, he recovered less quickly from each successive barrage. His fists seemed heavy and sagged down toward his waist. His sweat-suit, dark red like venous blood, clung to him. His long wet hair hung down, like shreds of muddy rags, in front of his frightened eyes. He looked like a doused rat.

"Had ... ee ... nuf?" Frankie asked, backing away and bending over to catch his breath.

"Just getting warmed up," Jake countered. Moving his big fists in unison, he beckoned to Frankie to step forward, daring him to resume the fight.

Frankie straightened up. His twisted features, though unbloodied, told of injuries lower down. He began hopping, shuffling sideways, one step to the right, one to the left. The net result was a slow, backward movement away from Jake's menacing fists. Lowering his dazed eyes, Frankie looked at Jake's atrophied thigh. "Gotta ... pretty fucked-up ... leg ... there. How ... did ... it ... hap ... ."

Jake moved quickly, straight forward, with small, deliberate steps. The methodical movement gave his squat, compact body an air of solidity, of ineluctable purpose, despite the asymmetry of its lower half. Before Frankie could finish his wheezy question, Jake blurred inside what was left of Frankie's defense and hammered his body. One fist smashed the ribs. The other sunk into the soft abdomen, causing Frankie to bend at the waist. The first fist flashed up and under, slamming into the forward-falling sternum, straightening Frankie and propelling him backward, his arms wind-milling, flinging circles of sweat into the air. As he twisted sharply to one side to keep from falling, his momentum sent him reeling through an open door and down some steps, into the boys' locker room.

Jake unhurriedly followed Frankie into the locker room. Spectators streamed in, a new circle curdled around the adversaries.

The now familiar pattern was repeated once more but at a slower tempo: Frankie, moving like a man under water, danced, his jitterbug slowed to a waltz, and Jake advanced, a shark smelling the blood of a meal to be eaten at leisure. After an exchange that even the blood-thirstiest spectators must have prayed would surely be the last, Frankie, the wind knocked out of him, teetering like a just-scythed weed, was saved from falling to the blood-speckled floor by the wall behind him, as if even the bricks had taken pity on him. Against the damp red wall, his goggling eyes and his pale bloodless unmarked face hovering above the occulted carnage like a bodiless ghost, he looked like he might fade into the kindred backdrop and be gone. Then, finally, he caught his breath; to the relief of the onlookers, he gasped and his midriff started heaving. With his arms exhausted and hanging limply at his side like flightless wings, he looked down wistfully like a spectral vulture at the road-kill of Jake's upturned face, and whispered, "Let's rest ... for ... a ... min ... nit." He seemed to be searching for a glimmer of kindness in the slits of Jake's savaged eyes. As Frankie spoke, his voice strained and hoarse, the expression on his ashen face put Billy in mind of a contrite lover, caught red-handed, making a silent hopeless plea for mercy. The trembling fingers of Frankie's right hand felt their way down Jake's left arm to Jake's fist which was jammed against his navel. With his other hand he groped the air, trying to reach Jake's other fist which was cocked back like the hammer on a loaded six-shooter, poised to strike; failing in that, he wrapped both hands around the fist pressed against his mid-section. It was a gesture of tender surrender, an abductee's adoring acquiescence to the instrument and the *fait accompli* of her undoing.

"Hell no! We finish, *then* we rest," Jake barked. "You finished, motherfucker?"

Frankie nodded. His head falling forward, his forehead brushing against Jake's crewcut, Frankie West was defeated.

Jake butted Frankie's head away. "You stay away from my friend, you bullying son-of-a-bitch?"

Frankie grunted assent. As he slid down, slowly like a gob of bloody spit, to the dirty floor, his soggy sweat shirt caught on the rough bricks and bunched up like foreskin under his arms and across his chest. When his butt touched the dirty floor, he let his head fall back against the wall. The light from a little window near the ceiling lit his pain-stricken face. It was then that Billy noticed how emaciated Frankie was and that Arthur—his big sad face thrust into the window niche, framed by weeds out of reach of the all-leveling mower blades—was peering down at Frankie and ... at Billy.

15

It was the Sabath, hot and humid. At one end, the hard rough-hewn chair on which Billy sat was having his ass for Sunday dinner. At the other end, his swollen face, half-in and half-out of the shade of a large colorful umbrella, was so dark and discolored you couldn't tell shiner from shadow.

The canvas umbrella was one of several that, thrusting up through wooden tables bordering a grassy area by the pool at Magnolia Park, looked like humongous jungle flowers or gaudy surreal mushrooms sprung up in the steamy heat of the early-afternoon sunlight. The tall surrounding trees, densely packed together, appeared to have been shoved out of the way to make room for the tables and the umbrellas and the grass—their remaining, un-pruned limbs had the air of being pulled back in horror of being sullied by the intruders.

Spread out on the grass, three young women in bikinis were sunbathing. Struggling not to look in their direction, Billy shifted his gaze between the dance pavilion across the pool—where Jake was bussing the small tables that encircled the dance floor—and the bar extending over the dam-waterfall at the far end of the pool. The bar and the pavilion, built in a niche cut for them out of the high north bank of Flagon Creek, or Cold Bayou as some people call it, were added to the park in the thirties at the end of Prohibition. His eyes compromised by the bright sunlight and the pummeling Frankie gave them the day before, Billy could barely see the dark form he knew was Jake's moving around in the unlit pavilion.

The three young women, lying on towels on the short grass, were being overtaken by the encroaching shadows of the vengeful trees. Parts of oily, sweaty arms, legs, and backs glistened in the rays shining through the dense foliage of cypress, oak, and, higher up on the steep north bank of the creek, pine. Ever so often Billy's head swung in the self-proscribed direction. His battered eyes swept, like a brace of mangy morose scavenger birds reconnoitering carrion, along the line of their buttocks, a neat row of notched hillocks.

This cheeky assemblage, this cocky troika of cannons abreast, this trio of up-jutting mounds dappled with sun and shadow like the knuckles of a camouflaged fist, seemed to be beaming back at Billy as good as they got, causing the virgin-voyeur-victim to wince and turn his head away from this feline Cerberus, this six-domed Demiurge of degeneracy.

As the sunlight crept across his face, the pleasure of its warmth gradually outweighed the discomfort of the rough-hewn wooden chair and he dozed off from time to time; his uneasy thoughts gave way to erratic dream-like images of the kind that sometimes pop in and out of the mind's eye in the intermediate state between sleep and wakefulness. So that his pre-sleep musings—these switched back and forth between deciphering Brother Johnson's sermon and untying bikini strings using only his teeth—were replaced each time he dipped below the threshold of sleep by a plague of pestering pictures: fists, battered faces streaming blood and contorted with rage, and basketballs zooming in like Texas-sized asteroids toward his face. Driven by the barrage of menacing mirages and intimidating images, he popped back up through the sphincter of sleep into the real world, his whole body jerking like a galvanized frog leg or a freshly-aborted embryo. He had not slept well the night before.

Snatched into full awareness by a particularly forceful spasm, Billy was surprised to hear voices nearby. He sat up. Charlie West, wearing bathing trunks, and Jimmy Garrard, in shirt-and-tie, were sitting a couple of tables over. I must have been asleep when they came over, Billy thought. Charlie and Jimmy seemed not to have noticed him.

"Any trouble getting it?" Charlie asked.

"Piece a cake," Jimmy said. "What are you gonna do with it?"

"Haven't decided yet. Where is it now?" Charlie glanced over at the three women and around at Billy. "No, on second thought, don't tell me. I'll call you later. Better yet, I'll drop by your place."

"Your cousin looked like somebody's little sister in the gym yesterday, Charl," Jimmy said. "Today he must look like a train hit him."

Jimmy and Charlie, flanked by the three nearly naked women and the wincing and crestfallen Billy, glanced across the pool from time to time to where Jake was emptying ashtrays, clearing off beer bottles, dirty dishes, and uneaten food. To Billy's jaundiced eye, they appeared to be affecting the air of two aristocratic rakes idly watching the inconsequential muddling of a plebe at work.

"I told you, don't call me Charl. It's a dead give-away." Charlie again looked over his shoulder at Billy. This time he nodded. It was both a greeting and a way of calling Jimmy's attention to a potential audience to their conversation.

"Look at my little brother over there. Slaving away."

"I hear he got kicked out of cop school." Charlie glanced across the pool and then back at Billy.

"Yeah. Now he has my old job. I'm sure he'll be better at it than I was. If 'Uncle Toe' told him to eat shit he'd do it."

"Hey! What's come over our born-again Christian?"

"I gave that up."

"So you keep saying, but a person couldn't tell it by the way you carried on in church this morning."

"You were there! What were you doing? Spying on me?"

"Just wanted to see the beast in its natural environment. What's going on with you? You go through more changes than a girl getting ready for her first date."

"What you saw this morning was just a show ... I used to have hopes of ... plundering Dixie's treasure trove. Now I just do it to piss her off."

"Looked pretty convincing to me. You wanted to impress *someone* with your religious fervor, but I don't think it was Dixie. You may have thought it was her in the beginning, when you first went off the deep end with that religious stuff. But that was just you fighting the inevitable. What ... you start out thinking your love for Jesus was purely ... what? Platonic? Spiritual? Next thing you know you're jacking off to crucifixion pictures. Then you had to tell yourself that if you played at both ends of the court, you weren't *really* ... ." Charlie reached for a cigarette from the pack on the table. "I told you, Jimbo, just because *I* swing both ways doesn't mean you have to, too. You don't even realize who you were putting on that show for this morning, do you?"

"Okay, Dr. Freud, who do you think I was trying to impress?"

"Let me put it this way: Who were you kneeling down in front of an hour or so ago? I don't think it was the Holy Spirit 'moving in your heart'. The only thing moving was further down, in your pants." Charlie nodded toward a large manila envelope on the table. "Take a look at those." When Jimmy had looked at the photos in the envelope, Charlie said, "Now tell me those turn you on more than what was a few inches from your face just before noon today."

"Okay, okay! I just happen to like 'em well-endowed." Jimmy blushed and then gestured toward the photos. "You have to admit she looks good. How'd you ever talk her into letting you do it?"

"Not hard, I assure you."

"Did you ... ?"

"Get serious. Frankie find out ... well ... ." Charlie shook his head. "With her ego ... and her temper ... she wouldn't be able to keep quiet about it. First big fight they had and out it'd come."

Who do you think you're kidding, Billy thought. She wouldn't fuck you if you were the last man alive, you pimply freak.

"Too bad about Frankie. He used to be some kind a hunk. What happened to him? Why did he let himself get like that?"

"Booze and cigarettes is what did it." Charlie lit the cigarette with his Zippo. "The reason he started drinking ... ? His marriage, I guess. Or at least that's his lame excuse. He's very jealous. He fucks anything that moves ... ."

"Nothing wrong with that."

". . . You sound like your brother ... but let her be five minutes late coming home from work and it's a federal case. He always thinks she's cheating on him. Nothing'll drive a person into adultery quicker than that."

"You think she made it with LeBeaux?"

"No question." Charlie again glanced back at Billy. Under his breath, he said, "With him and *for* him, if you know what I mean."

Billy blinked several times and shook his head, as much to make Charlie think he wasn't eavesdropping as to wake himself up. He didn't know what to do. Should he say something? Should he go over to Charlie and Jimmy's table? Under a bridge out of a Monet painting, two little girls were playing in the water flowing over the dam at the shallow end of the pool. Or should he just cross back over to the other side of the creek and go home? On the bridge, blocking his escape, were two large women standing watch over the little girls like mother bears guarding their cubs; Billy didn't relish having to pass that close to anyone, not with his face messed up the way it was. Should he wait for Charlie and Jimmy to invite him over? The little girls darted through the shiny membrane of the waterfall, disappearing, hiding in the dark space behind the dam. He should just get up and go over and sit down at their table like it was no big deal. The little girls burst back through the curtain of water, shrieking and giggling over the dull roar of the perpetually moving spill. Why should he care what two fat women—they probably hadn't even taken their kids to church this morning—thought about his blood-shot eyes—otherwise they wouldn't have been able to be at the park so early—or his puffed-up lips—unless they were from out-of-town and had rented a cabin for the week—he could always tell them you should have seen the other guy, but that would be a lie.

"You want my opinion," Charlie said, "Frankie's main trouble is he's living in the past. Even he knows that his life will never again be as exciting as it was when he was playing basketball. That's all he was ever good for. He's hoping to get a job with the Sheriff's Department, but he has a record and that may stand in the way. By the way, did you get your hands on the results of those tests?"

"Tests? I didn't know there was more than one."

"He's had a bunch done lately, but you know the one I mean."

"Right. Yes, I managed to get my hands on it."

"And ... ?"

"It says he's shooting blanks."

"When will he know?"

"Mailed on Friday. He probably got it yesterday afternoon .... First my little brother uses him as a punching bag ... then he goes home and that good news is waiting for him. Yesterday wasn't old Franko's best day."

"My heart is breaking. I say Frankie had it coming, what Jake did to him," Charlie said. "There's no excuse for hitting someone in the face with a basketball like that. It was a cheap shot. I don't care what Billy did to provoke it." He glanced around at Billy. "Look at his face, for Christ's sake. I oughta go thank Jake."

One of the three sunbathers raised her head and looked at Billy. She seemed to be scrutinizing him, studying his face. Remembering what that face looked like, Billy looked away. She looked like she was about to wave, he thought, like she wanted to send me a message. Maybe my face is so messed up she can't tell who I am. Maybe she thinks I'm someone else. He looked back and was pretty sure she smiled faintly but then she turned away and laid her head back down, using her folded arms as a pillow.

"Actually, he did pretty well considering the shape he's in," Jimmy said. "Frankie, I mean. It might have turned out different if he was in better conditioning. Maybe if he hadn't lost so bad to that colored guy ... ." He looked around at Billy for the first time. His expression reminded Billy again that his own face was a mutilated mask of gaudy bruises.

Jimmy turned back, his head and shoulders shuddering as if he were chilled. After a pause, he said, "That guy was good, wasn't he? And hung, too."

Seeing Jimmy's reaction to Billy, Charlie glanced back at Billy. He frowned and faced forward again. After a couple of beats he tuned back into the conversation. "Maybe. Frankie has a big hang-up when it comes to coloreds. The worse he feels about himself, the more he hates them. Same with women. Things go well, he's as charming as you please. But when he's down, he pouts, picks fights, acts like a real prick. Only he's not acting."

Charlie looked again at Billy. "You okay, Mayden? Come sit with us." Billy didn't move. "Frankie didn't mean it, you know. For what it's worth he likes you about as much as he's capable of liking anyone besides himself. Let me put it this way: He hates you less than most. I see you've fixed your glasses." When he added, "What's that, adhesive tape?" Jimmy snorted.

The same young woman looked again at Billy.

"Who are those women?" Charlie had noticed the woman looking at Billy.

"They work for some associates of my old boss, Theo Jeannsonne," Jimmy said.

"What kind of work do they do?"

"You really don't know? They're from New Orleans. That tell you anything?"

"What are they doing here?"

"Getting fixed, probably. Plus working. There's that party tomorrow night and some folks like to start early."

"Hey, why don't y'all move over there where there's more sun?" Charlie asked the women.

One of the women raised her head and said, "The grass is thicker here."

"Makes a better bed, eh?" Charlie leered.

The woman turned away and nestled her head on her arms.

Billy got up and went over to Charlie and Jimmy's table. "Where's Frankie's cabin?"

"Watch, I'll show you." Pointing, his hand moving up, past the lush foliage of the trees skirting the deep end of the pool, and over, through an opening in the shadows of the tall pines on the hillside on the other side of the creek, Charlie said, "See that blue roof through the trees over there?" Waiting for Billy to nod, he gestured upstream. "His cabin is the next one up thata way."

Jimmy stood up as Billy was sitting. "Well, I gotta go. See you at the party tomorrow night?"

"Does Mary love Jesus ... ?"

Standing close behind Charlie, Jimmy looked over at the sunbathing women. None of them looked his way. He put his hand on Charlie's head and ruffled his greasy hair. "Stay loose, Charlene," he said and walked away, wiping his hand on the front of his shirt.

"Let's go for a swim," Charlie said after Jimmy had gone.

"Yeah, sure. I'll just strip butt-naked right here in front of everybody."

"Hey! It's me, Billy. It wasn't me that beat you up. Don't take it out on me." Charlie stood up. Jogging toward the deep end of the pool, he looked over his shoulder. "Come on, man. Come keep me company, anyway."

Billy stood up and walked in Charlie's direction. Taking off his shoes and sitting on the edge of the pool with his feet dangling in the cold water, he watched Charlie climb the ladder to the diving board. Bouncing high off the board, Charlie dove into the cold brown water.

"Good dive!" One of the three young women yelled when Charlie had surfaced and swam over to where Billy was sitting. It was not the one who had been looking at Billy a few minutes earlier.

"Let's go talk to those girls, Billy."

"They're too ... old." Billy put his socks and shoes back on over wet feet.

"Too old for what? They're probably younger than you are. Come on."

The young woman who had complimented Charlie on his dive moved over and made room for him on her towel. "I'm Charlie." He pointed a hitch-hiker's thumb over his shoulder: "That's Billy."

To Billy it looked like Charlie was calling him out at home plate. He probably would just as soon I left, he thought, and, with feigned indifference, he looked toward the bridge over the waterfall.

"Billy Mayden. What's left of him."

Billy squatted a few feet away. Feeling self-conscious about the dark bruises on his face, he looked down and then away from the young women.

"You guys hear the one about the dog that ran under the train?" Charlie asked.

"Us *guys*? No, we haven't. Least I haven't," one of the women said.

"There was this dog, see. He wants to get across the tracks real bad. There's a girl dog over there he wants to ... , you know. But there's a train on the track."

"Is it moving?" one of the other women asked.

"Is what moving?"

"The train."

"Yeah. Wouldn't be any joke if the train wasn't moving. Anyhow, the dog darts under the train. He gets all the way across the tracks, but the train cuts off the tip of his tail."

"What happened to the girl dog?" The first woman asked.

The woman who had looked at Billy hadn't spoken yet. She didn't seem to be paying any attention to Charlie's joke. She stole a glance at Billy.

"What girl dog?"

"You said ... ,"

"Never mind what I said. Forget about the girl dog. The dog sees the part of his tail that got cut off under the train. So he goes back to get it. This time the train cuts off his head. Know what the moral is?"

Charlie squeezed one of the huge pimples on the back of his neck and looked at the pus on his fingers. Then he sniffed the pus and wiped it on the towel.

The two women listening to the joke looked at each other. One of them shrugged her shoulders. They smiled in mild disbelief. "No, what is the moral?" They seemed more amused than disgusted.

"Don't lose your head over a little piece of tail."

The women laughed. Billy stood up. He started toward the bridge.

"Where you going, Billy?" Charlie said. He got off the ground and ran after Billy. When he had caught up to him, he put his arm around his shoulder, made him stop walking. "Going to see your friend Jake? Whatsa matter? Don't you like the company? You don't really *like* that guy, do you?"

"He's alright," Billy said, remembering the fight. "I can't believe you told that joke to those girls."

"Why not? It was just a joke."

"I'm sure God will forgive you. I'll see you later, Charlie."

The sunbather who had looked at Billy sat up. She said something to her two companions and stood up. Picking up her towel, she overtook and passed Billy before he got to the bridge across the creek. She looked back at Billy twice, once before she reached the bridge and once while she was crossing over it to the other side of the creek.

Crossing back over, Billy stopped in the middle of the bridge and looked down at the water spilling over the dam. The two little girls playing there had been joined by three others; ten blue lips shivered with cold. This place will be a mad house in an hour or so, Billy thought, when Sunday dinners and naps are done. He wondered where the two mothers had gone; probably to the bar to drink beer. Should he hang around to make sure the little girls were okay, at least until more people showed up? No, what would it look like, him with his Halloween face, loitering around little kids like that.

Billy remembered being at church earlier. The object of much concern among the perfumed and dressed-up women, he had little heart for trying to explain without lying what had happened to him. After church, not wanting more of the same—Stella had alternately glared at and fussed over his facial injuries from the moment she saw them—and feeling nauseated at the prospect of chicken and dumplings floating in yellow chicken fat, he told his mother he wasn't hungry. That was not a lie then and was still true now. Vetoing the notion that maybe he should get something to eat anyway, he turned his thoughts to Brother Johnson's sermon:

Brother Johnson shouted to the congregation: "A man came up to me

the other day ... a member of this church ... and this man said to me
... ." Then he lowered his voice to hoarse confidential whisper, "'Tell me,
Brother Jay, if there is so much sin in New Orleans ... in that modern-day
Sodom and Gomorrah ... that Den of Inequity ... that Great House of
Satan Himself ... ,'" back to shouting, "'If there is so much sin there, why
didn't God just leave you there where you were?'" Then in his normal loud
voice, "'Why didn't he let you fight the Devil *there*? In his own bailiwick,
in his own domain? Why would God send you to *Tioga*? There ain't no
heroin *here*! There ain't no devil weed for our kids to get hooked on *here*!
There ain't no whores and pimps and gigolos *here* to wreck our homes
and destroy our marriages! Not here, there ain't. There ain't no perverts to
insinuate themselves into our lives and to shatter our morals! Not *here* in
Tioga! There ain't no strip joints and porno factories here, where women
debase themselves and open wide the Gates of Hell to suck in the hard-
working men of our community to their eternal damnation.

"'There's no place *here* where the consequences of prideful lust can
be gouged out with a coat-hanger ... no place where innocent, helpless
unborn children are murdered in their mother's womb ... children that our
Most Precious Father, heedless of their own selfish desires, but mindful of
their immortal souls, gave these women to love and bring up as Christians
soldiers in the war against Satan. Not in *Tioga*!'

"This man and plenty of others like him, and women, too, seem to
believe that because there are so many of what they consider *horrible*
sinners ... over *there* ... down *there* ... up North ... in the big city ... in
Baton Rouge ... in New Orleans ... in New York City ... in Moscow ... in
Communist China ... always in some *other* place ... that where they live
is somehow *immune* to sin ... that, compared to those *other* places, where
they live is a veritable Garden of Eden ... that those *other* places are so bad
that they must keep Satan so busy that he won't have *time* to come into
their town, into *their* community, into *their* congregation, into *their* homes,
into *their* hearts, into their *bedrooms*.

"Steeped in our sinful Pride, we are blind to our own shortcomings.
And this allows us to think that somehow we are better than your dope-
dealers, your prostitutes, your pimps, your gigolos, your strippers, and
your ho-mo-sexuals."

"Amen!" someone yelled. It was Jimmy Garrard.

"And I say to you this morning, these *are* terrible things. Drugs,
prostitution, homosexuality, and strip-joints are all terrible things.
Abortion is a terrible thing. But there are some sins that are even worse
than these terrible things. And these sins that are even worse than these
terrible things are committed ... not by drug dealers ... not by prostitutes

and pimps and gigolos ... not by homosexuals ... not by strip teasers ... not by untrained butchers wielding coat-hangers ... but by people like the man who accosted me ... by people who *believe* that they are *Christians!* By people who go to church every Sunday morning and every Sunday night and who wouldn't dream of missing a Wednesday Night Prayer Meeting. By people who tithe. By people who stand up in church and offer up some of the most beautiful, most pious-sounding prayers you would ever want to hear, prayers that bring tears to your eyes. People who can sing our sacred hymns so beautifully it sends your heart soaring up to Heaven. By people who *look* and *sound* like true Christians. In fact they look and sound so much like real Christians that you and I cannot tell them apart from *really* true, honest-to-God, born-again believers who will most certainly someday be with Our Savior in Heaven. The only people who can tell them from real Christians are the people who see them late on a Saturday night, in the wee hours of a Sunday morning, in places that should *not* be allowed to *exist* in a Christian Community. But then *those* people don't care if they're Christians or Buddhists or, what is closer to what they really are: Worshipers of the Devil Himself. *They* don't care about their *souls.* All *they* care about is their *money.*"

"Amen." Jimmy Garrard again.

"But these so-called Christians will never see the Throne of God. They will never live in a Heavenly mansion. They will never feel the nail-holes in Jesus's hands, or feel the scars from the wounds in His side and on His precious brow. No sir! These so-called Christians will burn in hell, right along with Judas ... and Pontius Pilate ... and King Herod ... and Adolph Hitler ... and Joseph Stalin ... and *Martin Luther King!*

"'Why, Preacher?' you ask. 'What have these people done that is *so* bad? How bad can they *be* if, as you say, they go to church ... if they tithe ... if they offer up beautiful prayers to God in the presence of *real* Christians ... and us *true* Christians can't even tell that they are *not* true Christians, just like ourselves? And even if they do stray a bit now and then on a Saturday night, is not God a merciful God? Didn't Jesus forgive even the thief on the cross?

"Well, folks, I won't keep you in suspense. These so-called Christians will burn in Hell for eternity *not* for what they do in the *bars* and *brothels* on Saturday but for what they do *in church* every Sunday morning. For what they do *in church* every Sunday night. For what they do *in church* every Wednesday night at Prayer Meeting. Because all these other praiseworthy things that they do ... things like tithing and offering up beautiful prayers and singing beautiful hymns, prayers and songs that inspire us to praise God for His wonderful bounty ... they do just so they will *appear* pious in the eyes of their fellow men. They do all these *wonderful* things because they *believe* other people look at them all dressed up on Sunday morning and think, 'Oh! Brother So-and-so is such a *fine* man.' As they *pretend* to pray to God on Wednesday night, with their heads bowed and their eyes closed, they *imagine* that other people sneak a peek at them and say, 'Look at Sister So-and-so. She is such a *good* woman.'

"These people know that by *acting* like Christians they can fool other people. But that's not the worst of it. The worst of them have worked out a way to fool *themselves*, because there is a place where the worst kind of sinner actually believes he can *hide from God!* It is a place he goes every chance he gets, a shameful place he *knows* is wrong for other people to go to, but he has somehow twisted things around in his mind so that is okay for *him* to go there. Where is this evil place? What does the skin-deep Christian do there? That place is his *heart* and what he does there is *love himself*. That's right! He loves himself to the exclusion of all else. You might even say he makes love *to* himself. For the pleasure he gets by going there is as worldly and as intense as *carnal pleasure* could ever be. For he only does it when he is *alone*. Or *thinks* he is, because we are *never* alone. God is always there. For he does it, not in the bright sunlight of the Sabbath morning or even the dim red lights of Saturday night, but in the muck and murk and mire of the pit of prideful privacy and the cesspool of self-centered secrecy, under the cover of the most utter Darkness, the Darkness of the human heart ... .

"Well, let me tell you now, good people, no amount of praying and singing and tithing; no amount of money spent on expensive clothes to cover weak and lustful bodies—money that *could* be given, that *should* be given, to God's church and used for God's work—will ever hide from Almighty God the *corruption* and *hypocrisy* that is in the human heart. For it says in the Bible, *Jeremiah*, Chapter 17, verse 9: *The heart is deceitful above all things and desperately wicked: who can know it?*"

Brother Johnson paused and wiped the sweat off his face with a big white handkerchief. He looked out over the congregation. "Well, friends, the Bible is the Word of God, so God knows what is in the deceitful, the *hypocritical*, human heart, and God hates *hypocrisy* more than he hates *murder*. More than he hates *rape*. More than fornication. More than adultery. More than thievery. More than dishonesty. Even more than blasphemy."

"Amen! Amen!"

Poor Jimmy, Billy thought, he doesn't know that Baptists only say amen at the end of prayers, never in the middle of the sermon.

"And what does God hate almost as much as hypocrisy? Do you know, my friends? Do you know what the twin sister of hypocrisy is? It is *pride*.

These fine people, these counterfeit-Christians, are guilty of the twin sins of *pride* and *hypocrisy*. Pride and hypocrisy. The song they sing on the radio and the television says *love* and *marriage* go together like a horse and carriage. Well, let me tell you, *brother*, pride and hypocrisy go together like the two halves of that horse's rear-end. And the people in that carriage, you and me and all the other decent folks, have to look at that ugly mess every Sunday as it comes slinking out of the swamps and fleshpots of Saturday night. And *God* is not fooled by these hypocrites, these proud peacocks that parade before you each and every Sunday in their fashionable clothes and their pious expressions and their perfumes that they hope will cover the stench of their debauchery.

"And now these same people have started implying in so many words that I ... accusing your preacher behind his back ... that I ... who God called to bring His Word to your community ... that I have knowingly and deliberately brought individuals into our very midst who are poisoning our families ... individuals who *they* say should have been left in the gutter where I found them ... in the gutter where *they* say they deserved to be in the first place ... in the gutter where *they* say they were destined to end up from the day they were conceived in sin and born out-of-Holy-wedlock. And, according to these same people who presume to judge ... these Pharisees, these Sadducees, who think that they can usurp the power of God Himself ... these serpents who come sneaking up to me after church and in-*sin*-uate that they know what's best for this community ... according to these people, when a young man is called away, it is God's way of punishing him for his sins and we shouldn't mourn that young man's passing. They say that if there is living amongst us a talented and beautiful woman who was raised in another faith and whose folks are of another nationality, we should shun her and exclude her from our fellowship, lest her talent and beauty and her papist past seduce and pollute us and bring us down to her level. These same people whisper behind your preacher's back that he, your preacher, is being punished through his family ... his own beloved wife and his own flesh-and-blood daughter who sang that inspirational old hymn, *The Old Rugged Cross*, a while ago. *They* say that we, the Johnson family, is being punished for helping this fine young man and this fine talented woman and others like them in their hour of trouble and need and misguided faith. *They* say that by helping them I and my own wife and daughter have been corrupted and are corrupting others.

"If you ask these hypocrites: '*Why* do you think you are better than this unfortunate young man who God has seen fit to take back to Himself? *Why* do you think you are better than this brave woman who is seeking to abandon her wicked ways and find solace in our midst?' If you ask them this, they'll pound their chest and pat themselves on the back, practically throwing their arms out of socket, and say, 'Why, Preacher, it is *because* I haven't done the terrible things that *they* have done or believed the evil things they have believed, that God has *made* me more fortunate than them. My material blessings are *proof* of God's favor.' To justify this monumental self-regard, they even go so far as to espouse the papist heresy that the fate of each and every one of us was determined once and for all on the Day of Creation, and that, if, *unlike themselves*, a man is not already saved, there is nothing that he can do that will change one whit the fact that he is going to Hell ... a belief that is diametrically, diabolically opposed to *John* 3:16.

"Well, let me tell you this morning, it is the *Devil* who uses worldly goods to win men's souls, *not* God. *God* couldn't care less about whether your car is bigger than your neighbor's or whether your wife has all the modern appliances in her kitchen or whether you have a television set or not."

"Amen, Brother Johnson, amen!" People looked around and frowned at Jimmy Garrard, but he kept his eyes on the preacher and seemed not to notice the irritation he was causing.

"John 3:16 clearly states that God so loved the world that He gave His only begotten Son that whosoever *believeth in Him* shall *not* perish but will have *everlasting life.* There's nothing in John three-sixteen, or any place else in the Bible, that says that you can not be saved *even* if you *murdered* someone, *even if you killed an innocent child.*"

"Amen!"

"There's nothing in that most holy of verses or anywhere else in God's sacred Word that says Adolph *Hitler* himself could not have been saved, if, before he died, he believed in God ... . I don't care how many Jews he killed."

"Amen!"

"Now I know a lot of you good folks are gonna disagree with what I'm about to say, but I believe that John three-sixteen even applies to coloreds. That's how merciful *my* God is. I've heard it said that a nigger is like a pig: You can wash a pig and dress him up, but he's still gonna be a pig. Well, my God is so powerful and merciful that if that pig was *capable* of believing in God *in his heart*, that pig—and we all know people like that pig, black *and* white—that pig would go to Heaven, no matter how dirty he was.

"But, ladies and gentlemen, there is nothing in that verse or anywhere else in the Holy Bible that says that if you believe in God He will give you a bigger paycheck or a bigger house to live in.

"Now I'm gonna ask our accompanist, Mrs. Vonderheim, to play and the choir to sing, very softly, *Just As I Am.*"

As soon as the music started, Jimmy Garrard went up to the front of the church and knelt in front of the preacher. The preacher acted like he didn't see him. Baptists don't bow before *any* man, Billy thought. Doesn't Jimmy know that?

"You say to me," Brother Johnson continued in a softer, less preachy tone, "Preacher, I believe. I've accepted Christ as my Savior. Where do I go from *here*? What do I do *now*? How should I live my life? What should I do when I see people sinning all around me? What should I do when the bad things that people do threaten me … my family … my community … my country … my very Way of Life?' The answer is this: Ask yourself this one question: 'What would Christ do if *He* was in my place?' After all, *that* is what He became a man of flesh and blood and came to this earth for: To set an example for us as human beings … as creatures of flesh and blood … with all the potential for greed and lust and duplicity and immorality that is inherent in our fallen state as descendants of that evil woman Eve and poor old gullible Adam … as creatures who by our very nature are mired like maggots in the corruption … the putrefaction … the rotten slime of this world. Jesus came to this earth to set an *example* for how we should live out our allotted span in this evil place. You must remember that we follow Jesus's example not for salvation … salvation is not something we can earn by good works or by anything we *do*, other than believing in Him … but to have peace of mind and to enjoy to the fullest the serenity that comes to us when the salvation and the divine Grace of God, that comes with surrendering our hearts and minds to Him, is bestowed upon us.

"Now, what is the one thing that Christ did … the one quality than even atheists and agnostics acknowledge He exemplified most … that is the best guarantee for earthly joy? He *forgave*. *Jesus forgave*. Jesus had for*give*ness for *all* sinners. So, if you would be Christ-like, then forgive those that trespass against you."

While he was saying these words about forgiveness, Brother Johnson glanced down and frowned a couple of times at Jimmy Garrard who was still kneeling in front of him.

"But you say, 'Preacher, you mean I should forgive *every*body? No matter who they are and what they have done?' And I say, Jesus loved everybody. He never said He loved some people more than others. He didn't set up some big fancy church … and most of you know what church I'm talking about … ," he pointed in the direction of the offending church for those who didn't know, " … a church for rich people to go to to show off their wealth and refined taste in fashion … and this … ," drawing a circle in the air, he encompassed all those present, " … smaller, humbler church for the rest of us. He ministered to the so-called dregs of society, the so-called scum of the earth. He didn't think He was better than them. He Who Was Without Sin laid down His life for everybody. He gave His All. He gave the very flesh and blood of His precious body for everybody. *Every* body. *Ev-er-ry* body! That is why, when we celebrate the Lord's Supper, we eat His flesh and drink His blood."

As he finished speaking, the preacher took Jimmy Garrard's head into his hands like it was a melon he was about to slice and serve. He put his lips close to Jimmy's ear and appeared to whisper something. At which point Jimmy got up and ran out of the church.

$$* \qquad * \qquad *$$

On the other side, Billy walked along the concrete apron of the pool past the wooden steps that ran the length of the canopied dance floor. Rounding the corner at the end of the pavilion, he collided with Jake who was coming down the long set of stairs that went up to the parking lot at the top of the hill where a big pick-up bin for garbage was kept.

"Hey, motherfucker!" Jake said. He had dropped the empty garbage can he was carrying and, squared off and fists raised, he was ready to fight. Seeing it was Billy, he lowered his arms. "Watch where the fuck you're going."

Seeing Jake's bruised, discolored face up close, Billy remembered the young woman who had seemed to be studying his own face. She had crossed over ahead of him. Where had she gone?

Billy felt dizzy. He sat on the steps.

"What's wrong with you, motherfucker?" Jake said. "You look pale as a ghost."

Billy didn't answer. Jake sat next to him.

"What were you doing over there?" Jake jerked his head toward the other side of the pool.

"What do you mean what was I doing?"

"You know what I'm talking about, shithead. You were over there sucking up to that prick Charlie West and that asshole brother of mine."

"I was over there before they were, *shithead*."

"I *saw* you talking to them, prick. Don't tell me you weren't."

"I wasn't sucking up."

"Then how come you were trying to hide under that fucking umbrella, like you didn't want me to see your chickenshit ass? After what happened yesterday you must be some kind of asshole to wanna hang around with that dicklicker Charlie West."

"I wasn't hanging around him. I merely asked him where Frankie's cabin is. I figured he'd know. He's his cousin."

"That's a fucking lie. I saw you watching the motherfucker showing off on the diving board and the two of you talking to those three whores."

"He only dove one time and who says they're whores?" Thinking what Stella would think of the sheer quantity of naked flesh, Billy conceded that Jake was probably right. "And, even if they are, so what? Jesus loves everybody, even whores."

"Yeah, yeah, yeah. Why do you want to know where that bastard's cabin is? You wanta get your ass stomped some more?"

Just then, the young woman sunbather who had looked at Billy with such interest came around the corner. Smiling at Billy, she stepped between him and Jake. At the top of the steps she looked back and smiled again. Then she took the path that went in the direction Charlie said Frankie West's cabin was.

She's going to Frankie's cabin, Billy thought. Only then did it sink in that she had put her hand on his shoulder as she passed him on the stairs. She wants me to follow her.

"You see the way that bitch was smiling at me," Jake said. "I'm a good mind to say fuck this job and go up there and fuck the dogshit out of that cunt. They say whores never get enough. I get my hands on her she'll have enough, I'll guaran-damn-tee you."

"I want to go see if Frankie's okay." Billy decided the best way to handle Jake's delusional remarks was to ignore them. "Maybe apologize. Ask for his forgiveness."

"Apologize! For what? For not catching the ball with your *mouth* when he threw it at you? Or injuring his fists when he pounded on your ugly-assed face?"

"He has a lot on his mind. God loves all sinners."

"So what! That don't give him the right to take it out on you. *Let* God love the son-of-a-bitch and you won't have to. Your 'love' would be superfluous, wouldn't you say, Old Chap?"

Billy stood up. "I'll see you later, okay?

16

The cabin, in dense shade, looked dark and empty. The wind hissed in the trees overhead and, below, the roar of the waterfall was being gradually drowned out by playful noises as the pool filled up with children. Unsettled by lingering dizziness and uncertain about what he was up to, Billy looked in through the screen door into the front room of the cabin. He saw the flickering light of a television set. After several seconds, he made out three little boys sitting in wheelchairs watching a preacher pounding a pulpit.

Billy, in no mood for kids, went around to the side of the cabin and looked in the bedroom window. The grass in the front of the window had been trampled down and there was a vaguely familiar smell in the air, but if Billy noticed either of these things, they were both immediately suppressed, crowded out of his mind by what he saw inside: Frankie West was curled up on a bed, his eyes closed. The young woman who seemed to have been enticing Billy to follow her to Frankie's cabin was sitting in a wheelchair next to the bed. Looking up, she saw Billy. She stood up and motioned him around toward the front door.

"I'm glad you're here," the young woman said, holding the screen door open. She was wearing white short-shorts and a red blouse. Billy started up the steps. "Wait, let me get rid of these kids." She patted one of the little boys on the head. "You boys go somewhere else, okay? Frankie's not feeling very good. He can't watch the game with you today."

"Ain't no game on today, anyhow," one of the boys said, "It's Sunday."

The three little boys, blinking and looking up at Billy, were pale and disoriented in the outside light, reminding him of stunted cave-dwellers confronted by a mean, ugly giant.

In the cabin, in the living room, Billy stood just inside the door. The young woman motioned him to follow her to the kitchen, which was across the room from the bedroom. Standing in the doorway between the two rooms, Billy watched as the young woman opened the refrigerator. She bent over, putting a strain on the already-tight fabric of her short-shorts, spreading her buttocks apart and showing him where the fit was at its snuggest. Her rear-end aimed at him, Billy thought of a rosebud about to flower. His eyes locked onto the little crescents of soft flesh, the bottommost part of her buttocks, overflowing their over-taxed receptacle.

Still bent over, the young woman said, "You want a beer?"

Billy's glazed-over eyes shifted back and forth between her butt and her upside-down face.

"Hey, Billy! … . Like what you see?"

Surprised and thrilled that she knew his name, Billy said, "Yeah."

"Yeah what? You want a beer or you like what you see?"

Remembering the time on the school bus when the pretty girl told Jake she hoped he was getting his eyes full, Billy tried, and failed, to think of something risqué to say, lamely settling for: "Both."

Handing Billy his beer as she went past him into the living room, the young woman said, "Let's sit." Standing next to the bunk bed against the wall opposite the front door, she patted the mattress of the bottom bunk. "Here."

Billy sat where he was told. Staring through the screen door, watching the little boys discussing what to do next, he thought he recognized them. They were the kids on Frankie's team in the calamitous game the day before. Then, shocked, he realized one of them was a girl, Brother Johnson's younger daughter, Tommy Sue. Brother Johnson had wanted a son and Tommy Sue was the next best thing, a tomboy.

"How's Frankie doing?" Billy took a swig of beer and wondered again how people could drink the stuff.

"Not so good," the young woman said. She sat next to Billy. "He vomited up some blood. I tried to get him to let me drive him to the hospital, but he wouldn't do it. He took a bunch of aspirins and went to sleep."

"How come you're glad to see me?" Billy manfully took a bigger swig of beer. "And how did you know my name?"

"Frankie told me what happened yesterday. Then when I overheard you guys talking a while ago down by the pool, I realized you were the one Frankie … beat … threw the basketball at. I almost said something, but … I don't know … I didn't want to say anything in front of Frankie's cousin Charlie. Frankie's not what you'd call fond of him."

Billy took another big swallow of beer, which, aptly and not altogether unpleasantly, tasted of sin, kinda like what he imagined chilled urine from a beautiful woman might taste like. "Wadgy want to say?" Already dizzy to begin with, Billy was feeling even more woozy from the beer, and his speech was slurred.

"I wanted to tell you that Frankie feels real bad about what happened."

The young woman moved closer to Billy. Their thighs touched. "He wants to make it up to you."

"Whaya mee, makie up to me? Howsy gone do that?"

"Oh, I'm sure we can think of something." The supposed whore bumped Billy with her shoulder. Just joshing, she seemed to be saying, leaving Billy confused as to her meaning. Acutely aware of the warmth of her bare tanned thigh, he didn't say anything.

Just then Frankie stumbled into the room. Bent forward, he looked up without straightening. He looked at the empty wheelchairs, then at the young woman and Billy. "Where are my teammates?" His voice was thin as if constrained by pain.

"I told them you weren't feeling good."

"Where'd they go?" Frankie frowned and went to the front door. He looked outside. He turned back and looked at Billy. "How you doing, old buddy?"

"Funny yousha ask." Billy's head was spinning.

"Yeah, I know. I lost it up there. Tilly's gonna make it up to you."

Billy looked at the young woman.

"Short for Chantilly." The young woman bumped Billy again. Catching a whiff of her loud perfume made him even more dizzy. "My stage name is Chantilly Lace."

Frankie, moving slowly, stepped outside and stood there, motionless, as if immobilized by the bright sunlight and the din of the children's voices coming up from the pool below.

Tilly stood up and went to the door.

Looking both ways along the path, Frankie asked, "Did you see which way they went?"

"I think they went down to the pool, Frankie," the young woman said. She opened the screen door and took a step, stopping half-in and half-out. "You're not going down there, are you?"

Appearing not to hear, Frankie headed off.

"You wait here," Tilly said. "I'm going to make sure he's okay. I'll be back in a bit, okay?" She walked over and stood in front of Billy. Billy looked her up and down. Bending forward, she held Billy's head in her hands. She kissed the bruises on his face. "We're gonna make it all better. You'll see."

Tilly left, but the room was still full of her, her smell, her voice, her body. Billy could not banish from his mind the image of her in front of the refrigerator; bending over that way she had revealed … everything … the two faces of Eve. In a rush of self-pity and lust, he felt like crying. This is what Stella is always warning me about, he thought. I better get out of here before Tilly comes back.

He stood up. There it goes, he thought. His dick was stiff and painfully cramped. He would not be able to resist touching himself.

He glanced at the door. If Tilly comes back right now she'll see it. The thought of that made his dick even harder, bigger, more painful; but the apparently real possibility of her actually *seeing* it scared him. I'll go to my special place in the woods. No one will see me there.

Just then he noticed an odor. It was part locker room, part toilet, part hospital. Working on the aroused state he was already in, the odor brought to mind the little house Clinton had built by the fence in back of his property for his hunting dogs; where bathed in sweat and the stench of dogshit and—when the wind was right—the compound olfactory blessings of MacMannaman's slaughterhouse, and of the sewerage ditch at the end of Pugh Lane, Billy used to jack off. Until the ticks got so bad he had to find another place.

The odor drew him into the bedroom, to the bed Frankie had been in. The sheets and thin blanket were twisted, tattered, and grey with grime. Billy couldn't wait. He unzipped his jeans and let the prisoner out. He watched as, unconfined, his dick got longer and thicker and straighter. Then it started to curve upward. All without his touching it. It looks like a rooster crowing, he thought. It likes being out. His throat tightened.

Putting a knee on the dirty mattress and ducking under the upper bunk, he leaned across the lower bunk and pulled the window shade down. As he pulled back he thought he saw something, a face, eyes peering in at him through the gap between the shade and the window facing. But when he leaned forward to check there was nothing there. He remembered the scary eyes in the octopus picture the Faustpool girl had shown him in Theo's house.

The smells in the room began to cause Billy's throat to constrict ever tighter. Swallowing was exquisite torture. His breathing quickened. He looked down at himself. Though mesmerized by the sight of his own dick, he felt his eyes drawn toward the window. Someone else was looking at it, too! He was sure of it. Casting a quick glance toward the window, he was immediately aware of a thrilling new smell.

It wasn't a totally new smell, though. Was it déjà vu or had he smelled it before? If he had, he couldn't remember when or where. When had he first noticed it today? Had he been smelling it all along and was just now noticing it? He couldn't be sure, but he *was* sure that he had begun smelling it, or smelling it more acutely, when, right after seeing that face peering in the window, he recalled the octopus picture. Then, moments later, when he glanced a second time at the window, it had entered his awareness like an olfactory echo across the threshold of consciousness.

Surprised and pleased by the sweetness of these little self-discoveries, he was emboldened by the possibility that other eyes may be seeing and admiring what his own were now fixed on; rather than being inhibited by this idea, he felt his dick getting harder and harder. He thought: Let 'em look! There was no way he could forego the pleasure of touching himself, anyway. He dropped his jeans to his ankles. He sat on the bed. He leaned back against the wall, his body laid out in front of him. He covered himself with the damp, smelly blanket.

The very second he touched himself he heard a noise outside the window. Before he could even wonder what it was, he heard a woman's voice. "Get away from that window. Get on away from this cabin. I don't want you around here anymore."

It was Dixie Johnson!

Then he heard the front screen door opening.

"Jesus! What a dump!"

Billy lurched to his feet, pulled his jeans up. Before he could zip his fly or buckle his belt, the bedroom door started to open. He sat down on the bed and leaned forward. Doubled over, his chest flat against his thighs, he made like he was tying his shoe. When he looked up, Dixie was standing in front of him. Trying to suppress a guilty grin, he said, "Oh, hi, Dixie."

Dixie was wearing yellow shorts, sandals, and a short jacket made from alligator skin.

Billy sat up straight, which made him feel dizzy again. Crossing his arms on his lap, he watched Dixie's eyes.

"So you *are* here." Dixie glared, fists on hips.

"I was taking a nap."

"Are you sick?"

"No, I was feeling dizzy and ... ." Feeling like a convalescent on the deck of a ship at sea, he messed with the blanket; smoothing it over his legs, and pulling it up past his waist, he tucked it around his hips.

"And what?"

"And so I laid down. I followed Tilly up here."

"Who's Tilly?"

"Her full name is Chantilly Lace."

"So, *that*'s what she calls herself. Why's someone like you messing with something like that?"

"I wasn't messing with her."

"And you won't in the future. I told her to stay away from here, away from you."

Billy looked down at his hands. Was it Tilly Dixie was yelling at before she came inside? His fingers were interlaced, forming a zig-zag valley between two rows of white knuckles. Why would Tilly be looking in the window? Here's the church, here's the steeple. He leaned forward and touched his lips to the steeple. If it was Tilly, did she see what he was doing to himself? He raised up and turned his still-interlocked hands over. Look inside and here's the people. He saw his fingers, lined up, like facing like, jammed inside his meshed hands. The digits were red, swollen with trapped blood. His eyes crossed, doubling the number of people. He leaned forward, put his hands between his knees. He pressed his knees together, squeezing the little congregation, turning them purple. He began pounding his knees together against the backs of his hands, punishing the proliferating parishioners.

Billy looked up. "What did you mean, someone like me? What am I like?"

"You're about the only good ... adult I know, Billy. You're innocent. You have a good soul. You have been a good friend to Frankie and me. You're not like 'Daddy'." She wiggled her index fingers on either side of her face. "You make being good seem like a good thing. You're *happy* in your goodness." Dixie squatted in front of Billy. She put her hands on his knees, made them stop moving. "Oh, I know you're hurting, Billy. I know how much you like that sorry so-and-so. Or *did* ... ." Slipping her hands around his, she gently urged his hands apart and placed his palms on his knees. She stood up and sat on the bed next to Billy. She took his face into her hands and kissed his bruises. "I know how you feel. He's done the same to me more than once. But he'll never do it again. You look awful."

"Thanks." About to cry again, Billy didn't mean to sound sarcastic.

"Oh, Billy! I didn't mean ... . I guess I could've put it better. I heard what happened. I know you must really be hurt by it. I mean, more than just ... the physical ... . But he *does* like you. For what *that*'s worth. And *you* like *him*. No matter what happened up there, Frankie West will always like you."

"He has a funny way of showing it." Fighting back tears, Billy snorted and emitted an agitated laugh.

"I know. He's like a little kid who destroys things when he gets mad. You ought to be able to understand that, though. Right, Billy? It's like ... when the game wasn't going the way you wanted ... you started trying ... doing things ... to ruin the game for everybody else, right? Isn't that the same thing? Not as bad, but the same *kind* of thing."

"Who told you that?"

"I have my sources." Dixie knuckled her lip against her teeth and absently chewed on it from the inside.

"Was it Crystal?"

Dixie snapped to. "No it was Jimmy Garrard. Anyway, Frankie feels humiliated by what happened. As well he should."

"You mean him losing the fight?"

"Yeah, that too, but I meant what he did to you. I'm sure he feels terrible about hurting you. He's got to know what a cowardly thing it was."

"Has Jimmy been following you around?"

"Yeah, I thought he'd gotten over it when me and Frankie got married, but it's started up again. In fact it's worse than it's ever been. I've tried to make it as clear as I could that I didn't want to have anything to do with him. But Jimmy sees only what he wants to see.

"He says it isn't sex he wants. Says he only wants to 'serve' me. His feelings for me are 'noble' and 'exalted.' He 'worships' me. 'From afar.' He looks upon me as a 'Great Lady' and he wants to be my 'lowly knight.' I don't know how, but this is supposed to make him a better person. As long as he is 'chaste'. The man's coo-coo." She stopped wiggling her fingers and drew invisible circles around her ear. "A pervert."

"Doesn't it scare you, him acting so crazy?" Unable to bear looking at Dixie, Billy looked at his hands. His feelings for Dixie were exactly as she had described Jimmy's.

"A little, I guess. But, you know, I think it's all a show. I can't quite put my finger on it, but it's like it's meant to impress someone else ... himself maybe ... but not me."

Out of the corner of his eye, Billy saw Dixie raise her leather-sandaled feet. She seemed to be inspecting her toes. Billy's gaze moved steadily from her painted toenails to her freckled knees, followed the crevice formed by her thighs to the bulge in her tight yellow shorts. With great effort, he managed to look at her face. His eyes followed the line of her profile. The clear skin of her forehead. The slightly hooked nose. The full red lips, their color natural, no lipstick. When his eyes came to the shell of her ear, he heard roaring in his own ears. As his gaze slid down her long, slender neck, his throat squeezed shut like a fist.

Unable to breathe, he looked away. Gazing straight ahead, he tried in vain to recall what they had been talking about. Sensing that she had turned and was looking at him, he could not turn toward her. His neck was stiff, the head-turning muscles working at cross-purposes. His head felt like a heavy stone, delicately balanced. It felt like it could easily tip over, fall off his body, and roll across the floor.

He thought he saw her head moving toward his. The smell of her perfume made him dizzy, dizzier. He caught a whiff of her breath, felt it grazing his cheek. Any second now she would snuggle her face against his neck. The fist in his throat tightened, bringing tears to his eyes. He trembled, sending a tear rocketing down his cheek and onto his hand.

He threw his head back and saw the dark spots on the underside of the mattress of the top bunk. Catching a whiff of urine, he fell backwards, hitting his head against the wall.

Dixie gasped with surprise, then gave out an embarrassed little laugh. She looked back at Billy. "Are you okay?"

As the pain in his skull subsided, Billy thought, why did I do that? She was going to kiss me. Wasn't she?

A sinking sense came over him that what he was about to do was *very* ill-advised.

Yes, trying to kiss Dixie Johnson now would be madness. But it was madness whose time had come. If he didn't do something quickly, he'd miss his chance, maybe the only one he'd ever get. (Thank goodness he wasn't as drunk as he was that time before.)

Pushing himself back up into a sitting position and propping on hyper-extended arms, he let his weight rest on the heels of his hands on the mattress. Slightly behind her, out of sight, all he had to do was lean over and forward a little, and he could kiss her before she knew what he was up to.

Suddenly, he remembered: His fly was open! Was he still covered down there? Almost faint with shame and self-consciousness, he looked to see where Dixie was looking. She wasn't looking at his crotch now, but she may have already looked. Dare he look down to see what she may have seen? He could tell without looking that his erection was gone, but when?

Clinging desperately to what was left of his resolve, Billy squared his shoulders, turned, and flung his arms around Dixie. Surprised, she acted instinctively, pressing the palm of her hand against his throbbing chest. Billy thrust his head toward her retreating face, managing to brush his lips against her ear before she pushed him away and sprang to her feet.

Falling forward in her wake so she wouldn't see his open fly—What was worse, Dixie seeing his previous hard-on or her seeing him all shriveled up down there, which was the way he felt now?—Billy put his face on the mattress where Dixie had been sitting. The spot, still warm with her body heat, seemed moist against his lips and cheeks. Rubbing his face in the wetness and inhaling the smell of her pussy, he remembered the joke about the dog that lost his head over a little piece of tail. Without breaking the contact between his face and the mattress, he let his legs slide off the bed and knelt on the floor.

An apt position for prayer, he thought. Or a beheading.

Behind him, out of sight, Dixie undid her shorts, let them fall to the floor, and, bending over, pushed her panties down to her ankles. Stepping out of the puddle of her shorts and panties with her sandals still on, she grabbed Billy's hair and pulled him back, away from the bed. Swinging around, she got in front of the kneeling supplicant, standing between him and the bed. She lowered her bare butt onto the bed where Billy's face had been. She took off his glasses and tossed them on the bed. Bringing her knees up against his face, she made his lips pooch out. Slowly squeezing his cheeks, she made his mouth vertical, mirroring her vaginal cleft. Gently repeating the action, she observed—surely with keen anticipation of what was soon to follow—his mouth opening and closing like that of a rare fish peering forlornly back at her through the glass wall of its aquarium. Still holding his hair, she tilted his head way back.

Oblivious to the fact that his pants were down, his bare ass exposed, the thought running through Billy's mind was, She's Salome and I'm the head of John the Baptist.

Bending forward, Dixie gazed coldly into Billy's tearful eyes. Her face was a reptilian mask. Her dull eyes seemed to look inward, their light turned off. It was if she were tracking her prey by echolocation or the sense of smell. Grabbing another fistful of hair with her other hand, she slid her butt forward to the edge of the bed. Leaning back to balance the fulcrum of her lean body, she lifted her legs and draped them over Billy's shoulders. Digging her heels into Billy's back, she urged him toward her; spreading her thighs, she arched her pelvis upward till her pussy touched his face; at which point, her hips thrusting into high gear, she scrubbed his nose and mouth with the mossy red brush and the cleansing secretions of her power and her glory.

Then, she lets go his hair and falls back onto the bed. Straightening her legs, she squeezes his head between her thighs, locking him in a scissor hold; it is as if, husbanding her desire, she means to immobilize her quarry long enough to catch her breath, at the same time keeping the mouth of her votary within a hair's breadth of the epicenter of her reined-in quake, which is itself that close to erupting. Then, raising up and resting on her elbows, she glances through the veil of her pubic hair at his face. Reading the hunger in his cooped-up eyes, she uncrosses her ankles and re-opens her thighs, laying herself out *like a dewy spring morning in an alpine meadow, which, in full bloom, embraces a river, slowing it, letting it meander through before it plunges back into its headlong descent from the mountains to the sea.*

Billy wedges his hands under her buttocks, his fingers forming a bowl, a caldron, a smelter. Thrusting his head forward, he feasts like a toothless man eating watermelon. My trough runneth over, he hears himself thinking. Dixie anchors her feet and answers him thrust for thrust, *anointing his face with sacred balm; ushering him, unscathed like Dante, through the hirsute Gates of Hell; giving him a bowl of the hot, steamy Gumbo of the Gods; dunking him like cornpone in the Primordial Soup that is the Origin of the World.*

✳   ✳   ✳

After Dixie had put her clothes back on and left the room, Billy stood up. Pulled his pants up. Tucked in his shirt. Zipped his fly. Buckled his belt. Messed with his glasses, trying to get the tape to stick. The gasps of Dixie's orgasms still pulsed in his ears.

Standing in the doorway to the living room, looking down at Dixie—who was sitting, lotus-style, sandals off, on the end of the couch nearest the bedroom door—wondering what her post-orgasmic mood would be like, and only now conscious that earlier, when she was taking him down on Frankie's sick-bed—her expression and manner like that of a wrestler moving in and pinning a colluding opponent to the mat—he had been reminded of the blank look on his father's face on those occasions when soon after returing home from working on the railroad he would flog Billy with a switch for whatever offenses against nature Stella might have caught their back-sliding son at, he savored the sweet after-tingle of undeserved punishment.

Putting his hands in his pockets, he became aware of a major problem. In the chaotic aftermath, he had forgotten to pull up his shorts when he pulled up his pants. Bunched mid-thigh, they formed bulges that were visible through his jeans the way girls' panties are visible under tight knit skirts. VPL's, Billy thought, near panic, realizing how erratic his mind was and how blatantly his stupidity was on display. He felt his mushy pecker rubbing against the zipper of his fly; the cheeks of his ass being chafed by the starched fabric of his Sunday jeans; and the absence of anything to absorb the cold sweat breaking out and trickling down the sides of the crevasse of his butt-crack.

Dixie patted the couch cushion. Billy sat next to her. Feeling owned by her like a beloved but naughty pet, he trembled with anticipation. Having taken possession of him, having done with him as she willed, surely she wouldn't fail to sense how eager he was for further ill-use.

"I'm going to tell you a story, Billy. I'm not exactly sure why I'm telling it to you. Other than the fact that you're easy to talk to and I know you won't judge me. That and I think by talking it out I may be able to understand myself better."

She trusts me! Billy was surprised but exultant.

"Once upon a time there was a girl and a boy. They had everything anybody could want. They were good-looking. They were popular in school. They were both good athletes, had beautiful bodies."

This was going to be better than Billy expected. Dixie was going to talk about herself, reveal her secrets.

"The boy's childhood had been unhappy, but the girl's family loved him and took him in. It was after that that the girl and the boy fell in love. (I'm leaving out a lot.) Their love grew and so naturally when the time came they got married."

Billy squirmed, grinding his butt into the cushion of the couch.

"They didn't have much money, but they were certain that their love would endure any hardships they might have to face. And for a couple of years all went according to plan. But then it began to dawn on the girl that something was not right. She felt like Maggie the Cat. 'When a marriage is on the rocks, the rocks are in the marriage bed', or however that went. Eventually, the girl ... the woman, I should say ... became convinced she had a rival for her husband's love.

"Now, if her rival had been another woman like herself, no matter how beautiful, she would have known what to do. She would have known how the game was played. But, as she watched and waited and tried to make sense of what was happening, she had a growing sense that her rival wasn't another woman. Dum da dum dum.

"She asked herself if it was her husband's friends who had stolen him from her. They were a wild bunch and when he was with them he drank a lot. She thought maybe the booze might be affecting him. Diminishing his 'ardor' as they say in paperback novels. But he drank before they were married. In fact, she drank with him, as much as he did. And after they were married they continued to drink. It was about the only kind of fun they could afford. Other than the fun they had ... between the sheets.

"Oh, by the way, thanks for that in there." Dixie nodded toward the bedroom. "You made me feel clean again. Like a virgin, almost."

"Takes one to know one." Billy's brain was out of the loop. *His throat and rectum were spasming in contrapuntal harmony with the residual orgasmic reverberations of Dixie's uterus.*

"You mean you're still a virgin? You and ... you guys never ... ? Why can't we ever say her name?"

"You know why." Licking his lips, Billy imagined that he could taste the residue of Dixie's pussy juice and wondered what exactly the Faustpool girl had told Dixie about him.

"Yeah, I guess I do. She told me before she left that that last night was the greatest ... that what you guys did was the most wonderful thing that had ever happened to her."

"You don't have to lie like that, Dix." But if you can't say the same about what I did for you a few minutes ago, lie your head off.

"No, really, it's true. I still think about the two of you together like that. I was envious."

"Hence ... ," Billy nodded toward the bed room.

"Yeah! You were great!"

"Come on, Dixie. You don't have to say that." Incapable of sustained cynicism, Billy blushed with pride.

"No, I mean it. You're a natural." Dixie leaned over and kissed Billy on the mouth.

"Thanks, I think." Can she taste her pussy on my lips? Billy wondered. Her mouth actually *does* seem dirtier than her pussy, he thought, remembering something Frankie had said. Must be the cigarettes. Dare he hope he and Dixie would someday French kiss the way he and the Faustpool had done so much (and the way he and Dixie herself did that one time when they were drunk and Frankie was gone). "Didn't Frankie ever ... ," Billy glanced at Dixie's crotch, "... you know?"

"No, he wouldn't do it."

"He told me he did. I'd a never thought of it, if he hadn't brought it up." Which isn't true, Billy thought, remembering the pitifully few seed-words on the subject in Jake's sex book that had nonetheless taken root in his imagination.

"No, Frankie lied to you. Barbara ... there I've said it ... Barbara and I talked about it. We read about it in this book Frankie stole and we wondered what it would feel like. She seemed really turned on by the idea. After that we saw this picture at Uncle Theo's house. It showed an octopus making love to a woman. We laughed at the time, but later she told me that it was the sexiest thing she had ever seen."

"The two of you go there a lot?" Billy remembered now how the Faustpool girl had known just where to look for the octopus picture.

"Yes, we were *extremely* close." Dixie put her hand on Billy's cheek. "You weren't the first for either one of us." Kissing him, her nicotine-flavored tongue entered his mouth and felt around for his. After a brief engagement, it was gone, leaving him jilted. "But you were very very good."

"Thanks. Again. Any time." Savoring the taste of the kiss, Billy could still feel Dixie's tongue in his mouth and he thought of the serpent in the Garden of Eden.

"I don't remember how I came to mention our conversation to Frankie. Maybe I had the foolish hope that he might be open to something new. But good old suave, sophisticated Frankie thought it ... what you ... we ... me, you, and Barbara ... did was disgusting. Said he would only do it to a virgin."

It's called cunnilingus, Billy thought, savoring the wicked word, as he let sink in the consequences of Frankie's lies. Having never known, until after the fact, the part deception had played in the affair, he had no hard feelings toward him. The miracle had to have been wrought by some means and, having happened, it more than outweighed any sense of betrayal he might have felt as a result of Frankie's prank. "Then, you've known all along that I ... with Barbara?"

"Oh yeah."

"Why didn't you ... ? Why didn't we ... ? All you had to do was ask. You didn't even have to do that, as it turned out."

"I don't know. It seemed like it would be a desecration of her memory, I guess."

"You could've got someone else to do it, couldn't you?"

"It wouldn't be the same if it wasn't you."

"Thanks for the desecration."

"Anytime. Now, getting back to the story. It actually started before we were married, after he came out of prison ... he called it reform school, but it was just like prison."

"How do you mean? What started before you were married?"

"Oh, you know, there were times when he couldn't ... get it up, is the way he put it. I should have heeded the warning signs, but I was 'in love' and thought it would all go away after we were married ... and it did for a while. But things were sporadic, you know, it came and went. So, the eventual truth dawned on me only very slowly. At first I refused to believe what my eyes, and my heart, told me. Oh, my God! It seemed so dreadful at the time."

Putting her elbows on the arm and back of the couch, Dixie lifted herself up and turned her body toward the front of the cabin so that she now faced Billy, her legs still lotused underneath her. Uncrossing her legs, she put her feet together, sole to sole, and leaned back. "What did you say that made Frankie so mad?" she asked. "Yesterday, up there in the gym."

What with Dixie sitting in that position on the couch and him still stimulated to the point of stupefaction, Billy had no choice but look at Dixie's crotch. The taut fabric of her shorts was dark with wetness.

"Billy, look at me, at my face." Dixie tapped him on the arm. She took his glasses off and put them on the arm of the couch. "What did you say to Frankie that made him so mad?"

Billy looked up. "I don't know. I just said he was the king and ever body should bow down to him."

"You must have said more than *that*. That wouldn't have made him mad. He *agrees* with that. He would like nothing better than having people bow down to him."

Billy shook his head, as much to clear his mind as to tell Dixie he didn't know what to say.

"You don't have to be afraid to tell me." Dixie leaned forward and put her hand on Billy's arm.

Billy turned toward her, tried to meet her eyes, but looked at her crotch instead.

"Okay, look." Dixie put her hands on Billy's cheeks, made him look at her. "I *know* what you said to Frankie that made him mad at you. Crystal told me. You said something about Arthur Maxwell."

Billy didn't say anything.

"You know you did, Billy. And I know you've at least heard rumors about him and Arthur. They were spread by people who don't like Frankie, don't understand him. Not that he's all that complicated. He's not. But he has a talent for making enemies. *And* not that the rumors aren't true … . You ask me, though, Arthur stands for the only good thing Frankie has ever done. Except his singing and, of course, sports."

Dixie lit a cigarette. For what seemed like a long time, she gazed out the front door at nothing in particular. Billy studied her smoke-shrouded face.

"My God! Could he play basketball," Dixie said, still looking outside. "He had such grace. He had a perfect build. Tight little butt in that tight-fitting uniform. Gorgeous thighs, with those little muscles that pooched out over his knees." Shifting her gaze back inside, Dixie touched her leg to show where she meant. "And here," she added, dragging the thumb of the hand holding her cigarette across her abdomen just above her hip bone.

Billy's throat tightened.

Looking outside again, Dixie continued her eulogy. "When he jumped he exploded off the floor. *Soared* over the others. Nobody ever had a jump-shot like Frankie's. High-arcing, they used to call it. 'West's high-arching jumper seems to stay in the air forever before ripping through the net'. That's how they described it on the sports page of the paper, which is the only thing Frankie ever read, so you can imagine what that did to the size of his head. It's true, though. Every eye in the stands would be drawn to the ball as it went toward the goal like it was a full moon and they were a pack of horny hounds. And then, when it finally went through the hoop, it would hit the net and actually bounce back up a little bit, sometimes high as the rim, seemed like. You know what I'm talking about? Did you ever notice that?" She looked at Billy who looked down as soon as their eyes met. "And, Billy, the sound!" She touched Billy's arm. Billy looked up. His eyes locked onto her lips. "It's like that sound ... of the ball hitting the net ... was what everybody was waiting for. It was the spark that detonated the crowd. I mean they *exploded*. You could *feel* it. In the soles of your feet. In your skin. In the bones of your *skull*. It was three hundred prayers answered at once. It was deliverance. It was the parting of the sea. Out there on that court, Frankie was the closest thing to royalty those people will ever know. What girl wouldn't love him? What girl didn't?

"Now, of course, I'm so fed up with Frankie that ... . " Dixie closed her eyes and waved off the rest of the sentence. "Anyway, I was talking about Arthur. Frankie always felt sorry for the poor old thing. When Arthur was little and his mother still dressed him in girl's clothes ... before she ran off with that Bible salesman or whoever it was ... Frankie said he heard that she wasn't even his mother ... that his real mother was one of the patients that Dr. Maxwell had ... abused ... same one he was supposed to have 'loaned out' to the those awful Foster Brothers ... that she just kept Arthur around like he was a live doll or something. I don't know if I believe any of that stuff ... people will say anything.

"Anyway, Frankie wouldn't let people beat him up when he was around. Or make fun of him. And some people ... people that don't like Frankie ... took that kindness, or pity ... the only kind of kindness ... or love for another person ... I believe Frankie is capable of ... as a sign of weakness. They tried to turn Frankie and Arty's ... friendship ... into something it never was ... something sick and perverted. It was because of their gossip that he even got the *idea* of letting Arthur do that to him. That *that* was what Arthur *wanted* to do. Don't ask me where Arty got the idea. Probably from his father, if you can believe what you hear about the man. Or from the Foster's, if that rumor is true. Even then I had to explain it to Frankie and it was me who talked him into it.

"Or so I thought. Come to find out ... ."

"Into what?"

"Please, Billy, don't make me spell out all the wretched details, okay. I know you know what I'm talking about. I know about that time you followed him, for example."

"What time?"

"A few summers ago. At a softball game up at school. You followed Frankie down to the dumps. He knows you followed him. He knows you saw what happened."

Billy didn't say anything.

✳   ✳   ✳

It was between games. Billy's hand was throbbing in pain. Playing first base in the first game, he had been hit on the heel of his glove hand by a hard line drive. Despite the pain, though, he had been able to pick up the ball and make the game-ending out.

Frankie West, the player-manager of Billy's team said, "Great play!", and told him to come out to his car in a few minutes. He had something for him.

In the early evening midsummer light, Billy watched Frankie making his way through the people standing around waiting for the second game to start. He saw Frankie get into his red Fairlane Ford convertible. After a few minutes someone in a white dress got out of the car and ran off toward the nearby school buildings. The windows of the buildings were ablaze, reflecting the sun, low in the sky.

Inside the car, Frankie sat staring straight ahead.

What is he thinking about? Billy wondered. Before the game he had seen Frankie talking to a Sheriff's deputy. What were they talking about? Was Frankie in trouble again? There was a rumor going around that he might have had something to do with some plate glass that had disappeared a few days earlier from a building site. Everybody knew Frankie was down on his luck.

As Billy approached Frankie's car he saw him taking a bottle from under the front seat, saw Frankie take a swig. Billy stopped and waited for Frankie to notice him.

"Hey, Billy! Come get some of this." Frankie held the bottle up for Billy to see. "It'll take the pain away."

In the front seat Billy took tiny swig and made a face.

"Don't like the taste, eh? Here, I have a Coke." Frankie reached into the back seat and, rummaging around among the rumpled clothes and empty beer cans and discarded cigarette packs, found a Coke and opened it. Opening the car door, he poured some of it out, making room for whiskey. The liquid fizzed on the asphalt. "Don't want to be too obvious about this, eh, Billy Boy?" Frankie brought the two bottles together and slipped them under the steering wheel. "Don't want any of the good Baptists to see us drinking this nasty fire water, right?" Positioning the bottles between his legs, he brought their mouths together, re-filling the Coke bottle with whiskey. He handed it to Billy. "Here nurse this for a while. It'll take the pain away. That's what I use it for."

"Who was that?"

"Who was who?"

"That person in your car a few minutes ago."

"Oh … her. She's a nurse I know. Don't tell anyone you saw her, okay? It might get around."

After a few minutes, Frankie said, "You stay here as long as you like, okay? I gotta go see a man about a dog." He got out, closed the door and leaned forward against the side of the car like he was dizzy and needed to regain his balance. Casting a glance back at the field and the stands, he pushed away from the car and headed toward the dumps.

After drinking the Coke and whiskey, Billy followed Frankie.

The dumps was where high school 'hoods' went to smoke. At the base of the embankment that bordered the railroad tracks, there was a little house. Built out of creosote railroad cross ties, it was kinda like a log cabin. One room, one small window on either end of it, it had a roof of corrugated tin. Just off campus, it was out the school's jurisdiction. Among the regulars it was known as the butt-hut.

Billy had, of course, seen the dumps before, but always at a safe distance. There was an air of mystery about the place that made the stories of what went on 'down at the dumps' more alluring than anything that went on at school, in or outside of the classrooms. When he was in school, Billy would go down there, from time to time. Out of curiosity. Always in the morning before first bell. He never actually left the school grounds, going only as far as the barbed-wire fence at the top of the embankment, hiding among some scrub pines.

To Billy, looking down, safe and smug on the edge of school property, the dump-dwellers, all of them tall and lanky, or so it seemed, in their leather jackets, looked dark and menacing in the morning fog and the shadow of the steep embankment.

Billy had often fantasized swaggering into the butt-hut. He had even practiced his walk in front of his mother's full-length mirror. I'll show those guys who's tough, he would say to himself, still very much under Jake's influence. I can thumb my nose at authority with the best of them. When I feel like it. When they see how cool I am, they're gonna think, this guy looks like he gets more than his share of pussy. Hey, baby, he would say to the sluts that hang out with the hoods, I hear you like it more than any guy ever did. I hear you can't get enough of it. You're just the kind of woman I'm looking for. When I get through with you, you'll have had enough, by God.

He spat on the ground and headed down the embankment.

Stopping several yards from the butt-hut, he was on the point of turning around and going back when he heard a voice inside. Was it a woman's voice? Was it the person he had seen getting out of Frankie's car?

Maybe it was Jonnie Vonderheim! Jonnie was a nurse. Maybe it was her he had seen getting out of Frankie's car. That would explain the white dress. More than once, Billy had seen Frankie's car parked in front of her house, even, a couple of times, after he married Dixie.

Maybe I can sneak up closer, Billy thought. In his mind, he saw Frankie's hands on Jonnie's rear-end. He tried to imagine what it would feel like to run fingertips over the taut fabric of Jonnie's shorts. He pictured in his mind Frankie unbuttoning the button, unzipping the zipper. He saw Jonnie's buttocks jiggling as, balanced on the stilts of her red high-heel shoes, she wiggled her ass, molting shorts and panties together.

Creeping around to the far end of the little house, Billy looked in through the single dirty pane of the small window. At first, he couldn't see much. His face was reflected in the glass and his head cast a shadow inside. Gradually, he made out the top of Frankie's head.

The back of Frankie's head rested on the window frame. Billy was looking over Frankie's shoulder. Frankie's long wavy red hair, flattened against the pane, was close to Billy's cheek. He must be sitting on something, Billy thought, a low stool or maybe some boxes stacked against the wall.

Apparently naked from the waist down, Frankie's pale body was stretched out in front of him. His legs were spread wide apart. His pants and underwear were squashed like an accordion, or foreskin, around one ankle. A dark form, barely visible in the dim light, blocked Billy's view of the lower part of Frankie's body, except for the legs below the knees. The form's head wobbled rhythmically, bobbing up and down and twisting side to side at the same time, a rapidly-reversing spiraling motion, like it had the knob of a prancing drum major's baton anchored in its mouth.

Moving his head to the edge of the window to let in more light, Billy got a better look at the dark form. Long hair, head bowed. Was it the same person he had seen getting out of Frankie's car? Must be. Same white dress. Is she kneeling? Looks like she's praying.

Frankie put his hand against the side of the person's head. A tender gesture. The person covered Frankie's hand with theirs but didn't look up. The person's hand was bigger than Frankie's. The person was wearing rings on three fingers. Frankie put his other hand on the other side of the person's head. She—it *had* to be the nurse, Billy thought—kissed the palm of the hand she was holding. Frankie swiveled her head back, framing her face between his hands. Was it Jonnie? Billy couldn't tell.

Just then Frankie took his hands away and Billy got a good look at the woman's face. She was smiling, apparently happy. Lots of lipstick, rouge, eyeliner. Big lips, fat bumpy cheeks covered with heavy make-up. Thick eyebrows, dark hair combed straight back. Teeth, yellowish-green in the fading light. The most, the only, pleasing feature was her eyes, shining and dancing bright, giving her a playful look, a look of impeccable innocence.

It definitely wasn't Jonnie!

The woman's head went down again and resumed the pulsing-spiraling motion.

*   *   *

"Billy, look. What I'm trying to tell you is that way down deep there's some good in Frankie. There's some of you ... some ... quality ... or something ... that is like you in him. What the stuff with Arthur was all about is Frankie's way of trying to ... it was that little part of him that was good trying to ... . He was trying to find ... this is hard ... he always sensed ... he always knew that you had something that he lacked."

"What do you mean?" Billy noticed that Dixie was talking about Frankie in the past tense.

"I mean ... I think the thing with Arthur was Frankie's way of struggling with an idea he and other people ... even people who like him ... have about him. He always wanted to be a tough guy. To be seen that way by other people. But a part of him hated that tough part of himself, saw through it. Or, at least, he never felt totally comfortable with it. Less so as he got older. By letting Arthur ... do what he did ... what Arthur wants to do more than anything in the world, Frankie ... (at least this is how I tried to get him to see it ... he felt *so* ashamed and guilty about it ...) was repudiating the tough guy part of himself ... and, at the same time, letting another part of himself ... a better part ... the 'Billy' part ... express itself ... by doing something ... well ... loving. I can't think of a better way of saying it."

Dixie's face lit up. She excitedly lit another cigarette. "*That's* why he had to attack you yesterday!" She took a deep drag and nodded as if in agreement with what she was thinking. "I've been reading up on ... reading psychology books. Don't you see? Look at what happened. He had just been humiliated by a Negro. What could be worse? Defeated at the very thing he was supposed to be the best at by the kind of person he despises the most.

"So, to save face, his tough-guy side had to come out. He had to try to show everybody and himself, mainly himself, that he could still play. Then, when *you*, of all people, brought up Arthur, you became a threat. It's like you and Arthur blended together in his ... unconscious mind. You became a ... symbol of that part of himself the other part has always seen as weak. So, he hit you in the face with the ball."

Dixie took a drag off her cigarette and looked thoughtfully at Billy's face. Suddenly, as if re-excited by what she was thinking, her own face lit up again. "In the *face*! *Of course*! Don't you see it? Oh, this is beautiful, it has *so* many meanings. Your face was both the symbol of society's condemnation of his love for Arthur *and* the symbol *of* that love. And so he used another symbol, the basketball, a symbol of him at his best, as the King, to attack both society which condemned and rejected him, and, at the same time, to attack himself; himself at his worst, as the ex-King, the ex*iled* King, the *failed* King. *And ... and ...* himself at his best ... but also ... his *weakest* ... . In other words, himself as *you*. It's perfect. If it had been anybody else, he wouldn't have done it in quite that way. He wasn't attacking you, *Billy Mayden*, he was attacking all the things you stood for. He was attacking *himself*."

"You could've fooled me." Billy rubbed his face. "I didn't stand for anything when he finished with me. I was flat on the floor. Took me a while to figure out *where* I was, though. Or even *who* I was."

"O, you poor baby, let me kiss it." Dixie covered Billy's face with smoky kisses. When she was done, she continued her story. "But here's the thing about Arthur: I can't accept it. I'm okay with the fact that it happened in the past. I just don't want it to continue. Enough is enough. I mean, it was one thing when I thought I was the one who talked Frankie into letting Arthur do it. I even *watched* the first time ... I *thought* it was the first time ... . (We were in the bunkhouse behind my parents' house. He liked it there. We used to go there when he was having trouble ... getting it up. I guess he liked it because it was the scene of his first sexual triumphs.) But it was an altogether different thing to find out that, not only had it been going on for years, it was still going on; it had never stopped.

"Maybe if I could have done it as well as Arthur ... could have *competed*. Frankie wanted me to do it. I did it a time or two, but then I couldn't bring myself to do it. For one thing, I wasn't nearly as turned on by it as Arthur is. It's not because I don't think it's ... clean ... or anything. I mean ... it's just another other part of the body. A lot of women do it all the time. Some of them even *like* to do it.

"I guess what it boils down to is I don't like the idea of somebody hanging around all the time that Frankie would rather be with than me. That and the way most people are freaked out by that sort of thing ... some, many of them ... even violently opposed to it." Pausing to think, she put her cigarette in the ashtray, twirled it, sculpted it, revealing the glowing hot tip. "I wonder why it has to be such a horrible, disgusting thing when a man does it? Come to think of it, you could say Arthur isn't really a man … not *mentally* or *emotionally*. I don't know what you'd call him."

Dixie put her hand, the one holding the cigarette, on Billy's neck. One by one, she surveyed the features of his face, eyes, lips, ears, hair. Focusing on her lips, Billy envisioned Dixie and the Faustpool girl naked together, surrounded by all the dirty books in Theo's living room. Focusing on her eyes, he wondered if Dixie was thinking that he, too, wasn't really a man. Then, remembering the condition of his face, he pondered about which would hurt more: to be burned with a cigarette or hit hard in the face with a basketball.

"Frankie's just a child." Drawing back her hand, Dixie put the cigarette in the ashtray. "An innocent child. Maybe if I thought me and Frankie could love each other in that simple, innocent way him and Arthur love each other, I could get used to the idea. But I don't and I can't. In my mind I keep seeing the two of *them* doing it. After watching them, it wasn't the same when me and Frankie made love. In fact, even at its best, sex was never as good between me and Frankie as it was between him and Arthur.

"Now I think I shoulda never opened that can of worms. Maybe if I hadn't, I never would have gone back to … . Oh! I don't know what I'm trying to say. You know what I'm talking about, don't you?"

"You never would have gone back to what?" Billy asked.

"Oh Billy! How I wish I could tell you!"

"Tell me what?"

"The more I thought about Frankie and Arthur, the more I wanted what they had. When I tried to think what exactly it was they had … what there was about it that made it so incredibly alluring … all I could come up with was this: They were doing something utterly forbidden. Something dangerous that could destroy them if almost any other people found out. I think that was what set me off … to begin with, anyway.

"Funny thing was neither one of them … certainly not Arthur … but Frankie, too … seemed to understand just how much danger they were putting themselves in. What made it forbidden and so dangerous was the incredible sexual *pleasure* they felt. There's no place in this world … in society … certainly not in the South … for that kind of pleasure. I know that now. *And* … it works both ways … the pleasure is there *because* it is so dangerous. More so for men than for women, I think. The two feed off each other. (I wonder if Frankie ever looked at it that way. I doubt it.)

"And yet … they got away with it for many years … .

"I don't remember how it started but one day I became aware that I had once been and, now, was again fatally attracted to something just as dangerous and forbidden as what Frankie and Arthur were doing.

Something ... someone that had been there all along, right under my nose, you might say. I can't tell you any more than that. Except to say I never knew anything could be so exciting. I mean at every level, not just sexual, though that part was ... ."

"Was what?" Billy asked. He knew what she meant.

"No! I've said too much already."

"Out of this world?" What she felt is what Case 80 in *Psychopathia Sexualis* felt, Billy thought.

"Please don't ask me to say any more." Dixie looked into Billy's eyes. "I'm in deep trouble, Billy. I've got to make a decision that will determine the entire future course of my life."

"Is it gonna make it any worse to tell me? It might help to talk it out."

"Okay, but you must never ever tell anyone. Okay? Remember I told you that I watched Frankie and Arthur together? Frankie knew I was doing it ... I was right there ... Frankie likes to have people watch ... he's an exhibitionist ... it just added to the excitement of it for him.

"I have never seen anything like it and nothing has ever affected me as ... profoundly ... as that did. I couldn't believe how ... skillful ... there's no other word for it. (That's when I realized they had done this many times before.) I mean, on the one hand, Arthur was an artist at work. On the other hand, he was like a baby nursing at its mother's breast. That's how attuned he was to Frankie's ... manhood. He was able to control it like it was a part of his own body. They say a great artist gets lost in his medium and that when an infant is nursing he can't tell where he ends and the breast begins. How's that poem go about not being able to tell the dancer from the dance? The baby and the breast are the same thing. That's the way Arthur was with Frankie's ... plum ... that what it looks like. I mean it was like Arthur could keep it ... as hard ... for as long as he liked ... . He kept Frankie aroused just short of ... climax, orgasm ... seemed like for at least an hour. I have never seen Frankie or anyone so incredibly ... turned on. I wish I had a movie of his face. Seeing Frankie's face was another part of what made it such a fantastic thing to watch. It was like Frankie's soul had been ... drawn ... into Arthur's mouth. At the same time it was like Frankie's whole body was feeling what his ... what other men would feel only ... down there.

"It was like the two of them were the same person. Like the two halves of one soul had come together and been made whole.

"When Arthur finally ... brought Frankie to ... climax ... I have never seen such a thing. Frankie ... ejaculated ... seemed like ... like it would never stop ... coming out of him. It looked like someone had opened a bottle of champagne. Of course, Frankie loved to watch himself climax.

He never lost his fascination for it. For him it was the eighth wonder of the world. (That's why he would never used rubbers. And I think that's why he loved dirty movies so much. The 'money shot,' as they call it.)

"For days after that I was so aroused I thought I would go crazy. No amount of … masturbating … did any good. It just made it worse. And Frankie couldn't … get … an … he couldn't do it with me after that.

"I was desperate. Otherwise I wouldn't have done what I did next. I *had* to do something. So I took another lover. But it couldn't be just anyone. If it was going to have any chance of coming close to what Frankie and Arthur had it had to be dangerous.

"To make a long story short, I seduced Teddy."

"Who's Teddy?"

"Teejay. I call him Teddy. Uncle Toe hates that name. When he was in prison, they used to call him Teddy, then Freddy. I begged him to tell me what was so bad about being called Teddy or Freddy, but he never would. Anyway, I seduced Teejay, seduced him *again*, I should say. I'm as prejudiced as anyone else … I mean, even at fourteen he was well endowed … and I expected that as a full grown man he would be hung like a horse, as Frankie likes to say. I also expected him not only to be turned on by a white woman but … and this is what made it really, really exciting … to have something to prove to white society for what had been done to him and his kind. And my expectations were more than met … they were exceeded … on all counts. What I didn't expect was that he'd be so accomplished. He really knows how to make love to a woman. To top it off the man is actually well-educated.

"Now it's funny how things can sometimes come together in ways you never expect. Recently, I met a man named Lester LeBeaux. It seemed like at the time that it was just a coincidence that he turned up in my life at that particular time. Now I know different. Not only did he know Teejay, he knew my whole family, my parents and Uncle Theo. The three of them go way back. Teejay must have told him, or he must have guessed, what was going on between the two of us, because, after Lester had charmed my pants off, he talked … deceived … manipulated … got me to agree to do something I never should have done."

Dixie looked out the window. She didn't say anything for a while. Then, almost whispering and seeming to be talking to herself, she said, "I wanted to know what it would feel like being watched. I should've never let Charlie take those pictures. He's the one who put the idea in my head, the little creep. Called himself doing 'art photography'. Some bull-crap about some guy named Hugh Heffer, I think it was, who was supposed to have given Marilyn Monroe her start in Hollywood. Seeing myself that way gave me a taste of what it was like. After that I was an easy target for LeBeaux. I still believe the two of them were working together.

"Meanwhile, my ... sexual ... anguish ... there's no other word for it ... was as bad as ever. Now that I think about it, I realize it couldn't have been any other way. I wanted something as intense and dangerous as Frankie and Arthur and that's what I had with Teejay. At least now I understand what Frankie must feel. Here's this absolutely soul-devouring ... thing ... act ... whatever you want to call it ... that can never be revealed to the world. And yet, I let Lester LeBeaux ... . Oh Billy, I was caught in a trap of my own making! I couldn't see any way out. I was on the point of ... suicide.

"Then, I had an idea. An idea for a desperate plan. I would get pregnant. I thought maybe the change in my hormones might give me some relief. My plan called for me going back to the beginning, you might say. It was for me and Frankie and Arthur to repeat the situation that ... derailed me in the first place. And that's what we did. Arthur got Frankie ... ready ... and then Frankie entered me and ... ejaculated. And now I'm pregnant."

"Great! So the plan worked. Or did it?"

"Well, not exactly, but I'm sane now. I'll tell you why ... how ... in just a minute. My problem now is I'm not sure I want to be a mother, after all. Lester wants me to run away with him. He says he can eventually get me started in Hollywood as a make-up artist. Says he's sorry about taking advantage of me."

"So what are you going to do?"

"I don't know. That's what I have to decide by tonight."

"What happens tonight?"

"Can't tell you. I mean I *really* can't tell you."

"How did Frankie know I followed him?" Billy asked after a while.

"He saw you looking in the window of the butt-hut."

"He couldn't have. I was *behind* him."

"He saw your reflection in some plate glass that was stacked against the wall at the other end."

"Did he tell you what he was doing?"

"You mean in the butt-hut? He *said* he was talking to Arthur."

"Talking? Well, I guess we both know now he didn't do much talking."

"Right, but that's what he said. Supposedly, Arthur was upset because his father had burned all his girl clothes, so he couldn't dress up even at home. Frankie said he stole some nurse's clothes for him."

"What else did Frankie tell you?" Billy asked.

"He said after he and Arthur left they circled back to see what you would do. They saw you go inside the butt-hut."

"Did they look in the window?"

"Yes."

Billy blushed. He *had* gone inside the butt-hut. He had surrendered to the sweet and sour combination of the smells of Frankie's ejaculate and what he now knew to have been Arthur's fat sweaty body still permeating the air in the over-heated little room. He had sat right where Frankie had. He had leaned back against the wall and unbuttoned the pants of his softball uniform.

Embarrassment prevented his remembering beyond that point.

But now he knew where the déjà vu smell came from that he hadn't been able to identify earlier.

"And you're telling me all this because I'm easy to talk to?" Billy asked.

"Yes. That and the fact that I don't want you to give up on Frankie. He's gonna need all the friends he can get … if … ."

Billy's heart sank. "You're gonna leave him, aren't you?" And me, he thought.

"Maybe. I don't know yet." Dixie sat up straight, put her feet on the floor and her hands on the sofa cushions, like she was going to stand up.

"And you think I'm the kind of 'friend' Frankie needs."

"Yes, that and something else."

"What?"

"Arthur. If anything happens to Frankie, someone will have to keep an eye on Arthur. Promise you'll do that?"

"I don't know about that, Dixie."

"Well, think about it."

"You were gonna tell me how you got sane again … ."

"Oh, yes! How could I have forgotten! It happened while you were … while we were together in the bedroom. The perfect solution came to me."

"The perfect solution?"

"Yes. Billy, you are the most loving person I know. And, it seems to me, the thing you love most in the world is … women … the *essence* of women … ."

"Pussy, you mean."

"Well … okay … yes, and what comes out of them … ."

"What do you mean?"

"Babies! Children! You love kids. Look at you at church. You're always playing with little kids. Holding new babies … ."

"So?"

"While you were … you know … ."

"Eating your pussy."

"Yeah, while you were doing that, I felt like the great, ancient Mother Goddess. It was like you had come to worship me. You were kneeling at my altar. You had come for my bounty. You were entering my temple to take my baby. King Solomon said the baby should go to the one who will love it most. Until you … ."

"Ate your pussy."

" … I had *not* lost that terrible lust-anguish. But you have finally satisfied my desire. You have opened me up. The pleasure I felt opened me up and a part of me feels like I should give my baby to you. That if I do decide to leave I should wait until it is born. And then, after I have fulfilled my destiny, I should return for you and my child."

"Wouldn't Frankie have something to say about that?"

"It doesn't matter what happens to Frankie. He is husk. He has played his role. The really important role should go to you. Maybe this is your destiny."

"That's a lot to take in."

"I know. I still don't know what I'm going to do. Before tonight, I've got to make the biggest decision of my young life. I'm going some place where I can drink and think. Wanna come along? Here, don't forget your glasses."

"No, thanks. I don't drink." Billy had something more pressing he had to do.

∗   ∗   ∗

It must be better than fucking.

Why do you say that?

Because you get hard just thinking about it. Look at you, you've got an erection. That's more than you can do when we're both naked and laying in bed together.

Dixie could feel herself getting wet. Just thinking about watching Arthur do his thing with Frankie made her want to masturbate.

It's just different.

Was it better with me watching?

Well, you know how I am. I like having people looking at me.

Dixie had admired Arthur's skill. She envied his ability to enable Frankie to sustain a full erection indefinitely. She marveled at how closely attuned he was to the object of his enormous lust. He was able to control it as if it was a part of his own body—she was reminded of nursing infants who are said not to differentiate between themselves and the all-beneficent breast—keeping it hard and delaying ejaculation, all the while obviously savoring the tactile

218

sensations of its smooth plum-like head. It was obvious, too, that Arthur's intense pleasure was fully communicable. She had never seen Frankie display such excruciating sexual arousal, nor had she ever seen him come so much and for so long as when Arthur finally brought him to climax.

Afterward she was so aroused no amount of masturbation would assuage her. She came to believe that being in that prolonged state of unquenchable desire was what led her to agree to let LeBeaux film her and Teejay. That and the fact that she had had sex with Teejay before. When her sexual curiosity had first peaked, she had lured Teejay into one of the vacant cabins at Magnolia Park and seduced him. So, doing it with him now wasn't exactly what you'd call a <u>new</u> crime; it wasn't as egregious as doing it with a complete stranger, for example. And, too, Teejay was a known (and thus highly desirable) quantity. Under ordinary circumstances size would not have mattered. But in this state of constant and off-scale arousal the memory of his enormous and well-formed phallus made this unexpected chance for an encore irresistible. Besides, as far as she knew, she had never been watched and, knowing Frankie's fetish, she wondered what it would be like.

Seeing the movie of herself and Teejay drove her to the very edge of madness. Her sexual anguish increased to the point of considering suicide. In her desperation she wondered if she got pregnant she might not feel some relief. The change in hormones might help. To get around the problem of Frankie's impotence with her, she decided to talk Frankie into a threesome with her and Arthur. It was a pretty good bet that the chance to father a baby would not only be the hook—if a hook was needed—that would make Frankie go along with the 'experiment,' but would give Dixie the chance to end her relationship with Frankie on a positive note.

You know, Frankie, we've talked about having a baby. I've resisted the idea up to now, but I think I'm coming around. Why don't we do this: We'll let Arthur do his thing with His Majesty and then, just before you climax, you can switch partners, so to speak, and come inside me. And I'll take it from there.

Sounds good to me.

Long story short: It wasn't until that Sunday in the cabin, under the spell of Billy's artful tongue and lips, that Dixie's lust was finally slaked; and she was able to get on with her life and be the woman God meant her to be.

17

It was dark when something woke Billy up. He sat up, not knowing where he was. Then, hearing a voice and seeing the bright lines of neon light framing the bedroom door, he knew: He was still in Frankie and Dixie's cabin; the voice was Frankie talking to someone in the next room. When he tried to stand, the room started spinning and he almost fainted. Putting a hand on the bed for balance and leaning across it, he pulled the shade up, and looked out the window. It's just cloudy, he decided, not nighttime. I couldn't have been asleep long, he thought. So, why do I feel so groggy? Looking down he thought saw Arthur Maxwell crouched under the window, smiling up at him. But when he knelt on the bed and leaned forward to get a better look, Arthur was gone. If he had ever been there.

For a brief second it struck him that the face he thought was Arthur's looked a little bit like Stella's. No way, he thought, it must be the dream I was having. He couldn't remember what he had been dreaming about.

Crossing the room, he leaned against the wall next to the door which was slightly ajar. Without opening the door any further, he thrust an eye into the stream of light coming through the crack.

The three little boys who had been there earlier sat in front of Frankie. Hunched forward in their wheelchairs, oblivious to the half-eaten all-day suckers and half-empty Nehi's in their hands, they hung on Frankie's every word.

"Shit, man. I am fucked *up*." Frankie was sitting in a straight-back cane-seat chair and whittling ineptly on a stick with a switchblade knife. A small, open bottle of whiskey was on the floor beside his chair. "*Again*." Running three fingers of the knife-hand through his hair, he squinted against the neon light and the smoke from the cigarette bobbing up and down in the corner of his purple-lipped mouth. "I am fucked up and I fucked up." In the harsh light, his pale, stubbly face was lavender-colored with purple freckles. His hair, bright orange in normal light, was dull purplish-brown. "I am fucked up be*cause* I fucked up."

*   *   *

After Dixie left Billy had pulled down his pants, pulled up his boxer shorts, pulled his pants back up, buckled his belt and sat on the edge of the couch, staring at the blank, dark screen of the television set. After a while he stretched out on the couch and fell asleep. He dreams he sees a basketball, deflated and rotting, in a mud puddle in the road, Pugh Lane, in front of his house. As he approaches the basketball, it becomes the head of a little girl sticking up out of the water. Trying to rescue the little girl, he discovers that what he sees—her head—is all there is; when he picks it up, it is the hollow disembodied head of a doll; made of plaster, it is soggy and falling apart.

When he woke up he thought he was at home in Stella's living room. In the dark, all that remained of his dream was a feeling of deep sadness, until, under the impression that a doll—over there in that dark corner, in a basket full of his sister's toys, that Stella refused to get rid of, even though the little girl herself had hardly ever touched them—was calling out to him, he remembered the dream and realized that the little girl in the dream was his twin sister Sibil and that his dream was a near-repeat, minus the basketball, of the first dream he can ever remember having, dreamed the night after Sibil was taken into Pinecrest, never to return home again, and he knew why he was sad.

He got up and turned on the television. A preacher was ranting and raving. Billy turned the sound off and sat on the couch, watching the preacher striding from one side of the podium to the other, one hand holding an open bible, the other hand pumping out hell and brimstone. The only light in the room came from the television set. Billy stood up, unbuckled his belt, pushed his jeans and underwear down to his ankles, and sat back down. Bent over, his chin cradled in one hand, his elbow resting on his knee, he pulled back the foreskin of his flaccid penis with his other hand.

He wanted to masturbate, but in the television's light, his dick had the look of a dead, belly-up catfish. Besides, there was no way he was going to be able to jack-off in Stella's living room.

He glanced toward the window to see if anyone was looking in at him. He saw a face in the window. It was the reflection of his own face looking back at him. There were pine trees just outside the window, but they didn't look right, weren't in the right place. He realized then he was still in Frankie and Dixie's cabin in Magnolia Park.

All the sensations of eating Dixie's pussy came flooding back, and he thought maybe he would try to masturbate after all, then take a nap. He remembered Case 80 in *Psychopathia Sexualis*. Case 80 liked to imagine that a young lady he knew enjoyed torturing and whipping him; he, Case 80, masturbated while thinking about licking the soles of her feet and the spaces between her toes. One day, seeing a servant girl letting a dog lick her toes while she was reading, he got an erection and climaxed, without even touching himself. Soon after that *'he took the place of the poodle and ejaculated every time.'*

Billy fantasizes looking through a knothole in his grandmother's outdoor toilet and seeing Dixie. Naked from the waist down and wearing an alligator jacket, Dixie is laid-back, leaning against the back wall, reading and masturbating. Then, Billy is a fly on the wall inside the vermin-infested little house, a disembodied spirit at one with the hot, smelly air. Dixie is so absorbed in the book and her self-pleasuring that she hardly notices when one of Clinton's hunting dogs noses it way into the toilet. She wiggles her toes as the big dog licks her foot. Not looking up from her book, she reaches down and lets the dog lick her fingers. Baiting her fingers again with her own smell, she entices the dog to move closer. She clasps its head between her knees. Repeatedly easing up on the pressure, allowing the dog's head to advance a little ways, and then clamping down again, stopping the animal's forward progress, she optimizes the tension and maximizes the mutual anticipation of the moment of contact. Feeling the dog's high-pitched whine pulsating in his ears and hearing the sound grow ever louder and more fraught with need, *Billy* is the one vainly wooing the moon. Remembering a time when one of Clinton's puppies woke him up licking his face, giving him, Billy, an erection, he imagines the dog's tongue is his own tongue, darting in and out of his own mouth like a viper's forked ribbon, slithering over his own lips and licking his own flared nostrils. Just before its nose touches down, the dog is snatched away and Billy is magically in the mongrel's space: Billy *is* the dog; down on all-fours, straining forward, choking, his eyes tearing up, his nose just barely touching her pubic hair, he can *al . . . most* kiss the wet lips of Dixie's pussy.

It wasn't working. Why was it that, try as he might, he couldn't cash in on the very recent memory of eating Dixie's pussy? Why, now, with his sexual desire, his sexual *need*, at its highest peak ever, had his phallus deserted him? With his head filled with the dull buzz of erotic over-stimulation, he remembered the Faustpool girl, the only girl he had ever dated on a regular basis. When he was with her, even in the heat of making-out, he never had an erection; only hours later, in his own bed, would he be able to bring himself to climax.

He gathered from the stories Frankie and other boys told that most guys got very hard boners and could barely restrain themselves from raping their dates. And if you believed what they said, a lot of them didn't *have* to restrain themselves.

Billy wasn't that way. He remembered a time not long before Frankie came back; Dixie had given a party in the bunkhouse on the Johnson ranch. Some beer had been consumed and she and Billy had started necking. Dixie had unzipped and groped around in Billy's boxer shorts and what she found was—for all the good it was to her—*nothing!*

Was that why, taking him in that purposeful way on Frankie's bed, she was impervious to his dick? And was that what she meant when she called him good?

But what was the virtue in being *unable* to sin? Would he be able to resist fornication if every time he was with a girl he had the kind of boner he had when he was alone? He certainly *wanted* to be able to fuck, most of all when his dick was hard, was right *there* in front of him, *like some giddy manifestation of his very soul; a vest-pocket Messiah, a hand-held Christ Child—Jesus, Jr.—a palm pilot, sent from that place inside where God resides; Redeemer Redux Redux Redux, odd infant-item, come to die for/from Little Billy Mayden's sins, giving up the ghost, again and again and again. Oh, Jesus! There were times when He wanted so very much to be touched and loved!*

He thought about that last time with Barbara Faustpool; it was *days* before he was able to get a decent erection. During those first few days, he thought of almost nothing but that girl and her pussy. The dominant image was of her laid out like a sunny landscape undulating with warm pleasure, the pleasure he was giving her—his serpentine phallus was not in this truly Edenic picture. She was more vividly and more relentlessly on his mind during those few days than she would have been if he had been able to jack-off or even fuck her. Even later, when he was able to get an erection, his phallus was not part of the fantasy. *It, his phallus, the would-be Serpent in the Garden, was off-stage, off-camera; it was more like the handle of a magical hand-operated projector that splashed bright and lively images onto a movie screen in his mind—or like an erotic barometer whose ever-richer colors and swelling, thickening, outstretching expansion was, compared to the inner storm of his fantasies, little more than weak glimmerings on the walls of Plato's cave.*

An image of Tilly's ass ripening in front of the refrigerator flashed into his mind and he remembered the ass of a waitress in Galveston, Texas wearing short-shorts who had waited on him in the café near the motel he stayed in the night before he was supposed to attend a one-day conference, paid for by the church, for writers of religious tracts. He got the distinct impression that the waitress was attracted to him, but he hurried out after eating, and, in light of the reason for his being there, refrained from masturbating when he got back to his motel room. The next day, though, instead of going to the conference, he had gone to the beach and spent the whole day looking at women and girls in skimpy bathing-suits. As powerful as many of these sights were, and the effects on his libido were cumulative if not exponential, it was the waitress's ass he thought about as he stood naked in the garish neon light—not unlike that in Frankie and Dixie's cabin—in front of the mirror in the bathroom of the gas station where he had gone for a lonely meal of vending machine food, instead of going back to the café where the waitress worked. The upshot was no matter how obsessively he fantasized kneeling down in front of the waitress and slowly unbuttoning and unzipping her yellow shorts and lifting her naked ass up onto the lavatory into position for him to eat her pussy, he had been unable to rid himself of the dull buzz of over-excitation in his brain or to fill the vacuum into which his dick had vanished, because no matter how much he mauled himself he was unable to get a boner.

Billy was feeling that way now.

Then he remembered that after Tilly left he *did* have an erection. So that was different. Why? Was it because she was a prostitute? Was it because of the beer? Stella said that beer and whiskey opens the door of the soul for Satan to come in. Stella wouldn't be surprised if it turned out that Eve had been drunk when she ate that apple. Billy had also had an erection watching Arthur being abused that day in the boy's locker-room in the gym at Tioga school, first by that gang of boys, and then by Jake. Was he turned on by violence? Also, after watching Frankie and Arthur in the butt-hut, he had jacked-off, no trouble. Was there some of Frankie in him, same as Dixie said there was some of Billy in Frankie? He was pretty sure Arthur had been outside the cabin looking in at him after Tilly left. Was he an exhibitionist? Or was it Arthur himself? Was Arthur—or his smell!—the key to the whole thing?

Billy's mind jumped from Arthur to something Theo once told Jake and him. Theo said he heard about an inmate, a 'boy', at Angola, whose 'daddy'—a fellow inmate who protected the 'boy' from other sexually aggressive alpha males in the prison population—had forced him to undergo castration. Theo said that, after the psychological trauma of the surgery was over and physical recovery was complete, the power and magic of the daddy's phallus was greatly enhanced for the boy; the boy said he dreamed about his daddy's phallus; sometimes he even dreamed that it was his own phallus. When he was awake, the boy claimed to be all the more driven to love the phallus, to take it in, to be possessed by it, to be made whole by it.

Billy thought this came close to describing him and capturing how he had felt about Dixie's pussy.

(Theo said he heard that after the operation the boy was more attractive to other daddy's; that he ended up the punk of the biggest stud in the whole prison block; and that he had his new daddy castrate the one who made him give up his manhood, keeping the severed cock in a jar of formaldehyde as a keepsake.)

His thoughts circled around again to Case 80. Not only did Case 80 have an erection, he ejaculated, apparently without even touching himself. *'This caused in him erection and ejaculation'*. Billy wasn't sure he believed this. If Case 80 really loved sucking and licking toes, and if he really loved the girl whose toes they were, he wouldn't have allowed himself to be distracted by anything, including, or especially, his own sexual needs, because all his sexual energy would be drawn to the point of contact with the sacred objects, though, later, he might have felt ashamed enough of this to lie and say that he had had an erection and had ejaculated, because how weird is it to want to suck toes so much that you can't even think about your own pleasure, until some time later?

Billy thought about how he and Case 80 were alike and how they were different.

If it gave her so much pleasure, Billy wondered, why hadn't the servant girl sucked her own toes? It wasn't all that hard to do. And if Case 80 loved it so much why hadn't *he* sucked his own toes? Billy himself had never had the desire to suck anyone's toes, even the Faustpool girl's or Dixie's. Maybe he should try it if-and-when he ever got the chance again. Maybe he should have started with sucking the Faustpool girl's toes and worked his way up; maybe then she wouldn't have reacted so violently when his lips first touched her down there. Oh, how much better it had been with Dixie, who went after it, who loved it, kept it going for a long, long time, never giving a thought to what she might be missing by not having a dick crammed up her pussy! Her pussy had *wanted*, had *loved*, to be kissed, licked and sucked on and *only* that!

Billy knew, of course, that toes and feet were very sensitive. When he was little it felt wonderful when Stella used to rub his feet, shins, and calves with rubbing alcohol when he had growing pains and he couldn't go to sleep. How good Jesus must have felt when Mary Magdalene washed His feet and anointed them with oil and then dried them with her long flowing black hair!

Theo had a book with a picture in it showing a woman with her arms wrapped around the cross of the crucified Jesus, snuggling her cheek against His bleeding feet. Theo said the woman was Jesus's mother, the Blessed Virgin Mary. All you saw were Jesus's feet with a nail driven through them and Mary's face. The idea was that Mary, in her own small way, was comforting her Son.

(Theo said a priest told him that Mary's eyes were closed so that her face wouldn't compete with her Son's mutilated feet for prominence in the picture and to remind us that true piety is an entirely private matter, but Theo was sneering when he said it, so who knew what to make of it. (Theo told the joke: Please cross your feet, we only have one nail left!))

Theo said what made crucifixion pictures powerful for him was the contrast between the *inhuman* instruments of torture and *human* flesh and blood, which Jesus *became* to show the world what, ideally, human beings are capable of. The nails driven into His hands and feet, the spear thrust into His side, and the thorns piercing His scalp all stand for the Masculine Will, the drive to snatch power and accumulate knowledge. The spear, for example, might stand for the surgeon's scapel probing His heart in quest of the secrets of immortality. The thorns are the neuro-scientist's electrodes invading His brain, in search of the essence of the human soul. The nails are the scholar's quills that twist His words into cages for the human mind. Artists, colluding with churchmen, have made Christ crucified—pinned to the cross like a butterfly, the primal imago, the prize specimen in a macabre reliquary—into the perversely ironic and duplicitous symbol of a tyranny even greater and more cynical, imperishable, and exclusively *male*, than the pagans of Rome ever were.

Jesus's body, on the other hand, stands for Feminine Mystery, which, Theo believed, will forever evade all attempts at understanding.

Billy could see that he was expected to understand that Mary, the woman in the picture, knows she is worthy only of touching her Son's bloody foot. He understood that as long as she thinks about Jesus's pain and agony, she is a saint; to the extent that she feels sexual pleasure, she is a pervert. It seemed a very thin line—after all, the pain and humiliation of the crucifixion is called Christ's *Passion*—but Billy believed that it was essential for his salvation that the line be drawn and maintained. What a great difference there was between Mary and Case 80 in their love of feet!

He thought: I am to Dixie what Mary is to Jesus:

Mary relieved Jesus's 'passion' by caressing His feet. Billy relieved Dixie's sexual anguish by eating her pussy.

Mary grieved for her lost Son, but she knew that His death would save the world. Billy grieved for the strategic and temporary loss of his phallus (son), but knew that his inability to contaminate another two people—

Dixie and the baby inside—with his own sinful discharges might count in his favor come Judgment Day. The actual relief to Jesus who was crucified and to Dixie who had suffered the torment of a diabolical lust and the perhaps unconscious anticipation of the pain of childbirth, might not be all that great, but Mary and Billy were both willing to take on the other person's suffering, to the point that their own suffering at least approached, in intensity and quality, that of the sufferer; and the fact that it was all either of them could do only added to their own suffering.

Mary's caressing Jesus's feet relieved the pain of His crucifixion. Billy's cunnilingus perhaps prospectively relieved the pain of childbirth for Dixie; and both good deeds presaged new life, Jesus's resurrection and Dixie's baby, at least if she didn't get rid of it.

Billy thought of yet another way his and Mary's situations were similar: In Dixie's womb there was a baby; in Jesus's tomb there was a young man. *And entering into the sepulchre, they saw a young man sitting on the right side, clothed in a long white garment; and they were affrighted,* Mark 16:5.

He wanted to believe that eating pussy, Dixie's and the Faustpool girl's, was the equivalent of Mary's ministrations; and he wondered: If, like Case 80, I had had an erection, especially if I had ejaculated, would I have crossed the line, would I be a pervert, a sinner? Yes, he decided, he would, no doubt about it.

Standing up, Billy turns off the television and goes into the bedroom. He lies down on Frankie's bed. Drawing his legs up and wrapping his arms around them, he rolls over onto the dirty, smelly bed—a foetus in an edge-less, point-less watery world.

He dreams he is sitting on the edge of a bed. He brings his foot up close to his face. He looks closely at his big toe. His big toe has an opening in the end of it. He stares into the aperture, which opens up like dawn in a wilderness clearing, revealing the reflective surface of a pool. It is like looking down into a magic well. He sees a single face but there are two different people in the face (three if you count his own implicit visage). As his eyes fly over the surface, focusing on one feature, then skipping to another, he sees, and is seen by, two different people in the same face: His mother Stella and Arthur Maxwell.

Then Billy is holding his leg in his lap like a baby; his big toe is also his dick; like himself, it is sad and so choked with lust it is about to pop. It is his doppelganger, his double. It seems to be trying to speak, to express some deep ineffable longing and sadness. With nothing but that pouty-melancholy mouth for a face, it looks like a baby, or a foetus—a first approximation of a human being.

It *is* a baby, *his* baby. It is to him as he is to Stella; it is *of* his body, just as he is *of* Stella's body.

He notices that his phallus has somehow become detached and has been plugged into a bottle; it is an over-sized nipple of a baby's bottle.

Before he can start sucking, something wakes him up.

✳   ✳   ✳

Numbly observing the scene in the other room, Billy, feeling disembodied, is unable to move—the absence of feeling in his crotch has spread to his legs and chest. Lurid light, directed by shiny metal reflectors down, away from the ceiling, gives the mise en scene—Frankie, spectral in the discoloring glare, facing off against three little people in wheelchairs inside a bubble of harsh brightness—an aura of profound unreality.

Above, on the top bunk, looming out of the upper darkness, is Ralph, the diminutive deaf mute. The little guy is like a grinning cartoon-vulture on the highest limb of a dead tree shrouded in a black cloud, happily anticipating some great moment of edibility on the ground.

Billy knows it is Ralph from the sparkle of his bright pixie-eyes and from the ragged and dirty baseball cap he is wearing. Ralph's baseball cap was ancient, ten years old. It had been part of Billy's Little League uniform. Soon after the season was over, Ralph caught Billy putting on a condom stolen from Clinton's sock drawer. To keep Ralph quiet about the stolen rubber, Billy had to give Ralph the cap, the only item of the uniform which Billy was allowed to keep, as hush-money. Billy is touched that Ralph still treasures it enough to wear it.

When, with a knowing smirk of recognition, Ralph looks toward the bedroom door—his expression seems to say that not only did he know that Billy was standing there looking in, but that he knew, as well, what Billy and Dixie had done in there earlier—Billy's sense of unreality dissipates. It made him feel good to imagine that another human being might know that Billy Mayden was unmistakably, beyond all doubt, among The Elect; and even better that Ralph might have watched while he went down on Dixie.

Frankie closed and pocketed the knife. Taking a deep breath, he sat forward in the chair, situating his narrow blue-jeaned butt on the front edge of the ragged cane seat. He tilted back, stretching his legs out in front of him and crossing them at the ankles; all that touched the floor were the back legs of the chair and the heel of one of his ratty cowboy boots. Easing himself even further back and straightening his body, he reached back over his shoulder and groped until he found the end post of the bunk bed; resting his head against the wooden upright and letting his arms hang down on either side, he maintained a precarious balance.

If Ralph falls off that top bunk, Billy thought, he will land right on top of Frankie and they both will end up on the floor. Made dizzy again by this unstable scene, Billy decided maybe he should get on home. He wasn't sure how late it was and he didn't want to have to lie to Stella about what he had been doing that was so important that it would keep him away from the evening church service. Bending over to make himself less conspicuous, he eased into the living room, intending to slink on out the best he could, using the three wheelchairs on his left to screen his exit from Frankie's view. Headed for the front door of the cabin, he sensed, down, on his right, a close presence: behind the wheelchairs, sitting on the old threadbare couch right where Dixie had sat earlier, yet another person was watching Frankie. Curious to know who it was but too shy to stop and take a good look, he made a quick decision to stay, at least long enough to see who this person was. Maybe it was Tilly, waiting for him to come out and claim his prize. Making a sharp right turn and sitting on the couch, he picked up a magazine and hid his face behind it. For one fraught moment, he thought maybe Dixie had come back to tell him something she forgot to tell him before; that she was definitely gonna leave, for instance, as soon as she got rid of her baby. Glancing over, he couldn't see her eyes behind her wrap-around sunglasses, but he could tell the person was not Dixie or Tilly. It was some other young woman, vaguely familiar.

Ralph looked down at the top of Frankie's head. He made like he was going to touch Frankie's hair, but seemed to think better of it and withdrew his hand. He signaled to one of the little boys to get the attention of the young woman in sunglasses. Frankie, able to see Ralph's face in the mirror on the wall above the couch (the same mirror Dixie used every morning to appraise her own rear-end), watched as Ralph signed something to the young woman.

The dark glasses make her look bug-eyed, Billy thought, like an insect.

"Ralph-want-know-where-Frankie-gun-is." Bug-Eyes spoke in a monotone and her head did not move as she spoke. She seemed to be looking straight ahead, not at Ralph; but, unable to make out her eyes behind the dark glasses, Billy couldn't really tell where she was looking.

Frankie looked up directly at Ralph. "That *gun*, as you call it, *son*, is a *revolv*er. This is your rifle, this is your gun. This is for killing, this is for fun. Hey! I said that pretty good, did n'I? Snunner your fucking business, you nosey little shit-eater." Frankie turned to the three younger boys. "I don't want to talk to that turd. I wanna talk to you fellers." He pointed to each boy in turn. "You ... and you ... and you. You guys are my real buddies."

He took a swig of whiskey and wiped his mouth with the back of his hand. "Y'all like the treats Crissy got you, doncha?" Before they could say they did, Frankie emitted a mirthless laugh. "You better, else she won't suck you off."

Crissy? Who is this Crissy? Billy wondered. Was she one of the other sunbathers he had seen earlier?

As Frankie spoke, the young woman signed something to Ralph. Ralph made calming gestures and took a drink from an imaginary bottle, as if to say Frankie was drunk and she shouldn't leave or be hurt by anything he said. (Okay, so *she* was Crissy, Billy thought.) Then, checking to make sure Frankie wouldn't see him in the mirror, Ralph held up a pistol for her to see, winked, and quickly put the weapon back in its hiding place behind him on the bed.

"You lucky funch of little buckers ... , I mean, you luttle bunch of licky fuckers ... ." Frankie looked up and grinned. Taking their cues, the little boys laughed. "You ain't got a worry in the world. I mean, if you did happen to get a piece of ass ... which is *highly* ... ," he blinked as he searched in vain for the word he wanted, ". . . ain't gonna happen ... ." He squinted at the little boys. "You wouldn't have to worry about getting her knocked up, though. I mean ... ."

Way he looks, Billy thought, he doesn't even recognize who they are. He probably doesn't even know how they got here. Then, uneasy, he remembered that one of the 'boys' was Brother Johnson's daughter, Tommie Sue.

Frankie continued, apparently deciding it didn't matter what he meant. "I used to not use a rubber. Not the first time I fucked ... whoever Iz fucking. I'd just pull His Majesty out of her before I comed. If I wasn't too drunk to remember to do it." Frankie chuckled. "That first one was for me. I liked to come *on* her, not *in* her that first time. On her tits and in her face, not her pussy. The second time I fucked her I would use one. That second one was for her. I kept ramming him in her til she either comed or faked it. Then I'd take it off and come on her again. I never knocked anybody up. I thought it was because I almost always pulled His Majesty out before I came or I used a rubber. Now, I know the real reason why." He pulled a folded piece of paper out of his shirt pocket. Holding a corner of the paper and raising it over his shoulder, he lunged forward, flinging his arm down in the same motion, in an attempt to open the folded sheet. The front legs of the chair hit the linoleum with a dull thud. Frankie let his cigarette fall onto the floor and ground it out with a violent twist of his boot. He took a swig from his bottle and sawed away at his thin red mustache with the knuckles of the hand holding the piece of paper, which was still only half-unfolded.

Apparently not noticing what he was doing, he wadded the paper into a ball. He looked down at it as if he didn't know what it was or where it come from. After a moment, he stuffed it back into his shirt pocket.

Ralph tapped on the wood part of the bunk bed. He signed to Crissy.

"Ralph-want-know-what-means-knock-up." As before, the young woman's head did not move. "How-I-knock-up-someone?"

"By not using one of these ... ," Frankie said after a moment. He rocked over onto one buttock and took out his wallet. Bending forward and holding it close to his face, he opened the wallet wide and peered down into the leather crack for a long time.

He's forgotten what he's looking for, Billy thought.

Frankie poked a finger into the wallet. Looking up he sniffed his finger. Getting the cued laugh from his young audience, he pretended to be probing the inside of the wallet. "If can find the somitch ... . Where in the fuck is ... ?" Several dollar bills dropped out onto his lap and onto the floor. One of the little boys bent to pick up the spilled money. "Jus lea' 'em air."

Finally finding what he was looking for, Frankie took it out, letting the wallet and the rest of its contents fall to the floor.

Looks like a monkey dropping a banana peel, Billy thought.

Frankie stared at the fruit of his protracted search.

He doesn't even know what it is, Billy thought.

Frankie leaned his chair back against the bunk and held the object up for all to see. It was a condom, squashed flat in its tin-foil package.

Ralph reached down and plucked the rubber out of Frankie's hand. He signed to Crissy.

"Ralph-want-know-what-is-Frankie-thing."

"That, son, is called a fuck-rubber," Frankie said, wagging his head side to side. "Shit, all those times ... I didn't ee'n have to use the stupid thing. Coulda save myself thousands a dollars." He looked down at the shirt pocket he had put the wadded-up paper in.

Ralph tapped and, pointing at a picture on the label of the condom packet, he signed.

"That's a Trojan, my man," Frankie said when Crissy had translated Ralph's question. "The fuck-rubbers're called Trojans. Trojans're bad-assed motherfuckers."

Ralph signed.

"You ask too many questions," Frankie said before Crissy could translate.

Ralph signed and grinned at the others. He patted the big wave in Frankie's hair.

"Ralph-say-Ralph-still-not-know-how-I-knock-up-some-body,"

Crissy said.

Frankie lifted his head off his chest. "The usual way." His flung his head forward, digging his chin into his chest. "You stick your dick in her dirty little cock," he murmured. "Stupid Yankees call their dicks cocks. You little fuckers know that? Bunch a queers. Yankees, I mean, not you guys." Raising his head again, he started laughing, loud and forced. "It's not *that* little, come to think of it … *come* to think of it. Guess her ol' man musta tapped her a time a two. Might as well. Ever body else has." He snickered. "I uz half right, anyways. It is deffny dirty." After a long pause, he resumed. "Then you pump away for a while and before you know it you come a shitload into her pussy, and presto! Miracle of life … you're gonna be a motherfucking daddy." He laughed. "I guess ever daddy is a motherfucker, eh, boys?"

Frankie's head fell forward again and he muttered, "Musta been drunk or suhhum … forgot to saddle up … or … forgot to pull His Majesty out in time." Then he shouted, "Hell man! There uz plenty times when … I said fuck it and nothing happened. It's okay. Might be fun having the little fucker around. I'll teach him how to play basketball."

Frankie looked at the lump in his shirt pocket. He frowned and then his face went blank.

Like he was trying to remember something but gave up, Billy thought. Flipping through the tattered pages of the magazine, he tried to look like he wasn't listening to Frankie. Able to shut out the meaning of the words, he couldn't escape the voice; the grating sound triggered his suppressed anger. He imagined himself telling Frankie that he would *not* go along with any plan, whatever it was, that Frankie and Tilly might have cooked up to make it up to him for yesterday, and that was final.

Then, it hit him! The way Frankie was going to make it up to him was: Arthur Maxwell! That's why Frankie had left. To find Arthur and send him up to the cabin. But then Dixie had run Arthur off. Had he come back? *Was* it Arthur he had seen when he checked to see if it was nighttime? *Must* have been.

With a touch of the panic he felt at the time, he recalled the last time he and Jake were together in the old car. Other memories ran through his mind: he recalled the look on Dr. Maxwell's face that time Jonnie Vonderheim gave him a blow-job. (Ralph had to explain to him that Dr. Maxwell wasn't in pain; he was *enjoying* it, really, *really* enjoying it.) Then came a synergistic memory in which he was both peering through the window into the butt-hutt and was inside it himself, sitting where Frankie had been. In the build-up to a single, shared climax, he witnessed the convulsive jerking of Frankie's body and felt the same *in his own body,* nearly choking on the same rasping, throat-clutching guttural sounds he heard coming out of Frankie.

Looking at Frankie now with new eyes, Billy's groin was infused with new life. Recalling what Dixie had said about the look on Frankie's face when Arthur was sucking his dick, he felt all resolve to resist the idea of letting Arthur make it up to him petering-out. Still, it might be better if he held off on bringing up Arthur's name. If yesterday proved anything, it proved that. I'll just wait and see, he thought.

Frowning, Frankie slid his butt further forward on the front edge of the chair. He unzipped his fly and rummaged around inside his underwear. When he had fished out his penis and looked at the pale sleepy thing for a while, he looked up and around the room. Seeming to find no one in sight, a look of fear flitted across his face. Then, seeing that indeed all eyes were on his dick, he smiled, unbuckled his belt, and unbuttoned his jeans. Rocking side-to-side on the chair, raising first one buttock and then the other, he pushed the jeans down to mid-thigh. Lifting his dick by the foreskin, like he was picking up a dead snake by the tail, he reached into his jockey shorts; cupping his balls in his hand, he scooped them out and let them flop over on top of the elastic band of his shorts. He pushed his shirt up, exposing his badly bruised torso, his protruding ribs and hip-bones, his concave abdomen, and his red pubic hair which was brownish-purple in the neon light. His head slumped forward and he and the others watched as his penis grew in size. As it filled with blood, it swung around, moving slower than the second hand of a clock, slinking into the patch of pubic hair like an exhausted side-winder. It came to a stop at about five o'clock— taking Frankie's point of view, from which six o'clock would be the narrow trail of pubic hair that went up to the dark hole of his navel—and seemed to shrivel up a bit like a balloon with a slow leak.

The younger boys gawked at Frankie's tired, droopy pecker, porcelain-white and black-veined in the neon light. Ralph was grinning, but he was looking, too.

So was Billy; at first as much to avoid looking at Frankie's battered and apparently disease-ravaged body as to play the voyeur; but then, feeling himself coming back to life and remembering his own recent failure and disappointment, he *wanted* Frankie to succeed, *wanted* him to get an erection, *wanted* to see him ejaculate.

Crissy didn't look. Rocking back and forth, she seemed, behind her dark glasses, to be looking at nothing at all.

"It's about time you boys learned about the birds and the bees," Frankie said. "Now, you little peckerheads probably don't even know what come looks like, do you? I didn't neither when I was your age. But now, my come comes out in big white gobs. Looks like clabber or something. Leas' that's what a little girl told me one time. That's when you have to start using fuck-rubbers."

Reaching up toward Ralph, Frankie snapped his fingers. "Gimme that fucking fuck-rubber." Taking the packet and fumbling around with it for a time, he finally got the condom unwrapped. He put the two pieces of foil on the lower part of his abdomen near his pubic hair. "Just stay right there, you little fuckers."

The little boys glanced sideways at each other like they thought Frankie might be talking to them.

Frankie began trying to fit the balloon over the end of his penis. "See, Ralphie, old son ... you other fellows, too ... ." Without raising his head, he looked forward. Apparently satisfied that the boys were paying close attention, a smile flitted around the corners of his mouth. "This is how it works. You just roll it ... like you would your socks ... all the way ... *down* ... and it ... it's *supposed* to catch the come ... if I can get the motherfucker on ... ." Frankie's penis, never more than semi-hard to begin with, lost what little stiffness it had, and he was unable to get the rubber on. "Come on, you bastard! Get hard!" He slid the loose skin up and down the dispirited, half-gelled shaft. When his penis didn't do as it was told, Frankie swatted his genitals as if they were a noxious insect, knocking the rubber and the two pieces of tinfoil onto the floor and causing his shorts to snap up and swallow his dick and balls like a bass nabbing an unwary dragonfly. "No crown for you, you piece of shit!"

The little boys gasped.

Under the sway of an incipient, not quite conscious idea that he and Frankie might be in sinc, dickwise, Billy imagined he felt the pain he imagined Frankie felt; he crossed his legs and squeezed his thighs together.

Ralph tapped and signed.

"Waddie say?" Frankie wanted to know.

"Ralph-say-come-on-Frankie-I-can-do-it'."

"Yeah, I know I can do it. I don't need a deaf-mute white-trash pervert-pigmy to tell me that."

Frankie pushed his shorts down to mid-thigh and resumed the task of herding the spongy snake-head into the rolled up rubber bag which one of the boys had retrieved for him. After a lot of fumbling and cursing, he succeeded in sheathing the sulky surrogate. Then with a great deal of caressing and more cussing, he managed to bring the wet-suited organ back to its former level of semi-rigidity. "Keeps the come from getting inside the lady's *woooomb* ... when you *woooo* her. Otherwise known as the bitch's box ... the sister's snatch ... the main squeeze. Or the *man* squee*zer* ... get it?" Rolling the rubber back up, he held it over his head. "Here take it, you little queer-bait. I won't be needing it. Git rid of it." A tear rolled down his cheek. He wiped it away and laughed without mirth. "Fact I never did. *Now* I find out. Thanks to a little test I had done." Looking down his nose at his scrunched-up shirt, he put his hand over his heart like a shell-shocked Marine hearing taps.

Ralph motioned to one of the little boys to retrieve the two pieces of foil from under Frankie's chair. He reshaped the foil and fit the two parts together around the condom. Then he tossed the reassembled packet across the room. It landed on the couch next to Billy. Billy quickly picked it up and put it in his shirt pocket.

"How come you so drunk, Uncle Frankie?" The tom-boy asked.

"Boss fired my ass."

"Howcome, Uncle Frankie?"

"For drinking too much."

Ralph tapped and signed.

Crissy translated. The little boys giggled nervously and Frankie said, "Yeah, ha ha. I drink because I'm a drunk. You 'bout as funny as a crutch. But you're right *this time*, you little turd." Absently stroking his penis which was flaccid as an earthworm, he continued, "Well, don't matter now, does it? Might as well. He's already fired my ass. You can't get the death penalty more than once. Any more is ... water over the dam ... or some such shit. Boss-man says his brother, the good reverend, made him do it. Shit, man! Plenty a fuckers in that church get drunk all the fucking time. And they don't *need* a reason to drink. Cept to get drunk. They both know what goes on in that church and they don't do diddley. Fact, boss has a fancy house where all the deacons get together ... *without their wives* I might add ... and do a lot worse than drink. Course, the good brethren need a place where they don't have to mingle with ... or be seen by ... the riffraff. Oh yeah, there's a lot more than booze to be had, let me tell you. For a price. Course, up in the pulpit, Brother John says he don't *approve* of that kind of stuff, but, down on the ground where money talks and bullshit walks, he's all live-and-let-live."

Frankie thumped his penis so hard it swung over and landed with a loud flop on the other side. "Little piece of shit!"

Billy winced in vicarious pain; picking up the magazine in his lap, he tried to tune Frankie out.

Ralph tapped and signed and Crissy translated.

"No, I'm not gonna break it, you little turd," Frankie said. He took a drag off his cigarette and blew out smoke with a whoosh. "The poster boy of Christianity. Pulled out of the gutter like some mangy old dog and put in front of the fireplace to dry out. Then I'm supposed to be *grateful*. Don't look good, me being around there now … . Oh, fuck it!"

Raising his head and looking past the three little boys, Frankie said to Billy, "Hey! Billy! Nice glasses. You fix them yourself? Good job. How long you been sitting there? Sorry about … what happened … ," he gestured with his head, ". . . up air." He stared at Billy for a long time, apparently thinking, trying to remember something. Then, waving as if whatever he was thinking was a gnat, he said, "You coulda been a helluva baseball player, Billy. You coulda been the next fucking Babe Ruth. Make all those hot-shot niggers like Willy Mays and Jackie Robertson look like amma … teurs."

Billy looked up from his magazine. Remembering how it felt to be hit in the face with a basketball, he tried to resist Frankie's praise. Deadening his eyes to make them look like Dixie's, he gazed at Frankie, said nothing. Waiting until Frankie looked away, he returned to flipping the pages of the magazine.

"Hey! What kind of hair got up his ass, I wonder," Frankie muttered.

Ralph tapped and signed. Crissy translated, spelling out a long name and a couple of dirty words. The little boys laughed nervously. Ralph must think Crissy doesn't know the dirty words, Billy thought, or maybe he doesn't know how to sign them.

Frankie didn't react at first. Instead he again seemed to be thinking, remembering, turned inward. Then he grinned. "Tell you about Jonnie Vonderheim! Did I fuck her? Did I give her a what? B-l-o what? Blow-job, is that it? Did *I* give *her* a blow-job? Is that what you said?"

It occurred to Billy that if Arthur Maxwell were there he might help Frankie get a hard-on. He wondered what would happen if he suggested to Frankie that he talk about Arthur. Maybe this time bringing up Arthur might have a different outcome. For one thing, he wouldn't be caught off guard if Frankie took it the wrong way. He felt the last of his hurt and anger slipping away. Remembering what Dixie had said, he now believed he understood how Frankie might have felt threatened enough to lash out the way he did. Imagining Frankie and Arthur together, it suddenly bore in on Billy what Frankie's body looked like now. His starved body, once magnificent, seemed weak and defenseless. Gazing at Frankie, a strange feeling came over him. Frankie's face was sad, open, innocent. It was pretty, like a girl's. It could almost *be* the face of a girl. A pretty red-haired girl.

Seen in direct sunlight, Billy's mother's hair had a red tint to it.

Billy now let himself savor Frankie's saying he could have been a good baseball player, not so much *what* he said as *why* he said it. It was an olive branch. Frankie's way of saying he was sorry for what happened. When he sobers up I'll ask him to forgive me, Billy thought, vaguely aware of the notion that asking forgiveness can be like heaping hot coals on an offender's head. Or was it the other way around? Which was it? Asking or offering?

"It's the other way around, asswipe," Frankie said, coming out of his reverie—or stupor. He twisted his head up and back and gave Ralph a menacing, questioning look. Ralph grinned down at him. Frankie grabbed for Ralph's baseball cap, but Ralph jerked his head back before Frankie could get it.

Frankie stood up, tipping his chair over. He stared at Ralph until Ralph dropped the mocking smirk. One of the little boys picked the chair up.

"No way am I gonna put my mouth on *that* grimy pussy," Frankie said, sitting and sprawling out as before.

"Why not!" The words just popped out, to Billy's immediate regret. He couldn't believe himself; so much so that, for a second, it seemed like he might have just thought the words or that someone else might have said them.

What was Billy thinking? In the frame of mind he was in, it was inevitable that Frankie's remark would trigger an impulse to defend cunnilingus. He was bursting to tell someone what had happened with Dixie; it would have to be Jake as there was no one else to tell, except maybe Ralph, who probably knew already. He wanted to shout, to *sing*: *Oh what a beautiful morning. Oh what a beautiful day. I have a wonderful feeling. Everything's going my way.* Put it on his gravestone: *Here lie's Billy Mayden, who on such and such a date in 1957, achieved nirvana.*

Even more than Jake he wanted Frankie West to know that he had eaten Dixie's pussy. He had various motivations, some of them contradictory and not all of them conscious, for wanting to do this:

In the mutual conciliatory mood—and phallic empathy—he sensed between himself and Frankie, he wanted to tell him that because of the wonderful thing that had come into being between himself and the fantastic woman they both loved, Dixie was going to be alright after Frankie was gone.

Still flooded with—and addled by—the scent, feel, and taste of Dixie's body, he wanted Frankie to know that, now, they were an interwoven *trio*, a company of erotic players, an *aristocracy* of lovers. That he had taken the Faustpool girl's place on the tribunal first seen on the backseat of the Trailways.

He wanted, too, by way of a friendly turning of the tables, to tell Frankie that Dixie truly *did* enjoy having her pussy eaten and to suggest that *he*, Frankie, try it just once before he died. What better way to face the end of life than ensconced in the smell and taste of its beginning? Leave by the way you came in.

At the deepest level, below the threshold of awareness, he was enraged at Frankie for humiliating him. What better way to get back at him than by eating his pregnant wife's pussy in his own sick bed, thereby giving her pleasure much more intense that any Frankie ever gave her.

At the same time, Billy realized, of course, that his two-word outburst wasn't at all appropriate. It was Jonnie Vonderheim's grimy pussy that Frankie didn't want to put his mouth on; and who could blame him. Added to that was the fact that, in all likelihood, Frankie considered cunnilingus to be sick, dirty, and perverse, no matter *whose* pussy was involved. Plus, there were other people in the room who without a doubt shared Frankie's low opinion of oral sex.

Frantic, Billy could think of no way to talk his way out of the mess he had made for himself. He just hoped Frankie was so drunk he wouldn't pick up on his exclamation or if he did he wouldn't be thinking clearly enough to make a big deal out of it.

"Oh! So he is listening after all. I thought *that*'d get your attention, Billy Boy. Yeah, some guys like to eat the old hairy pie. Women, too, or so I've heard. Ain't you always saying you get past the smell, you got it licked?" Frankie laughed. No one else did. "Ha ha ha. Little joke there, boys. Say, do you know how a French woman holds her liquor?" He paused. Looking puzzled, he shook his head. "Never mind. Never did understand that fucking joke. Anyway you won't catch me putting my handsome face where some other man's dick's been. 'Course, in Jonnie's case, that would be *many, many* men. *Thousands* of men. Lay all their dicks end-to-end, they'd reach to the moon."

So much for telling Frankie the good news.

Closing his eyes and not saying anything for a while, Frankie used his thumbs and index fingers to push the loose skin of his penis as far down as it would go. Opening one eye, he pulled the fingers away, his dick slumping to one side like a child falling asleep in church, and watched the skin creep back along the droopy shaft like the pushed-up sleeve of a sweater inching its way down. He repeated the sequence several times, pulling the foreskin down and watching its lethargic relapse. With each repetition the penis reared up like a purple-headed embryonic reptile waking and stretching in the sun, its little mouth yawning, but it did not get any bigger or stiffer. Sighing and opening his other eye, Frankie grasped the shaft. He stroked and tweaked the head of his dick with the fingers of his other hand. For a long time, while his fingers twiddled, he frowned like he was trying to recall some important detail.

During the ensuing silence, while his observers waited to see what Frankie would do next, Billy closed the magazine and tossed it aside. Peering between two of the little boys, he saw the flaccid crown of Frankie's penis projecting out of the confining fist. I wonder what he's thinking about, Billy thought, waxing sympathetic, wishing him success. As if to extend some sort of telepathic aid, he imagined Frankie and Jonnie Vonderheim going at it, then Frankie and Dixie together. Then remembering Frankie in the butt-hut and the tender look on the face of the fat ugly 'nurse', he wished he and Frankie were alone so he could tell Frankie he understood about Arthur Maxwell. He imagined talking to Frankie about the incident in the boy's locker room in the gym that day in ninth grade when Jake attacked Arthur, kicked him while he was down. He even considered telling Frankie about the strange effect the incident had on him.

Racking his brain, trying to think of some way he could help Frankie, Billy recalled an incident from high school.

Out of the blue Frankie blurted, "Church choir!"

Everybody sat up, startled by the loudness of Frankie's exclamation.

Billy couldn't believe it: Frankie had read his mind! Sort of.

"*That*'s the place to find lots a good pussy." Frankie closed his eyes and let his hands continue their futile efforts. "I think it must have something to do with those robes they wear. It gets pretty hot under those things and it's not just because of the weather, either. I betcha some of those older girls don't wear panties or anything under there. That must make 'em feel sexy, like they getting away with something naughty."

There followed an even longer silence during which Frankie's head drooped forward as if by imitating his penis he might win its co-operation. Just when Billy was sure he had gone to sleep, Frankie's head reared up and his eyes popped open. He looked up at Ralph and over at Crissy.

Then Frankie looked right at Billy and said, "Oh! Oh! I gotta tell you boys what happened the other ni ... one time. You know that goody-goody twat? What's her name?" Frankie took one hand away from his penis and rubbed his fingers and thumb together the way some people do to signify money. "Oh, you know. Real stuck up little cunt. Little goody-two-shoes type?" Frankie picked up the whiskey bottle and put it to his mouth but didn't drink. Just held it there against his lower lip, trying to think, or so it seemed.

Billy, still thinking about the incident in high school, his remembering of which seemed to cause Frankie to exclaim, Church choir!, recalled that in mixed ensemble Frankie stood right behind the Faustpool girl. He recalled how Frankie would lean forward and whisper things in her ear that made her laugh.

Ralph signed and Crissy translated, spelling out one name, just as Frankie took a swig from the bottle.

Giving a snort, Frankie sprayed whiskey all over the little boys. "Sister Johnson! Whoa! That *would* be something, wouldn't it?" He milked the snot and whiskey out of his nose. He wiped his fingers in his pubic hair. "Tapping the preacher's wife right there in his own church. Right under his righteous-assed nose. No, not her."

Frankie looked over at Billy. He seemed to sober up and the brief excitement was gone. Glancing from Crissy to Ralph, he seemed frightened. Releasing his penis, he pulled on his lips as if they too had gone numb on him. He asked, "Who was the one with the scar on her face?"

Not looking up from the magazine he had picked up again, Billy said the Faustpool girl's first name.

"Who?" Frankie looked hard at Billy.

Billy repeated the name.

"What about her?"

Billy gave Frankie a look that he hoped conveyed that he knew all about Frankie and the Faustpool girl; that, as of a couple of hours ago, he was out of reach of Frankie's cruelty. He wondered if Frankie was so far gone, drunk and dying, that he didn't even recognize the name. He said, "Was she the goody-goody twat you were gonna tell us about?"

"You mean ... ?" Frankie slid a finger across his cheek. "Not bloody likely. Now *that* would be a nasty fuck. Have to dig her up." He took hold of his penis again. "Who gives a fuck what her fucking name is? They all look alike upside down, right? Just like a Jew is a nigger turned wrong side out. Anyhow, let me tell you about the other ... that time." Frankie took another swig of whiskey. "I was ... ."

Billy thought, He's trying to remember where he is, what year it is.

"Let me think ... it was ... ." Frankie gave the money sign to Ralph, as if to say, Help me think, or, What am I thinking?

Ralph signed and Crissy said, "In-choir."

"Yeah, that's it. That's where it was."

Billy and Ralph looked at each other. Seeing the sparkle in Ralph's eyes, Billy remembered the story of Frankie and Sharon Dodge.

Sharon was a couple of grades ahead of Billy; she played guard on the high school basketball team; she had a big, well-formed ass and liked showing it off. In the weeks leading up to the year-end holiday season, members of the high school choir came to school early, assembling before first bell, in preparation for the annual Christmas concert. Frankie told Billy that every morning during rehearsal of the Hallelujah Chorus, he would push his knee between Sharon's legs from behind and she would respond by rubbing her ass against his crotch. Then one night, Frankie said, he cornered her in the back of the bus after their teams had returned from games at another school and that she bled like a stuck pig. The story spread around school and, when a few weeks later the Dodge girl dropped out of school, a double-notch—one for the kill and one for knocking her up—was added to Frankie's ever-growing total, but since, word was, Sharon Dodge had fucked a lot of guys, including many of the hoods that hung out at the Dumps and even the driver of the school bus she took to school, the same bus that Billy and Jake took—she always sat in the first seat behind the driver and was forever whispering sweet nothings in the older man's ear—nobody believed the part about Sharon bleeding like a stuck pig, and Frankie missed out on the hat trick.

Eventually, though, after Sharon and the bus driver got married and had an eight-pound baby boy that everybody said was awfully big for a preemy and bore an uncanny resemblance to Sharon's new husband, the math was done and the common conclusion became that Sharon was already pregnant with the bus-driver's baby by the time the hanky-panky between her and Frankie in the choir started up; and that it was Sharon, knowing she was pregnant anyhow, so why not?, who seduced Frankie, not the other way around, and Frankie lost his double-notch. This new version of the story worked well for all involved, enhancing Frankie's reputation as a pussy-magnet—the thinking being that of all the guys at school Sharon could have picked from for her one-last-fling she chose Frankie—and giving her credit among her slutty girl-friends for a well-executed take-down of a big-time alpha-male.

"I-had-on-robe," Crissy said, watching Ralph sign.

"Yeah, yeah, that's right. Had my fucking robe on." Frankie had been drawn into the telling. "Let's see ... it's dark inside the church, like they're trying to save on electricity or something. Nothing but a bunch of candles. I can hear frogs croaking. Must be coming from outside. Anyway, I'm standing right behind this whoring bitch-cunt and ... ,"

"Crissy-thought-Frankie-said-she-was-goody-goody," Crissy said.

Frankie frowned, looked confused.

Ralph gave Crissy a look; frowning, he gestured for her to just go along with the drama; then he signed and Crissy said, "Or-was-Frankie-being-s-a-r-c-a-s-t-i-c?"

Frankie frowned, then brightened when Billy spoke the spelled-out word. "Yeah, I didn't really mean ... she wud no goody-goody ... she just wanted people to think ... ."

Billy was beginning to suspect that Frankie was too drunk to hold anyone in particular in mind.

"Where was I?" Frankie asked.

Ralph put his hand on top of Frankie's head and made eye contact with Billy. Frankie continued, "Oh yeah, I was standing right behind her. The more I thought about all that naked pussy under those robes, the hornier I got. Rows and rows of holy, horny pussy." Frankie paused like he was waiting for his thoughts and fantasies to organize and vocalize themselves. "So ... ."

"I-rubbed-my-knee-against-back-her-legs," Crissy said, as Ralph signed.

"Yeah, that's it. Whad I do next?"

"I-pushed-my-knee-between-her-legs."

Moving his limp penis to one side, Frankie lifted one of his knees as high as his jeans and shorts, still at mid-thigh, would allow. "Yeah, li-kiss." He jiggled the skinny up-lifted leg and let it fall back down. After a short pause, he asked, "Whad the bitch do?"

Ralph signed, Crissy spoke, and Billy understood: "The bitch spread her legs, leaned back and rubbed her butt against your crotch."

Closing his eyes, Frankie started slowly moving the foreskin up and down, coaxing, caressing. Ralph's and Crissy's and Billy's eyes were focused on Frankie's dick; they were addressing not Frankie but his dick, reminding it, enticing it, creating for it. Then Ralph locked eyes with Billy and signed. Frankie put Crissy's fractured translations and spellings into his own words, phrase by phrase: "She bent her knees ... . She moved up and down ... very slowly ... sliding her ass up and down ... her butt-cheeks were like two big lips kissing my dick. Her ass-crack swallowed up my dick like a weeny in a bun... and it felt like there was a long, hot tongue ... licking my dick ... ."

Billy wondered if this threesome had done this before and was pleased to be part of what was now a quartet. He felt a re-newed connection, a closer-than-ever kinship, with Ralph. With his little child's-body stretched out cross-ways on the top bunk, his head and arms hanging over the edge, Ralph was like a usurpuous rebel-puppet directing the actions of the humans below. It seemed right that he and Ralph—two old friends who had so often seen Frankie in action—were there, like gurardian angels, keeping an eye on Frankie as he neared his end.

Ralph had spied so many times on Frankie West and Jonnie Vonderheim while they were having sex that the illicit lovers not only accepted Ralph's voyeurism but missed it when he wasn't around. Eventually they wanted it, like some exotic, forbidden spice they had acquired a taste for, finally coming to the point of requiring it for their full satisfaction.

As if awakening to the images and warmed by the attention, the bashful star of the little drama slowly became fully erect, as did Billy's own dick. Billy thought of the knob and handle of a baseball bat. As if reading Billy's mind, Frankie, his eyes still closed, grasped his dick and put his thumb over the slit in the end of it. "I win." Opening one eye, he peeked at Billy. Closing his eye, he laughed, a loud and happy laugh, and licked his bedewed thumb-pad, as if inking it for prints, or starting a pleasant sorting task.

Frankie opened his eyes and looked at his penis and, as if speaking to someone he was glad to see, he said, "Man! It's a good thing I had that fucking robe on." He stood up and let his jeans and shorts fall down around his cowboy boots. "I mean, His Majesty ... must a been ... was ... out to here." He tipped his royal member toward each of the little boys, knighting each in turn with his rejuvenated scepter. Taking his hand away, he looked down and admired his stiff, free-standing *in extremis* extremity. "Gimme that crown," he said, motioning to Ralph.

Frankie took something from Ralph. It was a small gold-colored plastic crown. He tried balancing the bauble on the head his erect penis, but it fell to the floor.

One of the little boys jumped up and fled from the cabin. Brother Johnson's daughter got out of her wheel chair. She picked up the trinket-crown and tossed it up to Ralph. Then she pushed the other little boy's wheel chair out the front door. Only then did Billy realize that one of the boys was a real polio victim. The little invalid looked back over his shoulder; clearly, he didn't want to leave.

After the front screen door banged shut again, Ralph via Crissy said, "What happened then?" Billy sensed that the question was directed to him.

Frankie seemed not to notice that his audience was gone or that he was being asked a question. He was still looking at his dick, like some prehistoric Narcissus admiring the ultimate self-object—the mother of all signs—the thing that best stood for himself. After a while though, he said, "I'm getting to that. Let's see ... . Where am ... was ... I?" After more eye contact between Ralph and Billy, and signing between Ralph and Crissy, Frankie is able to enunciate Crissy's broken English: "Oh, yeah. I'm standing there with my dick practically up this bitch's ass, racking my brain ... trying to figure out how ... and where ... I'm gonna fuck her. I mean, I knew it was gonna have to be right there in the church somewhere. In one of the Sunday School rooms, or something. I cudna waited long enough to meet her somewhere after choir practice or any such shit as that." He spread his feet as far apart as the clothes around his ankles would allow and, after pumping away at himself for a while, waited for more narrative: "And neither could she, man. Even in the dark, I could see it on her face."

243

Pump, pump. "She was as hot as I was. I could practically *smell* the fumes from the bitch's pussy rising up, seeping up out of the fucking robe. I mean, she was in *heat*." Pump, pump.

"So what did you do?" Billy was hyper-aroused and impatient.

After a long pause, Frankie closed his eyes and swayed, looked like he might fall asleep.

"I whispered in her ear. The choir was still singing, so nobody heard me," Ralph-Crissy said.

"Yeah, I whispered in her ear," Frankie said, standing up straight and grinning.

"What did you tell her?" Billy asked. He was trying to hold back until they reached the end, *which, of course, was a foregone conclusion, but masturbation, like comedy, is all timing, if it's done right.*

"I told her to meet me in the church bus in the parking lot," Ralph-Crissy said.

Remembering Jake and the pretty girl on the school bus, Billy's erection intensified.

Frankie closed his eyes and repeated the sentence like a schoolboy reciting a poem in class. "I ... told ... her ... to ... meet ... me ... inthebusintheparkinglot."

Frankie opened his eyes and grinned, proud of his achievement. Then, bringing his feet together, he stood at attention.

Ralph grinned at Billy, as if encouraging him to join in, as if he knew that if Billy helped tell the story it would slow him down and give him better control of his arousal.

"Then what did you do?" Billy asked.

"Shit man, I can't remember." Pump, pump. "Something." Frankie looked up at Ralph.

Ralph looked at Billy.

Billy said, "I said I want your hot dirty pussy," and threw it back to Ralph.

"Then I went out." Frankie said, via Ralph-Crissy. "Pretending I was going to the bathroom to take a leak or something. I went out the back door. Nobody was looking. I went to the school bus." Frankie pumped harder. "In the bus I looked out the window. I saw her coming out of the back door of the church. She was holding her robe up with both hands. She was hurrying across the parking lot as fast as she could run. That made her pussy even hotter. She ran so fast I didn't have time to take off my robe. She came in. She wouldn't let me kiss her. She picked up her robe, and dress, and pulled her panties down. Her panties fell to the floor."

"Crissy-thought-she-did-not-have-panties-on," Crissy said, speaking for herself.

Ralph shushed her with a wave of his hand.

Ralph signs. Crissy says, "I-get-h-i-s-m-a-j-e-s-t-y-out ... ."

Frankie continues to translate Crissy's mangled speech into his own words. "I get His Majesty out from under the robe." Pump, pump. Frankie repeats with emphasis, "*She let her panties fall to the floor.*" Frankie stops pumping and looks hard at his dick, as if he doesn't know what to say next and is hoping his dick will tell him.

"You got His Majesty out from under the robe," Billy cues Frankie.

Frankie picks up the thread, "I got His Majesty out from under the robe," and continues speaking what Ralph-Crissy feeds into him: "Bitch reached back and grabbed him. Her butt was pointed at me like it was in the choir. She had a good grip on His Majesty. She bent forward. She was standing in the aisle, facing the back of the bus." Pump, pump. "She grabbed the hand-rail on the top of the seat to keep from falling down. She was still holding His Majesty with her other hand." Pump, pump. "I can't see him. It's dark. The robes are bunched up between us. I feel her put his ... ."

"Yeah, yeah, 'His Majesty.' Say it, don't spell it out every time," Frankie said.

"I feel her put His Majesty against her pussy and butt-hole. She said for me to take hold of it, but don't take it away. I grab hold of His Majesty. I hold it there. She grabs the seat on the other side. Holding on with both hands."

"Like this ... ," Frankie said, taking over the story-telling. To show how the fantasy-woman was positioned, he turned loose of his penis, bent over, and took hold of imaginary hand-holds atop make-believe seats in a fictitious bus.

"She-bent-over," Billy prompted, when it seemed Frankie was stuck again, unaware that he was imitating the way Crystal talked.

"Right, she bent over," Frankie said.

"I-am-holding-His-Majesty." Billy said, cosseting his own blue jean-swaddled erection.

"Yeah, I am holding His Majesty." Frankie grabbed his dick with one hand, and continued on his own. "Like this. And it is right there." He pressed the end of his phallus against the palm of his other hand. "His Majesty touches the lips of both her holes. Now I can ram it in or just stand there and not move because she starts backing up." He looks at Ralph and then at Crissy, waits for what comes next.

Before Ralph-Crissy can respond, Billy says, "She-is-going-to-put-her-pussy-around-His-Majesty. It-will-look-like-a-fur-collar-on-his-neck. I-am-all-ready-for-her-pussy-to-take-my-dick-in-and-start-sucking-on-it-like-a-calf."

Frankie slapped his thin pale thigh. He paused. He looked blankly at the empty chairs in front of him like he has seen a disappearing act at a magic show. He closed his eyes and shook his head, as if, by spreading things out on the table of his mind, he can zero-in and lock onto some elusive desideratum. Then, stiffening with resolve and sucking in a big breath of air, he motioned with his free hand for the boys no longer in front of him to move back. Flailing his free arm and rhythmically grunting, violently nodding his head faster and faster in time with his fist pumping harder and harder, he looked like a rodeo cowboy atop a bucking bramer bull.

At the moment of ejaculation his eyes opened wide; casting looks of thanks to Billy and Ralph and Crystal, he flung his head back—he was on his way up to heaven.

Billy stared at the gobs of thick white semen coiling out of the end of Frankie's penis. He watched it rolling over the fingers of his fresh-fucked fist like a clabber-fall, landing with a muffled splat on the linoleum, some of it dropping with a stifled whisper on the jeans and underwear piled atop Frankie's cowboy boots. The output was copious enough but the propulsive force of it was a far cry from the artesian geysers that Dixie had described. Billy remembered peering into the butt-hut and seeing a wad of Frankie's jizm splatter against the window pane, right in front of his eyes, like a shrimp-bug hitting the windshield of a speeding car.

Thrusting his pelvis forward, Frankie shook his penis, milked it, and watched the last drops fall to the floor. "Son of fucking bitch. Looks like I done come all over the back of her ass before I could get it in." He laughed, then sat, sighed, and leaned back in the chair, stretching his anemic legs out in front of him. The neon light shining on his purple-veined, atrophied thighs gave the puckered skin around his knees the look of bleached beef jerky. He clicked the toes of his cowboy boots together a couple of times and reached for a cigarette.

Meanwhile Billy watched Frankie's pink-purple penis fall back, a little off to one side like an exhausted worm. He noted how it withered, wilted, and waned, belly-up in a bed of red moss, a last drop of semen oozing out of its vacant eye-socket.

Frankie reached in his shirt pocket for his Zippo, lit a cigarette, and folded his hands behind his head. "Pissed me off. But nothing compared to her. I mean, she's standing there with hot come running down the back of her legs, right? Getting in her shoes, right? Man, she started cussing me for everything she was worth. I thought *I* could cuss."

After a while, Frankie pulled his jeans and shorts up, snapped and buttoned them. He bent over and retrieved the money on the floor. As he rose up, he grabbed Ralph's baseball cap. Pausing, he looked at the cap, seemed to remember something, and smiled. Then, snarling, he threw the cap on the puddle of semen. He stepped on the cap and ground it into the floor like he was wiping up a mess he'd just soon not get too close to. He kicked the cap under the bunk bed. He looked at Ralph, but Ralph only grinned.

"You look like Alfred E. Newman, you ugly little shit," Frankie said.

Ralph climbed down off the bunk and fished the cap from under the bed. Waving it to catch Crissy's eye, he put it on his head and signed.

"Ralph-want-know-who-I-knocked-up," Crissy said.

Frankie grabbed the front of Ralph's shirt and pulled the little man's face up close to his. "Listen, you little creep. I didn't knock anybody up and you know it. I've had about as much of you as I can stomach for one day."

Ralph doffed his cap and grinned. He signed.

Crissy: "Ralph-sick-me-too."

Frankie appeared not to have heard Crissy speak. He looked at Crissy and then at Billy. Something about the two of them had caught his eye. Rocking, swaying on the balls of his feet, he looked back and forth several times at one and then the other of the two guests sitting on his couch. "Hey! You two look alike. I never noticed it before. Is it the glasses? You look like twins."

Billy looked over at Crissy. She had replaced her sunglasses with regular glasses that had white adhesive tape wrapped around the bridge between the lenses. Only then did he realize that Crissy was Crystal, the alligator lady. Was she was making fun of him with those taped-up glasses?

Then, suddenly, Billy became acutely aware of the full majesty of his erect phallus.

18

It was late in the day by the time Frankie's performance was over. Low in the sky, the sun had come out again, turning the world into shadows and golden light. Down below at pool level, all was quiet. The little ones, the ones not already scared off by the weather, had been coaxed and dragged out of the water and taken home to eat Sunday supper and made to get ready for church. The gradual waning and waxing of the waterfall's roar and the shadows' patient, intermittent march across the grassy sunbathing area and slow ascent to the tops of surrounding trees—gilded ever-more-splendidly in the dying light—had been the unnoticed accompaniment of the children's noisy, storm-threatened, late-summer afternoon amusement, their innocence mercifully untainted by the dark and dirty drama inside Frankie and Dixie's cabin.

Billy's head was a hive swarming with images, his guts and groin a simmering gumbo of grief and lust, his cheeks aflame with the shame of his ineluctable phallus, his heart heavy with remorse for his cowardly neglect in the matter of Frankie's forgiveness.

Like some gravid creature, heavy with spawn, he had to find a place to hide, to be alone with his resurrected self, to glory in the patrimony, the birthright, of his newly-bestowed prowess.

He headed upstream. Between Magnolia Park and Darktown there were woods and swamp with many private places, where he could discharge unseen the tensions built up over the past two days.

Taking the creek-side path, which was alternately spongy and silky underfoot with fallen oak leaves and pine needles, he met Charlie West and one of the other sunbathers going the other way. With a lascivious grin, Charlie introduced him to the woman, Pussy Per Se. As they parted, Charlie looked back over his shoulder and gave Billy a knowing wink.

Continuing on, Billy soon came to a smaller, less-traveled path. He followed this second path along a small dried-up stream. In its wider and shallower places, where sand and gravel had been left in pale patterns by past rains, the streambed stood out, glowing in the deepening shadows like a mirage, as if exuding residual heat left over from earlier in the day when the woods had been bathed in sunlight.

Coming to an even smaller and more neglected path, this one all but obliterated by lush late-summer foliage, Billy plunged through a gate of his own making in the dense dusty undergrowth.

The weed-choked path seemed to be leading Billy further and further into the heavily-wooded flood-basin of Flagon Creek. Soon the path was no longer discernible. Drawn ever deeper into the wilderness and feeling ever-more lost, harassed and afraid, his thoughts were scattered and fitful; but his senses were sharpened—harnessed and blinkered—by his ever-mounting desire.

Going past stagnant swamp pools, shiny and smooth as black glass, he smelled the areolae of purplish-grey clay exposed by retreating waterlines. Big white water lilies, brown-fringed atop dusty dull-green lily pads, gasped for air and gaped for light in the close steamy heat. The doomed blossoms—their pink inner petals beaded with syrupy drops of drought-extruded sap and jeweled with the ebony shells of water bugs dropped by black-spotted yellow spiders—surrendered, exhausted and spent, in dimly-dappled shadows of insectivores' fly-littered webs.

Hearing snatches of sounds that might be voices and suddenly thinking that he must be close to the Foster Brothers' still, he felt himself being swept toward panic. He spun around one way and back around the other, unable to tell the way he was going from the way he was coming. Making himself stop moving, he leaned back against a tree trunk and tried to catch his breath. Looking up and around, he struggled to think methodically. Where was the sun? Had he been going toward it or away from it or had it been off to one side? Which side? Even if he had known the answers to these questions, it was too late to use the sun for guidance, anyway; even the treetops had been drawn into the sinkhole of the uniformly grey dusk. Either that or it was clouding up again.

In a rush of fear, he lurched forward in what he thought might be the direction of the setting sun. If he kept going in a straight line toward the sun, he'd have to come out *somewhere*. He had heard that, lost in the woods, a person goes in circles. He came to a rotting log-bridge over a shallow dry gully, a depression formed by the run-off of backwater from this area of the woods. Crossing the bridge and plunging through a flowered green wall of dusty foliage, honeysuckle he guessed from the smell of it—it was the only thing that can thrive in these drought conditions, he thought, errantly—he found himself peering into a small grassy clearing.

Listening for voices and hearing none, his mind settled somewhat.

Hearing a rustling sound and calm enough to be curious about what might have made it, he plunged into the clearing.

Suddenly, there was quiet. Looking around, Billy concluded that he may have been going in a circle after all. But maybe that was okay. Seeing and recognizing a huge oak tree just beyond the edge of the clearing, he was pretty sure he knew where he was. If he was right about the tree, he would be within shouting distance of the Magnolia Park pool. The voices he heard earlier must have come from there. Good thing he hadn't gone in a straight line. A straight line would have taken him God knows how deep into the woods. What was he thinking, anyway? *He'd have to come out somewhere!* Yeah, the Gulf of Mexico!

Years before, Ralph had chopped his and Billy's initials into the bark of a big tree somewhere in these woods. Ralph had made gestures which Billy took to mean that he and Billy were thereby 'married' to the tree. On the trunk of the big oak tree that Billy was pretty sure he recognized, there were some amorphous scars that might have at one time resembled an R and a B. Reasonably sure now that it was the same tree, he was flooded with pleasant memories. It had been, and seemed still to be, a place where, despite its nearness to the pool, a person could be alone with himself without fear of interruption. He and Ralph, entering from another direction, had jacked-off there on more than one occasion. Billy felt at home here, safe from the menace of the Foster brothers.

On one side of the clearing was something which hadn't been there the last time he was here: Two dead cypress trees, deposited by the rushing waters of past deluges, lay one partially on top of the other—their trunks at a slight angle to one another—bringing to mind two mounting (or dismounting) lovers. They had come to rest over a little gully like the one Billy had crossed earlier, suspended like coffins over a long shallow grave.

Making his way across the clearing through knee-deep grass, Billy hoisted himself up onto the lower, nearer cypress trunk. He leaned back against the top trunk. His feet, dangling over the side, reached below the top of the grass but did not touch the ground. Makes a perfect couch, he thought. He ran his hand across the soft, layered bark of the lower trunk. Stretching out full-length on his back on the bottom log, he rolled over toward the top log. With his face in the crack formed by the seat and the back of the natural couch, he breathed in the slightly-sweet smell of the cypress bark. He put his arm around the top trunk as far as he could reach and hugged it.

Rolling over on his back and putting his hands behind his head, Billy looked up at the patch of sky above. Pulsing on the highest leaves and limbs of the conjugal oak tree which partially canopied the clearing, fugitive snatches of sunlight that looked like gold medallions, faded and brightened as wind-driven clouds parted, regrouped, and passed like the foamy rapids of a cascading river in the sky. Birds, now habituated to the intrusion, flitted from branch to branch. In the air overhead, butterflies inscribed invisible arabesques on the tumultuous face of heaven. The chirp of cicada, or it might be crickets or tree frogs, could be heard. Tonight, Billy (no meteorologist, he) mused, this place, the sky and the woods, will sparkle with stars and lightening bugs. A good place to bring Chantilly Lace.

Yeah, and, if she didn't eat you alive, the mosquitoes would.

Billy closed his eyes. In a dazzling reverie, he was face-up under a golden shower of mesmerizing sensations. Headquartered in Dixie's pungent pussy, his torch-like tongue and octopodous lips ventured high and low; making excursions beyond the labial ramparts, he explored again the sweaty creases and smegma-coated crevasses of her fundament and pudendum. Nose-to-nose with Dixie's cleat-like clit—revolving weightlessly in space from prone to supine and back again—he was alternately deliriously abject and downtrodden—a faithful nag, ridden roughshod and put away wet—and jubilantly triumphant and all-conquering—an exultant charioteer plunging into a tumultuous and fragrant melee of flesh vibrant with life and smelling of death.

After basking a long while in the afterglow of the miraculous interfacing with Dixie, he let parade before his eyes a caravan of hoarded memories, his treasure trove of erotic images flashing like shooting stars across the internal firmament of his much-expanded consciousness. In the nuclear reactor of his over-stimulated mind, he saw simultaneously the woman sucking Sir Winston behind the bar, Jonnie Vonderheim giving Dr. Maxwell a blowjob, and the 'nurse' kneeling in front of Frankie West in the butt-hut, crowning His Majesty with thick voracious lips. He remembered Dixie and the Faustpool girl 'choosing sides', working their way up, hot-hand-over-sweaty-palm, to the dew-drop exuding out of the little mouth of Frankie's dick; a tear, shimmering in the cold winter light, it is on the point of plunging down the shiny smooth ski-slope of His Majesty's swollen grandeur. Then, out of nowhere and with surprising and chokingly erotic force, a grossly-splendored image—at once and indivisibly visual-tactile-olfactory-gustatory—of the white gunk on Jimmy Garrard's inflamed dick in the steamy shower behind the Garrard's house.

Focusing now, he re-lived and embellished the story he and Ralph and Crystal had used to help Frankie get an erection and reach what may be his last sublunary orgasm. He saw Frankie's jizm squirting, spurting with fictional force, peppering and pelting the not-so goody-goody's butt cheeks in the dark school bus. He saw again the real stuff—the feeble pulse of viscous white fluid oozing out of Frankie's pee-hole. (The minimal force of its labored, story-coaxed emergence reminded Billy of 'snakes', the tamest and least-preferred variety of fireworks; made in the form of little rat-turd pellets, they uncoil when lit into long grey wobbly spirals of brittle ash.) Its smell filled his nostrils and he remembered taking Frankie's place in the butt-hut.

Undoing his fly, Billy pushed his pants and boxer shorts down to mid-thigh. Opalescing in the light, his phallus sprung up like a jack-in-the-box, miraculously expanding yet one more skin-jeopardizing notch; it seemed to be inhaling, out of breath, as if it had been smothering in the confines of Billy's clothes. It is glad to be out and about; as happy as I am to be alive, he thought, remembering Frankie's desiccated and discolored body.

Supine on the log, he removed his glasses. Reaching up and back, as far as his arm would stretch, he put the glasses in the crack between the logs. He took Frankie's rubber out of his shirt pocket.

His hands trembled as—his head raised up off the log so he could see what he was doing—he fitted the condom over the knob and rolled it down the shaft of his stiff penis. The snugly-fitting device allayed any fear that his dick might explode and gave form to all that he was feeling; to all that, at that moment, he *was*. He savored the strangely erotic smell given off by the still-moist rubber.

It's never been bigger or harder, Billy exulted.

He was totally alone.

Hearing something swishing in the grass near the root-end of the logs, he sat up straight. Lifting his feet, he turned and let his legs dangle over the side of the log. At the same moment, the smell of Frankie's semen intensified in his nostrils and he smelled another, familiar smell.

Arthur Maxwell appeared suddenly and in dramatic fashion, like a hopped-up kid at Halloween or a grotesque stripper popping up out of a cake at a prank party. Bursting into the clearing through the foliage near the root-end of the two cypress logs, his reptilian eyes flashed, large and luminous in the fading light. Billy again recalled the octopus and knew that Arthur *had* been spying on him when he was in Frankie and Dixie's cabin.

Arthur was wearing Ralph's baseball cap and a black leather jacket. There was a big wet spot on top of the cap. He came over to where Billy was. He stood in front of him. He stared at his rubber-sheathed dick. When their eyes met, Arthur gaped and brought his hands to his face, a gesture of mock incredulity—another item from his Jack Benny repertoire. The ursine intruder frowned and shook a finger at Billy, as if to say, You naughty boy!

Locking his eyes again on Billy's phallus, Arthur backed into the center of the clearing; taking little steps backward and tilting his head forward with each step like a high-jumper choreographing his leap, he appeared to be pulling against invisible elastic constraints, which, at the peak of his resistance, at the moment of his surrender, would catapult him forward at maximum speed. Then, segueing into a different scenario, he minced forward, head held high, swishing his hips with the exaggerated movements of a model walking down the runway. Holding them low and in front of him, he flopped and flapped his big hands in rhythm from side to side. Stopping a couple of feet in front of Billy, he shooed away the adulation of some imaginary audience.

Focusing now exclusively on Billy's dick, Arthur pursed his lips as if to say, Well, well, well, what have we here! Then a ravenous look of hunger swept across his big face.

Arthur's looking so intently at Billy's dick made it get even harder, made it curve up toward his own face. It was like something, a baby, a foetus, had come up out of his groin, and recognizing its mother, was dead set on merging head-on with the one who had given it life.

When Arthur moved closer, turning the duet into a trio, Billy let his hands slide down onto the log on either side of his thighs. Making fists and inwardly bracing himself—like the goody-goody hanging on to the handrails inside the church bus—he prepared to succumb to what, astonishingly, he craved and dreaded in equal measure.

The clearing darkened as clouds gathered overhead like huge dark-grey faces peering into a pit at two tiny combatants.

Bending at the knees, still looking at Billy's erection, Arthur removed one of Billy's shoes and dropped it on the ground. He pulled Billy's pants down over his ankle and foot, freeing his legs. He rolled the condom up and off Billy's dick. Pitched aside, the rubber lodged in the crack between the logs. Taking hold of Billy's calves, Arthur pulled him toward himself, scraping the tender skin of Billy's butt on the bark of the cypress tree. Like a preacher baptizing a new convert, he put one hand behind Billy's head and one on his chest and eased him down onto his back. With his head jammed against the top log of his too-short bed, his chin jammed into his chest, Billy's eyes were pointed toward where the action was about to begin.

Hooking two fingers around the base of Billy's stiff cock, Arthur pulled it away from Billy's abdomen until it pointed straight up at a right angle to his body. With his head cocked forward at a sharp angle against the top log, Billy could see his phallus straining up out of its pubic patch like the stem and bud of a wild lily sprouting out of a bed of Spanish moss. Lifting Billy's legs, the seducer, by pressing his victim's knees against his pimply cheeks, squeezed the corners of his capacious mouth together, spilling a cascade of stringy slaver onto the front of his black leather jacket.

In a waking dream come true, Arthur's bright eyes sparkled and flashed like a siren's wind-whipped beacon fires.

Positioning himself so that his eyes and Billy's were on a straight line bisected by the head of Billy's dick, Arthur created the heaven he wanted: a cosmos in which the corona of the phallus was a star and their eyes were four planets; the phallus a planet, their eyes four moons; the phallus a tight wad of protons, their eyes electrons.

The quivering knob of Billy's phallus pulsates like a beating heart freshly ripped from its rib-cage.

Then, like two rival cats warily regarding a common prey from opposite perspectives, their eyes settled into steady saccadic movements, jumping from orb to orb to orb in antic anticipation, mutually certain of the communal plum, the undivided prize to come.

Billy's phallus is simultaneously exploding and imploding; a fist, full of red-hot super-glue, trying to open and, at the same time, straining to contain a detonating cherry bomb.

Overwhelmed by the smells of the jizm-soaked baseball cap and Arthur's fetid breath and malodorous unwashed body—sweating and heaving and alive with animal appetite under the borrowed bovine skin— Billy surrendered and let himself be drawn into the hot wet maw of the wild innocent creature that was programmed to devour him.

* * *

A noise in the bushes! Someone else was coming toward the clearing. An intruder!

"Hey, Billy. Where are you, motherfucker?" It was Jake.

Arthur raised his head, a frightened look of recognition and traumatic memory on his face.

Letting go of Arthur's hair, Billy motioned his fellatious paramour toward the end of the two logs, sending him back out the way he came in.

Billy didn't have time to sit up, let alone jump off the log and put his pants back on, before Jake barged into the clearing.

"I seh Old Top. Mind if I join you?" Jake was speaking 'British'. He crossed the clearing to where Billy was. In his normal voice, he said, "Looks like you've started without me."

"Jesus Christ, man!" Billy sat up. He made a feeble attempt to retrieve his pants, still around his ankle. "Are you trying to give me a heart attack? You scared the living shit out of me. How did you know I was here?" He tried harder to reach his pants, but they stayed teasingly out of reach.

"Shithole Charlie West said he saw you headed this way. You know about this place, too, eh? Scoot over. I'm so horny I'd fuck a snake if you'd hold its head."

"This swamp is the right place for fucking snakes." Relief replaced shock as Billy was finally able to corral his pants. Rocking his butt side to side on the log, he tried to zig-zag the jeans up over his hips. Reaching the tops of his thighs, he stopped; he just couldn't bear to re-imprison his still rock-hard, habitually recidivistic dick.

"Give me a hand," Jake said, wanting to be lifted up. Sitting beside Billy on the log, he spotted the rubber; he picked it up and put it on the log in the space between them. "Where'd this come from? You gonna wear that? Or are you and your fist planning a family?"

"How'd you know I was out here? We better go. Looks like it's gonna rain. There might be lightning."

Jake looked up at the dark clouds. "It'll blow over. I don't feel anything in my leg. I was waiting for you down by the pool. What the fuck happened with that prick West? You were up there half the fucking day." Not waiting for an answer, Jake said, "I've been shitting my pants, wanting to tell you what I saw. You know those whores of Uncle Toe's. I watched one of those bitches getting dressed. There's a peep-hole I never told you about. You talk about *pussy*! You should've seen the *hair* on it. Make a beaver look bald-headed. Guess what her name was: Rosy Ravine O'Hair. Can you believe that shit? Just thinking about my dick poking through all that hair like a big old snake makes me so horny I'm about to come in my pants."

Again? You should wear diapers, Billy thought.

Jake undid his belt, pulled his pants and underwear down to his ankles, and started masturbating. "Hey, what's a matter? Lose your hard? You wanna put that rubber on? Maybe it'll get you hot." Jake reached for the rubber and handed it to Billy.

Billy tucked the rubber back into the crack between the logs. I'll come back later for it, he thought. Determined to watch himself ejaculate, he leaned back and rolled his hips toward Jake so his friend could see his unflagging erection. "Well, look at it. Does it look like I've lost my hard?" After spoiling Billy's fun with Arthur, the least Jake could do was bear witness to what promised to be a great one. It would be a splendid outpouring worthy of Frankie himself!

"Touché."

"Hey, did you fuck that cunt that passed us on the steps?"

"Yeah, sure. You think I'd be here jerking off with you if I had?"

"Touché."

Just then it started to rain. The sky was very dark.

"Oooooh!" Jake yelled, his voice full of surprise and fear. "*Mother ... fucker.*" He jumped off the log and started jumping around, his movement hampered by the pants still around his ankles.

At first Billy thought Jake was frightened by the weather, but when Jake bent over—his bare white ass luminescent in the gloom of the fast-fading light—and looked under the log, he realized it was something else.

"Motherfucker took my shoe," Jake said. Then he shouted, "It's a fucking bear!" He jumped back and fell on his naked butt in the grass. Quickly pulling his pants up, he scrambled to his feet. Holding his pants up with one hand, he picked up a stick and began poking at something under the log. "You motherfucker!" he yelled, moving excitedly up and down along the length of the two logs. "It's so fucking dark I can't see shit. Oh, now I see you, you cocksucker." Dropping the stick and buttoning his pants, he began kicking at whatever it was under the log, using the still-shod foot of his good leg as a weapon. Coming in quick succession: a loud grunt from Jake, a crunching sound, a loud exhalation of air, and a stifled scream coming from under the log. Jake had made a direct hit.

His t-shirt now soaked with sweat and rain, Jake bent over and started pulling at something under the log, trying in vain to drag it out into the clearing. Whatever it was, it was whimpering and gasping like it was hurt and frightened, struggling to catch its breath.

Suddenly, Billy knew what it was under the log. It was Arthur! He had been hiding under the logs. He must have crawled into the little gully underneath the logs from the other side.

With Arthur back in the mix, Billy was suddenly aware of being exposed, still naked where it mattered most. What if someone was out there in the woods somewhere watching? What if they had seen him and Jake masturbating together? And, worse, what if they had seen what he and Arthur had done?

"Stop! Stop! It's Arthur Maxwell. Don't kick him again." Billy jumped off the log, pulled up and fastened his pants, and looked under the log. Arthur was lying face up in the gully, gasping for air, trying to breathe. Billy reached under the log and touched his chest. Even through the leather jacket and the thick of layer of fat, he could feel the muscles trembling like those of a frightened puppy.

"He grabbed ... my leg ... ," Jake said, breathing hard, rain and sweat dripping off his face. "Can't stand that ... . Scared the ... crap ... outa me. Is my fucking shoe under there?"

"You didn't have to kick him so hard. You kicked him right in the face, I think. It looks all bloody. You panicked." Billy poked his head further under the log to get a better look. Arthur was clutching his chest. Had Jake kicked his sternum in or was Arthur clutching something to his chest?

"Hell, man, I told you I was fucking *scared*. Scared to fucking *death*. I wasn't thinking. For all the fuck I knew it coulda been a goddamn *alligator*. I'm sorry."

"I think he's dead! His heart's not beating!" Billy didn't really think Arthur was dead. He certainly hoped he wasn't dead. He just wanted to scare Jake. The best part of the glorious thing that happened between Billy and Arthur before Jake barged in, aborting what was sure to be the greatest climax he ever had, had been the exhilarating epiphany he had right when he was … just … about … to … : *This will happen again and again and again.* Absorbing the impact of this loss of present and future joy and remembering Jake's attack on Arthur in the locker room, he momentarily hated Jake. He wanted to make him at least feel bad for what he had done.

But suddenly Billy had his doubts. What if Arthur really *was* dead? Pressing his palm against Arthur's chest, he couldn't feel his heart beating under the thick leather jacket.

"See if you can feel a heart beat."

"I'm not touching that filthy bastard. What do you think we should do?"

"Go tell Mr. Jeannsonne, I guess." Billy ran his fingers through his wet hair.

"No! Wait! We have to think this thing out. What are we gonna say? That we were out here jacking off together? How's *that* gonna look? Besides, I could end up in deep shit. Last month … first week of FBI training … wilderness camp … you don't know about this … I beat this guy up. Big fucking ex-football player. We shared a tent. Kept teasing me about my leg, so I stomped his ass. Fucker told the instructor. The instructor told the regional director and so on and so on. They said my temper was a potential liability to the Bureau and put me on probation. If I stay clean they may give me one more chance. I was lucky I wasn't charged with assault.

"Then there's what happened yesterday. That fucking West hangs around with the fucking cops. The Bureau'll probably find out about it. You put this on top of that and my ass is grass."

"What do you suggest?"

"Let's hide the body. At least for now. Give us some time to think."

"Hide it where?"

"We're out in the middle of the fucking woods! We should be able to hide a fucking Mack truck out here. Hell, we'll just leave it where it is,

in that ditch under those logs. Ain't nobody gonna see it under there."
Squatting, Jake began snatching at the tall grass, pulling it up by the roots
and tossing it on top of Arthur's body. "We'll just cover him up, that's all.
It'll be okay for now."

They filled the gully with grass the whole length of the logs so there
was no tell-tale Arthur-shaped mound to be seen.

The forest lit up with lightening. A loud clap of thunder sounded. Rain,
blown by a sudden wind, started coming down in sheets.

Jake, frantic, turned toward the open clearing and looked up at the
dark sky. Raindrops splattered on his frightened pretty face. He took off
running, wearing only one shoe.

Billy followed instinctively but stopped after a few steps.

"Where's my shoe?" he yelled out.

Jake was long gone.

Billy thought: Where's that rubber? Where's that stupid baseball cap?
He ran back to the clearing. He'd at least get his shoe. But it was nowhere
to be seen. Was *that* what Arthur was clutching to his chest? Not wanting
to undo the hard work of covering up Arthur's body, he thought: I'll get it
later when I come back to check on Arthur.

He didn't remember to retrieve his new glasses.

19

When he got home from Magnolia Park, Billy told Stella that he wasn't going back to the Bible College.

Then, starting that same Sunday night, the day before Labor Day, and every night after that—a little after 8:00 pm, when Channel 5 went off the air and Stella went to bed—Billy would camp out in the living room and wait for Jonnie Vonderheim's phone to ring. As he feared, Jonnie started getting more and more calls, mostly at night, and, as summer faded into autumn, the living room couch became Billy's bed away from bed. He put a pillow over the phone so Stella wouldn't hear it and be curious why there were so many more calls than before. At first he was afraid the pillow would dampen the sound so much he wouldn't hear it himself, but that didn't happen. Because of the fiasco with Arthur, what little sleep he got was never very deep, and, if he wasn't awake when the phone started ringing, he would be before Jonnie even had time to pick up.

God help him if Stella figured out what he was up to. She was already mad at him about the television: for not leaving the room with her when Clinton wouldn't let her turn the thing off when there was women showing their butts on the lil old screen—like them hussies *dancing* (!) half-naked on the *Hit Parade;* and for not telling her that he was going to buy it in the first place, even if it was his own money. So, she really hit the roof when Billy told her the reason he wasn't going back to college was that it had taken all the money he had earned writing tracts for the Evangelical Society to pay for the dad-blamed thing.

It seemed vital that Billy listen in on as many of Jonnie's calls as he could. Sleeping by the phone, he kept tabs on the *incoming* calls. Ones made by Jonnie herself were another matter. There was no way of knowing about them. All Billy could do was pick up the receiver every so often when he was awake—when he couldn't sleep, say, or when he had to pee—on the off chance she would be on the line.

Jonnie knew most of the big shots, and some not so big, in the twin-parish area who had a stake in the investigations into the events of the Labor Day weekend at Magnolia Park. Billy's fear that Arthur Maxwell might really be dead soon became an unshakeable conviction that it was just a matter of time before his body showed up; and her phone conversations were his only way of learning what the chances were of his spending the rest of his life in the state prison at Angola, which is what he faced if … ; better make that *when*, because he was as convinced that they would get to the bottom of what he and Jake had done as he was that Arthur was dead, and that they would eventually find his body.

What Billy was most afraid of, though, was that Stella would find out what happened between him and Arthur in the time leading up to his death. Some things are worse than being an accessory to murder: Like doing things that were so bad that if your mother found out it would kill her.

Thanks to Clinton's censure, the phone was something of a taboo object, subjecting anything remotely connected with it to its inhibiting influence. Otherwise, Stella might have been expected to ask her son why he didn't go out, why he never left the living room, except to go to the bathroom. As it was, when Stella was in the living room and Jonnie's ring sounded, she and Billy would stare at what had become a noisy bone of silent contention and at each other—kinda like him and Arthur and Billy's dick in the clearing, Billy thought—but neither would say anything.

Billy couldn't be sure Stella hadn't already overheard something or figured out a lot on her own. It occurred to him that she may have felt frustrated that, with him sleeping on the couch, she couldn't listen in on some of those night calls *herself*. In that case, Billy worried, her frustration might start his mother thinking and wondering why all of a sudden her son was spending so much time in the living room. In fact, the calls Stella would most likely want to monitor—her window onto the various ongoing soap operas of Jonnie's sordid affairs—were from Jonnie's regular callers who knew not to call before her husband Fred went to bed. (Frankie said that when his affair with Jonnie was in full swing, he would call from the public phone in the neighborhood grocery store and let it ring only one time, a signal for Jonnie to meet him outside and they would fuck in the spacious cab of Fred's beer truck. This still gave Billy much food for fantasy.)

So, even though it was highly unlikely that Stella would ever say anything, Billy nonetheless repeated the same excuse every morning for not sleeping in his own room: He had fallen asleep working on new tracts for the Evangelical Society to earn tuition money for the spring semester.

Pretty soon, Billy couldn't leave the phone unattended even during the day. He didn't really know why he sat there all day, like a dog skulking around its lucky garbage can. Lack of sleep probably had a lot to do with his paralysis; having to worry all the time about the business with Arthur most certainly messed with his mind, which made it hard to sleep, which made it that much harder to think straight, so that staring at the phone sometimes seemed the only way he could focus his thoughts. He told himself that a major break in the investigation could come at any time, which meant that a crucial call could come even during the day; so, his being there at least kept Stella from listening in on such a call.

The bottom-line truth, though, the real reason Billy was glued to the phone, day and night, went beyond any rational considerations: With its round ten-eyed face, its droopy black bulbous ears, and its sensitive clit-like activator-knobs, the phone had taken on the power of a Voo-Doo idol, requiring his undivided devotion.

✳   ✳   ✳

"Where are you?" Jonnie's voice.

"Office." A man's voice.

"Are we still on for tonight?" Jonnie.

"No, it can't be tonight. Has to be tomorrow night. Late. After the March of Dimes party. I'll see you there. When you see me leave the party, you leave. Okay?"

"Why the delay?"

"Something has come up. Will you call him?"

"Okay, I'll call him. He's not gonna like it."

"You can charm him, J.V. That's your specialty, your gift, charming the pants off men. God knows mine have hit the floor often enough."

"Keep your mind on business, Maximilian."

"Just remind Big Man that we are the ones taking all the risks. Make sure he gets in touch with her. She's supposed to be waiting for a call so there shouldn't be any problems. I told him to tell her that there may have to be some last minute changes in the plan. That it goes with the territory. You make sure he tells her she's to be blindfolded and driven around a lot before she is brought to the place and afterwards and that she understands that. Oh yeah, couple of other things: tell him to tell her that we'll be wearing masks and there's to be *no talking* the whole time."

"Usual place?"

"No. It's not safe there anymore. I overheard one of the swing-shift orderlies talking with one of the others about the lights being on in the O. R. late at night."

"Okay. Have you decided where?"

"Yeah. I'll let you know at the party."

"Is it where we talked about before?"

"Yeah."

"Does she know?"

"No."

"You gonna tell her? You better tell her. You know how she is. You'll have to get someone to go tell her."

"Who? Tell her what, J.V.?"

"I don't know, *Max*. Something. So she won't be surprised. She doesn't like surprises."

"Okay, I'll have to go myself. I'll try to get over there tomorrow afternoon."

"Do you think that's a good idea? You don't want to be seen by the wrong people. You're not supposed to be around her, you know. That was part of the … you're the reason she was moved away from Pinecrest, remember?"

"Yeah, you don't have to remind me."

"Besides, there's no telling what she'll do when she sees you. The less time you spend in her cabin the better from our point of view, right?

"I'll be careful. Don't worry. Who's gonna see me? They'll all be up here at the barbecue we've got planned to kick off the festivities for the patients and their folks."

"She's gonna know where she is, you know. She goes over there all the time."

"Well, I guess we'll just have to live with that, won't we, Jonnie? Or maybe we'll make her keep the blind-fold on … and stick a sock in the other one's mouth."

The next morning, Labor Day, Jake called Billy. Billy said they couldn't talk on the phone because of the party line. He said he was too busy getting ready to go back to college to meet him down at the park. He was still mad at Jake. For getting him in this mess. For interrupting him and Arthur. For what he did to Arthur.

That afternoon Billy tried to check on Arthur. The woods were flooded. He couldn't get anywhere near the clearing. In fact he wasn't sure now if he'd know how to get back to that spot. Maybe he'd been wrong about the oak tree. He decided to not worry about it. If push came to shove, he would just tell the truth, that Jake was the one who did it.

Jake persisted about the need for them to get together. They talked several times over the next couple of weeks, meeting each time in one of their old hang-outs, the old car in the deserted garage behind the abandoned mansion or the prison cell in Camp Livingston.

The first time they talked, Jake said he had gone back to the clearing. Arthur was not there.

"That probably means that he's not dead after all," Billy said.

"Think again, Einstein. It just means his body got washed somewhere else by the fucking flood. It's just a matter of time before they find it. We've got to come up with some kind of story, case some asshole saw us in that vicinity. They'll be questioning everybody that was down there that weekend."

"That weekend? How they gonna know when it happened?"

"They have ways of telling how long somebody's been dead."

A few days later Jake said he had checked at Pinecrest and they said Arthur had not been seen since before Labor Day.

"That looks kinda suspicious doesn't it, you asking around like that?"

"I didn't go myself. I asked Mom to tell them that somebody had left a leather jacket down at the park and could Arthur come down and see if it was his."

"What if somebody comes down to get it?"

"Well, then we'll know he is probably alive."

"Or that someone wants a leather jacket."

"Mom said that cocksucker Dr. Maxwell hasn't shown up at Pinecrest since the Friday before Labor Day. She thinks he may have hauled ass out of state."

"Think Arthur went with him?"

"Not likely."

Jake said he had kept an eye out around the park. He'd even gone to Frankie's cabin. Arthur was nowhere to be seen. In fact the cabin was empty. Frankie and Dixie seemed to have moved out.

$$* \qquad * \qquad *$$

Billy continued listening in on Jonnie Vonderheim's calls.

"Remember don't say my name." It was a woman's voice, unfamiliar. "You being on that party line worries me a lot, makes things very chancy. When are you going to get off it? I really wish there was some way the two of you could talk to each other. Anyone finds out I talked to you, it's *me* that gets canned, not you know who. I'm not supposed to know anything."

"Who's this LeBeaux?" Jonnie asked.

"He's a state senator. Or was. Nobody's seen him since Labor Day weekend. They found a wheelchair they think may be his in the swamp over by Darktown, but not hide nor hair of the man himself."

∗   ∗   ∗

"I heard a deal was made. Theo gives his brother Magnolia Park in exchange for his not being prosecuted for ... well, you name it ... prostitution, making dirty movies, selling illegal liquor, abortions. He's an ex-con, you know." Different woman's voice, vaguely familiar.

"I heard that rumor, too," Jonnie said. "Any word of his whereabouts?"

"Who? Theo? No, Vinny says he hasn't been seen since Labor Day. I would have thought that if anyone knew, it would be you."

"Why?"

"Come on, Jonnie. It's me. You don't have to be so closed-mouthed with me. I've known about you and Theo Jeannsonne for ages. He and Vincent are friends, you know."

Hearing Jake's father's name, Billy recognized the voice of the woman talking to Jonnie Vonderheim as that of Jake's mother, Mrs. Garrard, Dr. Maxwell's secretary. He wondered why Jake's mother would be talking to Jonnie. Linda Garrard didn't have much to do with other people in the neighborhood. Then he remembered that both women worked at Pinecrest.

"Then you're more likely than me to know where he is, right?" Jonnie said.

"'Than I.' Okay, be that way."

"I heard Mr. Jeannsonne was called out of town on urgent business."

"Yeah, *real* urgent," Linda Garrard said sarcastically, laughing. "*Way* outa town. Do you want to tell me what *really* happened, Jonnie?"

"What do you mean, 'What *really* happened'?"

"Okay, if you want to be that way, let me just tell you one of the stories going around."

"Going around where? In your own mind?"

"Okay, let's say I *am* making it up. Just for the sake of argument. A hypothetical story. Goes like this. A certain lady finds out that a certain Cajun 'gentleman friend' is having an affair with a certain preacher's wife, whose initials, the preacher's and his wife's, happen to be J. J."

"That..."

"Wait, let me tell you the whole story before you start denying it. We're just being hypothetical, right? Now suppose this certain lady didn't like this preacher's wife. Her animosity goes back to a time the wife and the preacher made a surprise visit to this certain lady's house. Way back before the lady was 'saved'. They were calling on all the sinners who never went to church. There was a big revival or something coming up and they wanted to get as many people as they could to impress ... and offset the cost of ... the fancy evangelist they had coming in."

"So they weren't being very choosy. Even the dregs of society were welcome. Is that what you're saying?"

"You said it, I didn't."

"Well, that's how it was. And I *was* ... I *am* ... saved."

"Yeah, right. Good sex does wonders for the soul. Anyhow, like I say, the preacher and his wife just show up at this certain lady's front door. This certain lady didn't even have time to straighten up. Oh, how angry she was about the way the preacher's wife turned up her nose. Acted like she was in a pig pen or something."

"Okay, yes, that's all true. So what? Why are you telling me all this stuff? Where is it leading?"

"I'm getting there. My point is, you've never been jealous of anybody but her, have you? When you believed she was sneaking around Magnolia Park at all hours of the night ... 'like some cat in heat' ... is how I heard you put it ... you flipped. You could put up with anybody else ... 'being with' ... that's as good a euphemism as any ... any of your men ... even that retarded boy's 'being with' Frankie West didn't bother you. But with *her* it was different. It wasn't *Theo* that you cared about. It was her. I know how you are, Jonnie. You hate with a lot more passion than you love."

"Again, so what?"

"Here's so what: You told the preacher the rumors you had heard. The scuttlebutt is you had ample opportunity to tell him. That the two of you 'being withed' each other brains out on a regular basis.

"At first he didn't believe you," Linda Garrard continued. "Or maybe he just didn't care. Didn't think he could be hurt by rumors. But when he saw that movie that caused all the fuss ... the pornographic movie that was shown at the March of Dimes party on Labor Day at Magnolia Park ... when he realized the *extent*, the *scope*, the *history*, of the betrayal by his own wife and brother ... how long it had been going on ... he just broke.

"Our good reverend could live with his adopted daughter ... 'being with' ... his adopted brother ... and her 'being with' that mulatto boy with only Theo's initials for a name. He could put up with you and our own dear old Dr. Max 'being with' each other ... that was just 'business' ... and even with the two of you getting rid of the ... issue ... of his daughter's union with the mulatto boy. But a man can take just so much, as they say."

"That last never happened. Me and 'dear old Dr. Max' as you call him didn't do that one. They took her out-of-state."

"So you say. Doesn't matter. Anyway, you knew ... or so goes the story ... that the preacher would be seeing that movie. All you had to do was to make sure that at that crucial moment ... when the rage hit him ... he would have the means to act. One version of the story has it that you had Frankie West give Reverend Johnson the revolver that he, Mr. West, had been issued in his capacity as a security guard at Magnolia Park. Another version has you getting the little deaf boy, Ralph what's-his-name, to steal Mr. West's weapon and bringing it to you and that it was you who actually put the gun into Reverend Johnson's hand. I like both these versions ... Theo being shot with his own gun. How ironic! In still another version of the story, you made Fred loan you the gun he got from the Foster Brothers when he became one of their distributors. Some have even hinted that Vincent's old luger that he brought back from the war in Germany somehow showed up for further duty."

"Why would I want John to shoot Theo? Isn't it *Janelle* that I'm supposed to hate so much?"

"Well, there's two trains of thought about that. One goes like this. You were incensed because Theo never told you that he had ... 'been with' ... make that plural ... that on multiple occasions he had 'been with' the preacher's wife. He told you everything else ... pillow talk, the Japenese call it ... but he never told you about her. This made you realize that Theo really loved her and that she must love him, too. Why else would he keep her a secret from you and why else would she risk so much?

"The other theory is that you needed Theo out of the way."

"Out of the way of what?"

"There's conflicting thoughts about that, too, but they all boil down to this. Reverend Johnson coveted his brother Theo's property, Magnolia Park. You coveted Reverend Johnson. Having been told by Theo that Reverend Johnson was his only living relative, you manipulated the situation so that the preacher got his and you got him.

"So, my dear Jonnie, my dear dark-eyed gypsy, the long and the short of it was you saw a chance to kill a veritable flock of birds with one stone. You could get your revenge on Theo for not telling you everything, for holding back. You could see to it that your lover got his inheritance sooner than later. But, best of all ... what really got your juices flowing ... was the chance to take something from your old nemesis Janelle Johnson ...

something so precious that she had repeatedly risked *every*thing for it.

"The beauty of it was that she would have to *live* with her sorrow, her loss. There wouldn't be a soul she could turn to. And you could watch her pain ... you could observe her as if she were a fly having its wings torn off, over and over and over."

"That's a great story. Why doesn't the Sheriff arrest John? I mean, what does 'the story' say about that?"

"Because he is thankful that Reverend Johnson did what he, as Sheriff, couldn't do? That he got rid of a vermin that is polluting our good Christian community? It *is* kinda like the preacher drove the serpent out of the garden, wouldn't you say? And who is going to believe that such an upstanding Man of God would ever do such a thing! All that and the fact that the body hasn't been found."

"Speaking of people being out of town, have you heard anything more about Max? What are people at the office saying?" Jonnie asked.

"Not a thing. Nobody seems to know a thing."

$$* \qquad * \qquad *$$

"They found Dr. Max's car. Don't ask me how. Pure luck, no doubt. It had been re-painted and sold for cash. They figure the good doctor was in need of ready cash to make his getaway. Certain people that I don't need to name must have found out he was in Crystal's cabin that night and he figured he'd better hightail it." First woman's voice. The unfamiliar one.

"Any clues in the car?"

"What do you mean 'clues'?"

"Oh, you know, anything that would reveal Dr. Maxwell's ... secondary interests?"

"Yeah, they found traces of blood in the fabric of the front seat and on the floor, both on the passenger side of the car. The scuttlebutt is that the blood must be from one of his ... patients, if that's what they're called. Clients, maybe? They figure he must have been driving her home from ... wherever."

$$* \qquad * \qquad *$$

"Yeah, it worked out perfect for us." Jonnie's voice. "She says everybody believes Theo made the deal *after* the party. Because of his alleged part in making that movie. Seems it was filmed in his house."

"So, there's no reason for anyone to snoop into your little operation, right? See, I told you Frankie would come through for you. He got all the evidence the Sheriff needed to convince Theo to sign everything over to me." Billy recognized Brother Johnson's voice. The preacher had called Jonnie. Billy had lucked up, picked up the phone after getting up to pee.

Jonnie: Him and *Chantilly Lace*. I love that name. I guess she kept Theo 'busy' while Frankie did the rest?

Brother Johnson: Yeah, something like that. What about your old boss? Heard from him lately? He's not going to be able to make any trouble for you, is he?

Jonnie: No. In exchange for my helping them get the goods on Theo they've agreed to grant me immunity, *if* any of that ever comes out, which, with any kind of luck, it won't. I can put a period on that part of my life, thank goodness. Never liked that business very much, anyway. I'm ready for my new life with you, you big lug.

Brother Johnson: Once a Catholic, always a Catholic. Is that it? Do you know where he … Maxwell … is?

Jonnie: No. His secretary says nobody at work has seen him since the day before Labor Day.

Brother Johnson: What about Junior?

Jonnie: You mean Arthur? He hasn't been seen since then either. I know for sure Max wouldn't have taken him with him. He considered him a millstone around his neck. There is something to tell about that, but I can't tell you on the party line.

Brother Johnson: Sounds like we need to schedule another 'choir practice'. My 'assistant' has some new songs. He wants to see how you 'feel' about them.

Jonnie: I can't wait to be 'filled in'.

"There was a bullet in the body but … this is choice … they don't think that was the cause of death." It was the unfamiliar woman's voice. "Something about the wound … no sign of bleeding … . Don't ask me how they could possibly know something like that after all that time in the water. They said it looked like the shot was fired after the body was dead to make it look like he died from a gunshot wound. And here's another little mystery for you. There were no bullet hole in the leather jacket. So, it looks like the jacket was put on the body after it was dead. Of course, this is all speculation.

They don't know what they're doing."

"They believe that it … the body … was male?" Jonnie.

"They're pretty sure it was. It had breasts, but they didn't look like a woman's. Too hairy. Of course, if there was that other thing, the alligators must have ate it. Either that or someone cut it off."

"Why would they do that?"

"Beats me. Revenge? You know more about that sort of thing than I do, Jonnie."

20

Billy is waking up.

Outside a thunderstorm rages.

Inside the phone rings. And rings. And rings.

Ripped out the embrace of a dream, twisting and turning, he struggles to stay under. It is the first really good, deep sleep he has had since Labor Day, and he doesn't want to stop dreaming.

Surfacing, his upthrust head, weaving and wobbling atop the sprung coil of his spine, feels like a heavy mass spinning in a crooked orbit. The lineaments of his neck and eyes are loose and inelastic, like the wires of a puppet come undone.

He cannot get upright but he dare not stay down.

In the real world now, eyes wide open, still no end of trouble. Something is wrong! Something *real* is really wrong! It is the ringing of the phone that is wrong. Often heard and long listened-for, the outer sound seems the same, but there is in it now an inner quality that is strange and alarming.

Putting his hand on the floppy pillow draped over the phone, Billy feels it vibrating. One clear thought crosses his turbulent mind, Why doesn't she pick up the phone? I can't pick up until she does.

Billy has heard the phone ring dozens of times over the past few weeks. What was it about this time that made it different?

Then his mind jumps to where he doesn't want to go. They have found the body! This is it! The jig is up!

Not wanting to accept a conclusion he has long dreaded, Billy turns over on his back and clamps his eyes shut. Interlocking his naughty, wandering fingers, he presses his palms against his drumming chest. Cleaving in this way to himself and twisting inward again, he conjures the desperate notion that it is the dream still fluttering around in his mind like a murder of crows and not anything real that makes him think that Arthur's body had been found.

He has been having strange dreams every night since the disaster. He is almost certain that he dreams a lot about Arthur, about what happened that day in the woods. He can never remember the dreams, but, each time, when he wakes up, he goes through the same sequence of emotions: fear, disgust, lust, shame, grief.

These are the same emotions he feels when, sometimes, often, something reminds him of that overwhelming moment of union. He spends a lot of time daydreaming about what led up to that moment. Reliving and unconsciously embellishing the memory of their merging has become an increasingly rich experience, and remembering the ensuing horror has mercifully kept him from defiling the epiphany. He burns with an intense love for Arthur. He feels the spiritual violence and mortal passion of lost first love, every bit as painful as Barbara Faustpool's death had been for him.

On that day in the clearing, Billy Mayden, 'with some degree of horror', came face-to-face with the sublime—nay, the holy.

Separating his hands and heaving his body up on one elbow, he decides, no, it's not the dream. That's just wishful thinking. Giving up on chasing down the elusive images, he tries to calm himself and pay attention to the ringing. Is that two longs and a short? Two shorts and a long? One short and two longs? One long and two shorts? The rings blur together and he can't parse the signal into its components. Which one is hers and which is ours, anyway? He has for so long assumed that any late night calls are for Jonnie that, heretofore, he has automatically picked up the receiver as soon as it was clear that the ringing had stopped, not needing to discriminate between the two sequences. In his sleep-deprived-but-hyper-alert state, he can neither count nor remember which sequence is which, anyway.

Like a farm animal that will not be coaxed nor coerced into the slaughterhouse, he fights off the idea that the call is for *him*. He puts his hand under the pillow and pushes down, hard, very hard, on the receiver as if that would stop the ringing, cancel the call.

The jig is up … that's something Jake would say. This is all Jake's fault.

He pushes down even harder on the receiver; it vibrates against his tingling palm like a thing alive. With clenched teeth, he *wills* the ringing to stop. Then, ever the escapist, he tries again to remember the dream.

Stop it!

He sends up a hopeless prayer and relaxes his grip on the phone. Now each ring inflicts a fresh wound. Vacillating between picking up the receiver and being ready to pick it up the second it *stops* ringing, he is suspended between surrender and bull-headed delusion, between the certainty of immediate relief for his tortured ears and the mirage of salvation. He can still feel the vibrations of the receiver, like tiny worms crawling under his skin. How long has it been ringing? Is she not home? Come on, Jonnie, pick up the phone.

Defeated and resigned, he flips the pillow away and picks up the receiver. This is going to be bad.

"Billy! They found the body!" Jacob Garrard whispers. Then, louder, "Hello! Billy? You there? Wake up, asshole. What took you so long to pick up the fucking phone?"

Oh shit! He *was* dead. *Is* dead.

With the falling of the other shoe comes a loud silence. Only then does Billy realize that the thunderstorm has passed. Was it all in his head?

"How do you know?"

"How do I know what? What are you talking about? Wake up, shithead."

"I mean, how did you find out? Who told you? *Who* found the body? You mean ... *him*, right?"

"No, I mean Earl Fucking Long, you asshole. Jesus, Billy. For someone who is supposed to be smart, you can ask some of the dumbest fucking questions. Just listen, and hold off on the twenty questions, okay? They found him in the pool by the dam. Must have been washed downstream by the high water from the storm last night."

So, the storm really happened. Thank God for that much!

"How did they *know* it was him? I mean, it's been a while. Plenty of time for ... ."

"His jacket. Remember he was wearing a black leather jacket? Well, he still had it on when they found him."

An image of a dark rotting leather-jacketed mass bobbing up and down in the water of the pool at Magnolia Park forms in Billy's mind. He imagines that the sour taste of his morning-breath is from some putrid liquid seeping out of his brain into his mouth.

"How did you find out?"

"I was working late for Uncle Toe down at the park. That weird woman ... the alligator lady ... Crystal something ... I don't know her last fucking name ... found it floating in the pool."

"What are you gonna do?"

"What am *I* gonna do? You mean *we*, don't you, you chickenfucker? You're in this shit up to your eyeballs just like me."

"How do you figure that? It wasn't me that kicked him."

"Don't start with that shit again, you shit-eating motherfucker. Besides it doesn't *matter* who did what to him. Let's just say, between the two of us, that we remember it differently and let it go at that. It wasn't like either one of us *wanted* to kill him. For all *we* knew he could have been a fucking *alligator. We* were acting on reflexes."

"'Reflexes'?"

"Don't go dumb on me, you white-trash son-of-a-bitch. The two of us together *chose* to *agree* not to tell anyone about it. The law says we're equally guilty no matter who did what. The important thing is that we stick to the story we came up with for the cops. We've been over and over this. Do you remember what we decided?"

Billy hears a click. Jonnie has turned the tables. She has listened in on *him.*

21

"Now, Billy, tell me what happened that day," the sheriff said as he turned on the tape recorder. "Just start with when you woke up that Sunday morning and tell me everything you can remember. Don't worry about whether it is important or not. Just tell me anything and everything that comes to mind about that day. The smallest thing, or what seems like the smallest thing, might just be the clue we need."

A few days earlier, right after Billy hung up after talking to Jake, the phone rang, someone calling Jonnie. It was Linda Garrard saying she needed Jonnie's help, that they thought Jacob may have been mixed up in, may have had something to do with the body they found the night before in the pool down at Magnolia Park. Jonnie said yeah, she heard about that and wanted to know why they thought Jake was involved. Linda's husband Vincent told her they told him that they got an anonymous call. This was some time ago. The caller told them they, the caller, who they couldn't tell was a man or woman, not that it mattered at this point, had seen Jake and the Mayden boy somewhere near Magnolia Park, in the woods, Linda guessed, and they were 'doing something', was the way they put it, with Dr. Maxwell's son, Arthur. As far as anyone could tell, Arthur hadn't been seen for a long time, since Labor Day weekend to be exact, and it was around that time they think the person they found floating in the pool died. So, they suspected that maybe the body with the leather jacket was him, was Arthur, and that Jake and the other boy may know something about it. Jonnie wanted to know how she could help. Linda didn't know, she just thought Jonnie might ask around, see what she could find out. Jonnie said, will do; she would make some calls and get back to Linda.

A few days later, an unmarked car came to Billy's house to take him to today's interview with the sheriff.

"Well, let's see," Billy began, "I went to church that morning. Brother Johnson preached about forgiveness."

"Forgiveness?"

"Yes sir. And I started thinking about what happened the day before at Pinecrest."

"Pinecrest? What were you doing at Pinecrest?"

After Billy told the sheriff about the fight, he said, "Anyway, Brother Johnson's sermon got me to thinking. Maybe I should . . ."—Billy started to say maybe he should ask for Frankie's forgiveness, but anticipating that he might be asked what he had done to Frankie that required Frankie's forgiveness and remembering Jake's ridicule of that whole idea, he thought it best to avoid as long as possible mentioning Arthur's name; let the Sheriff bring it up. "Maybe I should ... tell Frankie that I forgave him for what he did to me. So I went down to Magnolia Park. I'd heard that Frankie and Dixie were living down there."

"Who'd you hear that from? When?"

"Mr. Jeannsonne told me. Let's see, it was in the spring. During spring break. Or it might a been Memorial Day."

"Where?"

"In Mr. Jeannsonne's house."

"Did you go there a lot?"

"Not too much. Jake Garrard knows him better than I do. Every time I went there Jake was with me." Billy mentally crossed his fingers. It was wrong to lie, but he wouldn't know where to start explaining why he and the Faustpool girl had gone into Theo's house. The octopus picture, for example. What would the sheriff think about that!

"Okay, you went down to Magnolia Park. What happened then?"

Billy told the sheriff some of what led up to his entering the clearing and sitting on the log 'couch'. He didn't tell about Frankie jacking off and he didn't tell about the rubber.

"So, you're sitting there in the woods. Communing with nature, let's say. What happened then?"

"I heard a noise in the bushes. Somebody was coming."

"Who was it?"

"It was Jake Garrard."

"What happened then?"

"Jake said something like, 'I say Old Top. Mind if I join you?' Then I guess he looked up at the sky or something because I remember him saying something like, 'Looks like we're in for a spot of the old precip, does it nawt?'"

"He talked like that? Why?"

"He says it's the way British people talk. Then he told me to scoot over or something and said he was so horny he'd fuck a snake if somebody would hold its head. That's the way he talks. I said out there in that swamp he might get his wish."

"Then … ?"

"Jake said that he had seen some good-looking women by the pool. He said he was so horny he was about to come in his pants. I said something like, 'Not again. You should wear diapers'."

"Why did you say that? Was that was a joke?"

"Yes sir. Jake is always talking about coming in his pants any time he sees a woman or girl he thinks is pretty."

"What happened then?"

"Then Jake pulled down his pants and started masturbating."

"Were you masturbating, too?"

"No sir." This wasn't *exactly* a lie.

"Why not?"

"It's a sin."

"So is lying. Anyway, go on."

"Then, all of a sudden, Jake yelled out something like, 'Oh, motherfucker'. He cusses a lot. He jumped down and started jumping around, trying to pull his pants up. Then he looked under the log."

"You're still sitting on the log?"

"Yes sir. Jake looked under the log. He said, 'It's a bear!' Or, 'It's a *fucking* bear!' He tried to step back but he fell down on his butt. He pulled his pants up and buttoned them up. Then he started kicking and stomping at whatever it was that was under the log. I guess he didn't hit it, because he picked up a stick and started swinging at it with the stick. He kept yelling, 'You motherfucker'. He was running from one end of the log to the other. He said it was too dark to see what it was. Then he said, 'I see you now, you motherfucker', and I heard a noise. It was his shoe hitting something. Right after that I heard another noise."

"Another noise?"

"Yes sir. It sounded like somebody was trying to take in a big breath of air or let it out and couldn't. Then it sounded like they was trying to say something, or yell, or scream, but they couldn't because they couldn't catch their breath."

"Did you know who it was?"

"Not at first, but then I did. It was Arthur Maxwell. Don't ask me what he was doing under that log. I yelled, 'Stop! It's Arthur Maxwell. Don't kick him again!' I jumped down and did my pants. Then I looked under the log."

"How did you know it was Arthur Maxwell?"

Billy was silent for a moment. "I didn't until I looked under the log."

"You said you said, 'Stop! It's Arthur Maxwell', and *then* you looked."

Billy looked to one side. "I was just getting ahead of myself, I guess. I didn't realize who it was until after I looked."

"Okay, go ahead with your story."

"I reached under the log and touched Arth ... the person's ... chest. I could feel ... the person ... trembling. Like a scared puppy or something. Jake said, 'He grabbed my leg. Scared the living shit outa me'. Something like that. He was breathing hard and dripping wet. I don't know if it was sweat or rain. Must a been sweat, because it wasn't raining that hard. Not yet. I said, 'You didn't have to kick him that hard'."

"Wait. You said, 'Jake said, "*He* grabbed my leg".' You said, 'You didn't have to kick *him* that hard.' Did you know it was a 'he' or are you getting ahead of yourself again?"

Billy covered his mouth with his hand. "I guess somewhere in all the excitement I realized that it was Arthur. I don't remember just when I did. Anyway, I said, 'You kicked him right in the face'. Arthur was all bloody."

"So, it was Jake who kicked him?"

"Yes sir. It was like he panicked. He didn't know what he was doing, he was so scared. He said, 'Hell, man. I told you I was scared'. He said he was scared to death. He said he wasn't thinking. He said for all he knew it could've been an alligator. Then he said he was sorry. I said I thought he ... Arthur ... was dead. Then Jake said, 'Oh, Jesus! What are we gonna do?' I said, 'Go tell Uncle Toe'."

"Who's Uncle Toe?"

"Mr. Jeannsonne ... . Then, I said, 'Or the sheriff, we should tell the sheriff'. Then, Jake said, 'No, wait. Let's think this thing out. What are we gonna tell them?' I said, 'The truth'. He said, 'That we were jerking off together?' *He* was the only one jerking off. Then he said, 'How's that gonna look?' Then he said if this got out he might miss his chance to be re-instated in the FBI training program."

"What did you say?"

"I didn't say anything. Then, Jake said, 'Let's hide the body'. He said it was just for now, that it would give us some time to think. I said, 'Hide it where?' He said we were in the middle of the fucking woods. That we should be able to hide a Mack truck out there. That's the way he talks. Anything that is really big is always a Mack truck."

"What if I told you Jake tells it a little bit differently?"

"What did he say?"

"He said he came into this little clearing in the woods and he saw Arthur attacking you. Raping you, he thought. Or at least that's what he said. He said he thought you were in danger, so he grabbed Arthur and pulled him away from you. That Arthur fell down. That when he fell he hit his head on a log. He said he thought Arthur was okay but before he could tell for sure, you jumped off the log and kicked Arthur in the chest. After that, he said, he just lay there.

"He said that you said you didn't want anyone to find out. That you felt ashamed. That you believed that people would somehow think it was your fault, what Arthur did to you. That they'd think you *wanted* Arthur to do it, whatever it was he was doing.

"He said the two of you hid Arthur's body under the log you had been sitting on. That then it started thundering and lightning. That you panicked and ran."

The sheriff then put a brown paper bag on the table he and Billy were sitting at, across from each other. One-by-one he removed Ralph's baseball cap, Jake's shoe, Billy's tenny shoe, Billy's glasses, His Majesty's little plastic crown, and a condom.

Then the sheriff said, "Look, boy. I don't know what you and that Garrard boy were up to with that poor retarded boy. It looks like it had something to do with sex." Before Billy could protest, the sheriff said, "Look son, a minute ago you said you jumped down off the log and *did your pants*. Remember that? I can play it back to you if you want. Okay, now, that proves there was *some* kind of sex play going on. That's okay. It happens. I don't need to know exactly what it was. You and Jake keep your mouths shut and nothing'll happen to you. But, let me tell you this. If you or Jake *ever* say a word to *any*body about any of this, I will show these … items … to your parents and I'll tell them what I think was probably going on. You get me?"

"Yes, sir."

"Just remember I went to school with your mama. I don't have to tell you how bad she'd be hurt knowing her son, her only child, was messed up in something like this, do I?"

"No sir, you don't. It would kill her."

"Did you tell Frankie that you forgave him for beating you up?"

"No sir, I forgot."

"Too late now, huh?"

$$*\qquad*\qquad*$$

"Listen to this." Billy's father, Clinton, was reading the paper while the family ate breakfast. "*After weeks of speculation, local authorities have closed the 'Case of the Corpse in the Black Leather Jacket' as the mystery of the identity of the body found floating in Magnolia Park swimming pool late last fall has been informally referred to in the area media. Speaking off the record to a* Town Talk *reporter, one authority said the body was more than likely that of Arthur Maxwell, the son of Dr. Robert Maxwell, former Director of Pinecrest, a state-run facility for the mentally retarded. The unnamed authority said that it appeared that the young Maxwell had wondered off into the swamps near Magnolia Park and had been attacked by alligators. The man's father, Dr. Maxwell, was unavailable for comment as he has reportedly moved out of the area.*

When his father had finished reading, Billy's mother said she heard that the preacher's daughter, Dixie, had been missing since some time around Labor Day and that a woman named Crystal something had been arrested in connection with Dixie's death.

22

Can I come in? Mr. Christopher … ? I'm Deputy Wade. Richard Wade. Oh, Mr. Chrisssstopher. Alright if I come in? I know it's late and all. Won't take but a minute of your time.

It's got Coke bottle glasses. Crystal don't move.

I know you're in there, Mr. Christopher. I saw you moving around in there just now. I'm Richard Wade. Me and you was in the same … we graduated … well, actually, I didn't actually … . Anyhow we went to school together, remember? Used to ride the same bus? It went by Pinecrest to pick you and a couple a the other ones up? Parish Catholic School? I mean, I know … of course … you know what school you graduated from … I just … I'm with the Sheriff's Department, kinda. Here, I'm gonna hold my badge up. You can look at it through the glass wender in the door if you don't believe me.

Door knob's turning. Door's opening. Spring's making hurting twanging noise. Hurts Crystal's ears.

I'm coming in. You don't have to be afraid. I won't hurt you. How come you all wrapped up in that thang? Y'ain't cold, are you? What is that, some kind a mat? Looks like what they have in the gym to keep you from knocking your brains out when you run into the wall. Not that it ever happened to me. I mean I never did play basketball or nothing. Hope you don't mind me just coming on in … real slow … like this … no reason to get scared. Door weren't locked or nothing. I could oil that hinge for you, you want. You look like a big ole pig-in-a-blanket, you don't mind me saying so. You ever have one a them thangs? They's so good!

Crissy-in-a-blanket. *Close eyes. Crystal huddle in the puddle of the hugger-rugger.*

What's that? I can't hear you with that thang wrapped around you like that. Mr. Christopher … . Is that your *last* name? What did you say? 'Christy in a blanket'? Like Christy Mathewson, right? I didn't never play baseball neither. Bad eyes, you know. I don't know if you remember me. I'm Dick

Wade. You might remember me as Dick Wad. Ha ha. Used to get called that a lot at school. I'm a Deputy ... well, not really, but I will be purdy soon, I reckon. Got my application in. Me and you went to grade school together. 'Course, I played hooky most a the time. Quit 'fore I uz knee-high to a tummel-bug. Ha ha. Hey! You know why a dog licks his dick?

Coke eyes' boots on the wood floor.

'Cause he can! Ha ha. What's the next to the best thing?

Now on little rug. Sounds different.

Panties! Get it? Next to the best thing? I just want to ask you a few questions. Oh, there you are. Poking your head out like a turtle.

Get it out of here! It wants to hurt Crystal. If it gets any closer, Crystal roll out and get ready to fight.

I thank we went to school together ... Christy ... . Can I call you Christy? Well, I know we did. I don't know if you remember or not. You were one of the ... make that *the* smartest kid ... guy ... uh ... *person*, really ... in the whole school. We didn't hang around together or nothing, though. I reckon I don't have to tell you that.

I-am-not-a-bat. I-do-not-hang-from-the-ceiling-of-a-cave-or-from-a-gallows. *Crystal-joke.*

Well, well, well. We can talk after all. I was beginning to wonder if the cat got your tongue or something like that.

Unwrap. Stand up. Circle around. Keep the table between it and you. It wants me to do something. It wants me to do something naughty. Cats-can-not-appropriate-the-tongues-of-Homo-Sapiens. Ordinary-domestic-feline-mammals-are-normally-not-in-possession-of-enough-muscular-strength-in-their-jaws-to-dispossess-Homo-Sapiens-of-even-one-of-the-smaller-phalanges.

Look, Christy, calm down. I just want to ask you a few questions. Okay? I like your shades. You wear them indoors? You must have sensitive eyes. I'd wear sunglasses, too, if I could. All the guys in the Department wear them. But I can't. Can't see shit without my regular glasses. You ain't gonna need that knife. Here I'll put my weapon on this here table. Now you put your knife right next to it. No? Okay. You talk kinda funny, you know that? When you say ever word the same way the way you do, you're hard to follow.

Crystal-not-going-anywhere. Maybe-it-means-alligator. Perhaps-it-means-to-suggest-that-an-alligator-has-confiscated-Crystal's-organ-of-gustation-and-speech-articulation. It-is-a-physical-impossibility-for-an-alligator-to-seize-a-Homo-Sapien's-tongue. An-outward-appendage-per-haps-an-upper-limb-maybe-or-perhaps-a-lower-limb. A-penis-is-a-defi-nite-possibility.

Whoa! Let's slow down there. I caught that one alright. Don't wanna lose *that*! Ever hear the one about 'John's dead'?

Alligators-are-reptiles. Reptiles-had-the-first-penises.

If you say so. There's this traveling salesman, see … .

An-ear-perchance.

Oh no! That's enough! Turn loose a my ear!

But-not-the-organ-of-speech-as-in-the-phrase-mother-tongue-and-the-site-of-the-gustatory-sense. The-organ-of-olfaction-is-another-possibility.

No! Not my nose! Boy! Once you get going they ain't no stopping you, is they?

The-oral-cavity-of-Homo-Sapiens-is-normally-too-small-to-accommodate-the-cranial-width-of-an-alligator-or-other-crocodilian-inside-it-and-even-if-said-crocodilian-inserted-said-cranium-in-said-oral-cavity-said-crocodilian-would-not-be-able-to-open-its-anterior-opening-in-order-to-masticate-said-gustatory-organ. Maybe-a-small-alligator … or-a-caiman … unless-it-is-talking-about-a-Homo-Sapien-that-has-not-yet-reached-the-acme-of-its-physical-development … .

Hey, Christy! You don't have to hide behind the couch like that. Howcome you don't wanna look at me? You don't never look at a person's eyes when you talking to 'em, do you? I member that from school.

Let-Crystal-see-its-badge.

You like that badge? Me too. Here, you can touch it if you want to. What you doing there? Tracing the letters and pitcher with your fangers? I like to do that, too. Did you say Crystal? Or Christopher?

Badge-Madge-Bridge-Midge-Barge-Marg-Bargy-Margie-Bargy-Margie.

I beg your pardon. You lost me there, sir. I'm not following … .

It-is-right-there. Crystal-has-not-lost-it. It-has-not-moved.

What's that you say? Who hasn't moved? Did you say 'Crystal'? Oh, yeah, now I get it. You're talking about all them little glass animals you have all over the place. What's this one? Oh, yeah, it's an alligator. No! Now, Mr. Christopher. You can't have that badge. How did you get that thang outa my pocket so fast? Give it back to me. Come on now. Don't make me have to shove this here table up against the wall to get at you. I'm not leaving till you give me my badge back. Jeez, you didn't have to throw it like that. You break it my ass is grass and the Sheriff is the lawnmower.

The-consistency-of-the-mammalian-gluteus-maximus-is-of-a-different-consistency-than-that-of-grass. To-attempt-to-reduce-its-size-by-passing-a-grass-cutting-machine-over-it-as-one-would-a-lawn-would-in-all-probability-result-in-a-disorderly-circumstance. The-oxygen-carrying-fluid-and-fatty-tissue-and-muscle-tissue-would-in-all-probability-prevent-the-cutting-devices-from-rotating-properly. However-there-are-in-all-probability-surgical-procedures-that-would-minimize-the-loss-of-blood-and-maximize-the-potential-for-survival.

Huh?

It-is-not-leaving-it-wants-something.

Okay, I understand. You stay over there. Right where you are. But you really don't have to worry. I won't bi ... . I mean, I won't hurt you. It's okay for you to stay over there. I ain't gonna come no closer than you want me to. I just wanna ask you a few questions about Dixie West. And I can do that from over here. She used to go by the name a Johnson before she married Frankie West. She's Brother Johnson's girl. You know her? Mr. Jeannsonne said you might be able to tell me something about her. Said she hangs ... comes over here a lot.

Crocodylus-johnstoni. Australian-crocodile. John's-son. Jean's-son.

What's that? John? Jean? That's Cajun for John, right? Oh yeah. They names *are* kinda alike. Jeannsonne's same as Johnson in Coon Ass ... . I mean Cajun ... . I reckon. Come to thank of it! You're right, by gum. They are *half* brothers. One's Cajun, though. Not a bad feller, though.

Half-a-brother-half-a-brother. King-Solomon-cut-the-baby-in-half-and-gave-each-mother-a-portion. Does-it-know-the-direction-of-the-dissection. Vertical-or-horizontal.

What's that? Direction of the what?

Die-section. Die-section. Die-section.

Oh! I get it! I said they was *half* brothers. Say that's purdy damn funny. Here's one for you: This here pregnant lady steps out in front of a big ole Mack truck, right? The truck driver slams on the brakes. Stops just in time. Then he sticks his head out of the wender and says, Hey, lady, you can get knocked *down*, too, you know. Get it? Knocked *down*. See, the lady was preg ... .

Coke-eyes-is-going-to-hurt-Crystal. Talking-about-cutting-people-in-half. Stealing-my-tongue. Running-over-women-with-trucks. Go-away-coke-eyes.

Look, mister. I can't help it about my glasses.

Go-away-coke-eyes.

Well, I reckon that's enough questions for today, sir. I thank I'll just pick up my gun and mosey on back to the office. Write up my ree-port. Hey, now wait a minute! You ain't gonna need that. What is that thang? That's what they call a machete, ain't it? Big ole spic knife. Cut sugar cane with it, don't they. That's what it looks like. Looks like you keep it pretty sharp. Where'd you get it?

Mash-Eddie. Mash-Eddie.

Okay! I'm going. Been nice talking to you ... .

∗   ∗   ∗

Crystal, it's Auntie Jonnie-Jon. Are you in there? I know you're in there. I'm gonna let myself in now, Crystal. Don't be frightened. It's just me. Auntie Jonnie-Jon. You can come out of that thing now, Crystal. Come on, Crystal, I mean it! You can wrap yourself back up after I leave. Sit down. Auntie Jonnie-Jon needs Crystal's help. Look what I have for Crystal if Crystal will help Auntie Jonnie-Jon. Isn't it beautiful? It's a jacket made of alligator skin. Your cup of tea, eh?

Crystal-can-make-a-cup-of-tea.

No, that's okay. Maybe later. No, no! Crystal doesn't get the jacket until after Crystal helps Auntie Jonnie-Jon. Now, listen very carefully. If anybody asks you, we never had this conversation. Say that. Say, We never had this conversation.

That-say-we-never-had-this-conversation.

Great! You are *so* smart. Now, you know how you used to like to memorize weird stuff? While you were still at Pinecrest? How we used to test you to see how much you could remember after looking at something, a medical file, say, for only a minute or two? That's how Auntie Jonnie-Jon knew how smart Crystal was. That Crystal belonged in a regular school. Isn't Crystal glad Auntie Jonnie-Jon helped Crystal get an education?

That-say-we-never-had-this-conversation.

That's right. Now look at what I'm gonna write on this piece of paper. There. See that? Now, I want you to try to remember every medical file that has that written in it. This should be pretty easy for you. The only files that would have that ... this, what I have written on this piece of paper ... take a good look, Crystal ... the only files that have that written down *anywhere* in them ... on *any* piece of paper inside the file folder ... are files with *girls'* names on them. Okay? *Girls only.* So, just let yourself see only girl's files. Close you eyes and concentrate. Got it? Now tell me the names of any girls whose files have this written in them anywhere, on any piece of paper inside the file folder. After we have all the names I'll tell you what I want you to do.

Sara-Abbott-three-times.

Great! Let me write her name down. Now, one thing I forgot to tell you. Some of them, like the one you just gave me, will have it written down more than one time. In more than one place. On more than one page. As soon as you see it, the first time you see it, tell me the name. You don't have to look through the whole file folder in your head once you've seen it. As soon as you see it, say the name. And, Crystal, look at me. Crystal, I need for you to look at me. I know how you hate to look at people's eyes, but I have to be sure you hear what I'm about to say. See, that's not so bad. Auntie Jonnie-Jon isn't gonna hurt her darling Crystal. Now, repeat after me: Crystal never had a conversation about medical records with anyone.

That-say-we-never-had-this-conversation.

Right. Now I'm going to write the new one that I told you just now down on a piece of paper. There. Read that.

Crystal-never-had-a-conversation-about-medical-records-with-anyone.

Good. Now here's your diary. Copy it on this page. That's good. Now, open your diary to this page and look at this sentence at least five times a day so you will never forget it. Now, tell me the next name.

Amy-Ackers.

Hello, Chris, it's Dee Jay. Is this a bad time? I know you like to stay up late. Is it too late? I could come back later. Why don't you have Uncle Theo do something about that door? Makes an awful racket. Needs a new spring. Guess what, I'm going to be in a movie. Well, maybe. I met this real nice man at the sanitarium. He knows a Hollywood producer. They're going to send out a camera crew for some screen tests. He's gonna call the producer *tonight*! Isn't that great! Aren't you happy for me?

Crystal-is-happy-for-me.

Well, yeah, I know what you mean: Look out for number one. You have your own way of putting things, but you're absolutely right. That's me from now on. A woman can't depend on a man to take care of her. All a man wants is to keep you at home, tied to the stove ... and the bed. Barefoot and ... how's that saying go? Something about big ... . Big and barefoot! That's it.

Dee-Jay-is-big.

No bigger than you are, Miss Priss. We wear the same size. Half my clothes are over here and vice versa. Of course, you don't like my girly clothes, but you look great in them. Oh by the way, I want to borrow your alligator-skin jacket. I know how much it means to you, what with you and your alligators and all. But I'll take good care of it and I won't keep it long. I'm hoping there's still a little animal magnetism left in it. Not enough to start a fire in the loins of that lazy husband of mine, of course. It'd take all the alligators in Louisiana for that. That's history anyway. But it'll make me look good in the movie, maybe.

Crystal-has-matches.

Okay, make your little joke. You don't know how crazy it has made me trying to figure out what was wrong with him. I just wish it *had* been that kind of fire that was needed. I tried everything. I poured out his vodka. I diluted it with water. He figured out what I was doing and started putting it in a special blue bottle that he hid in the kitchen. I finally gave up. He gave up on himself. Wait a minute! What did you say? 'Dee Jay is big'? Crystal! How'd you know that! Jesus! A girl can't keep *any*thing from you. I wasn't gonna bring that up. Could you tell from my coloring? Of course, you know about these things, I guess. Taking care of all those mother alligators, looking after their eggs and babies, and all. Oh, I don't know what I'm talking about. I'm so excited about being in a movie I can't be expected to make sense. Look, don't get mad or anything, but I may not keep it. What with all that's happening. Not everyday that something like this lands on your doorstep. Frankie'll be hurt, or he would be if he knew, but why should I be expected to take care of a baby all by myself? Frankie wouldn't be any help, even if he wasn't … in the condition he's in. I just wish he'd quit scheming behind my back. But I know he never will. It's all he has to live for anymore. I've already agreed to let him … I'm talking about the man I met at the sanitarium … he's going to shoot some preliminary footage … that's what he called it, 'preliminary footage' … with his little eight millimeter camera. That's what they call it when they film something: shoot some footage. Oh my God! I wonder if I show already. They say you look ten pounds heavier on film anyway.

Crystal-will-put-a-bandage-on-Dee-Jay's-foot.

What are you doing? Why are you taking off my boot, Crystal? Oh, I see. You want me to take off my clothes so you can see if I'm showing. Good idea. If it was anybody else … any other woman … I wouldn't do this … too creepy … but with you … you're so comfortable with your own body. I've never seen you embarrassed. What do you think? Can you tell? I don't know how far along I am. Frankie could tell you, I bet. He's always sniffing around my dirty underwear. He'd know the last time I had my period. Of course, the only reason he does it is to look for evidence that I've been with other men. He learned that from my old man, the Good Reverend. He used to do that, too. What do you think they'd think if I announced in church that the preacher liked to sniff his alleged daughter's dirty underwear?

This-is-Crystal's-jacket.

Hey, looks pretty good. That'd make a great shot, wouldn't it? Me with just this little piece of alligator skin on. Grrrr. Grrrr. This man I was telling you about? He was asking me if I'd be willing to be filmed in the nude *if* the artistic integrity of the movie depended on it. He says the movie will have all kinds of 'social relevance'. Got to have that social relevance. I told him I would think about it. Meanwhile, I'll test this out with Uncle Tuh … Frankie, I mean. If it does the trick with him, maybe I'll wear it for the preliminary shots. Whata ya think, Crystal?

Think-Crystal! Think-Crystal! Think-Crystal!

Now you sound like my old man. Just be glad you aren't a preacher's daughter. Listen, the real reason I came over is so you can help me play a trick on Uncle Toe. The man I met at the sanitarium wants me to see if I can make myself look like a certain woman he says he used to know. He gave me a picture of her. Look. He wants me to make myself look just like she does in this picture. She's some kind of movie star, I guess. She looks sort of familiar, doesn't she? But I don't remember ever seeing her in any movies. Do you? She must a had only bit parts. At least up until the time this picture was taken. Of course, she may look a lot different now. They can make you look anyway they want. I oughta know. I'm a make-up artist. The man at the sanitarium said if I don't make it as a movie star, he'd help me get a job in Hollywood as a make-up artist.

Janelle.

Hey, you're right. It does look a little bit like my dear old mother. That gives me an idea. Tell me what you think. I'll make myself over to look like the woman in this photograph. And *then* when I'm with Uncle Toe I'll give myself the personality of my old lady. They used to know each other many years ago. Before I was born. Before she married old Stone Face. He makes Mount Rushmore look like a bunch of clowns. Not me! *My* face isn't stone! Don't, Crystal! That tickles. You can't just put your hands on people like that! I can't believe he and Uncle Toe are half-brothers. I just wish Uncle Toe was my father. Where's my stuff? By the way, thanks for letting me keep it over here. There's no closet space in that stupid cabin of mine and Frankie's. Besides, Frankie'd have a shit-fit if he knew how many clothes I have. Thinks I should give all my money to him.

Cryssstal. Where's little Crystal? My sparkling little Crystal? Oh, I wonder where she could be hiding. What's this? Looks like a very big blanket. Gee, Little Red Riding Hood, what a big thick blanket you have. Okay, I'll just wait until spring. Until Sleeping Beauty comes out of hibernation. Dr. Maxy Waxy hasn't been to see Snow White since she moved into this little cabin in the woods. I wonder where the seven midgets are. Dr. Maxy Waxy wants a little kiss. And Dr. Maxy Waxy's little Froggy Woggy needs a little kiss, too, so he can turn into a handsome prince and go exploring inside Crystal's magic caves. Come on out Little Froggy Woggy. Oh, he is a thad widdle fwoggy. Look, little Froggy Woggy's head is hanging low. Okay, I'll come back tomorrow night. There's a big party in the park tomorrow night and you know how you hate big crowds of people. So, you just stay here, safe and sound in your cabin, and you can help me and Auntie Jonnie-Jon with something we have to do, just like you used to do at Pinecrest ... . That's what you call her, right? Auntie Jonnie-Jon? But Dr. Maxy wants to hide something here until tomorrow, okay? See, it's made of alligator skin. Isn't it pretty? It's got Dr. Maxy's doctor stuff in it. Me and you and Auntie Jonnie-Jon will use Dr. Maxy's doctor stuff to help a lady make sure she has a healthy baby, okay? Just like we used to do when we were a team. Can little Crissy keep a little secret? There's a good place, right under Crystal's bed.

Oh Crystal? Are you in there? Let Dr. Max in, okay? That's a good girl. Arthur! What are ... ? Where were you hiding? You spying on me, you creep? Your face looks like shit. Who beat you up this time? Why are you wearing that ridiculous leather jacket? Don't you know it's summer, dumbo. Dumbo, the elephant. You're big and fat enough, but *sow*'s more like it. You've started hanging around with Frankie West and those other hoods again, haven't you? Don't bother to deny it. Is that how you earned enough money to buy that jacket? How much do you get? Two-bits a throw? Or should I say 'blow'? I shoulda shipped you off years ago. Take it off. Give it to me, damn it. I don't want no kid of mine being thought of as a hood. It's enough that everybody knows you're a queer. Okay, keep the damn thing but get back in the other room. Crystal and I have things we have to do. Okay, Cryssstal, where are you? Auntie Jonnie-Jon isn't coming, so it's just you and me and Froggy makes three. Is that my little Crystal I hear inside her big thick blankie? Dr. Maxy Waxy is going to take Froggy Woggy's clothes off now. There. Now widdle Froggy Woggy isn't widdle anymore. Froggy Woggy can breathe. He still needs a kiss. Here, let me unwrap this big ole blankie so Crystal, the beautiful butterfly can come out of her cocoon and land right on little Froggy's head. Hey! For God's sake, Crystal! Put that thing down. Come on, now. Okay, okay. I'm leaving but I have to have that bag that I hid under your bed and the stuff you and Ralph took from my office. And I don't have to remind you, I can still make life pretty difficult for you if I want to. You still have to be evaluated once a year, you know. One of the conditions is no incidents of violence. I might have to mention in my next report that you tried to cut me with a machete. Hey! Wait a minute! It's not here. What happened to it? And where are those files you took out of my office? Why are you standing in front of that closet? You stupid cunt. You gave yourself away. Arthur! Turn me loose! I told you to stay in the other room. You stink like a pig. I'm warning you two. If anyone finds out that I've been here, I'll know who tipped them off. And one or both of you may find yourselves floating face down in that swimming hole out there. Come on, Crystal, give me my pants back, damn you! Ahhhh! Goddamn it! You've cut me real bad! Oh Jesus! I have to get to a hospital!

$$* \qquad * \qquad *$$

Crystal! Holy Jesus! God help me, Crystal! I'm in deep, deep trouble. Crystal, open up, it's Dixie.

Heeey ... good lookin' ... . Whaaat you got cookin' ... ?

I'm serious, Crystal. Deadly serious. So, please don't sing anymore. You've got to help me figure out what to do. Turn off the lights. I don't want anyone to know I'm here. Jesus! Look at all the blood! What happened in here? One of your alligators get hurt? Oh, never mind. You can tell me later. Just turn that light off so I don't have to look at it. Good, that's better. I've got stuff to talk to you about, stuff that can't wait.

How's about cookin' suuumethin' up with meee?

Come on, Crystal, I'm not kidding. How come you sound norm ... natural when you sing?

I got a hot rod Ford and a two dollar bill ... .

You know I've been wracking my brains, don't you, trying to decide whether or not to keep this baby. I had just about decided that I was gonna keep it. I was gonna give it to Brother Billy ... that's what Frankie's taken to calling Billy Mayden ... . Do you know him? Billy's mother wants him to be a preacher ... . Oh, Crystal, I'm so scared I can't think straight. Where was I?

I-was-right-here-still-am.

Come on now, Crystal. Stop joking around. I may have done a terrible thing and I need your help. This man ... who you don't know ... don't need to know, anyway ... was supposed to call me today and tell me where to go to ... get rid of it ... but he never called. Which was okay because I was gonna keep it, anyway. But then tonight at the March of Dimes party ... why weren't you there? Oh, don't answer. You can tell me later. Something happened at the party ... someone ... this awful movie ... .

Crystal, I thought Frankie was the father of the baby. Now, I think that it may be someone else. Someone whose baby I could never have in a million years. Not that I hate him or anything ... . Oh God, why am I ... it doesn't *matter* what I think of him. Crystal, you have to help me get rid of this baby. Didn't you used to work with Jonnie Vonderheim? I heard that she sometimes helped girls out who got into trouble. A friend of mine ... . What is that? That's a doctor's bag, isn't it? Made out of alligator skin? Never seen one like that. What's in it? What's that noise! Someone's at the door. Here, wrap me up in this thing.

$$* \qquad * \qquad *$$

It's me, Miss Crystal. I know you're in there. I saw the light go off a little while ago and besides, I can see you through the window. Come on, now, you've *got* let me in. I'm in deep trouble.

Mr.-Jeannsonne's-boy. *The colored one. Mr. Jeannsonne's boy. Same lips and nose. Same large gluteus maximus.*

I'm not anybody's *boy*, okay? Let me in, dammit.

Mr.-Jeannsonne's-boy.

Thanks for letting me in, Crystal. I mean it about that boy stuff. Who was that woman I saw come in here?

Miss-Crystal.

I was calling you that because I didn't want anyone hear me first-naming a white woman. White folks are real touchy about that. Some of 'em. Sound carries all over this place at night.

Touchy-touchy.

Okay, stop feeling me up. You're not my type. Touchy doesn't have anything to do with actually touching anybody. It means ... . What's that wrapped up in your mat? Good God! What happened in here! I'm gonna turn on my flash light, okay? Who is that? Jeeesus! Look at the mess ... is that blood? Here let's unwrap whatever this is and have a look at it. It's a woman, obviously. I see boobs. How'd this ... ? What ... ? You didn't ... ? Oh, I see what happened. Old Maximilian and Elvira really messed this one up, didn't they? That explains the trail of blood I saw outside. How long's she been here?

Maximilian-you-are-welcome. Maximilian-you-are-welcome.

Don't start with the words. I think this woman's dead. If she is, you're in the shit as deep I am ... if we don't get her out of here p.d.q. and clean up all this blood. Let's take this wig off and get a look at her face.

Frankie and Dixieee were sweeeet hearts.

Holy mother of God! You're right. It's her alright. *That*'s who I saw coming in here. She must have been delirious or something and wandered over here by mistake. Now I know for sure we've got to get her out of here, clean this mess up, before anybody else sees it. I came over here to hide out for a while, but looks like I done jumped out of the frying pan into the fire. I get caught here now it really *is* all over. Curtains for sure. Goddamn that bastard LeBeaux! I know I never should've listened to no white man. He didn't tell me ... no wonder he said don't worry none about getting her .... Dead knocked-up white girl and a nigger. Makes that business with the dirty movie look like a Sunday School lesson. They gonna yell murder and rape so loud you'll be able to hear 'em in China.

Alligator-sinesis-Chinese-alligator.

What are you doing? Don't take that thing off of her.

It-is-Crystal's. Crystal-wants-it. Crystal-is-the-alligator-lady!

Okay, hold your voice down. You're yelling loud enough to wake up the dead. Stop shaking her. That's just an expression. Loud enough to wake the dead. Means very loud. Just give me a minute to think this thing out. If I let you keep that jacket, will you keep your mouth shut about me being here? You have to promise, okay. And you have to hide it. Anybody else sees it they'll take it away from you. Do you promise? Okay, good. Go ahead and take it off her while I look for something to wrap her up in. A blanket or something. Here, this'll work, I think. First I'll just take these things off her. It'll take longer to identify her if she's not wearing anything. Buy me a little more time. *She* ain't gonna be needing clothes and jewelry and wigs anymore. These earrings are nice. And this dress is *very* nice! Looks like basic black, at least with this flashlight. Blood oughta wash out pretty good.

Crystal-has-alligator-skin. Crystal-looks-good. Crystal-in-the-mirror-looks-good.

What in the name of all that is holy are you doing, Crystal?

Crystal-looks-good-just-like-Dixie.

Well, yeah, you do look pretty hot alright. But not now. Put your clothes back on. You can get naked and look at yourself in the mirror after we get rid of .... Here, give me a hand.

Here-give-me-a-hand.

Stop it now, Crystal. You know what I mean. Why do you always have to take everything so literally? I mean *help* me. That's what 'give me a hand' means. It doesn't mean to actually give someone a hand. Looks like someone smart as you are could understand that people don't always mean *exactly* what they say. I gotta tell you, this business with this dead white woman plus the trouble that dirty movie has made for me has got me scared. I gotta slow down. Catch my breath. Let my heart stop pounding like a woodpecker. Here, help me wrap her up in this blanket. While we're doing that, let me tell you what happened last night. I was waiting outside old Max's office. He'd asked me to drop by for something. Can't remember what it was. He's always wanting me to drop by his office. It's never anything very important. I think maybe he's a little, you know … .

Old-Max-hurt-Teejay's-hand.

No, that's just means he likes boys same as he does girls … . The door to his office wasn't shut all the way and I heard him on the phone. So, I waited and listened to him talking to whoever it was on the other end of the line. I didn't catch it all. Said something about you being the only one who could have remembered all the names of … patients maybe … or different kinds of procedures … . I didn't catch that part. Then something about there not being enough time for anyone else to go through the files in the amount of time between such and such a time and some other time. Didn't you used to work in the records department at Pinecrest? Before they took you out and put you in a regular school? Anyways, best I could figure, the old bastard had it in his head that you took some medical records from Pinecrest hospital and he was going *after* your ass. I ran over as quick as I could to warn you, to tell you he was on his way over, but I couldn't outrun his car and he got here before me. I did wait around till he left, just to make sure you were okay. I peeped in your window and you looked okay, so I took off. There. I'll take her outa here and you can start cleaning up the blood. What's that noise! Someone's coming! Help me put her under the bed! No, she's not going to fit. Here, we'll put her in the corner and put the table in front of her. There, that'll have to do. I'll go out the back. I'll come back later if I get a chance and help you clean up that blood. You hide till whoever it is goes away. I just hope they didn't see my flashlight or hear us moving that table.

Mr. Crystal, it's Richard Wade. Remember? We talked earlier. There's some more stuff I have to ask you about. Just one more thang, sir. No, that's alright. You don't have to unlock the door. I'll just tell you standing out here. Can you hear me? I don't know if you been out yet or not, but they's blood in front of your cabin. I seen it with my flashlight. Fact is there's a long trail of it leading up to your front door. I don't know if you noticed it or not. How long's it been there, do you know? Oh, thank you for letting me come in.

It-wants-Crystal's-alligator-jacket.

Jacket? What jacket?

It-is-Crystal's. Crystal-is-the-alligator-lady. Dixie-is-not-the-alligator-lady. She-has-never-taken-care-of-any-baby-alligators. She-can-not-be-an-alligator-mother. Not-now. The-one-with-the-overly-large-posterior-said-Crystal-could-live-here-and-take-care-of-them.

Oh, I get what you're saying. I thank. You mean, Mr. Jeannsonne, right? You shore have a strange way a putting thangs. Can we have some lights on in here? No? That's okay, we'll just talk in the dark.

Crystal-did-not-put-it-anywhere.

You don't have to stand in front of the closet like that, Chris ... . Christo? Is that what you've been calling yourself? Or is it Christol? What kinda name is that? That one of them wop names? Anyways, I ain't gonna take your jacket or whatever it is you're going on about.

Crystal-will-trade-its-badge-for-it. Badge-Madge.

Don't start that again. Is that blood on your mat? I'm gonna turn on my flashlight, okay? Look, it's covered with blood. And, my goodness, there's blood all over the floor, too. They's blood ever where! What's that under the table? It's somebody! A woman, I thank. She must a been hurt real bad! Do you have a phone? No? You wait here while I run down to the bar and call the sheriff's office and have them send out an ambulance.

23

Now, Miss Crystal, please, if you will, tell us what happened next? You took off the decedent's jacket, didn't you? It's right here in the deposition. Which you signed, did you not? Let the record show that the witness shook her head in the affirmative. Now, Miss Crystal, we have been told that you suffer from a mental condition. Is that correct?

Your honor, the defense has stipulated ... . This has been explained in great detail in the material we provided for the court *and* the District Attorney's office. Everyone even remotely connected with this case has been in possession of this material, has had ample time to read it, and, furthermore, has had many chances to ask questions of counsel, of this witness, and of our expert witnesses, including, Mrs. Juanita Lopez Vonderheim, who has been the Head Nurse at Pinecrest during the whole time that Miss Crystal was a resident there which was most the first twenty-one years of her life.

Your honor, all I'm trying to get at are the facts. More specifically, I'm trying to get at this witness's *motivation*, her state of mind.

Proceed. This is just a hearing, counselor.

Now, Miss Crystal, you have a college degree, is that correct? Let the record show that the witness shook her head in the affirmative. Where did you take your degree?

Home.

'Home'? What do you mean, 'home'?

Your honor, learn-ed counsel knows that her degree is from Louisiana State University.

Rephrase your question, counselor.

Miss Crystal, you graduated from LSU, is that correct? Let the record show ... .

Counselor, I think we can dispense with your saying 'let the record show' every time the witness shakes her head yes. Save it for those times when she answers in the negative. Like I told learned counsel for the defense, this is just a hearing. If and when we go to trial you will have full leeway to parade your pedantry.

Okay, your honor. And, please, your honor, allow this humble counselor to thank his honor for his wise guidance in these intricate proceedings.

Get on with it, counselor.

Now, Miss Crystal, in what field of study were you trained?

It-was-not-in-a-field.

I beg your pardon. 'It was not in a field'. Is that what you said? What do you mean?

It-was-in-the-lowland-marshes-and-swamps-of-the-coastal-regions-of-the-state-of-Louisiana-and-the-Big-Cypress-National-Preserve-in-the-state-of-Florida. Crystal-conducted-the-first-study .... .

I'm sorry, Miss Crystal. I only meant .... You have a degree in Veterinary Science, do you not? No? Let the record show .... .

Your honor, Miss Crystal's degree is in Wildlife Management. Counselor knows that.

Okay, your honor, my mistake. I apologize for any harm or insult I may have caused to the witness's delicate psyche.

Objection!

Sustained. Counsel will please cease with the sarcasm.

Miss Crystal, did you or did you not take *courses*, three to be exact, in Veterinary Science? Yes? Now isn't Veterinary Science a branch of Medicine? Doesn't it entail your learning the same kinds of information that a medical doctor, a physician, if you will, would be likely to acquire in the course of his becoming a physician?

Objection!

Overruled.

So, it is safe to assume, is it not, Miss Crystal, that you are, or would be, in a better position to determine the medical condition of an injured person than the average person?

Objection!

Overruled. I want to see where this takes us. Repeat your question, counselor.

Would you or would you not be in a better position to assess the severity of the injuries sustained by the decedent than the man in the street?

Yes-because-he-would-be-dead.

Who would be dead? What are you talking about?

A-Mack-truck-driver-said-you-can-get-knocked-down-too.

Your honor!

Counselor, go to your next question. At this rate we'll be here till Mardi Gras.

Okay, your honor, but I reserve the right to come back to this question. Now, Miss Crystal, *before* you *stole* ... .

Objection!

Before you took the jacket off the person of the person who was lying on the mat on the floor in your cabin. The person whom you could not have known at that point was alive or dead ... .

Objection!

... Did you make any effort to determine the medical condition of that person who *you* say wandered, drunk, in a state of delirium, to your cabin ... did you even check to see if this midnight visitor was alive or dead *before* you removed her jacket? Or were you so enamored of her alligator jacket that you could not be bothered with such a minor detail as whether the person whose jacket it presumably was ... the person who was wearing the jacket at the time ... whether this person was dead or alive?

Your honor, counsel is badgering the witness.

There-are-no-badgers-this-far-south. These-carnivorous-burrowing-mammals-genera-*Taxidea*-and-*Meles*-range-from-no-further-south-than ... .

Miss Crystal! You will please refrain from these wildly tangential remarks. They're irrelevant, impertinent, and immaterial. Counselor, please repeat your last question in a more direct and less verbose manner.

Miss Crystal, did you check the *pulse* of the person who came to your cabin on the night in question? No! Did you look at the person's eyes, to see if they were open, closed, or blinking ... did you check to see if there were tears ... did you look to see if the pupils responded to light? No! Did you put your ear or a mirror, maybe, close to the person's nostrils to see if the person was breathing? No! In other words, although you are, or should be, given the extensive and expensive education that you received at the taxpayers' expense, more competent than the average person to make a determination of the state of animation of said decedent, you did nothing! You just took the jacket, is that correct? Miss Crystal, maybe you can tell me and the other people in this court room what kind of person is so cold-bloodedly avaricious that they would steal the clothes off the back of an injured person who is a guest in that person's own house, albeit uninvited on the night in question, but a guest nonetheless, and a frequent one at that, judging from the fact that many of the decedent's possessions were found in your cabin, unless, of course, you stole those, too, *and*, Miss Crystal, maybe you can tell me and the other people in this court room whether or not such a person is more or less likely to be capable of actually *causing the death* of such a person in order to acquire a coveted article of clothing.

Objection!

No more questions, your honor.

Stay where you are, Miss Crystal. Do you recall that I mentioned to you earlier that I may have a few questions of my own?

Yes-your-honorable-mention.

In your deposition you say that someone named Teejay took the … body … away. Have you been in contact with this Teejay since the night in question? No. You also said that this Teejay told you that Dr. Maxwell, who is … or was … the director of Pinecrest, told him … told Teejay … to go to your cabin that night to get some sort of medical records. Is that right? No? Oh, I'm sorry. You said that this Teejay said he over*heard* Dr. Maxwell talking to someone on the phone about some sort of medical records. Is *that* correct? Yes. You also said that this Teejay said that Dr. Maxwell said that you were the only person who could have compiled these records. Is that still your testimony? Yes. Did you know what Dr. Maxwell may have been referring to? Yes. Were you ever in possession of any medical records? No. Did you compile them? Yes. You compiled them, but you were never in possession of them, is that correct? Yes. At any time in the last, say, two months, did you go to the hospital facility of Pinecrest and take any medical records from said facility? No. Well, Miss Crystal, can you tell us the nature of the medical records which you have testified that you know Dr. Maxwell was referring to?

They-had-names-on-them.

Well, yes, of course, they had names on them. What I mean is when you were compiling these records … on what basis did you … how did you know which ones to compile?

Names.

Okay, what names.

Sara-Abbott. Amy-Ackers. Helen-Adams. Julie-Agnew. Hessie-Ahrens … .

Wait. Hold on. Where did you get the names? Who gave you the list?

Crystal-never-had-a-conversation-about-medical-records-with-anyone.

I beg your pardon.

Your honor, if I may … .

Yes, counselor, please do.

Miss Crystal was told by whoever it was who asked her to compile the medical records not to tell anyone who that person, the one who told her to compile the records, was. The terminology that person used was what Miss Crystal said: 'Crystal never had a conversation about medical records with anyone.' That sentence appears several times in her diary, in her own handwriting. So, in her mind, in Miss Crystal's mind, she never had that conversation.

You're telling me ... .

Yes, your honor. It is literally as if Miss Crystal never had the conversation.

Counselor, I'm giving you fair warning. I'll hold this witness in contempt of court if she doesn't identify who gave her the list of names.

But, your honor, as our expert witnesses have testified in the depositions, she simply *cannot* do that. It is as if she never had the conversation. If she never had the conversation, she cannot identify with whom she had the conversation. That's just the way her mind works.

$$* \qquad * \qquad *$$

State your full name please.

Juanita Lopez Vonderheim.

What do you do, Miss ... .

Mrs.

I beg your pardon, *Mrs.* Vonderheim. What is your job, Mrs. Vonderheim?

I am Head Nurse at Pinecrest Institution for the Mentally Retarded.

You are testifying under an agreement of immunity, is that correct?

That is correct.

Now, Mrs. Vonderheim, tell us all you know about what happened on the night in question.

I got a call from my boss, Dr. Maxwell. He told me ... he ordered me ...

He *ordered* you? What do you mean?

He said if I didn't do what he said he'd see to it that I went to jail and that I would be fired from my job.

He said that he would see to it that you went to jail? Did you know what he meant? I mean did you know how it might be in his power to see to it that you would go to jail?

Yes.

Please explain.

Dr. Maxwell had a policy that called for abortions ... and sterilizations ... for any female patients ... residents ... who got pregnant.

Pregnant! How could something like that happen?

It is impossible to prevent male residents ... and staff ... from gaining access to ... .

Okay, I get your drift. Did this policy apply only at Pinecrest? Was it Dr. Maxwell's policy, or did it come down from higher up in the ... bureaucracy?

I don't know.

And you assisted Dr. Maxwell in these ... procedures?

Yes.

But if it came from higher up, then how could he use it against you?

Dr. Maxwell also performed abortions on other ... women.

Other women? What other women?

Women who wanted to terminate their pregnancies.

And did these women give Dr. Maxwell money for this service?

Yes.

Did you assist in these 'other' ... procedures?

Your honor, under the terms of the immunity agreement, my client cannot be required to answer that question.

But you believe, or believed, that he would have tried to implicate you in these ... other procedures?

Yes.

Explain.

Dr. Maxwell kept a record of these ... other procedures. He used the medical files of patients ... residents ... who had died ... .

What do you mean, 'He used the files of residents who had died'?

Instead of making a new ... separate ... file with the woman's name on it, he put data into the file of a dead resident.

Why did he do that? What data? Why did he have to write down anything at all?

I presume there were some things that he wanted to keep track of. It might have had to do with drug inventories. He may have wanted to protect himself in case of one the ... patient's ... one of the women's relatives ever tried to make trouble for him. He always required the woman's father or husband to be present. Maybe he wrote down their names. I don't know.

Drug inventories?

Yes. The ... procedure ... calls for the administration of phenobarbital and we are required to keep track of how much we use.

Were the records ever ... audited ... to see if the books balanced, so to speak?

No.

So, the good doctor may have thought that in the unlikely event he could ... what? Change the date of death on the records of the deceased patients and hope that no one noticed?

I don't know. Something like that, I guess.

So, when Dr. Maxwell threatened to see to it that you landed in jail, you ... what? Thought he might somehow make it look like you willingly assisted in ... and perhaps ... profited ... from ... .

Your honor, my client ... .
I withdraw the question. What did Dr. Maxwell order you to do?
To help him terminate a pregnancy.
Whose?
Dixie Johnson West.
The alleged victim?
Yes.
And what did you do?
I told him I wouldn't do it.
That's it? You told him you wouldn't do it and he ... what? Dropped it?
Yes.

*   *   *

Now, ladies and gentlemen, I will summarize the testimony of the witnesses. Early in December of last year the badly deteriorated and half-eaten remains of an adult Caucasian male was found floating in the swimming pool at Magnolia Park. It was apparent that most of the body had been eaten away by something. Alligators, probably. All that remained, other than mostly bones, was the upper torso which had been protected by a black leather jacket. In an effort to identify the decedent, the Sheriff's Department had several of the alligators that are normally kept penned up near Magnolia Park sacrificed and the contents of their stomachs examined. What the examination turned up was some jewelry that witnesses have testified may have at one time belonged to Mrs. Dixie Johnson West. Upon further investigation the remains of a black dress were found in the pen where alligators are housed that witnesses have testified may have belonged to Mrs. West.

These results led to the search of Miss Crystal's cabin where a bag made from alligator skin was found, containing instruments which, according to the testimony of an expert witness, could have been used to perform an abortion.

Mr. Richard Wade, formally associated in some capacity with the Sheriff's Department, has testified that, on the night of last Labor Day, he saw what might have been the body of Mrs. West under a table in Miss Crystal's cabin. That it was Mrs. West, he says he is certain. As to whether Mrs. West was actually dead, he has said he could not be certain. On the basis of his testimony and other facts in evidence, Miss Crystal has been arrested and charged with the death of Dixie Johnson.

Because of certain events transpiring at a party at Magnolia Park on the night of last Labor Day, the dwelling of the decedent's husband, the late Mr. Franklin Leroy West, was searched. This search turned up some folders containing medical records from Pinecrest Home for the Mentally Retarded.

You have just heard from the Head Nurse at Pinecrest the relevance of these folders and I will not summarize her testimony.

The search also turned up a revolver which you have seen and which has been determined to have fired the two bullets found in the body found in the pool at Magnolia Park.

Mr. West, of course, is not a defendant in this proceeding, as charges cannot be brought against a deceased person, but you may want to take into account what part if any he may have played in the events under consideration here today. Did he conspire with the accused to kill his wife for alleged adultery? Did he conspire with her to terminate a pregnancy which was the result of a miscegenistic union? If so, was this what killed his wife?

There has been testimony to the effect that Miss Crystal is strong enough to have carried Mrs. West's body and dumped it into the alligator enclosure near Magnolia Park. Of course, if Mr. West was a co-conspirator, he might have aided in this gruesome task.

Gentlemen of the Jury, before I embark on the closing arguments for the prosecution, let me thank you for your patience throughout this long and arduous trial. I believe that when you retire to the seclusion of the jury room in order to consider, objectively and dispassionately, all the evidence and to weigh the prosecution's case against that of the defense, you will be impelled to conclude that the prosecution has proved beyond a shadow of a doubt that the person who goes by the name of Miss Crystal is solely responsible for the felonious death of Mrs. Dixie Johnson West.

It is my learn-ed guess that, at this point in this long and exhausting ordeal, each and every one of you is asking himself, 'Why do we have to sit here another minute? We are tired! We are angry! We resent the concerted albeit vain effort that the defense has made to confuse us and use us in its attempted miscarriage of justice'. Or, I should say, *abortion* of justice!

The defense has tried to distract you from the chilling fact that a heartless young woman, an *intellectual*, if the defense is to be believed, and, *on this one point*, the prosecution is willing to defer to the expert witnesses, took the life of an innocent young mother-to-be and her unborn child. I believe that even if at this *very moment* each and every one of you had to look into his heart and render your verdict, *without* hearing the prosecution's closing summation, *without* having to sit again through the rehashing of the confusing and misleading sophistries of the defense, and *without* the benefit of discussing among yourselves the merits of the two sides of this long and exhausting trial, you would not, you *could* not in depths of your souls, come to any other conclusion but that the defendant is *guilty as charged.*

However, I feel that in my role as upholder of justice in this parish it is my duty in the interest of completeness and for the benefit of closure to take you briefly, step-by-step, through the events that took place on that fateful night last summer.

The story is really a very simple one. A young and healthy and vibrant young woman, the daughter of a distinguished local clergyman, who was expecting her and her fatally-ill husband's first child was seduced by an unscrupulous politician who baited his evil trap with a promise of Hollywood stardom. This wicked man had no respect for that glorious and sacred institution of our glorious Southern Homeland, Southern Womanhood. This avaricious opportunist, who apparently has since absconded with a vast sum of taxpayer money, who by all accounts has gone to live a life of ease in some foreign infidel country, where in all probability there are no nigras ... this traitor to all our sacred traditions ... if you listen closely to his speeches ... would expose all our women and girls to the scourge of ... *miscegenation!* He would have all the tender young virgins of the White Race endure the lustful assaults of over-sexed and ... monstrously-endowed ... *animals* ... that were *legally* bred by our Christian forefathers to work next to and share the burdens of the beasts of the field.

Was it at the bidding of this opportunistic Othello that Dixie Johnson West went to the abode of the person known only as Crystal that fateful day? Was it for the sole purpose of ending the life of her unborn son that she took herself there to that ... abattoir ... that slaughterhouse ... on that momentous day? Had her ambition rendered her so vain of body and so immune to the natural concern for the salvation her mortal soul that she would exchange that soul and the life of the precious child, alive and growing in her womb, for the dubious honor of being the object of the salacious attention of the unwashed hordes?

No! In all probability she went there for counsel in her dire hour of need. In all probability she was still in the throes of a mighty internal struggle between the forces of Good and Evil. Between the satanic inducements of

Babylonian Hollywood and the sacred calling of Southern Motherhood. No, I believe she went there for help. For spiritual guidance.

Instead, what did she get? She got the Devil's Advocate! She got a willing accomplice. Not an accomplice for herself but an accomplice for the wicked man who sent her there. She got the sinister *sister-under-the-skin* of the man who intended to use her for the purpose of feathering his own nest. What she got was an *abortion*!

Let us look again briefly at the evidence. First, how do we know that Dixie Johnson West was ever in the hideaway cabin in Magnolia Park, where 'Miss' Crystal was apparently installed as the kept woman of two separate men, both of whom have seen fit to absent themselves from the state and probably from the country? I won't go over all of the tortuous and contradictory testimony presented by the defense to the effect that, on the one hand, since her body was never found and since no one the defense is willing to stipulate as a reliable witness ever saw her there, at least none who are still alive today to say they did, there is no proof that she was ever there, and that, on the other hand, the body was taken away by someone acting as an agent for the Sheriff's Department in order to conceal the existence of an abortion ring that everybody from the Sheriff on down was implicated in and profited from.

The testimony of the one witness who actually saw what may have been Mrs. West's lifeless body the defense has sought to have thrown out of court on the grounds that the witness, Mr. Richard Wadd, one, has such poor eyesight that his testimony is not reliable, and, two, he is lying in return for his being reinstated as a Sheriff's deputy.

I'll come back to this and the related and even more ludicrous accusation that some nefarious conspiracy was cooked up to cover up years of evil-doing by *all* the law enforcement officials of this great parish.

Let's look first at the ... . I won't call them facts ... . Let's call them, for lack of a better term, the suppositions or conjectures that the victim's body was never found and that there are no eye witnesses to her having ever been in that loathsome cabin that night. It is true that her legs ... her arms ... her trunk ... her head ... her beautiful red hair ... her sparkling green eyes ... her skeleton ... were not found. Why? Because the woman who calls herself the Alligator Lady *fed* Dixie Johnson West's legs ... arms ... trunk ... head ... her very bones to her repellent *pets*. And what appropriate pets they were! Vicious alligators! Perfect symbolic companions to the perpetrator of this heinous crime. But, let us not blame the alligators. *They* didn't know what *they* were doing. They can only be ... they can only *do* what God, in his infinite wisdom and boundless inscrutability, designed them to do. And, besides, they have paid with their lives so that Justice could be done.

They have been duly sacrificed on the altar of Truth so that the world could know what a monster 'Miss' Crystal is.

You've heard the testimony concerning Exhibit A. Exhibit A, if you recall, is Dixie Johnson West's jewelry that was found in the belly of Crystal's 'favorite' alligator and her black dress found in the alligator pen. You've learned that 'Miss' Crystal even had a name for this creature that she may have trained to crave human flesh, because there may have been many before this one: Cleopatra!

Cleopatra! Can there be a more diabolical name? Can there be any stronger testimony to the hideous character of this savage beast's worshiper, its devotee, its vestigial virgin, than that she would give it the name of the most infamous whore in the history of the world?

And how do we *know* that Crystal is perverted, degenerate, and depraved enough to feed human flesh to her reptilian companions like the crazed acolyte of some pagan deity? Because, as we have been told by Richard Wadd, soon-to-be *Deputy* Richard Wadd, of the Sheriff's Department, that when the enclosure where 'Miss' Crystal keeps these ravenous and insatiable beasts was searched the bones of at least five different bodies were found. And that when confronted with this evidence Miss Crystal freely admitted that she and an accomplice, an otherwise harmless retarded boy who on his own would never have dreamed of such a thing, fished bodies floating downstream from Darktown to the Magnolia Park swimming pool and fed them to the alligators. And what was her justification for this callous act? I quote: 'They were going to be eaten by *something* anyway, it might as well be my gators.'

This is what she *admits* to. What is more likely the case is that she and some number of accomplices may have gone to Darktown and *killed* those *at least* five innocent people and used the creek to transport them downstream like so many logs.

So, there is Exhibit A, the jewelry and the dress.

Next there is Exhibit B, the jacket. The jacket made of alligator skin. The jacket you have had the occasion to examine several times in the course of this trial. As I say, it is the item marked Exhibit B and I now show it to you one more time.

You have heard Deputy-to-be Wadd testify that he found this ... Exhibit B ... in Miss Crystal's cabin when, in the course of his investigation, he went there on the night in question. You have heard Deputy Wadd testify that he saw Dixie Johnson West wearing Exhibit B when he visited her and her husband earlier that same day. You have heard Deputy Wadd testify that he knew it was Exhibit B because he noticed a slight tear on the left sleeve. Right there.

(You will, of course, be able to examine this and Exhibit A at your leisure during your deliberations.)

Now, gentlemen of the jury, we are near the end of this trial, and it has been a trial for us all. You will soon be retiring to the jury room where you are required to reach a unanimous verdict. I put this crucial question to you to take with you and to ponder: If Mrs. West was wearing the alligator jacket, Exhibit B, in her cabin just across Flagon Creek in the afternoon of the day in question and this *very same jacket* was found by Deputy-to-be Wadd in the accused's cabin later that same night, how did it get there? You and I and everyone in this courtroom … including the fancy New Orleans defense lawyers and the defendant herself … we all know the answer: Dixie Johnson West was wearing it when she went to the last place she would ever go alive in this world.

So much for the preposterous idea that the victim was never in Miss Crystal's cabin.

Next there is the *blood*. You've seen the gruesome photographs of Dixie Johnson West's *blood*. You've seen the grisly images of what alligators can do to the human frame. I'm sorry … I apologize … for the necessity of showing you this dreadful evidence. But I'm confident that you understand that, in the interest of obtaining a whole and truthful picture, it *is* necessary.

There is the trail of *blood* leading up to the very door of Miss Crystal's cabin. *Blood* that proved beyond a shadow of doubt that, after losing so much *blood* that she was delirious and couldn't know what she was doing, Dixie Johnson West must have left and then, in an ironic twist of fate, gone back to the very place, the very den of iniquity, where a mortal injury may have been dealt her and her unborn son only a short while before. In other words, she was trying to save her own life, but in a state of delirium brought on by the loss of that very *blood*, was too confused and disoriented to know *where* she was.

There is the *blood* on the mat. The mat that, when she was having one of her fits, when she resembled nothing so much as someone in the frenzied throes of diabolical possession, Miss Crystal wrapped herself up in, apparently turning herself into some sort of symbolic sacrificial meal for her dangerous deity. It was on this very mat, stolen from Pinecrest Home for the Mentally Disabled, this mat converted into an altar of some idol resembling nothing so much as the devouring deities of the Aztecs, that Dixie Johnson West was slaughtered. It was on that mat that her womanhood was ripped out of her by a vicious psychopath.

There is the *blood* on the blanket the accused used to wrap the body in to soak up the *blood* so that there wouldn't be a trail of *blood* to the place where she fed the mortal remains of Dixie Johnson West to … to those cold-blooded alligators ... . Excuse me, gentlemen of the jury, for losing control of my tender emotions. Of course my job as your prosecutor *requires* me to take juries like yourself through heinous crimes step by bloody step so that together we, me and you, the jury, can bring the perpetrators of these atrocities to justice. But this crime has pushed even me to the limit of human endurance. I apologize.

Where was I? Oh yes, the bloody blanket. The defense in its desperate attempt to make this most damning evidence go away, like Lord Hamlet when he cried out, 'Out, out, damned spot', has insulted your intelligence with the suggestion that if Miss Crystal was guilty why would she leave this bloody blanket laying around her cabin where it was bound to be found. By now, thanks to the defense's own expert witnesses, we all know the answer: Miss Crystal is incapable of *feeling* guilt. She is incapable of feeling *any* of the higher human emotions.

I said I'd come back to the claim that it is not 'Miss' Crystal, but the Sheriff's Department, that is responsible for this crime and God knows what else. I come back to it in order to dismiss it summarily. Surely, I don't need to say more. Surely, none of *you* who know the Sheriff and all of his able deputies like you know your own kin ... in fact some of you *are* kin ... believe such ... fairy-tales.

The defense has suggested, more by innuendo than by anything remotely resembling hard facts, that a certain individual, an educated doctor of medicine, was in cahoots with the Sheriff and others in an alleged abortion ring. That it was he who actually performed the murderous operations to end the lives of unborn children. That these operations were usually carried out in the hospital where this man was the director. That on this one occasion he came to 'Miss' Crystal's cabin, not only to perform an abortion, but to seduce and sexually abuse 'Miss' Crystal, something that, according to the innuendoes, he regularly did when she was a patient under his care.

Gentlemen of the jury! I won't add any further insult to your besieged intelligence than that already perpetrated by the defense. I leave it to you to give these accusations the weight they justly deserve.

Thank you.

✳   ✳   ✳

What kind of person is Miss Crystal?

That's what this trial has been about.

That's the way it looks to me and must look to you, gentlemen of the jury.

Rather than attempt to discover the circumstances surrounding the possible alleged death of Mrs. Dixie Johnson West, the prosecution has proceeded as if they are more interested in persuading you to see Miss Crystal in a certain false light, so that you will assent to her being eradicated by the state like some evil monster.

That has been the main thrust of the prosecution's closing argument: Miss Crystal is an evil monster and your community will be a safer place without her.

They have tried every pernicious trick they can dream up out of thin air to force upon you a specific, and I say erroneous, erroneous in every detail, answer to that question: What kind of person is Miss Crystal?

So, I want to try and find the true answer that question.

But first I want to help you gentlemen reflect on what the prosecution has done. In trying to foist their answer on us, they have dredged Miss Crystal's past with a fine-tooth comb. They have gone over the haystack of medical and psychiatric records that have accumulated over the course of her troubled life for the needles of dirt with which they hope to pinion her like a monstrous, noxious insect in some mad scientist's bestiary.

What have they come up with? You've heard the stories of her temper tantrums some of which may have resulted in a few people being struck, but none badly injured, and a few inexpensive items of property being destroyed. You've learned of the harmless pranks she played on the members of her Pinecrest family and her school mates. You've heard about her sensitivities to certain kinds of noise and certain odors. You've heard of the unusual ways she has discovered to soothe herself, to ease the excruciating tensions that build up within her. I'm speaking, for example, of such things as the exercise mat she wraps herself up in when she feels overwhelmed or just needs to relax. Which, by the way, was *not* stolen from Pinecrest, which she loves as the only home she has ever had, or from any place else, but given to her by a friend.

You've seen for yourself the strange, and sometimes annoying, way she speaks and interacts with people. The way she confuses pronouns. The way she repeats what she has heard, sometimes days or weeks later, as a way of communicating about some aspect of the original situation in which she heard it. No doubt, you have observed … and this is important and I will come back to it in just a moment … that she dresses more like a man than a woman.

The prosecution has attempted to take these bits and pieces of a very troubled life and make them into some sort of proof that Crystal is a vicious monster capable of unnatural violence.

Now, gentlemen of the jury, I want you to take a moment and reflect back on your own lives. I want you to answer for yourself in your own mind these questions. Have you ever lost your temper and whacked some noxious bully or annoying pest of a school mate with your spelling manual or your geography book just to get him to leave you alone long enough for you to clear your head and get your thoughts in order? Have you ever felt so tense that the only thing you could do was to take a swig of whiskey, knowing that it wasn't the right way to handle the tension, but effective for the purpose, so you did it anyway? And, in addition to those questions, ponder these: Does the fact that someone is kinda weird or doesn't know quite how to act in public or gets confused if there is too much going on around them or overreacts to the smell of gasoline or the sound of squeaky screen doors ... . Do any of these peculiarities make someone a monster who is capable of murdering another human being?

The next question is this: If Miss Crystal were a man instead of a woman, what difference would that make? My guess is that most of you, all men ... and that's okay ... I'm not one of those who say that a man cannot possibly understand the mind of a woman ... my guess is most of you have done things no so awfully different from what Miss Crystal has done. Most of these things are more typical and more often tolerated in boys than in girls. When a girl does them we take more notice. When a girl acts in certain ways like a boy she is called a tomboy and we accept it. But if she acts like a boy in certain other ways, she is judged much more harshly than a boy would be. If, as she matures physically, she continues to exhibit some of these masculine traits she may get a reputation for being violent, whereas a man with those same traits would be considered 'manly' or 'forceful' or seen as someone who is not to be messed with. And God knows none of us want to be messed with.

Just something to think about.

Now let me tell you about the Miss Crystal that I have come to know. First off, she is a person that people find it easy to be with. People go to her. They go to her for many reasons, but they go to her mostly to talk about themselves. Just to have someone there as they mull over in their own minds their problems and the puzzles life has given them.

Now here's a funny thing: Crystal is easy to talk to, *because* she *understands* so *little* of what is said to her. She *remembers* almost everything. That's the way her mind works. It understands little, remembers everything. Just imagine how confusing that must be.

Because she understands so little, it is only with great difficulty that she has been able to tell us what is *relevant* concerning what was said to her by various people on the day in question and on various other occasions.

It is even more difficult for her to articulate the *implications* of these conversations and other types of interactions that transpired between her and the visitors to her cabin on the day of, and the days leading up to, the alleged death of Mrs. West.

Because so much is at stake, we must, in our efforts to understand what happened, give Crystal much leeway. She can't give us whole pictures. She can only give us fragments. Pieces of jig-saw puzzles. Or, perhaps, more accurately, Crystal can give us pictures, but she can't tell us the proper order in which to view the pictures.

Now, we would *like* to be able to put the fragments together and make a coherent picture. We would *like* to be able to put them in proper order, the order in which they happened in time. We would *like* to make a movie that would show every detail in its true relation to every other detail.

Unfortunately, we can't do that. The prosecution has *tried* to do that, but they have failed. It would take Sigmund Freud or maybe God Himself to do that. Unfortunately, neither of them is going to step in and do that for us.

However, it is my duty to point out to the members of the jury that, in order to convince you to acquit Miss Crystal of the charges that have been brought against her, the defense is *not required by law* to produce, so to speak, such a movie. To require such a movie would be going way beyond what is minimally incumbent upon the defense to prove. All we really have to do is to show that the prosecution's movie, their picture of events, is incomplete, puts things in the wrong order, leaves things out, puts things in that didn't happen. In short, to show that their picture is a false one, that it is not true. That it is not true beyond a reasonable doubt. That a reasonable man might reasonably doubt what the prosecution says is true.

So, with that caveat in mind, let us start with an examination of some of the basic elements in the foundation on which the prosecution has tried to construct its case. I think when we do this the prosecution's case will crumble into a pile of rubbish like the house of Roderick Usher in Edgar Allan Poe's classic tale.

First of all, the prosecution has made much of the trail of blood that was found outside Crystal's cabin. Now just imagine if you will ... or better yet ... recall the photographs that were presented of this ... what shall I call it? This detail. When you have the image of it clearly in mind, ask yourself this question: Which direction was the person going who left that trail of blood? Was he or she dripping blood as he or she was *leaving* the cabin? Or as he or she was *going to* the cabin? Can you honestly say that you know the answer to that question just from the photographs you were shown?

No, you can't. Nobody can. Not even our astute prosecutor can tell.

So, in a pinch, what does he do? He *postulates* that the blood was left by someone who was both coming and going.

Who can blame our poor prosecutor? With a case so impoverished of fact, what else *can* he do but postulate? However, as the loyal opposition we call a spade a spade. As Bertrand Russell once said, 'The method of "postulating" what we want has many advantages; they are the same as the advantages of theft over honest toil.'

So. Coming or going? I submit that little question sums up precisely what the prosecution has not known it has been doing since this trial began.

Since the prosecution has relied so heavily on the trail of blood outside Miss Crystal's cabin to build its case, let's look again at what we've learned from the interrogation, taken in deposition, of Miss Crystal, conducted by the court-appointed specialist in the kind of mental disability from which she suffers. What did we learn from that deposition? We learned that a certain doctor of medicine was in Crystal's cabin on the day in question and the day before. That on both occasions he tried to sexually assault or abuse her. That he had been suspected of similar behavior when Crystal was under his care in the institution of which he was the director and while she was working in the office of medical records of the hospital that is a part of that institution. That on the night in question Crystal defended herself against this man with a knife that she had in her possession. That in the process of defending herself she inflicted a wound on her would-be assailant. That he bled onto the floor and onto the mat that Crystal uses to soothe herself when she is overwhelmed by too much stimulation, a symptom of the rare mental disease from which this very same man diagnosed her as suffering. That the man left by the front door.

As you ponder the implications of this evidence, gentlemen of the jury, I'd like you, if you will, to ask yourself why the prosecution chose not even to mention what was revealed in this deposition; why, even though they were full party to the deposition, they chose instead to ask the judge to disallow it, unsuccessfully thank goodness, on the grounds that this man, which the prosecution has tried to paint as a paragon of virtue, is not here to defend his honor and his reputation. It's okay if there is no body, but not okay if a potential witness cannot be found? It's okay to go down a road that might lead to an innocent person being convicted of murdering someone who for all we know is still alive, but if a known child-molester, a sexual predator of the most vicious variety, is not here to defend himself, then it's: Oh! *We can't go there!* What kind of justice is this?

Now, I would like you also to ask yourself if there might not be some other reason, over and above his depraved sexual motives, why this so-called healer, who as a doctor of medicine is under the paramount obligation to *do no harm*, was in Miss Crystal's cabin that night? Recall, if you will, that Miss Crystal worked in the records department of the hospital at Pinecrest. Mightn't *this* have something to do with the prosecution's avid desire to keep you from knowing the contents of the deposition? What if, among other reasons, Dr. Maxwell went to Miss Crystal's cabin on the night in question to get some piece of damning evidence, evidence that he believed had come into Miss Crystal's possession in her capacity as a worker in the medical records department ... sensitive medical records, for example ... medical records that contained information he could use to blackmail certain powers-that-be who might want to bring him to justice? What was there in those medical records that was so threatening to the established power structure that it had to be kept under wraps at all costs? And most intriguing of all: *Where are those records now?*

Okay, anyway, back to what *is* in the deposition. Let us consider *that* together. If, as she says, she had to defend herself against his sexual advances, mightn't the blood *inside* the cabin have been his? Mightn't *that* be how the trail of blood *outside* the cabin came to be where it was? I don't recall any prosecution evidence that indicated that the blood *had* to be the alleged victim's. Do you?

But, let's say, for the sake of argument that the prosecution *had* shown that the blood in front of Crystal's cabin and on the mat inside the cabin *was* Mrs. West's blood. Does that prove that she was *first* injured inside the cabin and *then* left the cabin? Couldn't she just as easily have been injured somewhere *else* and *then* gone to the cabin? (The defense's contention, of course, is simply that the prosecution has not even proved that she was ever there, let alone made a plausible case for the manner in which the blood, whose ever it was, was left there.)

Let's examine carefully another of the foundation stones on which the prosecution has sought to build its precariously tottering case: Exhibit B, the alligator-skin jacket. This really is too easy! Opposing counselor's argument is nothing less than an insult to the intelligence and patience of you good gentlemen of the jury. But let's break it down anyway, for the sake of protocol, if for no other reason. I want to read to you verbatim the question the prosecution put to you concerning this item: If Mrs. West was wearing the alligator jacket, Exhibit B, in her cabin just across Flagon Creek in the afternoon of the day in question and this very same jacket was found by Deputy Wadd in Miss Crystal's cabin later that same night, how did it get there? (For the record, the man's name is *Wade*, not Wadd.) The prosecution's answer, of course, is that Mrs. West was wearing the jacket when she went there.

But does this really *prove* that Mrs. Dixie Johnson West was in Crystal's cabin that night?

I don't think so and I'm sure that you members of the jury don't either. For example, by way of analogy, that suit jacket you see there draped on the back of that chair is mine. You have seen me wearing it. (It's so hot in here I had to take it off just as you gentlemen have done.) If later tonight you went to the house of my honorable opponent, the District Attorney, and saw my jacket hanging in his closet, would you know *beyond a reasonable doubt* that I had been in his house sometime between then and now? Of course not. The District Attorney, thinking it was his, may have inadvertently picked it up and taken it home with him. Or one of his staff may have given it to him and, he, not knowing whose it was or what else to do with it, may have taken it home with him for safe keeping until he could figure out whose it was.

Or having come to believe what he has hinted, implied, and asserted as fact on more than one occasion over the past few weeks, namely that I pay more for my clothes than he and you gentlemen do, he may have concluded that my jacket was worth stealing. I'm joking, of course, about that.

So, not to belabor the point, if I am not here tomorrow and my jacket is in the District Attorney's closet, it does not prove that I was ever in his house, now does it?

What's next? Ah, yes, Exhibit A. The jewelry and the dress. The jewelry found in the belly of the beast, the dress in her evil lair. Good old Cleopatra.

I have to agree with the prosecution that there are fascinating questions concerning how these items ended up in that alligator's intestinal tract.

First of all: Whose jewelry is or was it? Was it Dixie Johnson West's? Could be. Has the prosecution proven that it is? No. If we had to guess, given what we have learned, what would we say? I'm no expert but my guess is that a beautiful woman who wanted to be a Hollywood star and who was allegedly being wooed by a rich man would not be wearing these particular items? It's your call. But I say she wouldn't be caught dead wearing them, so to speak, which of course she wasn't.

Secondly: How did these gew-gaws get inside an alligator? We've already been told that these alligators may have eaten at least five people. I want to come back to the prosecution's calumnious accusations concerning this evidence in just a moment. But for now, consider this: Might not one or more of those five people been wearing one of more of the items making up Exhibit A? The apparently inferior quality of the jewelry suggests that it was may have been owned by one or more of the many indigent citizens of Darktown. And even it isn't of inferior quality, who's to say it wasn't stolen by one or more of those five people or given to them by those who did?

Here's another thing: At or around the same time the events are alleged to have occurred in Miss Crystal's cabin in Magnolia Park, a young Negro man went missing. His body was never found, either. Because he was black and not white, no one bothered to find out what became of him. You say, 'So what? Who cares about what happened to a colored boy?' Ordinarily, I might agree with you. I'd say that's neither here nor there. Except for this one fact: This young man is reputed to have liked to dress up in women's clothes and wear cheap costume jewelry. In fact, he may have been so attired when he met his demise at the hands of persons unknown. Could it be that *he* was fed to the alligators? Not by Miss Crystal, but by them that done him in? By the same ones that could have disposed of the black dress in the same way? I don't know. Your call. But I would ask you whether or not this doesn't raise a reasonable doubt in your mind as to the soundness of the prosecution's case.

Now let's come back to the accusation that Crystal fed those five bodies to the alligators. All the prosecution has produced by way of proof is the hearsay evidence that Miss Crystal said, 'Something was going to eat them anyway', or words to that effect. All the rest of that story has been gratuitously tacked-on by the prosecution. There is no proof that she had anything to do with how those bodies came to be where they are alleged to have been. Some of them may have been carried there by flood waters. Some of them may have been dumped there by whoever it was caused their demise in the first place, someone hoping the alligators would hide or destroy any evidence by which their victims may have been identified. Some of them may have been put there by their relatives or neighbors who didn't have the decency, the inclination, the time, the money, or the just plain gumption to provide a more decorous disposal of their remains.

Now let's talk about what the prosecution has *not* presented. Let's call it Exhibit C or better yet Exhibit X. X is more appropriate. It is *most* appropriate. X stands for the Unknown. X stands for what is to be proven, but which has not been proven in this case. The prosecution hasn't presented Exhibit X for the simple reason that they don't have it. What is Exhibit X? It is the dead body of the alleged victim, Mrs. Dixie Johnson West.

Before we consider Exhibit X, just as an aside, let me say a few words about Mrs. West. The prosecution has painted a very pretty picture of her as the 'flower of Southern Womanhood'. But the facts are these: One, photographs of Mrs. West posing nude were found in Miss Crystal's cabin. Two, Mrs. West voluntarily performed sexual intercourse in front of a movie camera. And, three, she may have willingly submitted to an abortion. If what the prosecutor says is true, she did. This is the one part of his case I am inclined to believe, but that is neither here nor there.

Now, I don't know what kind of woman Mrs. West was. But, good or bad, she wasn't the saint the prosecution wants you to believe she was.

Okay, enough of that. The prosecution has said, 'Well, we can't present Exhibit X because the alligators ate it'. 'Teacher, the dog ate my homework'. Bad alligators! Bad Cleopatra!

Now gentlemen of the jury I ask you: What if the alligators *didn't* eat the prosecution's homework? What if the prosecution didn't *do* its homework? What if in its laziness and ineptitude and disinclination to resist the influence of the powers-that-be who want *somebody* to pay for the mayhem that threatens to overwhelm us all, the prosecution stole the homework of the class dunce and tried to palm it off as its own? What if the class dunce, true to form, got it all wrong? I'll leave it to your imagination who the class dunce is, or *dunces* are. There seems to a whole confederacy of them in this case. What if the prosecution really is dunce enough, or dense enough, to believe that you gentlemen of the jury can be duped into believing anything the prosecution wants you to believe, such as: Jewelry was found in the alligator; Mrs. West wore jewelry; *therefore* Mrs. West must have been eaten by the alligator.

Now, gentlemen, I have nothing personally against Mr. Wade. But let us briefly go over two important things we have learned about him in direct examination that you must keep in mind as you analyze and evaluate his testimony. First of all, we have learned that Mr. Wade has very poor, astonishingly poor, eyesight. His eyesight is so bad that for the longest time he couldn't even tell if the defendant, Miss Crystal, was a man or a woman. In light of this crucial information ... after all Mr. Wade is proffered as an *eye* witness ... we have to ask: Did Mr. Wade see Mrs. West in Crystal's cabin or did he see someone else? If it was Mrs. West whom he saw, did he see blood or did he see red hair or something else, water stains, for example? Remember, the cabin has neon lights than change the color objects seem to be. If he saw blood, whose blood was it?

The second thing we've learned about Mr. Wade is that he isn't a deputy at all. That he had no connection with the Sheriff's Department at the time of his great 'discovery'. We've learned that he was palming himself off as a private investigator, a private eye. That this was his first 'case'. That Frankie West had hired him to snoop around and find out what he could about his wife's suspected infidelities.

Now, a man, even a man with more upstairs than Mr. Wade, is prone to see what he is looking for. Could it be that, having Mrs. West in mind, he was in a frame of mind that *predisposed* him to believe that who*ever* he saw in Miss Crystal's cabin was her? Or is it more a matter of his being led, by the way *later* events played out, to *want* to believe *in retrospect* that it was her? Or might it be that Mr. Wade is lying about what he saw? After all, for a 'detective' in search of 'clues', something, even something bogus, is better than nothing.

Or, which is also possible, does this case involve something much more sinister than a few lies wheedled out of a man as easily manipulated as Mr. Wade? Sadly, I must raise this final and most frightening question: Has Mr. Richard Wade been promised a long-coveted position in the Sheriff's Department if his false testimony helps convict an innocent person?

These are all questions which, of course, the prosecution has not even raised, let alone tried to answer. They are questions, though, that, in the mind of any reasonable man, should cast grave doubts as to the soundness, or lack thereof, of the prosecution's case.

I won't drag this out any more. I think you see my point. But it raises an interesting question: Where is Mrs. Dixie Johnson West? What efforts if any were made to locate her? If as the prosecution alleges her alleged seducer has absconded with boat-loads of taxpayer money, mightn't he have taken his young paramour, his protégé, with him?

And there's another possibility to consider. The claim has been made but never proved that Mrs. West went to Miss Crystal's cabin that night to get an abortion. An attempt, as clumsy as it was desperate, was made by the prosecution to insinuate that what was *presumed* to be Mrs. West's corpse was seen by a *real* member of the Sheriff's office but then the body was somehow mysteriously lost track of. Our honorable and able judge has ruled that *at best* this bald-faced maneuver was based on hearsay evidence and has not allowed it, as well he shouldn't. But it should make us all wonder why some people feel compelled to attempt such subterfuge.

What if the powers-that-be want somebody to blame, not only to provide false security to a community battered by tragedy on every side, from above by the Federal Government and from below by the greed and mendacity that is endemic to the human condition, the human soul, but to hide their own role in this whole dirty affair? What if they have 'volunteered' Miss Crystal to be their unwilling Sydney Carton, who, you may recall from *A Tale of Two Cities*, died in another man's place, to take *their* place on the scaffold?

What if they believed that Mrs. West's dead body was such powerful evidence of one of their nefarious and greed-driven operations that it couldn't be entrusted even to the alligators, but had to be taken elsewhere and handled in some more foolproof manner?

If Mrs. West got an abortion *some*one had to have performed it. If someone performs them *some*one has to permit it and profit from it and protect the abortionists. These things don't happen in a vacuum.

I submit that these two possibilities are enough to cast a shadow of reasonable doubt on the prosecution's already opaque, lusterless case, a case as impervious to light as the tenth ring of Hades.

24

For me the whole thing centered around the black leather jacket the dead man they found floating in the swimming hole at Magnolia Park one morning in the early part of the winter was wearing. December I reckon. Did you ever have to try and put clothes on a kid that's asleep? I didn't never have to do it, but I reckon I know what it's like.

Way I see it if it had not a been for the leather jacket they would a figgered it was just another nigger got drunk and fell or got killed and was throwed in the body of water that's called Flagon Creek by the rednecks and Cold Bayou by the coonass Cajuns and that would have been the end of it. But the alligators couldn't eat the part of the dead man under the jacket I reckon because the leather was too tough for them to chew it. Or else they didn't have no appetite for cow hide. So when they took the jacket off of the dead man they seen that he was white. That meant there had to be an investigation. Which led straight to Crystal's trial which you know about already except for the end which I'm gonna tell you later.

At first the Sheriff and ever body else figgered that the dead white man in the black leather jacket was one of the three big shots that went missing around the time they figger Leather Jacket which is what I'm gonna call him was killed and that which ever one it was he was probably killed on account of the dirty movies ever body got showed at the big Labor Day party that Theo Jeannsonne gave at Magnolia Park to kick off the March of Dimes whether they wanted to or not.

See somebody switched movies on them and you ain't never seen such a mess.

Theo Jeannsonne is called Uncle Toe by people what knows him. Uncle Toe owned Magnolia Park. He wasn't my uncle. That's just what they called him. Uncle Toe. Kinda like a nickname. As ever body found out that seen the dirty movies, he was also called Teddy the Toad, and Freddy the Frog, on account of his being Cajun, I guess.

It was during the worst of the polio season near the middle or the end of the 50's. In them days seems like every day here come a nigger floating down Flagon Creek. Specially in the summer. Most of them was caught before they got down to where Uncle Toe's white customers could see them by the catfish net he put up to keep the snakes out. White people didn't like swimming with snakes and dead rotten niggers back in them days. Ever so often though the catfish net broke and a nigger got through and they'd find it a bumping up against the dam which is where they found Leather Jacket. The dam was built in the 30's. It was a CCC project. It made the water of Flagon Creek back up and made it wider. They made the wide part of it into a swimming hole that along with the bar and the crummy cabins was about all there was to Magnolia Park.

The Cajuns called Flagon Creek Cold Bayou. They had a different word for just about ever thing.

The reason for all the dead niggers was mainly on account of the Supreme Court giving them they civil rights and the rednecks taking them back with what later on in the 60's and 70's was called extreme prejudice. Back then it was just called rachel prejudice. Little joke a mine. Of course white people didn't cotton too well to nigger bodies dead or alive. They would just fish them out and turn them over to the parish to get hauled off somewhere where they folks could get them if they wanted to and if they was quick enough about it because they wasn't kep around too long. Ain't nothing smells worse than the meat of rotting people, black or white. I figger that's one way niggers and whites are equal. Of course most of the time the niggers was burnt so bad or the alligators had chewed them up so bad couldn't nobody tell who they was. Not even they mama.

Polio was the best thing that ever happened to Theo Jeannsonne. I don't mean he had it. I mean it was polio what put Magnolia Park on the map after it put Hot Springs Sanitarium on there first. All through the 50's people brought they kids to the Hot Springs for the healing of the hot rusty water coming out of a hole in the ground just up the hill from Magnolia Park. A lot of the daddy's of the polio victims used to go down the hill to the bar while they wifes was back up at the Hot Springs soaking they kids crippled legs in the hot water that was supposed to be good for them. I reckon that led to a lot of people knowing about the park that didn't have no kids with polio.

When I say ever body got showed the movie I mean ever body. Because ever body was there. All the big wigs from Hot Springs Sanitarium which is right next to Magnolia Park was there. All the not so big wigs from Pinecrest was there. Pinecrest was the place where they said they put feeble minded kids in but back in them days really it was where just about anybody what didn't nobody want and what couldn't take care of themselves was liable to end up. Not a bad place. Better than a bunch. Better than Magnolia Park for sure. I know because I was there before fatass Doctor Maxwell kicked me out when he caught me spying on him fucking the nurses and stuff. I used to hate that fatass Doctor Maxwell. Nearly as much as I loved Frankie West.

The beer was free. That was Uncle Toe's doing. Of course all the Catholics was there because Catholics can drink and still go to heaven. But the Baptist preacher Brother Johnson was there too and a lot of people from his church. Usually the Baptist wouldn't get caught dead in the same place with the Catholics, beer or no beer, but I guess Brother Johnson told them this was different. I guess he said it was for the poor little crippled kids. Wasn't nobody there from any of the other Baptist churches around here though because of the dancing and beer.

Dixie was there with that fellow LeBeaux. She tried to act like she wasn't with him but I knowed she was. Of course Charlie West was there, so Jimmy Garrard was there too. Crystal wasn't there. She don't like people. Both Sheriffs was there but none of they deputies and wifes and kids and stuff which makes me wonder if they didn't know about the dirty movie ahead of time. This old lady that used to work for Uncle Toe was there. Jonnie V. and Fred were there. I didn't see Fred but I seen this here beer truck in the parking lot blocking a bunch of cars so I reckon it was his.

Billy Mayden wasn't there but Jake Garrard was.

That reminds me. After they opened Crystal's alligators up to see what was on the inside of them and didn't find nothing that would have told them who Leather Jacket was the paper claimed Leather Jacket was Arthur Maxwell. Ever body knowed Arthur wasn't nothing but a big old dumb queer that didn't never talk none. And they said Billy and Jake was the ones that killed him except they left they names and what they done out of the paper. They was supposed to have took him or left him somewhere in the swamp and he got washed downstream by a heavy rain that came along in December and turned Flagon Creek into a river for a couple of days. Which ain't nothing new, this being Louisiana. If you don't like the weather in Louisiana wait a while and a flood will come along.

Come to think about it it must a took more than one rain to get 'Arthur' tore loose from where ever Billy and Jake was supposed to have left him. You should a seen the shape his body was in by the time he reached the swimming hole. I put them little squiggle marks around Arthur's name because me and Crystal told Billy he oughtn't to believe ever thing the paper says and that maybe Leather Jacket wasn't Arthur at all and he oughtn't to blame himself.

According to the Sheriff Billy and Jake didn't mean to do it so they wasn't nothing done to them. They was let go on and finish out the rest of they college if they wanted to. Which if they did would a give them 16 more years of schooling than I ever got. In them days wasn't nobody cared much about the deaf. Good thing Jonnie V. seen to it me and Crystal learned to sign. Crystal liked signing because that way she didn't have to look at people's faces when she talked to them.

At first me and Billy used to be friends. I stole things for him. Then he switched over to Jake. Then to Frankie. Then back to me after Frankie died. I knew we'd wind up friends again when he asked me to steal Jake's sex book from this here old car him and Jake used to jack off in usually with Jake's brother Jimmy spying on them and jacking off at the same time without them a knowing it. Didn't any of them know I watched all three of them and jacked off right along with them. Billy used to read the sex book all the time. I called it Billy's Bible. Wasn't no pictures in it.

I started out signing this with my hands to a couple of my cousin's boys or my brother's boys who can hear. Then when I got better at reading and writing I worked on it some more. My daddy was Adolf Foster or his brother Rufus Foster. They used to make whiskey before somebody shot them. Any body one of them fucked the other one fucked too practically as soon as the first one's dick come out so can't none of they kids tell who is a cousin or a brother or sister. My mama was a deaf Pinecrest patient who they took home and kept around to fuck and corn hole and make her suck they dicks. Fatass Doctor Maxwell didn't never try and get her back because he was chickenshit of the Foster's. I don't guess I ever will forgive fatass for that. You probably thinking well you wouldn't be here if he'd a kep her away from them but I don't see it that way. When my mama was about to have me they took her back to Pinecrest. They dumped her out in front of fatass Doctor Maxwell's office one night. I talked my cousin's boys or my brother's boys into coming out here to what's left of Magnolia Park and write this story down. One of them said out loud what I signed and the other one wrote it down. We was in my jack office at the time. That's a little joke of mine. See, we was in a toilet. Get it? That's where I am now and where I do all the work on this here story. It helps me think better.

This here is some of what I remember about what happened. I ain't telling everything exactly the way it happened because I want to make it interesting. Besides I may have forgot some stuff or what come before what and what come after something else. Maybe I'll get Billy to look at it and see what he thinks.

I took Arthur to stay with Adolf and Rufus after Jake kicked him that second time. I was helping Arthur get back at Jake for kicking him that time and another time. I guess the three of them was really happy together.

Adolph, Rufus, and Arthur, I mean.

They never did tell how Billy and Jake killed 'Arthur' except to say it was an accident. Worked out real good. Just about everybody was satisfied a little bit with that story and some was more satisfied than others. Whatever satisfaction they was didn't tip nobody over into the happy category though. It wasn't a very happy time. But the story served its purpose. Which is all you can ask a story to do I reckon. Its purpose was to make people think that was all they was to the story. But let me tell you they was a lot more to the real story than that. A whole lot more. More than even I know. Don't worry, I will tell most of it good as I can.

Whoever was behind what was in the paper knew that as long as they didn't know any better even white folks wouldn't care enough to ask any embarrassing questions as long as they believed the thing floating in the creek was Arthur Maxwell. Wouldn't care no more than they would if they believed it was nigger. The only reason it got in the paper was because his daddy was the head of Pinecrest and ran off around that time. Fatass Doctor Maxwell who I hated. Pinecrest was where Arthur should have been. But I guess his daddy felt sorry for him or ashamed of him and let him go just about anywhere he took a notion.

When they killed some of Crystal's alligators and looked on the inside of them, instead of finding what they were looking for, which was something that would tell them who the dead white man wearing the black leather jacket was they found what I reckon was Frankie West's wife Dixie's necklace and rings and stuff. That gave them the idea to look for other things of hers and they found pieces of what they figgered was her black dress in the nest of an alligator name of Cleopatra.

Her mama and daddy called her Dixie because they liked the South so much I guess. Brother Johnson was her daddy. They tried to pin that one on Crystal. That's how come she had a trial. They said she was in cahoots with a man who by that time was dead and couldn't stand up for himself. Frankie West. Best man I ever knew. And I loved him. And it don't make me no queer to say it neither. They said because some of fatass Doctor Maxwell's folders was found in Frankie's cabin that proved him and Crystal was in cahoots. I will explain what little I know about the folders later.

Even if they had not a found Leather Jacket floating in the swimming hole people would a quit coming to the park any more any how. I done told you about the civil rights movement and the dead niggers in the pool. Even Cajuns didn't like the idea of that. The main thing I reckon though was they come up with a cure for polio and people stopped bringing they kids to the hot springs. And another thing was the alligators that got out and multiplied so much while Crystal was in jail they couldn't never get them all back in they pen.

Here's what I know. They's a lot of gaps which you will have to fill in by using your imagination. Which is the only way anything ever gets told if you ask me.

To kick things off let me say that ever thing that come before I started signing to my cousin's or my brother's boys was written by Billy Mayden and that includes the stuff about Theo Jeannsonne and Crystal. Some of the stuff that was about him and Theo and Crystal he tried to tell the truth. The other stuff he made up but he tried to make it square with what he knowed was solid facts. Now I will add what I know more or less as good as I can remember it.

The first thing that Billy Mayden didn't know anything about was what happened at the big March of Dimes party because he wasn't there. I was. Right outside the bar on the walkway that went along side one of the big windows of the bar. It was on Labor Day night.

They was supposed to be a movie showed. It don't matter what it was about. Probably it was about the March of Dimes. Pictures of cute little kids in iron lungs and stuff. But somebody switched the movies and put in another one. It matters ever thing what that movie was about so I'll just tell it now.

Somebody turned the lights off. This here nigger T.J. was supposed to be operating the projector because wasn't many white people knew how and T.J. did. For a nigger T.J. knew a lot. He was sent to school by Uncle Toe and this here fellow LeBeaux. Then he got a job at Pinecrest which is where he learned how to operate a projector I reckon. Mr. LeBeaux must have got him the job. He treated T.J. like his own son which in this case wasn't so bad. When he wasn't working at Pinecrest T.J. worked for Uncle Toe toting garbage and cleaning up vomit and shit that ended up on the floor of the bar or any of the cabins. Stuff no white boys would have wanted to do for the kind of money Uncle Toe was willing to pay a nigger. So I reckon you could say Uncle Toe treated T.J. like his own son too. They both had big butts and the same initials so T.J. could a been a junior, which sometimes gets called by his daddy's initials to keep from getting them mixed up I guess.

Anyhow T.J. ran off at the last minute and they had to get Charlie West who was Frankie's cousin to operate the projector. Charlie was at the party anyhow so it didn't slow things up much. Come to find out later Charlie was the one who helped Mr. LeBeaux make the March of Dimes movie what didn't get showed. Charlie is a professional photographer.

Now I can tell you for sure it wasn't T.J. that switched the movies. That will be plain as soon as I tell you what was in the movie that was showed.

Like I say the lights was turned off. Then this here big picture is up on one of the walls of the bar. At first it's some writing and then an old timey movie. Black and white and lots of spots and hairs and stuff jumping all over the place. There is a white man in a striped suit like the prisoners in Angola wear and a white lady wearing a black dress and a pearl necklace on her hands and knees in it. You can't see they faces at first. All you can see is a dick sticking out of the fly of the striped pants and going in and out of the pussy of the lady on her hands and knees. Doggy style it's called. Then whoever is running the camera backs up and you can see the lady's face. You can't see the man's. About all you see is his dick. His dick comes all over the lady's butt and back. Then it jumps to where the man is kneeling down back of the lady and you see him licking and kissing her butt cheeks and sticking his tongue in both of her holes and you can see the side of his face and he ain't got on the prisoner clothes anymore and you can't see the lady's face anymore, just her butt and pussy from behind and her still on her hands and knees. It would a been hard to recognize either one of them unless you knowed them because the movie was so old and who ever it was would a changed a lot by then. Part of the time the lady's face was all scrunched up and her mouth was open. It was supposed to look like it felt real good having a dick in her pussy and butt hole but you could tell the lady was just play acting because at different times she would stop making out like it was fun and look over where the camera was like she wanted it all to be over or something. The man that was kneeling and sticking his tongue in the lady's holes had a big ass that stuck out and a mustache and rings all over a bunch of his fingers. The lady was black headed and her string of pearls dangled down and flopped back and forth because of all the humping they was doing. Her black dress was throwed up on her back to make room for the man to get at her to stick his tongue in her pussy and butt hole.

Billy says that of all the ways two people can make love stimulating the anus and penetrating the rectum with the tongue is the most democratic because ever body has the equipment to play either role. That's the way Billy talks, at least now he does. He didn't used to. (Billy ain't gonna like it but I stuck something at the end of this so you can see what he used to be like. It's the last thing he ever wrote for the Evangelical Sociey.)

Oh yeah, I forgot. Billy said the writing that was up on the wall before the fucking and sucking started said the name of the movie was Righteous and Randy or Convicts in the Convent. Billy said the first part must a been a take-off on Amos and Andy. (Getting back to the way he used to be he said gash and puncture was convict talk for pussy and butt hole don't ask me why he said it because nobody asked him. That's just the way he was around the time he quit writing tracks.) He said the writing also said starring Jane Littlepiece as St. Teresa of Avila, and Hairy Johnson, alias Teddy the Toad, as Fryer Frog. He had a very long tongue. Maybe that's howcome he had the name of Frog. Or maybe he was Cajun.

The second part of the movie was new and didn't have no writing to tell the name of it or who was in it and it was colored. And so was one of the people in it. That's a little joke of mine. It was a light complected nigger and a white lady. High class folks call niggers colored. It started out like the black and white one. All you saw was a black dick going in and out of a white pussy. Well the dick was not really black. I knew it was black later when the camera man backed up and I seen they faces. And now I remember it like it was black. I remember it a lot. I think about it when I jack off. Then the man comes all over the lady's butt and back but they was white stuff already coming out of his dick before he took it out because his dick was jerking like when a dick is coming and you could see the white stuff coming out real strong when it come out of her pussy. What was left in it after it come out squirted all over the lady's pussy and butthole. Then the camera backed up like before and you could see both of their faces.

This time it wasn't hard to recognize who they was. It was T.J. and Dixie. She had on a black wig and dress and a pearl necklace just like the lady in the first part but you could tell it was Dixie because of the red hair on her pussy.

I said the second part was like the first part except for the nigger and the color. At least they started out the same. Well the second part was different in a couple of other ways too. First thing was Dixie looked like she really liked being fucked by a nigger. She looked like she wanted to keep fucking forever. Ever time he would try to take his dick out of her pussy she would shove her butt back at him and reach back and try and grab his butt and wouldn't let him take his dick out. That was how come he was coming before he could get it out. Matter of fact I can say for sure she liked it because I ain't hardly never fooled by people's faces. I can tell what they are really thinking. Comes from being deaf. I have watched a lot of real fucking when the people fucking didn't have to worry about no camera and I know what it looks like. T.J. didn't look at the camera none neither. He just kept his mind on what he was doing. And it looked like he knowed what he was doing. But you could tell it was him.

They was rumors that Dixie and T.J. was fucking before her and Frankie got together. They was even a rumor that T.J. knocked her up. Her mama was gonna have a baby around the same time Dixie was gonna have hers and they both went off together some where where didn't no body that knowed them knowed where they was. I reckon they wanted to try and make it look like Dixie's mama had twins. According to the rumor they killed Dixie's baby because it come out black.

It wasn't never figgered out who switched the movies. This here fellow LeBeaux might have put the first old-timey part in the movie to get back at Uncle Toe and the preacher's wife Janelle Johnson. It come out later that it was them in that first part when they was young. And it came out later that LeBeaux had paid to have a bunch of movies showing both of them fucking but never each other except in the one they showed at Magnolia Park that night and the way that one was patched together it could have been nigger-rigged to make it look like they was both in it and fucking each other when they wasn't. It could have been somebody else in the striped suit, not Uncle Toe, because you didn't never see the convict's face and you didn't see the lady's face that Uncle Toe was sticking his tongue in the pussy and butt hole of. At least not at the same time he was doing it. I reckon LeBeaux might have been mad at them for something and he might have figgered a good way to get back at them was to make it look like they was fucking each other and he was sticking his tongue in her pussy and butt hole in front of ever body what knowed them.

I don't think LeBeaux would have put the colored part in because he liked T.J. and Dixie. It could have been done by Charlie West because Charlie hated his cousin Frankie. Frankie was good at sports and he always outshined Charlie even though Frankie was a lot dumber than Charlie. I think Charlie figgered there wasn't nothing that would have made Frankie madder than for ever body to see a nigger fucking his wife.

It could a been Charlie who put both parts in. In the first place it might have been him who helped LeBeaux make the movie of T.J. fucking Dixie. He was already working on the March of Dimes movie so it would have been easy for him to put in anything he wanted to at the last minute without LeBeaux knowing. In the second place I reckon Charlie figgered he could get a way with it because he knowed LeBeaux was going to have to make himself scarce after than night. And somebody might have helped him. Helped make himself scarce I mean. In fact they might have done it for him. Real scarce, if you know what I mean.

In the third place Charlie wanted to be a movie director. So he may have wanted people to see how much better the movie he made with T.J. and Dixie was than the old one.

Billy seen the colored movie later on when I stole it and the other one that he also seen out of the Sheriff's office and he said that the colored movie was a great work of art because it captured real sex between two people who really liked fucking each other on film. He said that wasn't something you got to see ever day. Like I already said I seen it a lot myself.

If Charlie wasn't the one who helped LeBeaux make the movie of T.J. fucking Dixie doggy style I don't know where Charlie got a hold of it. If I had to guess I'd say Jimmy Garrard found out that Uncle Toe was showing his brother Jake dirty movies and went over to Uncle Toe's house and found it. Jimmy worked for Uncle Toe for a while and probably knowed how to get in his house without no key. They was a gold statue of a dick with wings in the movie just like one Uncle Toe had in his house. That tells me that maybe Uncle Toe was in on it and that the movie was made in his house and probably that was where they tried to hide it.

A year or so after this Charlie and Jimmy went to New Orleans and lived together. Turns out they was both queers.

Something I forgot to say before is I thought it might have been T.J. and Dixie in the first movie too. T.J. and Uncle Toe looked a lot alike in the face. Didn't nobody never say anything about it but that was because one was white and one was a nigger so people couldn't see it but I could. T.J. was light complected and he had a big butt just like Uncle Toe. All Dixie had to do to make herself look like her mama when she was young was to put on a black wig and a black dress. Wasn't nothing she could do about that red pussy hair I reckon. But Billy says I'm full of shit. That it was really an old-timey movie just like it looked like it was and that Uncle Toe wasn't T.J.'s daddy. But I think Billy is full of shit hisself.

I reckon it was Charlie who told T.J. to run off like that because he didn't hate niggers the way Frankie did. Didn't look like it done T.J. no good though because he was caught later. Least that's what most people believed any how at the time. I will tell more about that later when I tell how Crystal's trial ended.

After that the party stopped being what you would call a regular party. Most people couldn't get out quick enough. You should a seen them running like a bunch a bugs. Them that stayed behind had themselves a different kind of party. Least that's the way it looked.

A few days later the two Sheriffs and they deputies went to the bar and found a big mess. This part is true cause I seen it with my own eyes. Tables and chairs was turned over and broke. Them two big old wenders was broke out. Glasses of beer and whisky and gin bottles was broke and the beer and whisky and gin was soaking the carpet.

And they was lots of blood.

It was on account of the blood that the Sheriffs and they deputies went to the bar and after a while they finally figgered out that the blood got there some time after the March of Dimes party. Later that night or the next night. They was blood on the wall where the movie was showed and the floor next to it. Lots of blood. They was two big gobs of blood high up on the wall with streams of blood running all the way to the floor. There was some nails drove in the wall in the middle of them two gobs of blood. Lower down between them was a place with an even bigger gob of blood. Think about it this way. If the streams running down from the two littler spots was creeks the one running down from the lower down place was a river. The river ran into a lake on the floor. That's how I remember it.

They was a dick and a lady's ear ring somewhere in all that blood. In the lake of blood I reckon. There was also a broken chair leg with a bunch of shit and blood on.

Billy said the Sheriffs and deputies finally figgered that somebody had been crucified on that wall. Billy got all his information from listening to Jonnie Vonderheim's party line. Maybe upside down and backwards. By backwards I mean they was facing the wall. In other words the opposite of Jesus. Except the jews didn't cut Jesus's dick off and stick a chair leg up his ass which is what Billy said the Sheriffs and deputies figgered must have happened to this here artificial Jesus. That's what Billy said he was. A artificial Jesus.

There wasn't no body though. One dick and lots of blood and an earring and a shitty chair leg. A peter but no Apostle Peter. That's another joke of mine. Git it? No Apostle Peter. See, Peter was crucified upside down. Least that's what I heard. Except I can't hear but you know what I mean.

Billy said when the Sheriffs and deputies finally got around to asking them, somebody that was at the party told them more about the movie and then they figgered they knowed who the crucified man was. That person that didn't want their name given out said T.J. was fucking a white woman in the movie. Billy said the Sheriffs and deputies figgered T.J. probably tried to hide in niggertown but must have been found and brought back to the scene of the crime. He said they figgered those who brought him back must have looked in his house and found some of Dixie's clothes and jewelry. I reckon that's how come the earring was in the lake of blood. Either that or T.J. was wearing it when they crucified him and it fell off on the floor.

Of course because it was a nigger the Sheriffs and deputies didn't do nothing else like look for the rest of the body and wasn't nothing put in the papers about it Billy said. I guess they figgered a nigger without a dick couldn't cause much trouble, dead or alive.

I would a liked to a been the one that went to Frankie's cabin and told him about the movie. He was too sick to go to the party but I knowed he would a wanted to know what T.J. did to Dixie. But they was something Jonnie Vonderheim told Crystal to put in his cabin the night before that could a got him in trouble that I wanted to get out of there and give to Jonnie before he found out it was in there because I didn't want him getting mixed up with what Jonnie and fatass Doctor Maxwell was up to because he already had enough trouble of his own without getting some of theirs if they got caught. He didn't know nothing about it because when Crystal put it there he wasn't home or was asleep or something. I don't remember what she said and I reckon I was too busy the whole next day to tell him about it. Plus they was something I had to put back in his cabin without him knowing it so I had to wait for him to be gone. So I waited. Pretty soon some body else come by and I guess they told him about the movie because he went over towards the bar and I reckon he got showed the movie so he could satisfy hisself that it really was Dixie and T.J. that was fucking in it.

Now I wish I had told Frankie about the stuff Crystal put in his cabin but I was still mad at him for putting come on my baseball cap. Maybe that's howcome I didn't have time to tell him about the folders.

When the Sheriffs and deputies was trying to figger out whose blood was on the wall they asked ever body what was at the party what they seen and heard. They couldn't find three of the biggest wigs what was supposed to be there to ask them what they seen. First they was fatass Doctor Maxwell. Then they was Lester LeBeaux. And then they was Uncle Toe whose real name was Theo Jeannsonne. After talking to a lot of people they decided fatass Doctor Maxwell hadn't ever been at the party. Which I could a told them but didn't nobody ask me. Don't nobody never ask deaf people nothing. Which I'm glad they didn't because I don't like to lie. If you believe that there's some swamp land I want to sell you. Ha ha. That's another one of my little jokes.

On account of the dirty movie what was showed at the March of Dimes party one of the Sheriffs looked for Theo Jeannsonne and Lester LeBeaux for the next week or two but couldn't find hide nor hair of either one of them. When what was left of the body with the black leather jacket showed up the Sheriffs figgered it might be one of them two because best they can tell Leather Jacket died close to the time of that March of Dimes Party give or take a day or two. Or it might a been fatass Doctor Maxwell because he disappeared around that time too.

I already said you can't believe what the paper says about it being Arthur.

They was more than one person that wouldn't a shed a tear if nigger lover Lester LeBeaux and whoremonger Theo Jeannsonne died. And in the mess that took place after the movie was showed just about anybody what was there could have killed anybody else what was there and who would a knowed any different. And a lot of them what wouldn't a shed a tear if Uncle Toe or Lester LeBeaux died probably figgered they was in thick enough with one of the Sheriffs that if they was to take a notion to kill one of them they could a got away with it. Fact they might be looked at as heroes because of how bad them two was. Of course they would a probably had to hand over a gob a money come election time.

Lester LeBeaux and Uncle Toe was bad men. Except when it come to T.J. that is. They both of them treated T.J. good as you and me would a white man. Take away T.J though and they was both bad men. And I would put fatass Doctor Maxwell in there with them.

All three of them men was big. So was Leather Jacket best they could tell from what was left of him. So who ever killed which ever one that was killed would a needed help dragging him off into the swamp. I figger they must have drug him off into the swamp because it took so long for Leather Jacket to get washed down to the park. They was at least two big rains between the party and when Leather Jacket showed up in the pool. One the night of the Labor Day party and one the night Leather Jacket was found.

Now who ever drug Leather Jacket off into the swamp could have dumped him in the alligator pen and he could have got washed out of there by a really big rain. Or they could have dumped him somewhere else and the alligators got him one of the times they got out of the pen. The gators was all the time getting out and scaring people what was swimming in the swimming hole. Uncle Toe had to hire somebody that didn't do nothing but keep an eye out for alligators when they was people in the swimming hole. Wasn't too many people liked to swim in it nohow because it was cold and dirty and because of the nigger bodies I already told you about. Except kids. Kids like to play in water no matter what. Crystal was supposed to be keeping the gators in the pen but she liked to let them out ever so often because she said they liked it. And because she give them just about anything they wanted if she could lay her hands on it. Don't ask me how she figgered out what a alligator wanted. She didn't like folks too much but she sure loved them gators. Uncle Toe made her not let them out until after Labor Day. The park was closed after Labor Day ever year.

I figger the alligators got out and found Leather Jacket tied to a cypress knee or some thing some where in the swamp and broke the rope he was tied with. If he had a been throwed in that pen they would have ate him jacket and all in that amount of time. But that don't matter. Swamp or pen. Take your pick. Either way the gators did their work.

I don't know no more about it. After they found Leather Jacket me and Billy and Crystal all put our heads together and tried to figger out the whole thing just on what the three of us knowed. After a while I will tell what we come up with if I don't forget.

Right now I reckon I will tell what happened at Crystal's cabin between her and fatass Doctor Maxwell. It ain't got any thing to do with what happened in the bar where the dirty movies was showed I don't reckon. But there was them that figgered Leather Jacket could a been fatass Doctor Maxwell so I will tell what I seen going on in and by her cabin.

Me and Crystal done some thing Jonnie V. wanted us to do. We both loved her like she was our mama. We would a both done any thing for her. She wanted Crystal to get some thing from fatass Doctor Maxwell's office and I was gonna go along to keep a eye out case any body showed up while Crystal was in his office. Crystal knows how to pick locks. Case we got caught we didn't have no keys. Jonnie didn't want it to look like her or fatass Doctor Maxwell give keys to me and Crystal or that they was stole because if they was stole it might look like her and fatass Doctor Maxwell knowed that some body might get into his office and should a told the Sheriff or done some thing to stop it.

Now I was supposed to be keeping a eye on T.J. for Frankie, too. Frankie was mad at T.J. for beating him in a game of basketball and wanted me to see if I could find out some thing Frankie could use to make trouble for T.J. Frankie hated that nigger more than any other nigger and Frankie hated niggers real bad. T.J. worked at Pinecrest and when me and Crystal got there I seen him. He was in the hall propped up on one of them beds that's got wheels on it that they haul patients around on. T.J. was reading a book. He didn't see me.

I told Crystal to go on in and I would keep a eye on T.J. I got where I could see if any strange cars come up and keep a eye on T.J. at the same time. She used a flashlight so wouldn't no body know she was in there.

After a while Crystal come out. She had some folders. Vanilla folders. Crystal could remember any thing that was wrote down if she seen if just one time. That's how she knowed which folders to get I reckon. Crystal used to be an inmate at Pinecrest when I was there. I showed her how to sign. She liked signing more than she liked regular talking. For a long time she worked in fatass Doctor Maxwell's office and helped him and Jonnie when they did stuff at night. I figger she had seen just about every folder in there at least one time.

I told Crystal to go on and I'd stick around for a while. We was supposed to take the folders to Frankie's cabin and that's what I told her to do.

After a while fatass Doctor Maxwell's car come up and parked in the parking lot. After a minute the light come on in his office. T.J. must a been waiting for Doctor Maxwell to come to his office because he went and stood by the door. Me and Crystal was lucky neither one of them didn't see us.

I waited a while watching T.J. watching fatass Doctor Maxwell. Then I went outside and around the building to peep in the window.

There was folders all over the place. I guess Crystal had a grudge against fatass Doctor Maxwell or some thing and throwed a bunch of his folders on the floor. She growed up in Pinecrest and maybe he tried some thing with her or some thing. He tried it with ever body else including your truly. Any how she left a big mess.

Fatass Doctor Maxwell looked at the mess. I could tell he was mad. He sat down and picked up the phone and started talking. I seen T.J. listening to him talk on the phone. The door was open just a crack and I saw his big white nigger eye in it.

Next thing I know T.J. come running out in the direction of Magnolia Park. Then fatass Doctor Maxwell jumped in his car and went that way too. I reckon T.J. knowed where he was going on account a some thing he heard Doctor Maxwell saying on the phone. Niggers can run faster than white folks. I knowed right off Doctor Maxwell wasn't going far because the road quit at Magnolia Park which ain't far from Pinecrest.

I got scared fatass Doctor Maxwell knowed Crystal had messed up his office and was going to her cabin and I still wanted to keep a eye on T.J. so I jumped on a girl's bicycle I seen and rode over to Magnolia Park fast as I could. I got there just in time to see fatass Doctor Maxwell going in Crystal's cabin without knocking or nothing. I was gonna go up there and watch through the window but I seen T.J. already looking in so I watched him instead.

I hate fatass Doctor Maxwell. I guess you figgered that out already. When I looked in his car in the little parking lot in the back of Crystal's cabin I seen the key in it so I took it just to make him mad. Didn't too many people know about the parking lot in the back of Crystal's cabin but it had to be there for trucks to haul stuff in for the alligators or a alligator had to be hauled in and out when she got a new one or one of the old ones had to be hauled off for some reason or another like it was dead or had to be took to the animal hospital at LSU.

After a while fatass Doctor Maxwell come out. He didn't have no pants on and was holding onto hisself like his balls was hurt or something because he was bleeding all over the ground and it looked like he was trying to hold his pants up against hisself to stop the bleeding or something but he kept stumbling and finally just throwed them down and went on without them. I reckon he tried some thing with Crystal and she kicked him in the balls or cut him with one of her knives or something.

When fatass Doctor Maxwell got to his car he got in on the wrong side. I reckon he was hurt so bad he was mixed up and believed Jonnie was driving like she usually did. Of course he couldn't a started it anyhow because I had the car key. I seen T.J. go look in the car and take off through the woods. I followed him far enough to see he was heading to niggertown.

Then I went back and got fatass Doctor Maxwell's pants and went to his car to check on him. He was asleep. At least that is what I thought then. I opened the door to the car and put his pants in with him and locked it again so couldn't no body mess with fatass Doctor Maxwell or his car except me because I had his keys.

After that I had a idea and so then I went to Crystal's cabin and looked in the window. I wanted to see if Arthur was still there. I needed him to help me with my idea. I figgered he might be there because before that I was out in the woods and it started to rain and I seen Jake and Billy running like a couple of scared rabbits or something. It was by the oak tree where me and Billy used to jack off in so I went there and found Arthur covered up with grass and leaves under two logs. I got under another part of the logs where he couldn't see me to get out of the rain and waited to see what he would do. Pretty soon he got out from under the logs and went in the direction of Crystal's cabin.

Turns out Arthur was in Crystal's cabin. I told Crystal to tell Arthur to stay there till I got back. Then I went to Frankie's to get his pistol. He said don't call it a gun. He said a gun was a dick.

Okay that's most of what I seen. I may a left some things out but not much. Now I guess you know why fatass Doctor Maxwell wasn't at the March of Dimes party. Not after what Crystal done to him. Anyhow didn't nobody ever see him after that. They say he went off to another state and got another job. I doubt it.

All I have left to tell is what happened at the end of Crystal's trial. While everybody was waiting for the jury to come back and tell if Crystal was innocent or guilty this here lady with a scarf on her head come into the court carrying a baby. Didn't nobody know who the lady was.

The lady went up to the judge and said could she make a statement. The judge said okay but she would have to swear on a Bible. A man gave her a Bible and said state your name. My name is Mrs. Franklin Leroy West she said. Then the lady took off her scarf and ever body seen her red hair. Then they knowed it was Dixie. I reckon didn't nobody think it was Dixie when she first came in because they had done got so used to thinking she was dead. And because she had that scarf on her head.

Then Dixie showed ever body her baby. The baby had red hair. Just like on Dixie's pussy.

That was the end of Crystal's trial.

After that Dixie said T.J. wasn't killed. She said her and T.J. made it look like somebody was crucified. They wanted everybody to think it was T.J that was crucified on account of the movie so they wouldn't go looking for him or nothing. She said the jewelry they found in the alligator wasn't hers. She said she made T.J. throw away her black dress because it made her think of the horrible movie of her and him fucking like dogs. She said he must a throwed the dress in the alligator pen or he maybe throwed it in the creek up by niggertown and it got brought there by high water. She said him and her run off up north. She said when she heard about Crystal's trial she come back to tell the truth.

They was some that figgered Dixie might a been lying. They said she might a wanted ever body to think T.J. wasn't dead and wouldn't think her son had a murderer for a daddy. They said maybe Frankie and them couldn't find T.J. that night and maybe they hauled another nigger back down to the bar and done all that stuff to him and maybe Dixie just said her and T.J. made it look like he was the one that was crucified so wouldn't nobody think T.J. was the cause of a innocent person's death. They said maybe it really was T.J. that was crucified and Dixie stole somebody else's baby or adopted one so it wouldn't look like she had a nigger baby.

I reckon I might as well believe ever thing she said though.

I reckon the way I wish the hardest for this story to end is that Frankie really is that baby's daddy. Same goes for Billy and Crystal and Arthur because they all three loved the baby and Frankie as much as I do.

Dixie give the baby to Billy and left and ain't nobody seen her since. Billy raised the baby and his name is Frankie Arthur Kennedy West. Kennedy was stuck in his name after President Kennedy was killed in Dallas, Texas. Some people said that make the baby FAK West. Get it?

Billy figgered him and Jake was brought in and bullied into keeping their mouths shut because the Sheriff figgered if they talked about it people might figger out it wasn't Arthur that was floating in the swimming hole. Billy figgers J.V. blackmailed the Sheriff into doing it. Billy figgers J.V. believed Brother Johnson killed Theo Jeannsonne for fucking his daughter. Or for fucking his wife in a movie. And so Billy believed Theo was Leather Jacket. Billy said Brother Johnson might not a cared about the movie if it hadn't been showed to ever body and they brother. J.V. and the preacher shacked up after that. The preacher's wife left and took her daughter Tommie Sue with her. Which the preacher didn't care because he said he wasn't her daddy. Everybody figgered it was because of the movie that the preacher's wife took off, but they's some what thinks Theo was not killed and her and him run off somewheres and shacked up theirselves. In which case what happened to Tommie Sue?

Billy said he didn't want to think about it any more so I guess that's it and I won't show him this until he wants to think about it some more if that ever happens.

Except I want to say me and Arthur and Crystal helped Jonnie by what

W. A. Moltinghorne

we done because fatass Doctor Maxwell might have spilled the beans. And we helped Dixie and T.J. too because fatass Doctor Maxwell didn't have no more use for his dick anyhow. Or his car neither. Unless they's roads in hell.

THE END

CODA

❀

A couple of years ago, Billy had the following dream, transcribed here verbatim from his dream diary:

I am sitting on the edge of a bed. I see Jake Garrard approaching; he is naked. I look at his crotch without really seeing his penis. With a mixture of fear and desire, I think to myself that I will suck him off. Then he is sitting, then lying, on my lap, at right angles to my legs, his butt resting in the crevasse formed by my thighs. Now I see his dick, his phallus, that is, because it is erect. It is very big, eight or nine inches long and thick as a woman's wrist. It is well-formed. It is beautiful, brownish-purple in color. It takes my breath away just to see it, a mixture of intense desire and envy. I take it into my left hand (my jack-off hand): it is strong, heavy, hard, and hovering. I know I will suck him off. He, the rest of his body, is small; he is young, like an adolescent boy. I do not see his injured thigh; in the dream he is whole, undamaged. His body is beautiful, not grossly muscled as it was in real life. His face is his own, but more feminine. He has his characteristic/signature crew-cut. I say something like, 'So you fucked so-and-so.' With a facial gesture, he dismisses the deed, discounts its value as a conquest, saying something about the noise and surrounding commotion the woman's kids were making in the house while the act was taking place. Without looking at my own crotch, which is anyway hidden from view by his body, I feel my own dick. It is completely flaccid, soft, hardly more than a flap of skin.

It strikes me that this dream—a tender, devotional prelude to fellatio—is telling a Frankenstein-Love story. Libidinal desires, sexual wishes, if you will, which in 1957 would have been too monstrous to imagine, finally achieve an integration, a paradoxical sublimation, an aesthetic form, if you will, in 2008, which allows their conscious expression in a dream; and we may speculate that the dream is itself both a compromise and a trade-off. It is a compromise because homosexual felattio, consonant at last with contemporary standards of decorum, *is* allowed, but only in *thought*, because even in our permissive twenty-first century, good taste still dictates, at least for this dreamer, that genital sex between men must remain off-stage. The dream is a trade-off because, complicit with the dreamer's depleted libido, it is 'only' a dream, which he can dismiss more easily than he can a 'real' conscious wide-awake attraction to a potentially available object, thereby protecting his subjectively-more-acceptable sexual identity as a *heterosexual* cunnilinguist. (In one session he called himself a 'male bull-dyke'.) By appeasing youthful, undying desires, the dream drains off their energy, thereby thwarting, or at least postponing, their consummation in 'reality'.

It is a Frankenstein story because it centers on a composite figure made up of parts of three male bodies. The head is Jake's. The body is Ralph's. The phallus is Frankie's. To the young naïve Billy, Jake was the smart one, a veritable intellectual, a lover of words, a would-be wielder of their power; his short stature, his deformed leg, and his expressive and rather feminine face all worked against his masculinity, despite his compulsively compensatory muscularity. Ralph's deafness retarded and restricted his emergence into society; voiceless and thus by default confined to and defined by his diminutive body, he had to talk with his hands, drawing public attention away from, and diminishing the subjective priority of the face—his and others'—the focus, the locus, of mind and social identity. Frankie was a phallic figure par excellence, a veritable Priapis; the sport in which he excelled is rife with symbols of masculine conquest of female sexuality: Frankie was the point man of a team of males on a mission of rape, of violation of the opponent's rectal chastity, if you will.

It is a Love Story because Billy loved all three of them. Because of their obvious flaws, moral, physical, and spiritual, and the forces of repression and homophobia, rampant in that time and place, Billy's erotic attraction to them was displaced, constrained, whatever, and his love was physically, somatically, unrequited, which, of course, is why it was still operative in his unconscious, still alive in his heart, if you will, at the time of the dream.

Theo Jeannsonne is in the dream, too; he is Billy himself, an alter ego, an avatar of his lack of genital competence, represented in the dream by Billy's 'flap of skin'. You could say Arthur is there, too; a kind of homo-erotic Holy Ghost, he is represented by Billy's cathexis of the brownish-purple phallus.

That leaves only one 'monster' to account for: Sibil, a.k.a. Crystal, Billy's twin sister. Might she be the woman Billy asked Jake about in the dream? Did Billy's dream censor equip the lone feminine presence in the dream with a sex drive and give her children to throw off the over-zealous interpreter?

Was the oneiric expression of companionable curiosity concerning coitus between Jake and a decoy baited with a nameless, off-stage stand-in for his own twin sister (who is a stand-in for Billy himself) as close as Billy could come to an awareness of his own feminine position vis-à-vis Jake?

W.A.M., Ph. D.

GIRLS ARE GOD'S DOING: A GUIDE FOR MOTHERS OF YOUNG GIRLS
Or
AN OUNCE OF PREVENTION
Or
THE BIRTH OF EVE AND THE DEATH OF JESUS: MAKING A CONNECTION

By
Billy Mayden

Yes, you read it right: Girls are God's *Doing*. Why not say: Girls are God's *Work*? We say: *Boys* are God's Work. Why not say: *Girls* are God's Work?

When we do something we are proud of, we say: That is my *work*. But when someone does something that we don't quite approve of, or does it in such a way that it is always having to be done over again because it wasn't done as well as it should have been the first time, what do we say? We say: Is that your *doing*?

Now, I know that most of you mothers of small girls probably either look the other way and dismiss your daughter's misdeeds against nature as innocent 'experimentation'. You believe that what Saint Athanasius said about people in general goes double for little girls: *'All things are pure to the pure'*. He lived a long time ago and was Bishop of Alexandria—Egypt, not Louisiana. But a much greater saint wrote: *'Nothing so much casts down the mind of man from its citadel as do the blandishments of women, and that physical contact without which a wife cannot be possessed.'* Those are the words of Saint Augustine, Bishop of Hippo, which I guess must be in Africa somewhere. You've heard it said the child is the father of the man? Well, the same applies to women. *The child is the mother of the woman.*

Now before you get all hot and bothered, just remember your Genesis. God created Adam after He had created everything else and He gave him dominion over all the earth. But God soon realized that something wasn't quite right; this wasn't going to work. We might say He didn't do the job to the best of His abilities. Maybe His mind was already moving on to something else by the time He created Man.

What was wrong with God's Creation? All the other animals had ways of keeping their kind going. When a woolly mammoth or a saber tooth tiger or a dinosaur got sick and died or got killed and eaten by something, other mammoths or tigers or dinosaurs come along to replace them. (It's called Preservation of the Species, among many other things.)

But Adam was alone. So, if Adam was going to beget sons, and if there was going to be a human race to *replenish* and *subdue* the earth, God had to do something, something more, something He should have done in the first place.

Another problem: because Adam was alone, al*one*, there was only *one* of him, just *one* human being. And, of course, there was only *one* God. So, in that *one* respect, Adam was like God. As things stood, you could say that the gap between Adam and God was not big enough and the gap between Adam and the other animals was too big. Now, God was a jealous God and He didn't want anything or any*one* to be anything like Him, in any way, shape, or form. So, in addition to solving the 'replenishment' problem, God naturally wanted to do something to make Adam less like Himself and more like the other animals. He had to supply the missing link in the Great Chain of Being that would connect Adam, who was too far 'up here', to the rest of the Animal Kingdom, which was 'down there'.[1]

Eve then was God's first *afterthought*, 'a thought coming too late, after the occasion for which it was apt', as my dictionary puts it. God had to create Woman to make up for an *oversight*—'an unintentional, careless mistake or omission'—on His part.

So, what did God do? The Bible says, *And Lord God caused a deep sleep to fall upon Adam, and he slept; and he took one of his ribs, and closed up the flesh instead thereof. And the rib, which the Lord God had taken from man, made he a woman and brought her unto the man.* For a long time this account, which is in Chapter Two of Genesis, was taken literally and people even used to believe that male humans had one less rib than female humans. But why would God go to all that trouble when all he had to do was *create* Eve, in the same way He did Adam? Just do it, God!

In fact, if you look in Chapter *One* of Genesis you find that that is exactly what God did: *So God created man in his own image, in the image of*

*God created he him; male and **female** created he **them**.*
But there must have still been something missing, something wrong with Eve: she still wasn't quite human, because *she didn't have a soul.* How did Eve get a soul?[2]

If we want to pinpoint how Eve got a soul we have to read between the lines. The key to this whole business is to be found in the very next verse in Chapter Two: *And Adam said: This is **now** bone of my bones, flesh of my flesh: she shall be called Woman, because she was taken out of Man.*

There are two key points about this verse I want to focus on. First of all, it was *Adam, not God,* who said *This is **now** flesh of my flesh,* etc. The second point has to do with the word *now* and that is why I have made it bold. Apparently, Adam had just finished doing something that allowed him to say, **Now**, this, i.e., Eve, is flesh of my flesh. At some point between when God gave the soulless Eve to Adam and when *Adam* said, *This is **now** flesh of my flesh,* etc., *Adam* did something[3] to Eve to give her a soul and make her human.

What did Adam do to Eve that gave her a soul? In 1949 a *woman*, a Frenchwoman, wrote: *Christianity gave eroticism its savor of sin ... when it endowed the human female with a soul.* Now, I'm not exactly sure just what she meant by these words, but it is clear that she sees a connection between sin and the process by which the human female acquired a soul, which is borne out by the fact that it wasn't until *after* she got a soul that Eve 'ate' the 'apple', which is when 'eroticism' got its 'savor of sin'.[4]

I think if we substitute the word 'Adam' for the word 'Christianity', we will be one step closer to understanding the whole story of what happened in the Garden of Eden. *Adam endowed the human female with a soul.*

How did Adam 'endow' Eve with a soul? Aristotle taught that the soul was in the 'seed' and that the 'seed', which is white, went from the man's brain, which is also white, through his bone marrow and his testicles,[5] and into the woman's womb, and Aristotle ought to know because he was the *'Father'* of Western Civilization.[6]

Now, where does that leave us? Adam took the soulless woman that God gave him and planted his seed in her and voila! Eve had a soul.[7]

Now, let's dig down to the next level of detail. In order to make this jerry-rig work on a long-term basis, women had to be 'attractive'—O, perfidious word!—and they had to be 'receptive'.

To make them attractive, God gave women those attributes that make flowers attractive to bees, outfitting them with bright colors in strategic places, velvety surfaces, and alluring odors. Granted, something of that nature was necessary, but look *how much* of the female body, from the face and hair down to the feet and toes[8] , had to be brought into play to correct God's mistake; as opposed to *how little* God had to fiddle with the male body, i.e., nothing more visible or vital than the organ of liquid excretion had to be pressed into momentary duty for this dirty business of procreation.[9]

So far, so good. But the device by which Eve and her female descendants were made 'receptive' or willing—the 'on-off' switch, if you will—is what sabotagued God's perhaps otherwise Perfect Creation. The damage that has resulted from this little mischief-maker makes me think that by this point in the game God had lost interest in the whole project. Chances are He didn't see the need for the device. After all, being God, it wasn't like He had a whole lot of experience with this sort of thing. So He probably delegated to Satan this last little step of making Eve receptive. After all, it wasn't like God was above letting Satan meddle in the affairs of Man, if for no other reason, to spice things up a bit for Himself when things got too boring in Heaven—just look at the Book of Job. Or, yet again, maybe Satan did it when God wasn't looking.

How ever it happened, the end result was a machine that could turn *itself* on! Not only could this machine turn itself on, it could do it many years before it was ready to do the job that it was created to do. And it could do it for no other reason than its own enjoyment!

Which brings us to … .

The Parable of the Pearl. A grain of sand, a parasite, or some other small foreign irritant gets inside an oyster's shell and, the oyster, in order to protect itself, forms a pearl around the intruder. In other words, a pearl is an abnormal, unnatural, and unnecessary growth, taking energy and material away from the organism, forcing it to secrete precious bodily fluids to deal with a danger not of its own making, while doing nothing to preserve the species or even its own host; at best it is superfluous, at worst a liability.

Now, the pearl is a perfect symbol of the state of mind of a person, man or woman or boy or girl, who is in a state of concupiscence.[10] (Yes, I said girl, because little girls are notorious for interfering with themselves.) A pearl is cloudy, opaque; diverting but draining and, most of all, deceptive or even deceitful because, like a hooded chameleon or a bonneted coquette, it readily takes on different colors and it does it promiscuously, which means, among other things, indiscriminately, without plan or purpose. What does a pearl resemble most? Answer: A soap bubble, like the kind that children love so much. With its dainty iridescence and delicate evanescence, a *bubble* is the very symbol of the transience of earthly life. Compare the pearl to the diamond: The diamond, a.k.a. 'ice', is cool; it is crystal clear and able to clarify light, to break it down into distinct colors, as opposed to the muddle of colors that the pearl makes of light; it can cut to the heart of any matter and so is much more than just an ornament; it is the very stuff of Life in its ideal form; it is eternal ('A diamond is forever'.); it is the perfect symbol of the many-faceted mind of the Man of Genius.

The 'Pearl' of Passion vs. The Diamond of Dominion.

It should have been no contest, but, in fact, it was all downhill from there. Given the pearly inch, Eve ran with it, taking—'laying hold' if you will—the manly mile. Let me explain: What they say about idle hands applies even more to that nervy little pink pop-up piece of protean protoplasm; you could almost say that particular proverb was made-up with it in mind. It was the Devil's grain of sand in the oyster of Eve's weak female brain that grew into the Pearl of Envy, leading her to covet, coax and capture Adam's lowly but loyal attaché-worm, which she proceeded to flatter and provoke, giving it the big-head and pumping it up into a treacherous serpent-mole, a secret agent, an ever-present in-house nemesis of Man's higher strivings; bursting with brio but short on savvy, it became a blood-bloated tick-pawn of her sublunary schemes, always at her beck-and-call; rather like a mesmerized cobra under the spell of a snake-charming mongoose.[11]

End result: The 'pearl' got passed on and now inside every woman is a little girl wired to be both cunning and irresistible; inside every little girl is a demon whose only goal is to isolate Man from God, alienate men one from one another, and to divide each man against himself, thus giving Woman a disportionate, disruptive, and **demonic** influence over the affairs of Man.

Yes, it was all downhill after that. I am willing to give God the benefit of the doubt and assume that it was Satan who coaxed apart the valves of Eve's oyster and deposited his little grain of sand Down There. No doubt The Man Up There was busy with more noble endeavors, which we scum could never understand. Blame who you want, the damage was done.

Now, some people say it wasn't *Eve*'s fault that she 'ate' the 'apple'. Had to be Devil who made her do it, they say. Well, *I* say, Satan or one of his agents *was* there in the Garden of Eden, alright, but *not* in the form of a serpent. And there *was* a 'serpent' there, hiding under a certain fig leaf, who would come out when Adam was asleep and Eve could play with 'him' to her heart's content without Adam being any the wiser. Unless he was playing possum, which I doubt, but if he was it was because he was too afraid to open his eyes for fear that he was dreaming and it would all go away if he opened his eyes and then by the time he woke up or wised up, it was too late, because he was too far gone to think rationally, what with all the blood AWOL from his brain.

No, Adam's 'serpent' was not Satan's agent in the Garden of Eden. It was just a pawn.

Let's look at another Bible story involving a serpent. One time God asked Moses what he had in his hand. Moses said it is my 'rod'. God told Moses to throw his 'rod' on the ground and Moses threw his 'rod' on the ground and it turned into a snake.[12] This scared the you-know-what out of Moses and he ran away, I guess because he didn't want to be bit by his own 'rod'. Then God told Moses to take hold of the snake's tail and when he did *'it became a rod in his hand'*.

So, if God can mess with Moses' mind and make him think his 'rod' is a serpent, why can't Satan can use that little grain of sand that he planted in Eve's 'oyster'—think of the small remote-controlled electronic devises you read about in science fiction stories that are planted in somebody's brain in order to control them, or the little homunculi that were once believed to dwell inside men's brains, directing various actions and bodily processes, only think of the device being placed in or the homunculous dwelling in that part of the female body which is so much more dominant than the brain in determining the actions of women and girls—to seduce Eve into harkening unto his voice and putting forth her hand and turning Adam's 'rod' into a flute, a fife, a pipe, on which she played the tune that brought forth all the children of the world?[13]

So, even though the 'serpent' was more attached to Adam than 'he' was to Eve, Satan used her to make it like her more, to go to her like a pet dog, so Satan could steal Adam's 'seed' and to convert it into poison, which he then used to unloose a scourge of suffering and death upon the earth, a scourge that has gone on for lo these six-thousand years and that will keep on going on for millennia to come, until Judgment Day.[14]

Or maybe you want to say: God created everything, including Satan, so really it's God's fault. Everything comes from God, right? Satan was just God's tool, right?

Well, I don't know about that. I will grant you this: Satan is a clever Devil and the point is he knew where the weak link was; he knew where God had dropped the ball.

No matter who you blame, though, we're stuck with little girls and little girls are trouble waiting to happen and the question is what do we do about them in the meantime to minimize the damage to the rest of us, the human race.

Okay, grab hold of your seats, because I'm about to make a big jump ahead in time. I want to go from the creation of the Eve Problem to a possible solution. To go from the Birth of Eve to the Death of Jesus, and to suggest a possible connection between the two. And when we get there I want to raise the question: Why did God choose to let His only Son die on the Cross?[15]

Let me begin our consideration of the question by expanding it: Why did God choose to let His only Son die on the Cross, and why are there so many *pictures* of Jesus on the Cross? Why did God and Jesus want us always to be looking at Jesus dying on the cross, with nails through His hands and feet, so He couldn't even have scratched His nose if it started to itch or kicked a dog away that was about to use Him as a fire hydrant; with a gash cut in His side that must have made Him look more like a woman than a man[16]; and with a crown of thorns mashed down on His head so hard that so much blood was running down His face and getting in His eyes and mouth and ears that … ? Well, you get the picture.

I'll be honest with you: I don't know the answer to the question of why God wants us always to be thinking about the crucifixion.[17] It's one of the biggest questions that ever was, both in the sense of importance to our salvation and in the sense—thanks to all the crucifixion images—of the number of people who have contemplated it throughout the ages. And God made it so big so none of us mere humans would ever be able to answer it, but would never give up trying to answer it, and that way would always be thinking about Jesus and God and not the things that Satan tries to slip in our back door, so to speak, or that he starts growing in our wet, leaky basements, to stick with the architectural comparison.

(The immensity of the question calls to mind the parable of the blind 'wise' men groping the elephant.) [18]

Okay, you say, what does Jesus on the Cross have to do with the trouble inherent in little girls? Well, that's what I'm about to tell you. It has to do with the Ounce of Prevention mentioned in the subtitle of this tract.

Go get a picture of Jesus on the Cross, one in color if you have one. Or, if you don't have one or can't lay your hand on it right away, just imagine Jesus on the Cross. In your mind, look at every part of Jesus. Imagine that you are a fly on the aforementioned elephant and you are going from wound to bruise to gash and drinking in the horror of the Death of God.

Using your imagination to the fullest, look real close at where they hit Him on the head and body with clubs, and try to conceive, for example, what it would feel like to be hit upside the head with a baseball bat as hard as some big Roman soldier could swing it. See in your mind's eye where He got hit in the mouth. Do you see where His teeth got knocked out? Look, some of His teeth have cut through His lip and His lip is bleeding and hanging down. Do you see where His teeth have cut through His tongue so bad that part of it has fallen off? Can you hear Him crying out something that might be, Why Me, Lord?, but it sounds more like someone speaking a foreign language because of his messed up mouth? The words dribbling out of the bloody hole in His face are so garbled that you suspect that even

God Himself can't make out what His Son is saying.[19]

If you look real close you can see where they whipped Him a whip with nine tails with pointy barbs on the end of each one of them; the barbs are kind of like the jacks that your sweet little daughters play with, except the points are filed to a fine point. You can see where the jacks cut into His flesh, where they took all the skin off His muscles so that His quivering muscles are exposed. [20] Imagine what *that* would feel like!

Now, even the Bible can't hold everything, so spend a few minutes thinking about might be hidden under His loincloth; I suspect some of the things they did to Jesus were so awful they had to be left out for fear of the effect it might have on vulnerable minds, especially little boys, to read about such barbaric practices.[21]

Now, as you thought about those things, did you even for a second have the slightest desire to make love to your husband?

Here's my point: Contemplating Jesus on the Cross is a marvelous way to get your daughter's mind off certain parts of her body, and, later on, when there'll be times when she has to partake of fleshly things in order to start a family and it'll be hard not to think about fleshly things more than is absolutely necessary to start a family, she can contemplate Jesus on the Cross to *control* the way she feels. And when she's by herself and feels like she will surely explode if she doesn't interfere with God's Work, she can just remember the nail driven through both of Jesus' feet to keep his legs together. Can you *imagine* how *that* must have felt! Can you imagine what kind of twisted soul could think about that and still want to interfere with themselves?

Let's talk more about *interference*. That's what we've been leading up to: Interference with God's Work. What all females, even little girls, feel in their bodies in a certain secret part, a part smaller but more powerful than a cherry bomb, goes back to God's Doing; to the Weak Link in God's Great Chain of Being that Satan never tires of exploiting in his neverending crusade to snatch men's souls. Who will dare say they could have done better? It simply was the best way He could come up with, under the circumstances, short of starting all over from scratch, to keep the supply of boys and men up to the level that is needed to do His Work here on earth, namely, first of all, to keep the colored infidel races from over-running the earth, and second of all to spread the Word of God to these same infidels so they can take their place on God's Great Ladder to Heaven, on the rung just below (science tell us) the white woman, and one notch above male orangatangs and the other male monkeys.

Now, if you're baking a cake in your oven, you don't open the oven and stick your finger in the un-cooked cake and scoop out some to eat just because it gives you pleasure to do so, now do you? If you did, what would your cake look like when it finally got done cooking (assuming there was something left in there after all that interference)?

Well, the same thing will happen to your daughter's baby when it comes time for her to have one. And, remember it is *your* grandsons whose future is at stake.

You know what … I'm tired of writing this shit

ENDNOTES

1 Of course, when Eve 'ate' the 'apple' and Adam realized how sons are begotten, he knew he was a long way from being like God. That's when he went running for the fig tree. And this goes double for Adam's offspring, which of course includes us and every other human being. Who among us, knowing where he came from and how he got there, can fail to realize just how far down the Great Chain of Being we all are from God?

2 I suspect that is what the business of the 'rib' in Chapter Two is all about: God is trying to explain how Eve got a soul, without going into all the unsavory details that aren't fit to be talked about in church and around children.

3 —something involving 'flesh' and 'bone', which is why God didn't want to spell it out when He wrote this part of Genesis, which is appropriate, because, after all, this was *before* Eve 'ate' the 'apple' and while the world was still innocent.

4 For those of you who don't know, let's just say 'eroticism' is a fancy word for Preservation of the Species, which is itself a fancy way of saying you-know-what.

5 And his you-know-what.

6 'Western' means Europe and America, not a John Wayne movie.

7 Perhaps the way to put this in words that a modern reader could best understand, without changing the Bible too much, would be something like this: Adam's 'rib' was 'taken out' and 'turned' *into* Eve.

8 E.g., Chinese foot-binding.

9 Which is still another word for Preservation of the Species. No wonder Woman was called 'The Sex' by the early Church Fathers!

10 Another word for 'eroticism'; see note 4 above.

11 Helen of Troy launched a thousand ships; Eve launched the human race.

347

12 I think God must have been speaking to Moses in a dream, because this kind of thing only happens in dreams—it happens all the time in my dreams; back in those days I reckon people couldn't always tell the difference between a dream and being awake.

13 Over half of whom are *girls*, of course.

14 I wager that some of you object to my way of telling the Story of Adam and Eve, that you think it's too close to pornography. To which I reply: God is the Father of Pornography; its Mother is The Book of Genesis, in whose womb, a.k.a. The Garden of Eden, Eve and Adam, the first and greatest, albeit unwitting, of all porn stars, did the dirty deed for the first time *ever*. What else is there for a man and a woman held captive in a garden to do, once they discover that they are both anatomically correct? *They* didn't know that He was going to blab it to the whole world. *They* tried to hide it, for God's sake! The runners-up? God and Mary; that bit about the 'angel' of God appearing to Mary is a *very* nice touch—flashers are such shy guys! No wonder Mary was *sorely* afraid! Talk about your G-spot!

15 I have written a little poem which could serve as a bridge over the four-thousand years between The Creation and the time God became a Daddy for the first time, letting His 'angel' do the dirty work:

> John:Son of God
> In the biggening*
> Was the Wad.
> And the Wad
> Was with God.
> And the Wad
> Was God's Wad.
> And then God
> Shot His Wad.
> Why not?
> He got
> To screw
> The Jew.
> Down there
> Is where
> The Wad
> Is God.
> *The Big Bang

16 At least to those who are inclined to see filth everywhere they look.

17 I mean apart from the obvious fact that the crucified Jesus stands for the dead and wounded soldiers and the fallen women of the night— e.g., Mary Magdelene—who stand between you homemakers and the twin evils, violence and sex, not to mention the godless communists, lurking out there, just the other side of the door of your happy home, waiting to wreak havoc six ways from Sunday.

18 And I don't have to tell the mothers of small girls who fall into a certain category what part of the elephant we need to focus on.

19 How would it make you feel if your own father was unable to catch your drift?

20 Like what you might see walking home from church on a moonless evening through a shady part of town when a mental patient jumps out of the bushes and exhibits himself under a street light.

21 Speaking of vulnerable minds, is it because they are like vaginas that a kid finds other people's wounds, gashes, and cuts so fascinating and his own so frightening? Are these openings in the skin windows or gateways into the body of another person, and breaches in the ramparts of our own? Are bruises, especially the knots that pop up when a blow is delivered to the head, say, or a shin, or better yet, is a *boil* the unconscious equivalent of a 'pearl' or the larger (more functional) male counterpart: Sensitive to the touch, pleasantly responsive to gentle caresses; of colors ranging from pink and red to blue and purple; temporary, but making up in length what they lack in height?